**Praise for *The Book of Beloved***

"A tour de force from an accomplished writer who has a gift for delivering vivid sensory impressions to deepen the impact of her story...A powerful book you will not soon forget." —*Historical Novel Society*

"Carolyn Haines is a master wordsmith who has succeeded where so many in the horror/supernatural genre fall short. She has created a story that will haunt its readers..." —*Amazon Reviewer*

"This work is a slice of history, changing attitudes and a really good mystery all wrapped up in a well written story." —*Amazon Reviewer*

**Praise for *The House of Memory***

"What a page-turner! This book has it all. Ghosts of murdered young women, a haunted insane asylum, an antebellum house where evil lurks, and a still-living young woman threatened by human and superhuman forces. This is a classic and beautifully-crafted ghost story in the tradition of *Ammie Come Home* or *The Turn of the Screw*." —*Amazon Reviewer*

"This is a more than a mystery about spirits. The story is intriguing and cleverly plotted; it truly kept me engaged. Haines never disappoints!...Excellent series!" —*Amazon Reviewer*

"Again, Ms. Haines has written a book that holds your tight grip on it page by page." —*Amazon Reviewer*

**Praise for *The Specter of Seduction***

"Haines once again spins a Southern Gothic ghost story so wonderfully complex that when the human villains are finally exposed on the last pages, it's a total surprise, yet nonetheless makes perfect sense...a perfectly satisfying ending to a gripping book." —*Amazon Reviewer*

"A gifted storyteller, Haines writes with a direct, crisp style that is at once lyrical and often sensual. As the menace and dangers build, the pacing and tension increase exponentially. And, when the suspense and characters are so compelling, as in *Specter of Seduction,* one might lose track of the fine quality of the writing itself. But this is a book that shines with refined, sharp prose. Haines has a poet's ear for language and knows how to utilize words to set a tone, evoke a feeling, and capture a moment." —*Amazon Reviewer*

"This is a great read--one you will not be able to put down once you start." —*Southern Literary Review*

"Don't miss this 3rd in the Pluto's Snitch series and be prepared to be on the edge of your seat until the very end." —*Amazon Reviewer*

**Praise for *The Seeker***

"Inventive...Aine's struggle with her own illusions is genuinely effective." —*Publishers Weekly*

"This mix of thriller and ghost story is all about what is just glimpsed for an instant, whether physically or psychologically.

And the suspense is intensified by the fact that readers can't be sure whether they're following the thoughts of someone sane, unhinged, or in the process of coming apart...Great for both lovers of Thoreau and suspense fans." —*Booklist*

**Praise for *The Darkling***

"[A] spellbinding tale . . . eloquent evidence that Southern storytelling is indeed a very special art form." —*The New York Times Book Review*

*#6 on the list of 10 best horror novels of the year* "But it's Haines' knack for good, old-fashioned storytelling that truly sets *The Darkling* apart. The scares are parceled out sparingly, but assuredly. After the first few chapters, I found myself saving the novel for late nights, when I could pour a cup of coffee, light a lamp in a dark room, and allow the hyper-eerie visuals to seep into my bones. While Haines has found previous success with crime and romance, *The Darkling* may be proof of her true calling." —Ryan Daley www.bloodydisgusting.com *#6 on the list of 10 best horror novels of the year*

**Praise for Carolyn Haines**

"Like the heat of a Deep South summer, Ms. Haines's novel has an undeniable intensity; it's impossible to shake its brooding atmosphere." —*The New York Times Book Review*

"A writer of exceptional talent!" —*Milwaukee Journal*

"A masterful evocation of time and place." —*Kirkus Review*

# A VISITATION OF ANGELS

*Pluto's Snitch #4*

## CAROLYN HAINES

*For Helene Buntman, my talented friend*

# CONTENTS

# CHAPTER 1

The heat rose up from the baked clay road in a hazy shimmer. For September, the afternoon was brutally hot. I tried to discreetly wipe the sweat from my forehead and upper lip as the open car lumbered along the rutted dirt road. Only the cool breeze generated by the vehicle's movement made the journey tolerable. Even with the breeze I didn't know how much longer I could take the sun beating down on us.

Reginald Proctor and I had been on the road for several days making the difficult journey to a remote area of northeast Alabama, where the Appalachian foothills provided daring driving opportunities. During the time we'd been on our trip, Tennessee had voted to ratify the 19th Amendment. Women had gained the right to vote—but I feared my poor brain would be cooked in my head before I got a chance to cast a ballot. Not even my bobbed hair and a large straw hat helped.

Reginald, my friend and partner in our newly formed detective agency, rolled the big touring car to a stop in front of a huge mud puddle that covered the entire road and spilled into what looked like a slough on both sides of the road. In the afternoon heat, the stillness was instantly suffocating.

"I'm afraid the bottom of that puddle isn't solid and we'll get stuck." Reginald wiped his forehead on the sleeve of what had once been a pristine, starched white shirt. Now it was as wilted as my own clothes. Because of where we were going and what we intended to do, Reginald and I had both opted for the more conservative attire of the early 1900s. With his Brilliantined hair, neat mustache, and athletic grace, Reginald looked like a handsome movie star, even when wilted from heat. My modest skirt and white lawn blouse was stifling, but we would not risk more modern attire. Not in Mission.

There was no other road to our destination—Mission, Alabama, on Sand Mountain. We'd been called to help a young mother who found herself in a desperate situation. We'd been delayed leaving Mobile, Alabama by a bad storm that had blown in from the Gulf of Mexico with high winds that toppled trees, tore the roofs off buildings, and pushed torrential rains inland. The legacy of the storm was bad roads and dangerous river crossings, which had hampered our travels.

"Maybe if we back up and get a good head of steam we can power through that puddle." I was ready to get to our destination and get out of the hot car.

Reginald cocked an eyebrow, his sleek black hair winking in the bright sun. "You want to risk getting stuck here until someone happens by?"

"I don't like sitting here, but I also don't like the alternative." Reginald was the best sport and a fair man, but he did take pleasure in deviling me in small ways.

For all of his handsome looks and dandified ways, Reginald was a practical man, and one who took me at my word that I wanted to be treated as an equal. "Slip off your shoes, hike up your skirt, and wade out to see how deep the puddle is."

It was my turn to perform this chore. Perhaps the muddy water would at least cool my feet and lower legs. It was worth a try.

Reginald leaned against the door of my uncle Brett's car and lit a cigarette as he watched me kick off my shoes. He smoked while I stepped into the water. The mud squished up between my toes unpleasantly as the water lapped at my ankles. The puddle was lukewarm, not cool.

"Be on the lookout for leeches." Reginald spoke with wicked calm.

"If I see one, I'll catch it and put it on you." I hadn't been an English teacher of high school boys for nothing.

Reginald tossed his butt to the ground and crushed it, making sure the fire was out. The surrounding brush and trees were soaked by the storms that had tormented us for the past week. There was little danger of fire, but he was always careful. I liked that. "I've been thinking about this woman we're going to help. Elizabeth Maslow," he said.

I waded in a little deeper, the water moving up to mid-calf. "And?" For all that we'd been trying to get to Elizabeth Maslow for two weeks, we hadn't really discussed the merits of the case. My uncle Brett Airley and his fiancée, Isabelle, had not wanted us to take it up to begin with. Uncle Brett warned us that many of the residents of Sand Mountain were hardworking farmers who might be a little peculiar due to isolation. Good people, as he said. But there were other residents in the area, religious cults that had sought an isolated location that allowed them to practice a belief system that might draw legal consequences elsewhere.

"Raissa, please reconsider taking this case. Sand Mountain

is a strange place with a lot of...different beliefs. They won't tolerate an uppity woman." Uncle Brett had leveled his gaze at me and held me pinned. "You're outspoken, Raissa. I enjoy it, but there are groups who will not, and you'll be far removed from my help." He'd turned to Reginald. "They'll hang you, son."

Uncle Brett hadn't been judging, merely stating fact.

When Reginald didn't pick up the thread of our conversation, I glanced at him. His furrowed brow told me he was concerned. We'd discussed this before we left Mobile, but it still weighed heavy on my conscience. I'd overridden his concerns with my insistence. "She said an innocent man is going to be executed. We have to at least try to help. While I'm worried about this McEachern man, I'm equally worried about Elizabeth Maslow and her child. Superstitious people are capable of great harm. And she has no one else to turn to."

"And she knows this Slater McEachern didn't murder anyone because she saw the truth in a dream?" Reginald didn't hide his skepticism. He believed in the supernatural. In fact, our detective agency, Pluto's Snitch, specialized in cases with a paranormal aspect. But a woman who intended to stand up in court and say that she dreamed the truth was a bridge too far for him. "I can see why a judge or jury might find that problematic."

His words were ringing in my head as I made it all the way across the large puddle. The bottom was covered with a squishy residue, but beneath that the hard clay held. We could drive on without getting stuck.

I wasn't finished with the topic of dreams that foretold the truth. "No one wanted to believe me when I saw that soldier under the oaks at Uncle Brett's. I don't dream things, but I do hear the whispers of dead people who tell me truths." I said it softly, without challenge, but Reginald nodded.

"I know there are things in this world that can't be explained, and I believe in them. I believe in you, Raissa, but the legal system requires facts, not fragments of dreams. I'm not certain we can do anything to help Mrs. Maslow or Mr. McEachern." He flashed a grin. "And I don't particularly want to get hanged or see you on a gallows."

I answered with a grin of my own. "I can understand that, but this is 1920. We have powerful connections in Mobile and the state of Alabama. I can't believe you and I would be in real danger. Now Elizabeth and the child are a different story. We may not be able to change a thing, but we can at least try to help. I promised we would hear her out." I waded back across the puddle and went to stand in front of Reginald. "According to the map we got back at the grocery in Thomasville, we're not far from Mission. We're almost there. If we can't help, we can leave tomorrow."

Reginald nodded reluctantly. "Promise me you'll be careful in what you say. I've been around some people who...use what they believe to control others. If you threaten them, they can turn nasty."

Reginald was really worried. "I promise."

He nodded more decisively this time. "Then let's get going."

Our car cleared the big puddle and the road became steeper and more difficult. The silence between us was not strained, but we were both on edge. We'd left the open and cultivated fields behind and were deep in the woods, which were quite beautiful, but the sense that we were being watched festered and grew in me. We passed several streams that bubbled over the large stones that were scattered among the trees. This was not the lowland terrain I knew. I'd done a little research at the library on this region of the state and I knew the average elevation was over 1000 feet, the Alps compared to the flatlands of Mobile. When we came out of the woods into a clearing, a breeze swept over us, and I sighed in relief. The air was only marginally cooler, but the humidity of the lower elevations was much reduced.

Reginald slowed the car. A meadow on my right sloped to what appeared to be the edge of a precipice. Wildflowers were everywhere, an assortment of yellows and oranges. I spotted black-eyed Susans, one of my favorites. The goldenrod had also begun to bloom, the heavy gold fronds swaying in the breeze.

"It's beautiful here."

"It is," Reginald agreed.

He moved the car slowly forward. When we rounded a curve, he braked hard. He didn't have to say a word. I knew what stopped him. The sight was so ominous it made my breath catch in my throat.

More than twenty buzzards perched in the limbs of a tree that had been blasted black by lightning, leaving only a charred husk of what had once been a mighty oak. The large, black birds hunched their ugly red heads—heads that seemed always dipped in carrion. In my brain, I knew vultures cleaned up the dead creatures on roadsides and farther afield. They were benign, even helpful. In and of themselves, they were harmless. They weren't predators. Nonetheless, the sight of so many, waiting so patiently as they watched the road, disturbed me. The birds perched, motionless, until a few opened their wings and cried at us. The sight and sound tapped into the concern that had continued to grow as we neared Mission. I couldn't help but think the birds were an omen.

"I've never seen buzzards roosting like that," Reginald said.

"Me either." I saw a crudely made sign that had been nailed to the tree. Somehow, it had survived the incineration. *Mission, 2 miles*. Beyond the tree was a clump of hardwoods, and movement there let me know someone was watching us. "There's someone—"

"I know," Reginald said softly, his gaze focused on the copse of trees. "I sensed someone watching us about four miles back, though I couldn't be certain. But there's definitely someone here."

"Shall I call to them to come out?"

"No!" Reginald put a restraining hand on my arm. "Ignore them. Look at me."

I did as he requested. "What are we going to do?"

"Drive into Mission and pretend we didn't notice. I suspect the community doesn't get a lot of visitors. It's natural they'd be curious and cautious."

He was trying to allay my fears. And perhaps his own.

We drove past the copse and though I tried peering through the trees to find out who was spying on us, the woods kept their secrets. Finally we arrived on the outskirts of the town, where another sign greeted us: *Gypsies—don't let the sun set on you here*. A noose hung beside the sign.

"Gypsies?" I turned to Reginald.

"Some of these little towns hate anyone who isn't Anglo and of their same religious belief and background. Outsiders. Be aware, Raissa, this is not a welcoming place."

"No wonder Elizabeth Maslow wrote for us to come." His words affected me, but the sign and noose made me angry, not afraid.

Reginald drove into the village, which was a kind term for the sad gathering of buildings. There was a main street with a dry goods store, a place that sold hand-hewn furniture, a café,

an apothecary, a butcher, and a bank. The courthouse/jail was a
block over but since the settled area had been stripped of
trees, the stone building was easily visible. When I looked at
the jail, my stomach clenched. It was dank and dirty looking.
As we drove closer, I saw two hands wrapped around the bars
of a window. Could that be the man our client had asked us
to help?

"How are we going to find Elizabeth Maslow?" I asked.

Reginald parked the car in front of the courthouse. "We'll
have to ask, and I believe the smart thing to do is let the head
lawman know we're in town. Strangers clearly aren't
welcomed here and I don't want us to be a surprise to
anyone."

"Then maybe we should just keep quiet." Dread and
oppression had settled over us the minute we drove into town.

Reginald smiled and nodded to his left. "There's no keeping
this quiet. In ten minutes everyone in the settlement will
know we're here."

I glanced in the direction he indicated and saw two men
standing at the edge of the road watching us without any
attempt to hide their interest. Their *unfriendly* interest, judging
by the scowls on their faces. Reginald was right. Best to
confront this head-on, at least where the law was involved. I
was well aware of the power of lawmen to act as accuser, judge,
and jury in such isolated communities.

We got out of the car without hurry and sauntered up the
steps of the sheriff's office and jail. Though I was still dying of
the heat, I was glad I'd thought to wear one of my longer and
more conservative skirts. My blouse, a bit the worse for wear,
completed the look of a young woman who knew her place. I
took in the stone façade of the building. It wasn't a courthouse
as much as administrative offices. Behind the jail, hammers

rang out as they struck nails. Someone was building something with gusto.

Inside the dark foyer of the building, a sign sent us left into the clerk's office.

"May I help you?" A thin, middle-aged man sat behind a desk covered in ledgers and letters.

"Could you give us directions to Elizabeth Maslow's home?" Reginald asked.

The man studied Reginald, then me. "You have business with Elizabeth Maslow?"

"We need to speak with her." Reginald smiled pleasantly.

"Deputy Gomes will have to give you directions." It was clear he had no intention of helping us.

"Is the deputy available?" Reginald admirably kept his tone light and breezy.

"Office across the hall." The thin man nodded to the right side of the building.

"And where is the jail?" I asked sweetly, causing the thin man to startle so badly he upset a stack of papers that slid to the floor.

"Women aren't allowed in the jail," he said.

"Not even as visitors?" I pretended shock. I'd been down this path before in larger cities that should have known better. Here, in Mission, it was likely I'd discover that a woman was allowed in three places—her home, the grocery store, and church.

"Who you thinking of visiting?" the clerk asked cagily.

"I've come to spread the word of the Lord and save souls." I regretted the words the moment they came out of my mouth, but it was too late. Reginald gave me a stunned look that he quickly hid.

"You'd better see Deputy Gomes," the man said, slowly

9

standing. His face and neck were red, as if he knew I was playing him for a fool. I deeply regretted my flip remark, but it was too late to pull it back.

"Thank you for your help." Reginald took my arm and led me out into the little foyer that separated the side of the building. "What was that?"

"I know." I sighed. "I couldn't stop myself. He was so smug."

"You're smarter than that, Raissa."

"Obviously not." I did regret my blathering. I'd been raised in the Methodist church but if someone grilled me on my Biblical knowledge, I wouldn't pass muster.

Reginald kept a grip on my elbow—possibly hoping that somehow that would control my tongue—as we went into the office where Deputy Gomes ruled. It was a small room with a counter and a heavy book that I recognized as a jail docket. I was itching to open it but Reginald tightened his hold, reminding me to remain quiet and passive, like a good woman.

"Can I help you?" the deputy asked. He, too, was thin with thick brown hair and a handlebar mustache that was more in style last century.

"Could you direct us to the residence of Elizabeth Maslow?" Reginald asked.

The deputy rose slowly. "What's your business with Mrs. Maslow?"

"Personal." Reginald smiled. "We're relatives, and we also have some business in the area."

It was my turn to be stunned, but I didn't show it.

"We just discovered she was here. Elizabeth slipped away from our family, and now that we've found her, it's our Christian duty to help her," Reginald said. "We're in the area, so two birds with one stone and all."

Deputy Gomes studied us. "We've been worried about her," he said cautiously. "Her...mental state."

"Oh, dear! How so?" Reginald played it perfectly.

"She's been upset and some of the things she's been saying don't make a lot of sense. That and that baby she had." His tone had grown hard. "She came here and bought property, saying her husband would be along. He never showed, because he don't exist. She arrived with lies on her lips and fooled folks into selling her property in a place she don't belong, a town with morals and values. Hard for a solitary woman to raise a baby, much less one that's a monster."

"Monster?" I couldn't help it. Elizabeth had written us that her baby, a little girl, had been born with membrane between her fingers and toes, but that was hardly monstrous.

"Like something that lives in the water." He watched my reaction closely. "Like a frog." He held up his hands and spread his fingers wide. "The thing has webbed hands and feet. Like it ain't all human. I guess when she was looking for folks to help her out, Elizabeth didn't bother to tell you the truth of her situation."

Reginald's fingers dug slightly into the muscle of my arm, reminding me not to react.

"Could you tell us how to get to Elizabeth's house? We'd be most appreciative." Reginald was completely cordial.

"That baby comes from the devil." Gomes came to the counter and leaned on his elbows. "Satan's spawn. Nothing good can come of that. While you're doing your charity work with *Miss* Elizabeth Maslow—we all know she ain't married— you might convince her to give up the father of that baby. They both need to be punished. God does not love a fornicator."

"Who does she say is the father?" I asked.

Gomes tilted back his head and laughed out loud. "It sure beats all, but she says she was visited by an angel." He laughed again, and this time with a sharp edge. "It's bad enough to be caught in sin, but to claim it's the working of one of God's messengers, now that's something she'll be held to account on. Trust me, retribution is coming down the road at her."

The malice in his face told me how deeply Elizabeth was hated. Whatever the reasons, Elizabeth Maslow had gotten herself into serious jeopardy.

# CHAPTER 2

The deputy sheriff stood on the steps of the administrative offices and watched us drive away. He'd given us directions, and sneeringly told us to hustle Elizabeth and her 'git' out of town before legal action was taken against her. It was curious he was willing to let her escape with her sin—if she left Mission.

As we pulled onto the road, I had to ask. "Can they legally punish Elizabeth for having a child and not being married?"

"Fornication is a sin in Alabama. Any sex outside of marriage is illegal. Technically, she can be charged."

I snorted. "If that law were truly applied, a lot of men would be in jail."

Reginald rolled his eyes. "True. And those with influence never pay the price. Women are always the losers because they can't hide their guilt. A child." He swallowed. "The business with the infant's webbed hands and feet makes it a hundred times harder."

"It may be correctible with surgery."

"Logic doesn't matter. Some folks will say it's a sign." Reginald watched the road.

"Of what?"

"Of evil. Or something akin to evil."

I snorted again. "That's ridiculous. A baby can't be evil. You know that."

"Oh, I know it, but there are those who see it differently. We should try to convince Elizabeth to leave with us."

It wasn't a bad plan.

The cottage we sought was a couple of miles out of town down a narrow, sandy path between towering hardwoods. In places the trees canopied the road, lending welcome shade. When the house came into view, I took in the wide porch with a rocking chair and butter churn. In the back was a small barn. A horse whinnied from inside, but the paddock area and well-constructed coop were empty. Neat fields stretched behind the paddock and at the far end of the pasture was an open gate that led into a wooded area.

Before we could get out of the car, the front door opened and a slender woman with striking black hair stepped out. She was young, maybe twenty-two or three. She wore a long skirt and plain blouse and her hair, which had been braided in an intricate swirl, was pinned up. In all regards, she was a modest woman. And quite beautiful. Hauntingly beautiful.

Reginald was equally captivated. "Helen of Troy," he whispered.

She came toward the car and we got out to meet her halfway.

"Thank you for coming," she said.

"I don't know what we can do." Reginald couldn't stop staring at her. Her hair was blue-black in the sun, and her eyes were a tawny brown that seemed to drink in light and hold it.

The planes of her face were angled, high cheekbones widely spaced on either side of a straight nose. Her complexion was olive, and her square jaw held firm resolve.

"You can help me prove that Slater McEachern didn't kill Ruth Whelan."

"You say you know that this McEachern is innocent," I said, taking care how I worded my sentence. "How are you so certain?"

"Because I saw the killer in a dream."

Movement at the end of the field caught our attention. Two men were standing there, watching us. They'd come out of the woods and simply stood, hands at their sides, staring. They wanted us to know we were being watched.

"Let's go inside," Reginald suggested.

"Of course. Arrangements have been made for your stay. My neighbor, Hattie Logan, has a bedroom for you."

I wondered if Elizabeth had assumed we slept together, but that was the least important matter in front of us. We'd work it out when the time came. I followed her into the house with Reginald behind me.

The interior of the small cottage was cheery and the smell of stew cooking made my mouth water. A bassinet, decorated in yards of bright pink cloth interwoven with green and yellow ribbons, had been placed beside the kitchen table where Elizabeth had been chopping carrots when we arrived. She waved us into chairs around the table. "Coffee?"

"Yes, please." Reginald smiled. We both looked at the bassinet, but neither of us made a move to go to it.

"I named my little girl Callie."

"She is healthy?" I asked.

"Completely." She went to the cradle and picked the baby up. The infant wore a long muslin gown. Her head was covered with thick black curls and her eyes were lively and alert. Her little hands were in fists, but when she reached for her mother's nose, I saw the webbing between the fingers and thumb. The membrane was thick and in the sunlight I could see that it was transfused with veins. It could likely be removed, but it would take a skilled surgeon to be sure there was not too much bleeding or scarring that would render her fingers useless.

The baby cooed softly and pointed at me. Elizabeth handed her to me, and I took her with only a little apprehension. I'd taught high school children, but I'd never spent much time around babies. She seemed so tiny and fragile. The moment I touched the child, a series of images populated behind my eyes. I saw things in my mind that had no connection to me or any past I knew. In a flashing series of images I held a rifle in my arms, and I leaned into a dirt embankment, bullets exploding all around me. I felt my own tears on my face and tasted the dirt I tried to burrow into. When I looked at my hands, I saw Alex's wedding band. And I felt his terror and determination to live. A sob burst from me.

Reginald was instantly at my side. "Are you okay?" He was puzzled.

"Yes." I pushed the visions away, focusing on the kitchen and Elizabeth and the baby. Elizabeth watched me, and I had the distinct impression she knew what I was experiencing. I shifted the baby to a more comfortable position and the assault ended. Once she settled in my arms, I relaxed. Callie was content and happy, and I saw that her eyes were a dark navy blue. "She's beautiful."

"Yes, she is. She is my gift." Elizabeth picked up a carrot and began chopping it. "She's in danger here, because of her hands and feet. And because I'm not married."

"Yes, Deputy Gomes seemed affronted by the child. And by your conduct."

She scoffed. "They want to punish me, but they don't know what to do. Yet. I'm sure they'll come up with something."

"Because you claimed the father was an angel?" I asked.

"It isn't a false claim. Gabriel came to me in the night." She looked directly at me. "I have no human lover and you know this. You've felt it."

I busied myself with the baby. I'd been a married woman and a teacher. Babies didn't jump in a woman's belly out of thin air. An egg had to be fertilized, and there was only one way for that to happen.

"Why do you think the father is an angel?" Reginald asked.

"He told me. And because of the dreams." She stopped mid-chop and stared out the window of the kitchen. "Callie is his gift to me. That's what he said. She brought the dreams." She looked at Reginald. "I didn't ask for them. I don't really want them. But when an angel gives you a gift, you have to accept it and use it. Don't you think?"

There was no artifice in Elizabeth Maslow, but I wondered if she were completely sane. She was so sincere, so certain an angel had given her not only a child but the ability to see things in dreams. I didn't doubt that she had abilities, but coming from an angel was harder for me to accept.

"Tell us how the dreams work," I requested. "We have to understand to be able to help you."

She nodded, her hands busy once again with the carrots. "It's hard to describe." She got up and picked up the carrots to put into the stew that bubbled on top of the wood-burning stove. There was no electricity in Mission. When she sat back down, she smiled at her baby in my arms. "It's like this. I go to sleep and suddenly I'm somewhere else. I see things that have happened. It's like an...echo."

"And you saw the murder of a woman."

Her eyes brimmed with tears but she didn't cry. "It was horrible. Yes, I saw it. He struck her." She picked up the knife, but there were no more carrots to chop. She put it down. "With a meat cleaver. Again and again."

"And you saw the killer?" Reginald asked.

She shook her head. "No, not his face. Only his hands. It was like I was...inside him. Seeing what was in front of him."

"How do you know it wasn't this McEachern man?" Reginald asked.

"Slater McEachern almost lost the thumb on his left hand when he was a boy. They saved the thumb but it's badly scarred. I've seen his hands holding the hymnal in church. The man who killed Ruth has two normal thumbs. There was no scarring on his hands. They were...strong. Unblemished. It was not Slater McEachern."

I believed her. It didn't make any sense, but I believed her. "And you saw this in a dream?" I asked.

She nodded. "If not a dream, then some kind of altered state that I can't explain. When I came to, I was in the front yard. My arms, face, and legs were bleeding from where branches and thorns had torn at me. My head was pounding, but I remembered that my baby was inside, asleep." She touched her child's crown of dark curls. "I wouldn't have left Callie alone. Not for any reason."

"Whether we believe you or not," Reginald said, "no one else in town is going to. We need proof."

"That may be hard to come by," Elizabeth said. "People think I'm either a Jezebel whore or a crazy woman. No one will believe what I saw. No one will help me—or you, if you are my agents. That is why we must work alone. Callie and I will leave when this trial is done. Life here is only going to get harder and harder. If I can help Mr. McEachern, I will, and I hope you can assist me. If there's nothing to be done, then I must go."

"Is there anyone who can corroborate anything you saw?" I asked her.

She hesitated. "The man who killed Ruth was looking for something. He tore up her house, spilling drawers and looking behind things. If I knew what he wanted, that might help." Her voice quivered. "He stepped in her blood and tracked it all over her clean house. He didn't care at all. He had contempt for her things."

"Were you friends with Ruth?"

She looked at me with great calm. "I was. We shared a common...situation. Ruth was afraid to be my friend, but it didn't stop her. She helped me in the first weeks of Callie's life. We loaned each other books and shared a love of the forest. I was a danger to her, because my sin was public."

The horror of Elizabeth's life made me realize how very fortunate I'd been. My husband had been killed in France during the fighting, but Uncle Brett had stepped up as my protector. Elizabeth had no one. Her baby was more liability than benefit.

"Who might have wanted to hurt Ruth?" I asked.

She thought about it. "Ruth knew a lot of secrets. She didn't gossip, but she knew the weakness of the flesh." She stood up and went to stir her pot of stew.

Reginald exchanged a look with me. "We need to talk with this McEachern man. Is he anything to you?" Reginald asked her. "If you were involved with him we need to know now."

She shook her head. "No."

"Why has he been identified as the killer?"

"It's the land. Slater McEachern wanted it and tried to buy it, but she wouldn't sell to him. People think he killed her so he could get it." She looked down for a moment. "Women don't really own land in Mission. I lied to buy mine because I thought my brother would show up. He didn't have to be my husband, only a man. Ruth's husband died and the land was hers, but the town was pressuring her to sell it. There were those who desperately wanted it."

"Why is that land so important?" Reginald continued to question Elizabeth as I got up and went to stand beside her at the window. She took the baby from me before she answered.

"There's a spring on the land." Her smile was secretive. "Some people say it has healing properties."

"Healing properties?" My curiosity was instantly aroused, and I wondered if she'd tried the water herself.

"That's what Ruth told people." She shrugged. "I'm not a big believer in miracle water."

Said the woman who claimed her child had been fathered by an archangel.

She laughed at my expression. "Callie isn't a miracle. Not exactly. She is my gift from the divine. She was given to me, along with the dreams. Now I must honor my obligation and speak the truth."

Reginald leaned in closer to her. "You need to be careful, Miss Maslow. There is talk in town already about you. The best thing you can do is keep your head down and let this pass. Raissa and I may be able to help your friend, but you, more than anyone other than McEachern, are in a dangerous position."

She went to the stove and stirred her stew for a long minute. A delicious smell wafted from the little black pot. "I would like nothing better than to live my life in solitary pursuit with my child. I have no interest in public attention. But I know what I must do."

"No divinity would require suicide," Reginald said. He spoke softly, but it didn't lessen the harsh impact of his words. "If you persist in speaking out on McEachern's behalf, I fear you'll be swept up in the mob rule. They *will* hurt you."

Elizabeth didn't blink or avert her gaze. She held first Reginald, then me, in a steady look. "Then I must suffer what comes. The only way out of this that I see is for you to find the real murderer. That would save me, and my child." She came to us and put a hand on our arms. A tingle went through me, and for a split second I saw a golden aura shot through with azure around her head. It was gone even before I could truly see it. "If I'm injured or killed, promise me you'll take Callie away from here. They won't harm a child. At least not immediately. You'll have time to run with her. If they come for me, you must do that and send the sheriff from Victoria, which is the nearest big town. Promise me."

"Shouldn't we simply call the sheriff from Victoria now?" Reginald asked.

"He won't come." She walked to the window and looked out, her face a study in total acceptance of the choices before her. "Mission is a problem he ignores. Deputy Gomes doesn't trouble him with matters here, and he lets Gomes and the town leaders handle things their way."

The reality of what we faced made my stomach roil, but I wasn't ready to accept defeat without first trying.

"Shouldn't we all just leave now? Raissa's uncle can speak with the governor. He might have more success saving McEachern than anything we can do."

"There's no time now," Elizabeth said. "Events have been

set in motion. Just promise me you'll take Callie and leave if they come for me."

"I promise." Her courage sparked my own.

Reginald said nothing, but he didn't disagree. At last he spoke. "That's presuming we're not standing on the gallows beside you."

# CHAPTER 3

B y the time we finished eating a pleasant supper of
stew and cornbread in Elizabeth's kitchen, the sun
was sinking and the air cooling. We hadn't talked
about the details of why we were in Mission—Elizabeth stayed
on her feet, cooking, serving, tending the baby. When I
finished drying the dishes after she'd washed, she turned to
me. "I like to take a walk at this time of day. Would you and
Reginald mind walking with me?"

"We still need to go over exactly what you saw. In your
dream," I reminded her. I enjoyed her company, but I had a
demanding itch to get out of Mission as quickly as we could. I
wasn't afraid, exactly. It was more the sensation of impending
doom—something tragic just on the horizon waiting to roll
over us like the tornadoes famous for sweeping across the
Cumberland Plateau. Like any sensible soul, I wanted to run
from it.

"There's a place in the woods. It's cooler there. We can
talk then."

Reginald shrugged, and we both stood up to follow Elizabeth out the front door. Little Callie hugged Elizabeth's neck and looked over her shoulder, seeming to watch us as we followed in tandem. The child hadn't uttered a single cry or demand since we'd arrived. Elizabeth had taken her out of the room to feed and change her, but not because the baby had demanded food or attention. She was eerily self-contained for an infant.

Elizabeth moved gracefully down a narrow path that skirted a chicken yard filled with the soothing clucking of hens, an enclosure that once was a pigpen, and a paddock attached to the barn that held a buckskin mare. I caught the outline of a fine carriage sheltered in the barn aisle. The carriage was an incongruity on the hardscrabble farm.

Elizabeth glanced in the barn. "I had a fine driving team for the carriage and some cows and pigs when I first came here. I played the role of the wife with a prosperous husband on the way. I would never have been allowed to buy land and stay here otherwise, and I had to stay. At least for a while."

"Why do you stay?" I asked.

She ignored my question and continued to talk. "In the past six months, I've found people to care for the animals, and they've gone to new homes. There's only Mariah left—" Elizabeth gestured to the mare, "—and I'll take her with me when I leave here."

Reginald and I exchanged a look. She'd been working on her plans for a while.

The minute we left a fallow garden behind and stepped into the woods, I felt an immense burden lifted from me. I inhaled deeply, air sweet and pure and filled with golden light that filtered through the canopy of the trees. The temperature dropped at least ten degrees, and even Reginald relaxed.

In the center of the clearing was a mighty white oak, the

limbs spread wide and the leaves dancing on a breeze. Looking up at the tree, I felt the promise of fall, though there was no indication of the changing of the seasons. It was still hot as blazes. Yet fall was close. The tree seemed to whisper the upcoming change to me.

We were being watched, but this time I knew it was not by citizens of Mission. These were spirits of the long departed: Indians, settlers, trappers, explorers who'd crossed the Cumberland Plateau in the service of Hernando de Soto and others. Their shadows stood behind trees or in the dim swirl of light pooling beneath the branches. These ghosts were harmless, sad remnants of a long-ago past. Something held them here, but I had no sense they were ready to depart. They were biding their time. But I hadn't come to help them, nor did they want my help. I stepped up my pace to stay with Reginald and Elizabeth. Living with Uncle Brett and the luxury of a motor car at my disposal at all times, I'd grown a bit soft. Elizabeth strode down the trail carrying a baby without effort.

Even in a motor car, the journey to Mission had been long and difficult. I couldn't imagine traveling in a wagon with all my worldly goods and perhaps a few children. The early pioneers had been of stalwart stock.

I nudged Reginald as Elizabeth prepared a blanket on the ground for Callie. The placid infant didn't protest as Elizabeth put her down.

"Do you sense the spirits?" I asked my partner quietly. Reginald had a great gift for reading people. He could often see into a person's heart with keen understanding of his motives. But he wanted to be able to see spirits, as I did. When I knew spirits were near, I let him know so he could practice feeling the sensations of their presence. Sometimes it was like a breeze tickling my skin. Sometimes it was a warmth or a sensation of color or a vibration or even a smell. More often, I could see them, some more fully formed than others. And then there were the times that my heart squeezed tight from the malevolence that radiated off an angry or evil spirit. I'd met a few of those too.

Reginald stepped away from me, allowing the sensations to encompass only him. He closed his eyes. "There's peace here. Whoever is in the woods has accepted their fate. It's almost like nostalgia holds them here."

"Very good." I couldn't help but beam at him as if he were a star pupil. He was not a true sensitive, but he had abilities he could hone. He might never see spirits in the way I did, but he could certainly learn a more acute awareness. He was improving with each case.

Callie kicked her arms and legs and gurgled, and Elizabeth picked her up. "Excuse me." She stepped into the woods to feed Callie in privacy, and Reginald and I drank in the comforting solitude.


"NOW I'LL TELL YOU EVERYTHING," Elizabeth said, having returned to the clearing and put Callie down for a nap. "This is the best place to hear my story."

"Just start from the beginning. When did you first meet Slater McEachern?" I needed to get it clear in my mind. I still was uncertain why she'd called Pluto's Snitch to help her. She wasn't haunted, as far as I could tell. There was no danger to her from supernatural elements. The danger she faced was from very human sources—the people of Mission.

She took a seat on a stump and began. "I came to Mission months ago, leading people to believe my husband would be joining me, as I told you. The homestead had been abandoned, and the bank was relieved for me to take over, cash in hand. No one asked too many questions."

"Where did you come from?" I asked.

"It doesn't matter. It only matters that I was directed here. I settled in, making some cash from selling jams and soaps and sewing. For the first months, everything was good. I was accepted. And then I got pregnant, had my baby, and the dreams began. I didn't tell anyone or say anything. I was uncertain if what I dreamt was real and true, so I began to test it."

"How?" Reginald asked.

"The day after Callie was born, Ruth Whelan stopped by with some fresh bread and jam for me. She had a cut on her face." She touched her cheekbone. "Here. She said she'd tripped and hit her face on a cabinet door." She cleared her throat. "That night I dreamed what really happened. A man struck her. Punched her, really. His ring cut her face. A ring with a lion embossed in the gold."

"Who owns such a ring?" Reginald asked.

"I don't know. I've never seen it on the hand of a Mission man. This is a plain community. Neither the men or women here wear fancy jewelry. Displays of wealth, for most people, are frowned upon." She paused, then continued. "But I know what I saw was true, because the next time I saw Ruth, I told her I knew a man had hurt her and I described the ring. She went very white and almost fainted and told me to keep my mouth shut and to stay out of her business. She accused me of spying on her. Why would she think I was spying unless what I described was what really took place the night she hurt her face?"

She had a point there.

"It happened again a few days later. I dreamed that little Hildy Morse was lost in the woods. I could see her in the trees.

She was so scared and upset. She'd wandered away from home and gotten turned around. A young woman found her and led her back to the path. She warned Hildy not to tell it was her. And Hildy didn't. Her folks were so relieved to find her they never questioned her. But I saw her playing beneath an old oak tree after church one day and I asked her. She started to cry and begged me not to tell on her 'friend.'"

"Why wouldn't the woman want credit for helping a lost child?" Reginald asked.

Elizabeth shrugged. "Depends on what she was doing in the woods, doesn't it? The people of Mission judge harshly for the sins of the flesh."

"And you didn't see the young woman's face?"

She shook her head. "Only her hands. It was if I were inside her, looking out. I saw what she saw, felt what she felt. She was concerned for little Hildy, but she was also worried that Hildy would tell on her. It was very unsettling, to say the least. After one of those dreams, I wake up and I'm panting and sweating and I can hardly breathe. I honestly feel like I'm dying and I can't control anything." Just talking about it had made her forehead bead with sweat. As if the baby also felt her distress, little Callie began to pump her arms and legs and warble. It wasn't like a sound I'd heard any other baby make. Elizabeth picked her up immediately and soothed her.

"Do you dream every night?" Reginald asked.

"No."

"When do you dream? Is there something that triggers it? Had you seen Hildy or Ruth the day you dreamed about them?" Reginald had an ability to cut to the logical heart of a situation.

Elizabeth shook her head. "No. Not that I recall. Since Callie was born, I stay to myself as much as possible. I have money hidden away, enough to care for me and Callie's needs. If I thought the dreams were triggered by seeing people, I'd never go into town." She hesitated. "It's hard for me. I'm afraid that I'll die in the middle of the dream." She kissed Callie's head. "What would happen to my child? That terrifies me. I'd like to stop dreaming, and maybe if I can help Slater McEachern, I will. I think I *have* to help him—that this is what the dreams have been about. I had to learn to trust them so I'd be brave enough to believe in them and take a stand. Once that is done, I can leave here forever."

Nothing Reginald or I said to her would stop her from trying to save a man she claimed to have no real bond with. I knew the power of her compulsion. She reminded me of the stories my mother had told me about Joan of Arc, another mystic who believed her mission was more important than her life. For her troubles she'd been burned at the stake.

"Can you tell us about the dream where Ruth is killed?" I asked.

She looked away, deep into the forest as if she saw something there. Maybe she did. I was keenly aware of our ghostly audience, but I knew they meant us no harm. Looking closer, I caught a glimpse of Union and Confederate soldiers, standing together, the false hatred of the war long forgotten in death.

"It's terrifying to talk about because I kind of relive it. Let me prepare." She shifted on the stump, closed her eyes, and inhaled, exhaling slowly. She repeated the process several times before she nodded. "I'm ready."

"Tell us," Reginald encouraged.

"When the dream begins, I'm in the woods and it's very dark. I use my hands to brace against the rough bark of the tree trunks. The blackjack oak, the maple, the pine. I know the way. I've been here many times. My eyes have adjusted, and

I make my way toward a cabin with a light burning in the front window. I'm careful to be quiet, to make sure no one is about." Her voice lowered in register, taking on a more masculine tone. "Be quiet! Be quiet! Surprise is important. I knock on the oiled wood of the door. It's a solid knock. Not timid. I'll be welcomed—I know this."

I looked at Reginald. Elizabeth was slipping deeper and deeper into the memory. Her body was gently swaying back and forth, and her right hand made the movement of knocking. She seemed unaware of her actions.

"I hear her footsteps coming to the door. Ruth. She cracks the door, surprised to see me, but she opens up for me to step inside. I've disturbed her evening and she holds her knitting in one hand. At first she is glad to see me, but that changes when she realizes something is wrong. She is wary of me, as if she intuits my intentions. She backs away from me, saying she's tired. She wants me to leave. I move closer. She retreats. Her hands clutch her knitting and her fingers curl around one of the large needles. She knows. It's in her pale blue eyes, the realization that she is going to die. And that I will enjoy killing her.

She offers coffee, putting the kitchen table between us. Yes, coffee is good, I tell her. On the drain board near the sink I find what I need. When she turns to the stove to put the kettle on, I pick up the heavy meat cleaver she uses to dismember chickens. I've sat in her kitchen and watched her work many times before. Before she can turn around, I lift the blade high and wait. She faces me, sees it ready to strike. Her eyes go wide with shock but she doesn't try to flee or scream. The blade cleaves into her skull like splitting a ripe melon."

Elizabeth made a savage chopping motion with her right hand, as if she held the cleaver.

"I pull it free of the bone as she crumbles." She twisted her hand as if she were dislodging the blade from Ruth's head.

"I slash at her neck and shoulder again and again. The thud of the blade in the flesh is good, satisfying. Blood and brains have sprayed around the kitchen." She makes a motion as if to wipe the cleaver's blade on a towel or cloth. "Ruth Whelan will no longer be a bother to me."

Elizabeth slowly quits swaying. Her eyes open and she looks at us. "That's the dream. It's still as vivid as the night I dreamt it."

"Who is holding the cleaver?" I ask. Her eyes are still distant, as if she's right there, in the dream. If she tells us who she suspects, perhaps it will help us find evidence to aid Slater McEachern.

"I don't know. I'm inside his head. I can see everything he sees. I can feel some of his sensations, his emotions. But I can't see him. I don't even have a sense of his size, except in relationship to Ruth. He was several inches taller than her. He split her skull with one blow, which tells me he's strong."

Elizabeth's recounting of the murder had chilled me to the bone. She'd been so detached, so calm, as a woman she knew was brutally murdered. Almost as if she felt nothing. But then she looked directly at me and I saw how haunted she was.

"Ruth was dead by the time I dreamed this," she said. "I woke up that very night, snatched Callie out of bed, and ran to her house. When I got there, the front door was open. I stepped inside and saw that someone had torn her house apart, looking for something. Maybe they found it. Maybe not. I could smell the blood from the doorway. When I saw her, sprawled up against the stove, her back burned into it and her head split open and nearly severed at her neck..." She swallowed and gently rocked Callie. She drew comfort from the baby, as much if not more than she gave. Callie turned her head and watched us with those bright navy blue eyes that were almost black.

"Do you know what the intruder was looking for?" Reginald asked.

"I don't know. I think it might have been the deed to the land. Ruth didn't have anything anyone else wanted. That farm was the only thing of value. Both of her children died of a fever a couple of years ago. Not long after that, her husband was killed when a tree fell on him. Ruth was lonely. The killer could have waited. When Ruth died, the land would have gone up for sale. All the time she lived there, she never tried to stop anyone from getting the spring water if they wanted it. Now folks are acting like Mr. McEachern wanted that land because he thought it was valuable, saying the water could heal people."

"Healing water." Reginald spoke more to himself than us. "Who's been healed?"

"Several people claim they were healed by the water. One said her vision cleared. Another claimed the water helped her rheumatism. A little boy had a high fever and drank some of the spring water and his fever broke. The Indians believed the water had healing properties. Sometimes they'll slip by, filling skins with the water to take back to their villages. They aren't wanted here in Mission." A flush touched her cheeks. "No savages, no pagans, no gypsies."

I recalled the sign with the noose. "What's the issue with the Romany people?"

"Lucais Wilkins, the man who runs the town, says the gypsies are thieves. He hates them so everyone else follows suit."

"This Wilkins is the mayor?" Reginald asked.

Elizabeth only laughed. "There is no mayor of Mission.

The town is run by a board of governors appointed by the church. Lucais is the head of that board and the man who has enough money to buy his way whenever he wants. He hires the law officers. He sits as judge on trials. He runs everything."

Mission wasn't the only town that was controlled by a single person or even a handful of wealthy people. "What church is it?"

"Everyone in town is a member of the Blood of the Lamb Reformed Church. It's an offshoot of the Protestant faith, but nothing like the Methodists or Baptists."

Elizabeth was very well-spoken and apparently well educated. She was an outsider looking in on the town, but an outsider with a larger worldview.

"Where did you come from, Elizabeth?" I asked again.

The question made her sigh. "It doesn't matter. I've always been a vagabond."

Oh, but it did matter. It mattered a lot. "Why Mission, Alabama? You could have gone anywhere. You're educated. You could have worked as a secretary or maybe a clerk for a town. Maybe a lawyer's secretary. Why here, where there is no work for you?"

"I was directed here."

"By whom?" I asked.

"By the Divine." She smiled at my expression. "I'm not an emissary of God or some kind of pagan priestess. I just know that my being here is not an accident. Nor is the gift of the dreams. It's all toward a greater power."

The baby was watching her with rapt attention, as if she understood the ramifications of what Elizabeth claimed.

"God sent you here?"

She shrugged. "I wouldn't have said God, but that's close enough."

"What would you have—" Reginald's hand on my shoulder stopped me.

Reginald was kind but firm. "We came here to help you, and we came without the expectation of pay. What we do expect is your honesty. You're risking a lot for a man you say you don't have any bond with. He's not a relative or a lover or a business associate. So why does this feel so important to you? We need to know what's going on."

Elizabeth looked down at the ground for a moment. "Yes, I owe you that much. I suspect you've guessed some of it anyway." She faced us. "I'm Romany. I came to Mission looking for my brother. He came this way to sell pots and pans, and the last account of him was in this area. That was more than two years ago."

# CHAPTER 4

D arkness slipped among the thick trees as we sat under the white oak and talked. Elizabeth came from privilege. She'd had private tutors in Tennessee and spent summers in Europe with relatives. Her family could claim a direct line of descent from Kelly Mitchell, the Queen of the Gypsies. Mitchell had been buried in Meridian, Mississippi, and newspaper articles of her grand funeral had traveled all the way to Charleston. The stories of wishes granted were legendary for those who visited the gravesite and left behind a token of food, drink, or money.

"My parents died several years ago in the flu epidemic. It was only my brother and me left, both of us grown, but we'd been very sheltered. My brother had a yen for adventure, and he took part of his inheritance, bought a wagon and team, and set out to sell pots and pans in rural areas. He said he wanted to know what it was like to be a real Gypsy, not a city Gypsy. Ramone never saw danger. I tried to stop him, but he wouldn't listen."

"Hard-headedness appears to run in your family." Reginald said it, though I was thinking the exact same thing.

"If it weren't for Ramone, I'd be safely home in Chattanooga. We have property, money in the bank, a safe and comfortable life. None of that mattered to him. He was to join up with some travelers on the Tennessee-Alabama line. I had built a satisfying life around tutoring children and giving piano lessons. I thought eventually I would fall in love and marry. When I didn't hear from him for months, I tracked him to the group of travelers. One woman told me he'd had a dispute with their leader and Ramone had set off alone to sell his wares on the Cumberland Plateau. She said Ramone was talking about communities so isolated that they would gladly buy all their supplies from a tinker traveling though. It sounded exactly like Ramone's thinking—that he would go to the hardest place and make a killing with a captive audience." Pride and dismay mingled in her voice.

"How did you track him here specifically?" Reginald asked.

"I followed him to Victoria and a woman in a dry goods store where he'd bought material and sewing supplies told me he was headed this way. He left a letter for me, indicating this was his destination. He was to meet me here. So I followed. But not as a Gypsy. I traveled as the proper wife of a farmer. If the people of Mission knew I was Romany, they would have banished me. Or worse."

I didn't doubt it. Even just recalling the sign with the noose made me cringe. The people in this community didn't like *any* outsiders, but there were some outsiders they really hated.

"But you moved here?" I asked. "Why didn't you keep searching?"

"This was the last place I knew he was heading. I thought if he wasn't here, that he'd certainly come later.

Frankly, I didn't know where else to go. When I couldn't find him, I realized he would have to find me. I put jams and jellies in the local store with my name on them. I did what I could."

Elizabeth had chosen to remain in an inhospitable village on the off chance her brother might travel through?

"This isn't a safe place for you or your baby."

She didn't argue. She was out of arguments—and yet she flatly refused to leave without helping Slater McEachern. Whatever held her here was more powerful than the impulse to protect her child or herself. All she'd say was that it was a directive from the Divine.

"When this is done, I'll leave. You have my word."

That was presuming that Elizabeth would have an opportunity to leave. Dread had begun to creep over me with the night. The hoot of an owl told me that the nocturnal predators were out. I had a sense that once again we were being watched, and this time by the living. It was time for Reginald and me to find our lodging and to sleep. We all rose as if we were of the same mind.

"You'll find Hattie to be a lovely hostess. She has a room for each of you. I didn't know..."

"That's perfect," I said. "We're exhausted. I'll fall asleep as soon as my head touches the pillow. Tomorrow we'll talk with Slater McEachern."

"I'd like to come too." Elizabeth touched my arm. "They haven't allowed me to talk to him at all."

"It might be better if you didn't," Reginald said. "We don't want the appearance that you've collaborated with McEachern in any way."

She nodded. "A good point."

"And they don't even want Raissa to speak with him," Reginald said. "They seem to have a very clear idea of what a woman's place is in this town."

"And it isn't in a jail." Elizabeth and I spoke in unison, and for a moment the tension was broken. We laughed, and it felt good. In Elizabeth I recognized some of my own traits.

"My uncle warned me to keep quiet here," I told her.

"He's a wise man. There's no place in Mission for a woman with intelligence or opinion. I do my best to avoid expressing any thoughts."

Until now. When she was bent on taking on what served as law enforcement, the judge, and town rule. Essentially the entire male establishment of Mission. Elizabeth was not naïve or stupid. She knew what she was risking, and she had so many strikes against her. More difficult was the fact she was risking her infant daughter, though I hoped the townspeople would not take action against a baby. I couldn't be certain, though. When fear was invoked and whipped to a frenzy, people were capable of incomprehensible cruelties.

Moving as a group, we started back through the woods, the fallow garden that had played out with the summer heat, and past the barn. "Shall I hold Callie for you while you feed the horse?" I offered.

Elizabeth shook her head. "Mariah loves Callie." She looked over to the paddock where the buckskin came to the rail to greet us.

"We should go," Reginald said. He seemed edgy, and I wondered why.

"We'll talk tomorrow," I told Elizabeth before we headed to the car and the drive to our lodging.

MRS. LOGAN HAD LEFT a candle burning on the kitchen table

with a note telling us where our rooms were located. She'd already retired. Widow women worked long, hard hours, and Reginald and I slipped quietly to our rooms. We were worn out. I looked forward to a bed and the oblivion of sleep.

I snuffed out the candle and was almost instantly traveling the shadowy world of dreams. I walked along the shoreline of an ocean, the waves cresting white as they broke and then charged the shore in a whirlpool of foam, kissing my bare feet with warmth. I loved the sound, the feel of the sand sucking out from under my feet as the water shushed up and out. I didn't know this place, but I was at home here, alone against the huge void of winking sky and murmuring ocean.

As I passed between the sand dunes and the water, a breeze kicked in that brought with it an icy chill. The water, which had been warm and appealing on my bare feet, grew icy, biting into my flesh like angry fingers. The sand sucked and held me in place, making me panic as I tried to pull free. The harder I pulled, the deeper I sank. Sand covered my feet, then my ankles, and the water rose higher, tugging at the hem of my skirt. A force I couldn't see held me motionless. Behind me, I sensed the approach of someone but I couldn't turn around. I was mired in the sand up to my knees, my body held stationary. The surf pounded now, but not as loudly as my heart.

From behind me came the flutter of wings and a bitter wind. The softest touch, feather light, moved along the back of my arm, sliding down my back from shoulder blade to waist. Twisting and fighting to free myself of the cold grip of the sand, I only sank deeper, to mid-thigh.

"Behold the child." The words came from the blackness behind me and I no longer tried to look. I could not bear to see what stood only inches from me, because I was afraid.

"Leave me alone." I sounded pitiful and weak.

"You asked to see, and now you shall."

But I didn't want to see any longer. I wanted only to leave this place, to run down the shoreline and away to safety. I could not, though. I was trapped as securely as if I were held in chains. This was not a ghost or a spirit in the ordinary sense of the word. This was something that lingered in the dim shadows of sleep, between the worlds of the living and those who slumbered.

A hand grasped my shoulder, and numbness crept over me. It was a struggle to breath, my lungs unwilling to pull in the oxygen my body screamed to have. Suddenly the darkness of the sky and ocean disappeared, replaced by a rough brick wall with iron bars set in a window. Two hands gripped the bars. These were not the hands of Slater McEachern. The trimmed nails, the tapered fingers that indicated artistic talent—I knew these hands even though now they were grubby with dirt. Reginald's face pushed against the bars. His hair was oily and unkempt, and his eyes haunted. "They're going to hang me."

He looked directly into me, and I felt his despair and hopelessness. They would hang him for who he was, not for anything he did. I was helpless to save him.

Again, a hand grasped my shoulder, and I found myself in a shady cemetery. I recognized the graves, the graceful beauty of the burial ground at Caoin House where my uncle Brett lived. This past summer, I'd spent more time than I wanted in that cemetery, where so many ugly secrets had been laid to rest. What drew my attention was not the familiar tombstones, but something else. Two Negro men dug a grave, the sweat running down their faces in the awful heat. I sat in the dirt, my feet dangling in the grave, a shovel in my own hands. When I looked at my hands, I was shocked to realize I was also a Negro. My hands were heavily calloused from hard work, and I grasped my shovel and jumped into the grave, relieving one of the other men as I bent to the task.

The man digging with me spoke. He was in his fifties, lean and hard from work. "I heard Mr. Airley say to bury him fast. Took Mr. Brett a long time to get his body back. They kept him swingin' for two days. Keep diggin'."

We were burying Reginald. What was left of him, anyway, after the town of Mission had finished with him.

"Stop!" I fought the paralysis that held me in a grip so tight I could no longer feel my torso or legs. I had returned to the beach, to the suffocating sand that was now at my hips. The earth was swallowing me whole in one slow gulp.

Whoever, or whatever, had been behind me was gone. The sound of the ocean returned and the stars blinked on in the velvety night. Once again, the water teased my toes, warm and comforting. The grip of the dream had released me.

I awoke in a strange bed in a strange room, the hot night laying as heavy on me as a wool blanket. I was drenched in sweat and I sat up, hoping to catch a breeze from the open window. It took me a moment to remember that I was in Hattie Logan's home in Mission, Alabama. Even when I did, my anxiety didn't lessen. Had I seen the future? Was Reginald going to be jailed and hanged? Would Uncle Brett retrieve his body to bury him at Caoin House? It took everything I had not to give in to the overwhelming urge to cry. Tears had never been my friend, and I fought them back.

When I'd gathered my emotions sufficiently, I got up and went to the window to look out. Two big sycamore trees, the leaves still green though autumn was close, glowed white in the moonlight. The slightest movement made me look closer. A man stepped out from behind the tree trunk. He stared at the house, but I couldn't tell if he saw me in the window. I eased back, hiding. Was he a living human or something else?

I peeped out the window again and he was much closer. I could see him in detail, the shirt so white it glowed in the moonlight. He lifted his arms, and behind him two enormous wings spread open. Was I still in the grasp of a dream? I couldn't tell, and I felt myself slipping into darkness. He would be waiting there for me, in the land between the living and dead, and I was terrified.

I came awake gasping for oxygen. It was as if I'd been held underwater for a long time and was finally free to break the surface and draw in air. When I caught my breath, I stood up and went to the window. The sycamore trees shone like old bones in the moonlight, but if someone was out there, he remained hidden. I knew where I was. I knew that I'd been dreaming. Deeply dreaming. If this was "the gift" that had come to Elizabeth Maslow as part of her relationship with an angel, I wanted no part of it. I only wanted to get in the car with Reginald and drive home as fast as we could.

# CHAPTER 5

I got up the next morning when the sun was bright in the window of my room. I could hear Mrs. Logan busy in the kitchen. I'd finally returned to sleep in the wee hours of the morning. My room was small but comfortable, though to be honest I was so exhausted I could have slept in the backseat of the car. The horrible dreams I'd experienced were like an almost forgotten memory—just a faint lingering whiff of tragedy and danger.

I performed my toilet in a washbasin on a stand and put on another of my conservative dresses from my days as a school marm. The years of war had taught me to be frugal with all things, even clothes that were out of style in the broader world. They were perfect for Mission, and I thanked my uncle for his wise counsel in suggesting my wardrobe. I'd adapted a more modern look since I'd moved to Mobile, and the shorter skirts of the flappers would not be accepted here. Luckily I could keep my cloche hat on and cover the fact that my hair was bobbed. All of the women I'd seen in town had long hair worn in neat buns.

A knock came at the door and Mrs. Logan said, "Mrs. James, breakfast is ready."

I was eager for breakfast, and suddenly ravenous. When I opened the door I was assailed by the mouthwatering aroma of bacon cooking. I stepped into the kitchen to find Reginald at the table eating a hearty breakfast of eggs, grits, bacon, biscuits with syrup, and strong coffee. Before I could take my seat, a plate filled with food was in front of me. My eggs were scrambled, in contrast to Reginald's over-light. I didn't say anything but watched as Mrs. Logan stepped out the back door into the yard.

"I told her how you liked your eggs." Reginald was grinning. Food and a good night's sleep had clearly improved his outlook.

"What time is it?"

He checked his watch. "Just after seven."

"Good. We can get to the jail first thing."

"They won't let you talk to him." Reginald ate a bite of biscuit. He wasn't being contrary, just matter-of-fact.

"They may try to stop me, but I think I have a way."

He sighed. "Is it going to be worth it to get under their skin? They can make it harder on Elizabeth and they already know we're connected to her."

He had a point, but I needed to see this McEachern man for myself. Was he haunted? Did he carry residual energy from darkness? I needed to talk to him to be able to determine some necessary things.

"Look, if there's a window at the jail, I'll get him to go there and talk to you. But you have to remain outside, Raissa."

I remembered the hands I'd seen on the bars when we drove into town. Reginald's hands. The biscuit I was chewing stuck in my throat, but I washed it down with hot coffee. "A grand solution," I said, tucking into my breakfast with the same gusto Reginald had applied to his. I would not allow a dream to dictate my behavior or emotions.

Mrs. Logan returned with a basket of fresh eggs and refilled our coffee cups. When we asked about lodging for another night or two, she said that Elizabeth had made arrangements for the rest of the week.

"Elizabeth seems very...independent," I said, hoping she would open up about the woman we'd driven across most of the state to help.

"She's learned to take care of herself, and Callie. She's a good friend. I can't say that about everyone who lives in Mission. Now can I get you anything else?"

"No thanks. If I eat this I might pop like a big tick."

"You two be careful in town. Elizabeth is determined to help McEachern, if she can. She needs to keep herself safe."

"Mrs. Logan, did you know Ruth Whelan?" Reginald asked.

"Ruth was a good person," she said, keeping busy at the sink and stove. I had the sense she didn't want to look at us.

"Do you know why McEachern or anyone else would want to kill her?" Reginald continued.

"I don't. Slater McEachern is a big man plenty capable of killing her the way she died. It took a powerful man to sink that cleaver so deep in her skull. But Slater's never struck me as violent. He's a drinker, though. Folks that get caught up in Satan's snare of liquor can do terrible things."

"Did he drink to excess?" Reginald asked the practical question.

"Never to my knowledge," Mrs. Logan said. "The local men brew up some whiskey from time to time. Some folks just break the law."

"Drinking is illegal in Alabama by statewide decision, not a national law." I wondered if the folks of Mission thought Prohibition was a federal law.

"Any drinking at all in Mission is to excess. It's illegal here. It goes against the church and God's teaching." She rinsed out her dishcloth and wrung it before she looked at Reginald. "Folks who drink any amount walk with Satan. It's a danger to them and the rest of us. When a member of the community is weak or mired in sin, it drags the rest of us into it."

I wouldn't argue with her—didn't want to. I'd seen instances where alcohol was worse than the devil for destroying people's lives. Some folks couldn't stop. "Is Mr. McEachern a bad man?"

She thought about it. "I wouldn't have thought so." A slight flush touched her cheek. "He stops by here to check on me and helps with some of the chores like fence mending and plowing to put in the garden. Since my husband died, Slater's been a big help to me. To other widow women too. But good deeds don't excuse a man from hellfire."

"And Mrs. Maslow?" I used the title of a married woman, giving her that shred of protection.

"She has her peculiar ways, but she minds her own affairs. Like I said, she's been a good friend to me." She wanted to say more, but she stopped herself. "Now is there anything else you need?"

"No, thank you," Reginald said.

We finished eating, and while Reginald checked with Mrs. Logan about a place to buy gasoline for the car, I washed up the dishes and left them in the drain board. By eight o'clock, we were driving into town.


I OBEDIENTLY—AND under protest—waited in the car while

Reginald went into the town offices to get permission to speak with Slater McEachern. Reginald had parked beneath a tree, but the day was already getting hot. September held little promise of autumn in Alabama. As far as I could tell, there was only one season—pretty much Hell. I'd only been in Mobile since the summer, but Uncle Brett promised me that October was a jewel as the humidity lessened and the days chilled. Seeing would be believing.

I got out of the car and walked down the side of the road toward a general store. I didn't need anything, but looking at the items on the shelves would at least help pass the time. I wasn't twenty feet from the car when I saw two men standing outside the store watching me. They were the same men from yesterday. They stood perfectly still, staring at me. I kept walking. If they wanted a showdown, I was going to give it to them. I increased my stride, knowing my aggressive pace would annoy them.

When I was fifty yards from them, they turned left and started down a side road. I almost followed, but I knew I shouldn't provoke trouble with Reginald already at the jail. They might keep him.

I walked on to the store and spent ten minutes looking around, taking note of the neat row of jams with Elizabeth Maslow's name on the label. The proprietor ignored me, and I headed back to the jail. About halfway there, I knew someone was watching me. When I turned around, the two men were back, standing on the side of the road, hands hanging at their sides, just watching. Scarecrows. They stood almost like they were dead. The thought made me look more closely. But they weren't spirits.

I got back in the car and waited.

I was about to give up on Reginald when I saw two hands

appear at the jail bars. The sound of hammering had commenced once again behind the jail. It was so loud that I wondered if I'd be able to hear McEachern if he tried to talk to me. No way to find out but to give it a try. I hurried across the barren ground to the edge of the jail.

"Mr. McEachern?"

"Yes."

His voice was low and deep, casual, with a burr of an accent from his land of birth. Not what I'd expected.

"Is Reginald still with you?"

"He is." His hands gripped the bars, but not with urgency and I noticed the mutilation of the thumb on his left hand. "He said you had questions for me."

I wanted to see his face, to look into his eyes, but this was the best we could do for now. I could see his hands, the fingers long, well-formed—strong. The oval tips indicated someone who was sensitive to touch, to texture and feel. The calluses on the fingertips of his left hand and right thumb told me he played a stringed instrument.

"I don't know if Elizabeth told you what we do, Reginald and I."

"Mr. Proctor just filled me in," he said. "I'm not certain why Elizabeth thinks you can help me. The town is determined to see me hang." The slight brogue roughed up his bitter words.

"Did you kill Ruth Whelan?" He would answer no, but it was his voice I wanted to hear.

"I did not. I knew what Ruth was about, but I didn't begrudge her a living."

His answer confused me. "What she was about?"

"Your partner understands. It would be best if he explained it to you."

I hated to be treated like a child or simpleton—or a woman. "Why don't you tell me?" I said. "I'm not a pampered Dumb Dora."

"No, you're worldly. *Lonnsachadh*. A woman of culture and experience." His laughter was deep and rich and seemed genuine. "Forgive me, but I didn't want to shock you or talk inappropriately to a woman I can't even see. There's a wooden box on the other side of the jail. If you pull it around, you can stand on it and we can have a proper talk. Since I'm the only prisoner, I think we can safely talk for a bit."

"I'll be right back." I hurried around the building and stopped in my tracks when I saw what all the hammering was about. Three men were building a gallows. To hang Slater McEachern. He hadn't even had a trial but they were already building the mechanism to kill him. I had to agree with Elizabeth: his plight was dire and he could not expect justice in Mission, Alabama. The urgency of his situation was like a dash of cold water in my face.

I grabbed the box and dragged it back beneath the jail window that McEachern occupied. He was in a far corner of the jail, the most isolated cell as far as I could tell. When I climbed up on it, aware that I could easily be seen from the street if anyone passing cared to look, I was finally on eye level with the man. He was in need of a good bath and beard trim, but that didn't detract from the mischief glinting in his green eyes. He wasn't quite a ginger, but close enough to have earned his brogue. For all of the trouble he was in, he seemed amazingly lighthearted.

"A pleasure to meet you, Mrs. James," he said, extending his hand through the bars.

"Mr. McEachern." I took his fingers. The jolt that came with them was unexpected. I withdrew my fingers. Slater

McEachern was a man charged with sexual energy. It was as natural to him as his handsome features. I wondered first if he was aware of it and then if Elizabeth had told us the truth about her romantic involvement with him.

"Call me Slater, please. I haven't enough time left for formalities."

I couldn't argue with honest facts. "I saw the gallows. When is your trial?"

"Tomorrow. I expect to be dead before sundown tomorrow. It won't take them long to hear the evidence and render a verdict. I have no alibi. Lucais Wilkins believes he is ordained by God and that whatever decision best serves him is divinely inspired."

That was the second curious thing Slater had said, that the judge would benefit from his death. I'd go back to the first item on my growing list. "What kind of living did Ruth Whelan make that you didn't begrudge?"

"She gave comfort to some of the town's men." He didn't flinch or look away. "They gave her money. It was an honest exchange. The woman had no one to provide for her and she had to figure a way to survive. The world isn't kind to single women without family. Especially not a place like Mission."

I wasn't shocked, exactly. His answer was unexpected, but logical. "Why didn't she charge for the spring water that seems to be so special?"

He shook his head and a hint of bitterness crept into the tightening skin around his eyes. "I mentioned that to her, but she refused. She said the spring was God's gift, and she would not profit from something he gave so freely to all."

Yet she exchanged sex for money. It was a curious belief system. "Was it well known she was a street woman?"

"Yes."

"Were you a client?" I had to ask.

"I had been, in the past. But Ruth and I became friends. Just like I'm friends with Elizabeth Maslow. There are things on a farm that a solitary woman—a solitary person—can't do. I tried to help both women with some of those chores."

"Out of the goodness of your heart?" I was more worldly than he might believe. The milk of human kindness was rare to find and most often curdled.

"Ruth was a kind woman. I liked her. I've been fortunate in my business dealings, and I had time to help with her roof or well. I had employees I could send if I was too busy myself."

"And Elizabeth?"

"She reads tea leaves for me. She has a gift."

"And you believe in tea leaves?" Slater McEachern looked like a man who believed in hard work, fierce protection of what he loved, and his own set of values. That he believed in tea leaves or future predictions was a revelation.

"I believe in many things, Raissa James. I believe in what you do. I heard about you when I was in Montgomery last month. When you helped the Sayer family, as you did Miss Zelda, you develop a reputation that travels even to places like Mission."

I'd wondered how Elizabeth had even heard about Pluto's Snitch. Now I knew.

Slater continued to talk. "Let me see if I have it straight. You named the agency because Pluto is the god of the dead and you solve mysteries that often deal with the unhappy dead."

"That's true. And while Reginald and I are not formally trained as private investigators, we consider ourselves reliable snitches." I knew I sounded stiff and formal, but it was best to maintain some professional distance. "What I want to talk about is your whereabouts on the night Ruth Whelan was murdered."

"No prevaricating on your part. I like a direct woman." He grinned, and the sparkle in his eyes defied his sad circumstances. "I was at home, alone, when Ruth was killed. If I had an alibi, I'd bring it forward so I could get out of here."

"When was the last time you were at Ruth's house?"

He frowned. "The day before she was killed. I stopped by for some spring water and to help her fix a wheel on her wagon. I had to go into town and buy a hub band to replace the broken one."

"And did you tell anyone you were helping Mrs. Whelan?"

"I did. Just a casual mention to Vernon McKay. He owns the dry goods store."

A casual mention, but it was enough that McKay could be called to testify that McEachern had been at Ruth's house.

Clearly McEachern agreed. "I know it looks bad, and I have to tell you that if Lucais Wilkins puts pressure on Vernon, he will testify to whatever Lucais wants him to say."

"The man with the most power often gets his version of justice."

"You're more cynical than I expected. It's a good trait for a private investigator."

"I may be young, relatively speaking, and a female, but I'm not naïve."

"I can see that you aren't, and a good thing if you're going to help me. I'm sure Elizabeth told you I'm being framed."

"To what purpose?" I glanced back at the empty street of the town. Soon someone would come along and I'd have to climb down from my box or risk being arrested myself.

"A convenient scapegoat, but also it would put my holdings up for sale. There are those who covet what I've acquired.

They know the only way to force me to sell is over my dead body."

"Two birds with one stone," I remarked, thinking of how the murderer had rid himself of Ruth and freed her property, and now had also put Slater's lands on the auction block, probably for a pittance of their worth.

"You see the big picture, don't you, Mrs. James?"

"Who do you think killed Ruth Whelan? We need a direction to hunt for evidence if we're going to present a defense." I checked the street again. My good luck couldn't continue to hold.

"There are people who relish her death, but I never heard anyone mention killing her. She was quite...popular with a lot of the men. Ruth knew how to give pleasure and she wasn't stingy. She also knew how to keep her tongue from wagging."

I liked Slater McEachern. Even listening to the pounding of hammers that were building the platform to hang him, he was levelheaded and clear. "The way I see it, there are two possible motives at work here. She could have been killed for her property, which Elizabeth tells me has value greater than the land itself because of the spring. But there's also the possibility that Ruth was killed to silence her." I threw caution to the wind because the clock was ticking. "Do you know if she was seeing anyone who might feel threatened by her? Would she attempt to blackmail anyone?"

"Hold on there." I could see the temper flare in his expressive eyes. "Ruth wasn't that kind of person."

She was a prostitute, but she wasn't a blackmailer. Interesting. "Are you sure?"

"She was a kind woman. She did what she had to do to survive. She'd never try to use that to harm anyone."

I couldn't help but link the very strong attachment Slater

had to Ruth with the way Elizabeth protected Slater. It was an interesting triangle. "You seem very certain."

"There's not a man or woman breathing who hasn't had to do things they didn't like, either to stay alive or to care for their families. Ruth wasn't a thief and she didn't take public charity. She found a way to earn her own keep. I won't judge her on that and you shouldn't either."

I felt heat rise in my face. I was judging her and he was right to call me out. "Could you make me a list of the men who frequented her home?"

"I don't know for certain. Ruth didn't talk about the men she saw." He looked past me toward the street. "Get down. Someone is coming. Your friend is giving me the signal."

I didn't wait but jumped to the ground and dragged the old box to the side of the building. I had more questions for Slater, but I wouldn't get to ask them today. I straightened my skirt and headed toward the parked car, where Reginald joined me a few minutes later.

"I was outside the cell. I heard your conversation with Slater. Are we going with blackmail and revenge or the value of the property as the motive for Ruth's murder?"

"I don't know. I do believe Slater is innocent, but who else would want her dead?"

"We can wait to see who buys her property."

"Slater will be hanged by then."

Reginald nodded. "Let's—"

His suggestion was cut short when the lawman we'd spoken with the day before and three other men surrounded us as we leaned against the car.

# CHAPTER 6

"Did you finish your business with Elizabeth Maslow?" Deputy Gomes asked.

A piece of egg was stuck in his handlebar mustache and moved up and down as he talked. I couldn't make myself look away. Reginald, too, fought the compulsion to stare. He looked past Gomes to the men standing behind him. I let my gaze follow his and recognized them as my "watchers." It was becoming clear to me that there was a system of spies in Mission. Few things got past the nosy residents who all seemed eager to report to the law.

"We're enjoying our visit with Elizabeth and Callie," Reginald said, taking the lead in the conversation, as was proper for a man.

"That brat still alive?" Gomes asked.

"And in the pink of health," I said.

Reginald stepped in front of me. "Both mother and child are fine. Is there a reason they wouldn't be?"

"Deformed creatures often don't thrive. In the wild, the

mother would kill a spoiled baby. You know, to stop the suffering."

Reginald stepped backward just enough to trap the toes of my foot under his heel. He applied gentle pressure. "Well, there are no worries about little Callie. She's in grand health. Elizabeth said she grows stronger each day."

"Abomination," one of the men muttered loud enough for us to hear. They wanted to provoke a confrontation, probably so Gomes could tell us to get out of town. He'd mentioned earlier that we should take Elizabeth and the baby away.

"Tell me the evidence against McEachern in the murder of Ruth Whelan" Reginald said, and I admired his ability to hide his true feelings and to speak in a manner that made it seem as if he sided with Gomes. "That's a terrible thing. So much worse when the victim is a woman."

"A good woman," the tallest of the men said. "Ruth Whelan was butchered by that savage Scotsman. Now he's gonna swing." His glee was disgusting.

"I saw the gallows." Reginald was still conversational, still with his heel lightly pinning my toes to the ground. In another minute I was going to kick him in the back of his knee with my free foot. "Do you have to build a new gallows every time there's an execution?"

"We don't have much cause to hang people here," Gomes said. His suspicion of us was fading as he dug into a topic he enjoyed. "We might get more than one use out of this gallows, though." The men behind him laughed.

"I heard tell there was a traveling electric chair making the rounds in the South. Less trouble, I'd think." Reginald jumped right in, as if a public execution was just another picnic celebration.

"There's no electric source here. Won't be for years."

Gomes hooked a thumb in his belt and leaned against our car. "How much longer are you staying in town? You might get to see the hanging. Trial is set to start tomorrow. The evidence is pretty damning. I'd be willing to lay a wager that McEachern swings before suppertime tomorrow."

Reginald eased off my toe and pulled his wallet from his pocket. "Two dollars?"

"You taking the position that he won't hang?" the taller man, who appeared to be the only one that wasn't mute, asked belligerently.

"I'm taking the opposite side of the deputy's bet. If he wants to put his money on the possibility the execution won't take place, then I'll take the opposite of that."

Gomes snatched the money from Reginald's hand. "He'll hang tomorrow, and that's my bet."

"And if he doesn't, I'll get my money back and two of your dollars?" Reginald wanted to make it clear.

"That's right."

"We might have to attend the trial," he said, finally stepping to the side so that I could be a part of the conversation.

"No women in the courtroom," Gomes said. "They don't need to fill their heads with such things."

"I see," Reginald said, and to my utter fury, he winked at Gomes. "A very wise decision."

The three men behind Gomes—men I'd seen on the edge of town and standing in the road spying on us—laughed at my impotence. They obviously could see the anger in my face and knew there was nothing I could do. Men ruled, especially in an isolated village like Mission. These men didn't mind grinding a boot heel into the neck of the women they had the legal right to control. I wondered if the news that Tennessee had ratified the 19th Amendment on August 18, giving women the right to vote, had even made it to Mission. Women would cast a ballot in November for the presidential election. Would what happened in the broader world matter here? I had the sense that the laws of the United States were of little importance in this place.

Tension with the men was becoming more pointed, and Reginald reached into his pocket and drew out his billfold again, pulling out a few ones and handing them to me. "Why don't you go over to the dry goods store and see about getting those staples Elizabeth asked about?"

Elizabeth had asked for no such goods. Reginald was getting rid of me. While it galled me severely, I also knew he'd make more headway if I left. "Sure, I'm happy to do that. I love shopping." I gave them my brightest smile as I grabbed the money and walked away. I could hear them talking but I didn't turn around.

"She's a looker," Gomes said, "but she needs to learn to tame that mouth of hers."

"It's a process," Reginald said, as if I were some horse he was training to pull a cart. He would pay! I kept walking. I could no longer hear the exact conversation, just the murmur of their voices and the amusement that dripped off their words. I knew he was only acting to further the case, but it stung nonetheless.

Small puffs of dirt rose up from my feet as I made it to the store. I took a minute to lean against one of the posts, kick my shoes off, and dump the sand out of them. It wasn't the most ladylike thing to do, but I'd had a bellyful of propriety.

The grit poured out in a little pile on the porch. I used my bare toes to kick it off the unpainted boards. Mission didn't have a single paved road, and so far I'd seen only one other car. The town also made do without any electrical power. Hand pumps for water were in people's front yards, and women cooked over woodstoves, lugging the cut wood from a shed at the back of the property. When a woman put in a day's labor, she worked, hard. Men too. Those who farmed or cut timber went at it furiously, often heading for the fields or forests at daybreak and not stopping until dusk.

Two horses were tied to the rail in front of the store. I walked up to the nearest and let my palm slide over the silky muzzle. Life was hard for the horses and oxen that pulled the wagons, carriages, plows, and logs. This was a fine saddle horse, and one whose spirit had not been crushed by brutal training. It watched me with interest and alertness, welcoming my touch. Cars were slowly replacing the work horses across the country and that was a good thing. Progress was slow in such isolation, though. It would be a long time before motor cars or any kind of power or telephone grid came to Mission, and I suspected the men who ran the community liked it that way. Isolation was one of the best tools for keeping people "tractable."

I glanced down the street. Reginald was following the four men into the office building. He didn't look back at me. A flame of resentment shot through me, even knowing he was doing the smart thing. Reginald and I were true partners in the agency, and it stung for him to treat me as less than, even when it was for the case. I took a breath, realizing I had to control my unreasonable response. Were I in his shoes, I would do exactly the same and he would not bat an eye.

"Ma'am?"

The silky voice made me turn around abruptly to find a tall, slender man, clean shaved and wearing glasses, standing at my elbow.

"That's my horse," he explained, untying the reins from the hitching post.

The bay horse whinnied to the man, as if greeting him. "What's his name?"

He laughed. "Naming an animal is sentimental foolishness." He leaned closer. "But his name is Sir John Monash."

I laughed. It wasn't a name I was expecting, but one I knew well from the letters my husband had sent me.

"This horse has superlative good sense and so I named him after the Australian general who performed brilliantly in the war."

I hadn't expected his answer. "My husband was killed in France." I forced myself to continue, to find something less emotional to say. "Alex said the Aussy soldiers were teased about being either miners or cowboys, so they called them diggers." Even though I no longer cried every day, it was still hard to force the casual words out. I missed my husband, and at times like this, when I was startled into the memory, the pain was sudden and swift.

"I'm sorry." He tucked the few articles he'd bought in the store into saddlebags. "I lost a lot of friends myself."

"I'm sorry."

"Mrs...."

"James." I held out a hand and he shook it without hesitation, a mark in his favor.

"Michael Trussel."

"And you live here in Mission?" I asked. The sun pounded down on us, and I looked at the store's shady porch with longing. "Might we step into the shade?"

"Of course." He retied his horse and offered me his arm. He walked me to a couple of rockers that had been placed with a barrel between them. I'd seen the set up all over rural

Alabama. Someone would put a checkerboard on the barrel and men who were finished with work for the day would relax with a game. Often drinking was involved, but not in Mission.

"May I get you something cool to drink?" Michael offered. "It's September, but it seems no one has told the sun."

I liked the way he phrased things. Whether I admitted it or not, he was intriguing. "Some water, if there's any to be had."

He went into the store and in a few moments returned with two glasses of water. "Vernon keeps water on hand. The days are hot and hard for farmers."

"Is this the magic spring water?" I asked it with a casual smile but I wondered if this was the healing water I'd heard about.

"Ah, you've heard of the healing properties of the spring that's on Ruth Whelan's land."

I decided to press my luck. "I have. A magical spring that has the power to heal and also the prime ingredient of the best corn whiskey around." His eyes narrowed but he remained completely composed. "And I heard it might be a motive for Ruth's murder."

"Folks do love to gossip." Michael smiled, but only with his lips. "I heard some talk about you and that fellow you're traveling with." If censure was there, it was hidden. "You're family to Elizabeth Maslow."

"So we are. Such a lovely woman and that baby is a joy."

He nodded. "Elizabeth must have told you about the spring."

"She did. I'm not sure she believes it has healing properties."

"Oh? She and Ruth were friends. I figured they'd back up each other's stories."

I couldn't read Michael Trussel. Was he friend or foe? A believer or non-believer? I wished Reginald would come out of the building and stroll over. He was far better at seeing through the disguises that people threw up.

"Tell me about Mission," I requested. "How was this area settled? Timber, mining, what?" Reginald and I had done as much research on the area as we could, but it was always best to hear what the locals had to say.

"There are some caves north of town and there was a mining interest. Coal and some precious metals." A shadow passed over his face but was instantly gone. "Not for me. The extraction was too difficult. There are easier veins of coal to get to if one must mine." He shrugged. "The loggers came for the virgin timber. They're still cutting. It's hard to get the wood to market, though, and again, there are much easier places to cut logs."

"Is the soil here rich and fertile?"

"A little too alkaline, but a farmer who knows his business can do all right." He turned his full attention to me. "You know a lot about farming."

"Not a lot. I was a schoolteacher. I know a little about a lot of subjects."

"They never had schoolteachers who looked like you when I was taking my lessons. Maybe I can talk my old schools into importing a few."

I laughed at the overt flattery. "I understand wanting to explore new places, but why come here? Why this particular place?"

"I was hired to come here."

"I see." But I didn't. Now I knew to probe with caution. "May I ask why you were hired to come here?"

"I was a Pinkerton agent." He took off his glasses and

polished them with his handkerchief. "I was sent to search for a missing man."

I thought of Elizabeth's brother, Ramone. "And did you find him?"

"I did. He was heir to a Boston banking fortune, but his money couldn't help him. He'd been robbed and murdered. By a woman in Victoria. She'd buried him in her herb garden. I do believe it was the finest crop of basil I'd ever seen."

I laughed out loud. I couldn't help it. His irreverence was scandalous. "That's terrible."

"People do terrible things all the time." He stared into my eyes. "I suspect you've seen your share."

I looked down, grateful that I could use the guise of a demure young woman to break his inquisitive look. A proper woman always looked down from a direct stare.

"Are you still a Pinkerton?"

"Oh, no. I'm a...salesman. In fact, I was calling on Vernon in the store to see if he needed any of my wares."

"You sell pots and pans and tin whistles." I moved the conversation back to a lighter place.

"No, my wares are medicinal. I sell healing elixirs, compounds that can break a fever, the braces and wrappings for setting a leg, drawing salve, a potion for teething babies to sooth the gums."

"You're a doctor?"

"No. I merely sell the supplies that doctors need to work effectively."

"How did you come about this profession?" It seemed a stretch to go from detective to medical supply salesman.

"The young man I was paid to find. The one in the herb garden. It was his job. I took it over. I'd had enough of crime and tragedy. I decided on a new career."

I sat perfectly still, the many implications nudging against me. The sun was blisteringly hot, and it was so bright it burned the color out of the road. Even Sir John Monash, who'd been a dark mahogany bay with black stockings, was now a faded sepia. And standing just at the horse's shoulder was a young man. The side of his head was caved in, and blood had washed down his neck and torso and into his pants and shoes. He held a hammer in his hand. And he watched me and the man I talked to.

"Have you ever thought that you might be haunted?" I asked Michael.

His brow furrowed. "A lively change in the conversation, I'll give you that. Perhaps we could discuss this over dinner tonight."

The dead man stroked the horse's neck and I wondered if Michael had inherited the dead man's horse as well as his job. "I'd like that," I said. Michael Trussel knew things about dead people, and I wanted him to tell me.

# CHAPTER 7

Michael Trussel took his leave, saying he would call for me at six o'clock at Mrs. Hattie Logan's house. I had some trepidation, but Michael was an observant man who'd been in the area while looking for a murder victim. If he was any good at his job as a Pinkerton, he'd have observations about the residents of Mission, if not more substantial information.

I took the water glasses into the store and set them on the counter. Vernon McKay gave me a knowing look. "Mr. Trussel is popular with the ladies," he said.

"He has charm," I agreed. "And he seems to like women. That's not the case with all men." I met his gaze with a level one of my own as I talked. McKay's disapproval of me was clear. "Some men appear to consider us a necessary evil."

McKay walked out the front door and looked up and down the road in both directions before he returned to stand behind the counter. "You're of great interest to the people in this community. I hope you realize someone has been watching you since you came to town."

"I am aware. I just don't know why. I've never been of much interest to anyone except my family and husband, who died in the war." I got it out quickly. It was important that he know that I had been married but was widowed. "Why are these people watching me?"

"Not many strangers come to Mission. Even fewer stay. The town's in turmoil over the murder of a good woman. The trial of the murdering rascal who killed her begins in the morning."

It was good that Vernon McKay wouldn't be sitting on the jury for Slater McEachern. "I heard about the murder. A terrible thing. Who would do such an awful thing to a woman?"

"Someone who wanted her property," McKay said.

"And this man in custody is the only one who would benefit from owning that land?"

"He'd benefit the most."

"Did you know Mrs. Whelan?"

"I did. She was a good woman. Worked hard, came to church every Sunday. Helped out old Doc Wainwright with some nursing when he called on her. Good Christian woman."

The storekeeper had to be aware of the rumors about Ruth Whelan. He was merely choosing to ignore them. Or possibly he was someone who visited Ruth in the dead of night, looking for the sin that daylight should never expose. "She was a widow, I heard. That's a hard life even in a town with milk delivery, schools, and fresh produce. Out here, so isolated, how in the world did she make ends meet?" I kept my eyes wide and innocent.

"She took in laundry and sewing. She cooked for the sick and elderly. She made the best bread in the state. My wife often sent me to pick up a loaf for breakfast, fresh out of the oven."

"I'm sure it was delicious. And Ruth didn't have any children?"

"You sure are interested in a woman who was dead before you drove into town. If that's the case."

"What?" I didn't follow what he was saying.

"Meaning you could have been in town before Ruth was killed, for all I know."

It wouldn't be the first time that strangers in town took the blame for local scandal. "Impossible, since someone has been watching me since I arrived." I smiled. "Forgive me. Curiosity is unbecoming. I apologize. I got caught up in the drama of a tragedy." His disapproval of my unfeminine pursuit was clear. "Would you mind telling me about the gentleman I just met outside? Michael Trussel."

"He took a shine to you. I could see that right off."

"He has an interesting job." My cheeks ached from the false smile I wore.

"Yes, he's a traveling salesman of medicinal products. He's very knowledgeable about folk healing, using plants and such. He's not from around here, but he gets on with all the healers and doctors who buy from him." He arched an eyebrow. "He's been keeping company with Melissa Gomes, the deputy's younger sister. Take it from me, that's not an anthill you want to step in."

"Funny, he didn't mention anything about a romantic interest." I pretended I didn't understand that I was being warned off. I looked at the candies he had on the counter. Brightly colored jelly beans filled a jar beside Necco wafers, clove gum —a favorite of my husband's—and caramel creams. I picked up a pack of gum. "I'd like this and a pack of cigarettes. Camel's."

"We don't sell cigarettes to ladies. It's against the law."

"It's for my friend, not for me. And there's no law against women smoking."

"Maybe not where you come from, but you should take that up with Lucais Wilkins."

"Is Lucais Wilkins the sheriff?"

"Might as well be. He's the head of the church board. He and the board make the laws and the deputy enforces them. You don't want to get on the wrong side of Mr. Wilkins or Deputy Gomes."

"No, I don't. Like I said, the cigarettes are for my friend." I tried one more time.

"Then he can buy them."

It was pointless to argue even though I wanted to. I put the gum back. "Is there anywhere I can purchase some healing spring water? I'd like to take some to Elizabeth."

"She's gonna need more than spring water to heal that baby of hers." His eyes were as cold as a dead fish. "I don't think we have anything here in the store for you, Miss. You should wait outside."

"Thank you." I should have known not to ask for cigarettes. If I'd been thinking, I wouldn't have, because in this town the pleasures men took for granted were not permitted for women. If smoking could be considered a pleasure. I kept trying but didn't care for it. Still, I'd been hoping to surprise Reginald with a new pack. He'd smoked his last cigarette on the drive over. It would also have been an excuse for me to follow him into that office building. I was itching to find out what was going on.

The sun outside was brighter and hotter than before, if that was even possible. The high-collared, long-sleeved dress I wore stuck to my body with sweat. Even my shoes were hot. I longed for the short set I wore in Mobile with sandals. In this regard, Reginald suffered as much as I. Decent attire for a man included a long-sleeve, starched, white shirt and flannel slacks. A businessman would add a bow tie or tie, belt, or suspenders, possibly a waistcoat or vest and a jacket. I was about to sit down on the rocker and wait for Reginald when I saw him leave the administration building and walk toward me. Little spurts of ashy dust puffed around his feet.

I started to get up and meet him halfway, but he needed cigarettes. There was nowhere else to buy them. He dropped into the chair beside me that Michael Trussel had only recently vacated. "These people are unbelievable."

"I tried to get you some tobacco but they wouldn't sell to me."

Heat touched his cheeks and he shook his head. "I can't wait to get out of here."

I stood up and went back inside the store and asked for a glass of water. Vernon McKay gave it to me without a word. When I gave it to Reginald, he drank it quickly, wiping his mouth with the back of his hand.

"What happened?"

He lowered his voice to a whisper. Vernon was watching us through the open front door. "They're going to hang that man tomorrow. They don't care if he's guilty or innocent. They started building the gallows the minute he was charged. This is nothing short of murder."

"We should go to Victoria and send a telegraph to Uncle Brett. Maybe he can get the governor to intervene."

"There's not time," Reginald said. He wiped the sweat from his forehead. "There isn't any time to get official help."

"What are we going to do?" My only talent was talking to the dead. So far, I'd been useless on this case. I'd only stirred up the men of the town to dislike me.

"I don't know, but we have to do something." Reginald's misery was clear in his voice and eyes.

"Drive me to Ruth Whelan's house. Maybe there's something there, a clue, some evidence to the real killer." When Elizabeth had recounted her visit to the dead woman's house, I'd felt her horror. I didn't want to go, but I had to.

"Even if we found something, I'm not certain they would listen or accept it."

"We have to delay the trial. If they hold court tomorrow, Elizabeth will go there and try to speak for him."

Reginald leaned in closer to me, his body almost humming with tension. "If she does that, they'll hang her right beside him. Whatever is going on in this town has people looking for someone to blame. They're all angry. They hate outsiders, anyone different. McEachern and Elizabeth are considered outsiders, suspect by definition. That's one strike against them. McEachern came to town and became successful where others failed. He's independent and thumbs his nose at Lucais Wilkins's rules. Elizabeth is educated and without a man. These things, in a place like Mission, are enough to bring down a death sentence."

Reginald wasn't exaggerating. Growing up on the streets of New Orleans and in orphanages, he was very well aware of the dark impulses that motivated some people and always ruled a mob.

"I'll be right back." Reginald stepped into the store and I heard him ask for Camels.

"Might be best for you and the missus to leave town before dark," McKay said.

"I'll leave when I'm ready," Reginald answered, "unless you know a reason I should go."

"Nope, no reason. Just watch yourselves. There's still panthers in the woods and some wild boars. Easy to get hurt out in the woods and hard to get help."

"Thanks for the warning."

Reginald came out the door and signaled for me to walk with him. He lit a cigarette and offered me one but I declined. I was headstrong, but I didn't like smoking enough to make an issue of it on the public street. I had no doubt we were being watched. Almost as if I'd called them forth, I saw two men at the end of town. The same two I'd seen earlier. They stood at the side of the empty road staring at us. I noticed again how their hands hung at their sides and they stood perfectly still. Watchers. But what did they watch for?

We strolled, unhurried, to the car. Reginald opened my door and shut it once I was seated. In a moment he had the car started and in motion. I reminded him of the gasoline shortage in Mission.

"Good thinking," he said. "I'd hate to get stranded here."

"Let's check out Ruth Whelan's place and then drive to Victoria to fill up the tank. I am going to contact Uncle Brett and see if he can get someone up here. It's possible he can have some influence. What we need to do is come up with a way to delay the trial."

Reginald laughed until he glanced over at me and realized I was serious. "I suppose it can't hurt to try to delay the trial somehow. How do you think we can do that?"

"Maybe we can find something at Ruth Whelan's place that will throw doubt on Slater McEachern's guilt."

Reginald drove out of town and when the road forked, he

took the left-hand lane. At my questioning look, he explained. "Mrs. Logan gave me directions before we left this morning."

"I'm having dinner tonight with a traveling medicine sales-man. I'm hoping he might give us some information about what might have happened to Ruth. Who had a reason to want her dead. If Slater didn't do it, someone else did. That's what we need to focus on. Michael knows the area and he's an observant man."

Reginald gave me a look. "You work quick."

"It's not like that." My flush belied my words. Michael Trussel was a good-looking man.

"All teasing aside, are you sure it's safe to carry on with a man you don't really know?"

I shook my head, slightly embarrassed. "I suspect that an unmarried woman is scarcer than hen's teeth around here. I'll be careful. Besides, we don't have any other leads."

"Remember, pull information from him and don't give any. It's like a poker game."

"I wish you could go to dinner with him," I said and meant it. Reginald was far better at gathering information from the living than I was.

"Is he handsome?" Reginald asked with a wink.

"Very. And smooth. He was a Pinkerton. He came here looking for a man who was murdered. I thought at first it might be Elizabeth's brother, the missing Ramone. But Michael said he was an heir to a Boston banking fortune."

The humor dropped off Reginald's face. "Of course Ramone could have lied about who he was." He tapped the steering wheel as he thought. "Be really careful, Raissa. The Pinkerton agents have always been above the law. They have reputations as being more lawless than the criminals they pursue. They're dangerous."

He'd succeeded in unsettling me. "I will take care."

"Give away as little as possible. Play to his ego and extract as much as you can." He put a hand on my shoulder. "Now let's see what we can find at Ruth Whelen's place."

# CHAPTER 8

U nlike the farms that had been painstakingly cleared out of the thick forest, Ruth Whelan's cottage was set deep in the woods with no attempts to tame a yard. The trees grew close around the frame house with a porch just big enough for two rocking chairs and a butter churn. As we pulled to a stop, I saw someone inside the house, staring out at us. A woman.

"There's someone in the house," I said.

"Good. Maybe they'll have some answers for us." We got out and walked onto the porch, our footsteps ringing loud on the wooden planks with the sound of emptiness. I knew then there was no one inside. No one living. "Ruth is here."

"Can you talk to her?"

"I'm going to try." Reginald knew that spirits seldom communicated in a straightforward manner. They used symbols or feelings or mental pictures to send messages. I wasn't looking forward to what images I might receive from a woman who'd had her skull split with a meat cleaver. Still, it was why we'd come here. Elizabeth couldn't tell us who the killer was, but from what I understood of the murder, Ruth had faced her killer as he'd swung the murder weapon. Ruth had known her killer well, from what I'd learned from Elizabeth's dream.

The front door wasn't locked. Why would it be? Ruth was dead. Stealing didn't seem to be a problem in Mission. A first glance around her little house indicated that everything remained as it had been when she was alive. The small living room, complete with a sofa and chair near the fireplace, had several books on an end table. The works of Mark Twain. Ruth had been a reader. The hutch against the wall held dishes with a pretty floral pattern. Delicate. The arms of the sofa and chair were covered with tatted antimacassars that showed real skill. Ruth Whelan seemed to have been a very feminine woman.

In one corner the drawers of a desk had been dumped onto the floor, the contents scattered about.

As we went farther into the house, I saw the carnage. The kitchen table had been almost cleaved in two. A dark reddish stain crusted on the floor and over the sink and drain board. It would seem Ruth had been standing at the sink when she was attacked, just as Elizabeth had recounted in her dream. Glass was scattered on the floor where something had been broken. Suddenly a miasma of remnant emotion—violence and fear—hit me just below my ribs with a sharp pain. When I doubled over, Reginald caught my arm.

"I feel it, so I know it must be terrible for you," he said, eyeing me with concern.

"I'm okay." The impact lessened, but out of the corner of my eye, I saw things slither away. Not ghosts, but remnants of fear and anger. Ruth Whelan's house was filled with bad things.

A rhythmic creak came from a bedroom. It was a short shush, shush, creak. Shush, shush, creak. Shush, shush, creak.

Over and over, not slow but not fast. "Do you hear that?" I asked Reginald.

He shook his head.

There was no one alive in the house, but it wasn't empty, either. I took a breath and stepped toward the sound. Madam Petalungro, a talented medium in New Orleans who had decades of experience dealing with the dead, had taught me that I could withstand even the darkest energy if I took precautions. To that end, I wore a necklace with bits of iron on it. In a battle with a succubus, I'd learned the value of being prepared.

Reginald stepped in behind me as I moved toward the gentle sound. As I stepped into a bedroom, I saw my breath condense in front of me, though the house itself was hot and closed and nearly suffocating with the smell of old blood.

I stopped just inside the doorway, Reginald close up against my back. The room had been completely wrecked. The bed was flipped, the mattress gutted as if someone had cut it open to look for something. Dresser drawers were pulled open and the contents thrown on the floor. The things that Ruth Whelan valued had been trashed.

But that was not what kept my attention. Framed against a big window was a bassinet with yards and yards of blue gingham material. The bassinet slowly rocked, the material rippling and creating the shushing sound. There was no hand to rock the cradle—that I could see. But it moved to the left—shush, shush, creak—and then swung back to the right. Shush, shush, creak.

"What do you see?" Reginald whispered, his breath also condensing in the bitter cold of the empty room.

"A bassinet by the window. There's a baby there." I could hear the cooing.

"There was no baby here," Reginald said. "The deputy said Ruth was a widow and had no living children."

"I think that may not be true." I watched the little crib rock back and forth in a motion meant to soothe a child, the same motion a mother's hand might make.

"Why would Gomes lie?"

"Because Ruth Whelan was more than just a convenient companion for the men of this community. She also had some medical training. She helped the local doctors and nursed the sick." A sadness, so heavy, settled on my shoulders. I thought my spine might snap under the weight of my realization. "Ruth Whelan helped women get rid of babies they didn't want."

"I see." Reginald had spent years in New Orleans in a lifestyle that I knew little about. Abortionists were common to him in the world of prostitutes and grifters that had been his childhood. The flesh trade was a way to survive. He'd managed to stay above the worst of that life, but he was not innocent or naïve.

The little dead baby and its crib vanished. Heat flooded the room, along with the stench of blood and gore that had permeated the kitchen. I gagged and turned away, going out onto the porch and leaning against a rail as I coughed up the water I'd drunk at the grocery.

Reginald helped me to one of the rockers and lit a cigarette. "So, either the murderer was after something in the house, or someone else came here to search." He hesitated. "It could have been the deputy. I get the idea he'll do whatever he has to do to protect his master."

"Lucais Wilkins."

"The man who rules Mission with an iron fist."

I took a steadying breath. "He runs everything according to

the dry goods merchant. He runs the church, the town, the justice system. Mostly he has the final say on what women can and can't do. This is not a good place for a woman. I believe Lucais wants this property. Or something that is or was on it. He's willing to see a woman murdered and a man hanged to get what he wants."

"Do you think that man you met today, the Pinkerton agent, works for Lucais?"

"I do."

"Then you'd best be on your toes."

"I will." I stood up, feeling less nauseated. "Let's see what this house has to offer."

Now that I knew what to expect in the house, I was prepared for the smells and the oppressive heaviness that Ruth Whelan's murder left behind. Reginald and I began a search for a journal, diary, or list. I believed—and so did he—that whoever killed Ruth did so to remove information she had. It was possible she'd gotten too bold and attempted to blackmail some of her wealthier clients. It had happened before. If she was the town prostitute, she'd known plenty of secrets that a lot of people would want buried. If she also performed abortions, she would have had information that could lead to a death penalty. For all involved.

I pulled out drawers in the kitchen and checked to see if anything had been tacked to the bottoms of the drawers. I checked coffee and flour canisters. In the pantry, where so much hard work had gone into jams, preserves, pickles, jars of tomatoes, corn, and butterbeans, I held each jar up to the light to see if some paper had been slipped into the contents for safekeeping.

Reginald went through Ruth's clothes, checking seams and pockets, collars that felt a little thick. He patted down quilts and blankets, felt pillows and even a few stuffed animals he found in the back corner of Ruth's chifforobe.

"I'm going out to look in the shed." I needed to be alone. There was so much going on in Ruth's house that I felt bombarded by emotion. If I meant to connect with Ruth Whelan, I had to get out of the house and into a quiet place.

"I'll finish here and wait for you." He looked around the chaos of the house. "Someone has been through this place with a fine-tooth comb."

Reginald understood. It seemed to me that while he might never be a natural medium, he was developing more ability. And he was attuned to my needs, without explanation.

When I stepped out the back door into the yard, I became aware that I'd been holding my breath. The smell of death had made me sick, but in the clean air that sensation passed. There was a chicken coop in the back, the birds sad and hungry. I fed them some scratch from a barrel and shut them in the coop. Reginald could help me catch them and take them back to Elizabeth or Hattie Logan. I wasn't going to leave them there to starve or be eaten by hawks or foxes or other predators. People thought chickens were stupid, but I liked the happy cluck-cluck sound they made, and the way they minded their own business.

I searched the coop carefully, looking under nests and gathering the eggs as I went. They'd have to be broken and thrown away because there was no way to tell how old they were.

I found nothing in the coop, and even though I mentally invited Ruth to visit, she did not. I could sense her, the pleasure she took in caring for her birds, the satisfaction of the clean nesting area, the raked grounds around the coop, the solid fencing that protected the birds, at least until something tore it open.

"Ruth?" I spoke her name, hoping to entice her.

My gift for seeing spirits had come as a surprise this past summer when I'd arrived in Mobile, Alabama to visit my uncle Brett for the summer. The death of my husband, Alex, in the Great War, had left me at sixes and sevens. I'd taken a job as a high school literature teacher and loved working with the students, but a summer vacation at the beautiful Caoin House was too tempting.

It was on the grounds of Caoin House that I was made aware that Alex's tragic death had awakened a latent childhood ability that I'd suppressed. I could see and communicate with the dead. And what I'd also learned was that the dead were just like the living. Some were merely lost, sometimes unaware that they were even dead. Others had returned to this plane to deliver messages or warnings or threats. And some were evil, desperately clinging to this world, willing to commit terrible acts and inflict harm for a variety of motives as diverse as their living counterparts. Some were very dangerous, too, attaching to the living and feeding off their hopes and fears. The most powerful could manifest and move objects, or even attack the living.

As I walked down the pine needle-strewn path to the barn, I felt only peace. Ruth had loved her cottage, the woods. It was only in the house that I felt negativity and stress. Ruth's life there had not been so pleasant and free.

A horse clopped up to me from a pasture. The gelding looked good, and I found a halter hanging on a peg and captured him. He, too, would have to go to a neighbor's. Someone had to care for him. I led him into a stall and found the feed room and a barrel of grain. I gave him a small feeding. I loved listening to the sound of a horse eating, and I stroked his neck as he chewed.

He lifted his head, ears pricked forward. He gave a low whinny of greeting. When I looked at the open doorway of the barn, I saw her outlined against the white-hot sun.

She was a slender woman, petite, with a tiny waist. She wore her hair up in the old Gibson girl style, more 19<sup>th</sup> century than current, and a long-sleeved dress with a long skirt that suited the place. Mission seemed to be at least thirty years behind the rest of the country. The modern women that had begun to grace even the larger Alabama cities would be run out of Mission on a rail.

"Ruth?"

She came forward slowly.

"I'm so sorry."

As my eyes adjusted to her in the darkness of the barn, I could see that she was translucent. She wasn't strong enough to manifest completely, and I knew she couldn't stay long. It took more energy than she had. The horse went back to eating, ignoring her.

"Who did this to you?"

She raised her hands as if to ward off a blow, and a wave of fear slammed into me. She had died in terror.

"Find..."

The word came to me more as a thought than a sound. "Find what?"

"Find..." She sobbed and came closer. Her head was cleaved, and she'd lost an eye in the brutal attack. "Find!"

It was painful to look at her. "Find what, Ruth?" I kept calm, stroking the horse's neck, focusing on the soothing sound of his eating, the warmth of his hide beneath my hand. The little things kept me steady.

She bowered her head and sobbed. "No, no, no, no." She

mumbled the word over and over. I didn't know if she mourned her own death or something else.

"Who killed you, Ruth?" I tried again.

"Find...him."

I nodded. "We're trying. Was it Slater McEachern who hurt you?"

"No." She lifted her head at an odd angle. "Not Slater. Not him. Find..."

Her word was good enough for me. Slater was not her killer. Elizabeth, no matter how she came by her knowledge, was correct. There was no reason for Ruth to lie to me. The dead were not trustworthy in many regards, but I believed her about this.

"Why were you killed?" I thought she understood me, but the way she angled her head made me wonder if she truly did. She floated closer. Blood saturated her dress. "Why, Ruth? Can you tell me?"

"Because—" She looked up sharply and the horse snorted and pushed away from me, knocking me lightly into the stall. "Run!" In a split second she was back at the barn opening. "Go!" And then she was gone. I heard a car door slamming and a male voice call out.

"What are you doing here? This is private property." The man sounded tense, angry.

I waited for Reginald to respond, and when I heard his voice, I went to join them. The car was long and new, a fancy car. I recognized the make, an Aston Martin. Someone had paid a pretty penny for this car in a place where gasoline wasn't even sold.

The man standing beside the car was prosperous. He wore a freshly starched shirt, ironed to perfection. His moustache was waxed in a continental style, and he wore a fedora even though the day was like an oven. He looked me up and down and didn't bother with a greeting. He turned back to Reginald, who stood on the porch.

"You're trespassing on private property," he said.

"And so are you," Reginald offered casually. "Unless you now own Ruth Whelan's place."

"Who are you?"

"Reginald Proctor and my associate, Raissa James." Reginald waved me over to stand beside him. "And you are?"

"Lucais Wilkins." I supplied his name.

He gave me a searing look. "What are you doing here?"

"I suspect the same thing you are," Reginald said. He was his best in this kind of situation. He couldn't be ruffled or upset.

"I intend to buy this property."

"We're also interested buyers," Reginald said, supplying the false story we'd worked out with Uncle Brett. "A lot of people might be put off by the fact a brutal murder was committed here, but not us."

"I thought you were in town visiting a relative," Lucais said.

"Can't we do both?" Reginald asked.

"I'm going to town and I'll send the deputy out here to force you to leave."

"Afraid of a competitive bid?" Reginald asked, and I felt my heart catch. Lucais was no one to mess with.

"You'd better pack up and move along. This place isn't for you," Lucais said. "Take some friendly advice before it becomes unfriendly."

Reginald didn't move, but the front door of the house slammed with enough force that the panes in the window rattled.

Lucais started forward angrily but stopped when Reginald

came down the steps to meet him. "Someone wrecked this house," he said. "I wonder what they were looking for."

"I don't know how you did that, slamming that door without touching it, but I'm not falling for any of this bullshit you're selling. I don't know why you're really on Sand Mountain, but take my advice and leave while you're still breathing." He got in his car and drove away.

"Lucais Wilkins," Reginald said to me. "The man who runs the town. He's a bully and if he hangs Slater McEachern, he's a murderer."

"And the man who's going to make it a point to run us out of town."

"He can try," Reginald said. "He can try."

# CHAPTER 9

Reginald settled the chickens and the gelding at Elizabeth's place. The old boy had trotted behind the car without tugging on the lead rope once, and Reginald had made sure to go slow. I would have ridden him back if I'd been able to find a saddle. Elizabeth told us that Hattie would send her helper to get them before the night came on.

"Are you sure I won't be charged with theft?" Elizabeth asked. "Lucais would rather see those animals die of starvation and thirst than think I was benefitting from them."

"I'll speak with Gomes," Reginald promised. He sighed. "You haven't been honest with us about Ruth. How she survived. The things she did."

Elizabeth nodded. "No, I haven't. She was my friend. I didn't see the need to speak about it. She took no pleasure in what she had to do."

"Except that's probably why she was killed."

Elizabeth studied the ground before she looked up and held my gaze. "Yes. She knew everyone's darkest secrets. She talked about that sometimes, when she was feeling sad and alone. She said she carried the worst parts of so many people with her."

"So many men," I said.

"The men used her, yes, but the women did their part in making her feel excluded. She provided what many of them cared to withhold. She helped them hide their appetites and sins, the men and the women alike. They should have thanked her, not shunned her."

"We ran into Lucais Wilkins," I said. "He's planning on buying the property."

"I've heard that, but I don't see the natural spring as something Lucais really views as a valuable investment. He's not the kind of man who's going to be content selling jugs of water, or even moonshine, for that matter. Lucais doesn't see himself as a merchant or bootlegger. There's something else there."

"If Ruth had a list of her clients, the men she...serviced and the women she helped get rid of their pregnancies, where would she have hidden it?"

"I've thought about that a lot since she was killed. If she had something of value to hide, where would that be? I think I know."

"Elizabeth, I don't mean to sound harsh, but you need to be completely honest with us. We're wasting our time unless we know the whole story," Reginald said.

"Of course. There's a circle of stones in the woods behind her house. Big stones, not ones she could move herself. They've been there for ages. She liked to go there to think. She said the place held power left behind by the Indians."

"I'll go there right away." Reginald looked at me. "I want to go alone. If someone is watching the place, I don't want you caught up in things."

"No." My reaction was quick and firm. A faint glimmer of the terrible dream swept over me. Reginald could not get arrested. They truly would hang him. "It's too dangerous for you. You more so than me. I can go."

Reginald started to say something but stopped. He frowned. "Why are you saying I'm in more danger than you?"

Elizabeth nodded. "Because she's seen that danger." Her voice rose with excitement. "Gabriel came to her. He gave her a dream, a glimpse of the future. She met Gabriel and felt the touch of his power."

"Touch of what power?" Reginald was quickly getting upset. "Who is this Gabriel?"

"I had some dreams last night. Disturbing." Even as I talked about them they slipped further from my grasp, as dreams were wont to do. "At first it was just a regular dream. I was walking on a beach with the surf and the night. It was good. Peaceful. Then I was sinking in the sand. Reginald was in danger." A flash of the Caoin House cemetery, gravediggers hard at work, hit me and I blinked back tears, which Reginald didn't miss.

"It must have been some dream."

"Trust me. It was." I didn't want to talk about it. To speak of it made it too real. The terrible grip of the dream had caught me once again, unnerving me. I needed action, to do something to combat the sense of helplessness that made my limbs heavy and unresponsive. "Give me the keys to the car. I'll be back as quickly as I can."

"You can't drive." Elizabeth put her hand on my shoulder. "It isn't allowed. Women don't drive. If they catch you, they'll put you in jail."

"What do you mean women can't drive? Why not?"

"It's against the laws of Mission. Only men can drive."

"Even if a woman owns a car?"

"She cannot. And they will arrest you."

"That horse of yours. Is she ridable?" I'd get back to Ruth's and search the area around the circle of stones for a journal.

"She's very nice. Easy."

"I'm a good rider. I grew up riding. Is there a saddle?"

"There are two, but you'd have to ride sidesaddle. It's how things are done in Mission."

"I can manage that, though I have a better seat astride."

"I'll saddle her for you," Reginald offered. "But I still think I should go."

"No." I didn't want to tell him what I'd seen in my dream. I only knew he could not find himself behind the bars of that jail or he might never leave alive. "Maybe you could take Elizabeth on her rounds to deliver eggs. Meet some of the local women. See what they know."

Reginald wasn't pleased, but he wasn't going to fight me. "Brilliant. "

I leaned in and captured his gaze. "It's important that you do this. We need another suspect. The women will talk to you a lot quicker than they'll talk to me. Maybe you can find out if they've heard gossip, or have ideas of who really killed Ruth. You can charm them."

"Doubtful. They'll know that their husbands visited Ruth."

"That's what I'm counting on." I grabbed his hand and held it, remembering the hands I'd seen holding onto the bars of the jail. An artist's hands. "A lot of women are possessive. Sex is a duty to them, but it is also the hook another woman can use to catch their wayward spouses, if left…unsatisfied. To many of the married women, Ruth would have been a blessing because she was a woman who could take care of their husband's needs but who would never attempt to claim a man in marriage."

"And she knew how to avoid the trap of a baby," Elizabeth said. As if on cue, little Callie began to make gurgling sounds. I wondered if the baby could cry. I'd never heard her do more than the soft sounds of a baby lamb.

"Let me get the horse ready." Reginald stepped out of the house. His footsteps across the porch were quick and even.

"What gift did Gabriel give you?" Elizabeth asked eagerly. "I knew when I met you that you'd be able to see him."

Elizabeth's loneliness was apparent to me. She'd been so very alone in the birth and raising of her daughter, in running the farm. Her friend had been murdered, and she lived in a town that viewed her with suspicion if not contempt.

"Can you dream the truth?" She caught my hand and held it in a gesture of friendship.

"No." I frowned. "The dream was a nightmare. Terrible. I never want to experience that again. He touched my shoulder and I was paralyzed. Sinking deeper and deeper into the sand, and I couldn't move. I couldn't save myself. If that's what he considers a gift, I want no part of him."

"He touched you." Elizabeth's eyes were wide, the skin beneath them tense. She was afraid for me.

"Just a light brush more than a real touch."

"He has marked you."

I shook my head. "No. There are no marks on me." I'd washed myself before I dressed. Except for the sunburn on my arms and face, I was unmarked.

Elizabeth took my wrist and led me to a mirror near a hutch. She brushed back the fine hair beside my ear. Just in the hairline, so small I hadn't noticed it, was a red mark. In the poor light I couldn't see it very well.

"That's just a bug bite. Mosquito or fly." I rubbed it and it tingled.

Elizabeth pulled me toward the light from the kitchen window. She lifted her heavy black curls to show me a similar mark on her skin. I bent close. It looked to be concentric circles inside a red dot no bigger than a pencil's eraser.

I knew it wasn't a bug bite. And how did she know to look for the mark on me? Was it possible the creature from my dream had left a physical reminder in my flesh? The idea was terrifying. A few of the spirits I'd encountered were able to manipulate the physical world, but most could not. They were remnants of a dead time, spirits and emotions lost between the worlds of the living and the dead. But this winged creature, this...man or angel, had abilities I'd not yet encountered. The implications were frightening.

Elizabeth was watching me, seeing the truth of what she said sink in. "I'm sorry," she said. "If I'd known Gabriel could reach you in that way I would never have called on you for help."

"What does this mark mean?"

"I don't know."

"Do you know anyone else who has it?" I would find answers and come to a way to remove it.

"I've heard stories."

Rumors and old tales about angel markings were not what I wanted to hear. I didn't have another option, though. I couldn't even call Madam Petalungro to ask her advice because there were no telephones in Mission and possibly not anywhere on Sand Mountain. The terrain and isolation kept them insulated from the broader world and that was how they liked it. I'd hardly been in town twenty-four hours and the disconnection from the real world was already wearing on me. Now, I knew I was about to hear things that would further upset me.

"Tell me what you've heard."

Reginald came in the door. "Your horse is tied at the rail. You should go and get back as quickly as you can, Raissa. Don't go inside the house. Promise me."

"I promise."

Reginald checked his watch. "If you're not back in two hours, Elizabeth and I are coming to find you."

That would put Reginald *and* Elizabeth in danger. "It shouldn't take more than half an hour to ride there, an hour to search, half an hour to return. That's enough time. I'll drop the gelding by Hattie's on the way."

"I don't like this." Reginald could be as stubborn as I was.

"Reginald, I think we should visit Gaylen Brooks." Elizabeth smoothly turned the conversation. She bent to pick up her baby and little Callie cooed with pleasure.

"Who is Gaylen Brooks?" I got a glass of water and drank it down. It was hot outside and I had a solid ride in front of me.

"Her husband is Welton Brooks, Lucais's right hand man. A real brute if Gaylen's bruises are a testimony. Gaylen may talk to us about Ruth. Maybe."

I wiped my hands on my skirts and walked out the door with Elizabeth, Callie, and Reginald. I liked to ride horses, but I didn't relish this ride in the frying sun. No matter, it had to be done. Reginald retrieved Ruth's gelding and handed me the lead rope. I untied the reins and stepped into Reginald's laced hands as he boosted me into the sidesaddle.

"Will you be able to mount on your own to come home?"

The sidesaddle was tricky. "I'll find a stump or use the porch. Mariah is a calm horse."

"Mariah can run like the wind," Elizabeth said. "But she's easy to stop and she doesn't spook."

"I'll be fine." I clucked to the mare and we set out down

the road at a trot. She was easy to sit, and when we'd cleared the yard, she broke into a rocking canter. The gelding followed easily behind and I was at Hattie's before long. She came out and took the lead rope. She cast a concerned look at me but didn't comment.

"Thanks, Hattie. We'll see you later." I was off again. All I had to do was sit deep in the saddle, holding tight with my right leg. While I preferred to ride astride the horse, which was more secure, I'd learned sidesaddle and in the backward world of Mission, it was a lucky thing I had. My hand strayed to the place behind my ear where the red mark tingled. I loosened the reins a little more and let Mariah gallop. I couldn't get out of Mission fast enough.

# CHAPTER 10

I approached Ruth's house at a walk. Mariah was blowing, and she needed to cool before I let her graze in the abandoned paddock. When it was safe to turn her free, I loosened the saddle's girth but left it on her. I removed the bridle and put her in the yard beside the barn, then closed the paddock gate. She was secure but able to munch grass and get water from the trough. I hung the bridle on a post and headed to the woods, finding the path that Elizabeth had clearly described.

It was mid-afternoon, and the shade of the woods was welcome. I trudged along the path, eyes peeled for the circle of stones and also snakes or other wild creatures that might not mean me harm—except I was invading their territory. The woods around me were home to bears, wolves, and some wild cats like cougars and panthers. They avoided human contact at all costs, unless they were provoked or couldn't run. Every living creature had a right to protect their home. I just didn't want to be on the receiving end of that fight.

The chatter and activity of the wild creatures relaxed me.

They'd alert me if anyone else was about, and that was my biggest worry. If my suspicions were correct, Lucais had come to Ruth's before, searching for something. I had to take care that I didn't lead him to what he sought.

A limb snapped to my right and I dashed behind the trunk of a large white oak. Holding my breath, I tried to calm my pounding heart so I could hear better. I'd had a sense that eyes were on me. Watchful eyes. The woods suddenly went quiet. No birds or scuttling of small animals. The little creatures—the prey—knew someone dangerous was in their midst. I found a cedar limb the size of my arm and picked it up. It was better than no weapon at all. The stillness was more frightening than the sound of something rustling alongside me.

"Ruth?" I called to her. "I'm here to find your killer."

The wildlife noises resumed, and I hiked along an incline for about a quarter of a mile before I saw the circle of stones. It was unmistakable, as Elizabeth had said. Twelve stones created a circle, with one large stone in the center. The area was clear of all grass and leaves, as if someone had swept it only moments before.

The power of the place settled over me. This was an ancient gathering spot, a place where humans came to connect to nature and to spirit. My upbringing had been mostly traditional Protestant church, but as I'd begun to explore the spirit realm, I was learning that there were many ways to celebrate creation, many versions of the divine being I called God. And also many ways for religion to be used as a cudgel to batter people into servitude. Through the ages there had always been those who used religion to bully and belittle others.

This place harkened back to a time and people who didn't need the written word, interpreters, or buildings filled with riches and wealth. Here, the trees and stones were holy. Nature was the temple. The whisper of the wind contained a sense of a mighty creator. For the first time since we'd come to Mission, I was able to truly draw a deep breath. I was on sacred ground.

The tension in my shoulders fell away, and I sat in the dirt, leaned against a sturdy rock, closed my eyes, and merely listened. Not for the sound of an interloper or danger, but for the whisper of the divine. A raw energy from the earth shifted up through my bones, and I could feel it pass out the top of my head. Whatever it was, it was powerful and warm.

I realized that Ruth and Elizabeth shared more in common than I'd first understood. Yes, they were both outsiders in this strange community, but it was more than that. Both were connected to nature. Both walked outside the narrow world-view of Mission. Both were considered dangerous. Ruth had paid with her life. It was very possible that Elizabeth and little Callie would also.

I kept my eyes closed and tried to focus on where Ruth might have hidden a journal or diary. It had to be a dry place. Anywhere outside wasn't optimal. The heat and humidity, the almost daily rains, would quickly destroy paper. But if Ruth had reason to believe she was in danger, she might have found a temporary hiding place.

A small giggle came to me, and the hair on my arms lifted in response. No child should be out in the woods alone. Grown men didn't giggle, and if they did, I was in worse trouble than I'd anticipated.

I opened my eyes a slit, forcing my body to remain relaxed. If I meant to survive this—if it was an attack—I had only the element of surprise on my side. My fingers wrapped around the cedar club I'd found. Movement came from the north side of the clearing. Whoever it was crept slowly closer. In the narrow slit of my eyelids, I couldn't see anyone.

A twig close by snapped and it took every bit of restraint to keep from reacting.

"Hey, lady, are you okay?"

The little girl's voice held real worry. I opened my eyes to see a child in a blue gingham dress standing at the edge of the stone circle. She held a well-worn doll in one hand, her dark eyes wide open with fear and concern.

"Who are you?" I sat up and brushed the dust from my back. She didn't answer, and I tried again. "My name is Raissa. What's your name?" She had to be about seven or eight. What was she doing wandering around in the woods by herself?

"Hildy."

I recognized the name with a start. "You're the little girl who was lost in the woods, aren't you?"

She nodded. "Where's Mrs. Whelan?"

This was going to be difficult. "Have you come to visit her?"

She nodded. "We play dolls. She makes clothes for Lindy." She held up the doll, which wore a blue gingham dress made from the same material as Hildy's. "She makes pretty clothes, but I can't take them home. I'd get a strappin' if my daddy knew."

"Why would he be mad about doll clothes?"

"I'm not supposed to see Mrs. Whelan, but she's nice to me. She tells me I'm smart. And pretty." She picked at her doll's sparse hair. "She tells me about places far away. Good places."

"She sounds like a good friend." My chest tightened painfully. I could not tell this child that Ruth Whelan was dead. Hildy's loneliness was visceral.

"She is. But it has to be secret."

"I won't tell."

She glanced toward the house. "Where is she?"

"She can't come today, Hildy. She's...gone away."

Tears brimmed in the little girl's eyes. "Gone away? Forever?"

I didn't want to tell her the truth. I'd not intended to. Should I lie or break her heart? There really was only one choice. "Yes, forever." If Ruth Whelan was a forbidden friend, Hildy would eventually ask about her. And then she would face punishment.

"Where did she go?"

"To a place where she's happier. You don't worry about her. She sent me here to tell you goodbye because she didn't want to leave without telling you how much she cared about you."

"I wish she hadn't gone." The child didn't cry but her shoulders slumped in defeat. It was possible Ruth had been her only true friend. Life in Mission would be hard for any girl child, but for one as sensitive—and lonely—as Hildy, it would be hell.

"Me too. But she didn't really have a choice. She had to go."

"What about the doll dresses?"

I wasn't certain what she meant. "Where are they?"

"Hidden. So no one will know. Mrs. Whelan put them in the rock with her precious things. That's what she calls them. Precious things." She held the doll out to me but I didn't take it. She valued her dolly, that much I could tell. "Will you play dolls with me?"

"Sure." Hildy's plight touched me deeply, but I couldn't help a growing excitement. Did the child know Ruth's secret hiding place? "Where did Ruth hide the doll dresses?"

Hildy went to a mid-sized rock beneath a white oak with a number of gnarled roots. "Help me, please." Hildy pointed at the stone, and I pushed it away, revealing a deep indention in the tree roots. I reached into it and found a bundle wrapped in waxed butcher paper. I pulled it free and put it on the ground.

"That's the dresses." She smiled as she sat down beside them. "This one, the yellow, is the newest. My mother never let me have a yellow dress. She said it would show dirt too easily."

What possible difference could it make to give a child the color dress she wanted, dirt or no dirt? "You'd be very pretty in a yellow dress. Maybe when you grow up you can buy one for yourself."

She shook her head.

"Just a minute." I reached deeper into the hole and found something else, a slender book. It too was wrapped in the waxed butcher paper that would give at least a little protection from the damp. My heart pounded with the possibility that this was what I sought. "There's something else here." I pulled the bundle out and turned to show Hildy but there was no one there. The child had vanished.

Limbs crackled just down the trail—someone was coming. I shoved everything back into the hole and put the rock in place. When Lucais Wilkins came stalking into the clearing with two bearded men carrying rifles, I was sitting in the dirt, leaning against a rock.

"I told you once that you're trespassing," Lucais said. "What are you doing here?"

I held onto the reality that it was a much better thing that Lucais had found me here instead of Reginald. "I'm thinking of buying Mrs. Whelan's property," I reminded him.

"Women don't own property." He said it as if it were law, and possibly it was law in Mission.

"Oh, it's not going to be my property but my uncle's."

"And who is your uncle?"

"Brett Airley from down in Mobile. He runs a shipping company. His boats bring a lot of the supplies up the Alabama to the Tennessee for transport here." I swallowed, aware that my throat was dry and I was deeply afraid. "Uncle Brett loves the mountains." I was babbling and I forced myself to stop.

The suspicion on Lucais's face had lessened whatsoever. "What are you doing here? What are these rocks?"

"I was looking for the property boundary and I turned my ankle. I was giving it a chance to stop hurting so I could walk back." I pulled myself to my feet and hobbled a step or two before I sat down again. "Would you consider bringing my horse to me so I can get home? She's just back by the house."

He motioned one of the men to fetch the horse before he stepped closer to me as if he could sniff a lie on me. "Home?"

"I'm lodging with Mrs. Logan while I search for property for my uncle." It was good luck Uncle Brett had given me that excuse for nosing around the country. "My uncle is determined to have a place to come to next summer to get away from the big storms down along the coast. We just had a bad one. Twenty-four people drowned along the Alabama coast. You see, Uncle Brett has done so much for me, I offered to find a property for him." I continued to babble about Uncle Brett and the powerful people he knew and the parties he held. My goal was to let Lucais know that while he might control Mission, I had connections with people who had far more power in the outside world.

"And you somehow decided to look at the property of a murdered woman, out of all the places you could look." He drilled me with a penetrating glare.

"I didn't actually know that until I got here." I gave him my most innocent look.

"Then why this property?"

"It's the spring. I heard about the healing qualities of the water. Uncle Brett suffers from gout. I thought it might help him." The lies tumbled out of my mouth.

"I'm buying this property. You'll have to find another place."

I didn't have to answer because the man had returned with Mariah. I scrambled awkwardly on top of one of the stones, feigning my alleged injury. He brought the mare to stand so I could mount. When I had the reins in my hand, I thanked them for their help.

"Tell your uncle to find another property." Lucais was standing close to Mariah and he made the placid mare anxious. She danced and sidestepped to get away from him.

"I'll tell him, but you should know my uncle is a very determined man. With lots of money. I've never seen him set his cap for something and fail to get it. But I'll tell him." I nudged the mare into a trot and we left the clearing. I could only hope I'd left no traces of the hidey hole beneath the stone. And where in the world had Hildy Morse disappeared to? The child was there and suddenly gone. She'd probably heard the men coming since I'd been preoccupied digging in the hole. She was smart enough to know she couldn't be caught in the woods with me—that would mean serious trouble for her. Thank goodness she'd made her escape before Lucais saw her. I had no doubt her punishment for even speaking to me, a stranger, would have been severe had she been caught.

I passed the big touring car parked in front of Ruth's house. In the motorcar, Lucais could overtake me easily if that's what he decided to do. The idea sent a bolt of terror through me. Was he playing with me, like a cat with a mouse? Did he mean to let me get a ways down the road and then roar up behind me?

When I was half a mile from Ruth's cottage, I turned Mariah into a narrow dirt lane that wound through the woods. The thick, dense growth of trees wouldn't allow the car to pass. Nonetheless, I rode deeper into the woods before I stopped Mariah. I'd give Lucais some time to do whatever he was doing at Ruth's and then clear out.

Half an hour passed before I set Mariah back toward Ruth's house. I was torn between going back for the journal or riding back to Elizabeth's, but the possibility of a storm decided for me. I'd grab the journal and the doll dresses. Hildy set a store by those dresses and Elizabeth would know how to get them to her or leave them somewhere she could enjoy them. Much more pressingly, the journal might answer a lot of our questions. I had to retrieve it.

As I hoped, the big touring car was gone from Ruth's property, and I rode Mariah back to the circle of stones. She waited patiently as I got off and recovered the doll dresses and the journal. Any minute Reginald would be driving to look for me and I didn't want to put him at risk, so I didn't take time to look at the journal. I mounted using the rock again and pointed the horse toward home. I held one truth tightly—Lucais Wilkins might have been looking for the book, but he hadn't found it.

# CHAPTER 11

With the small leatherbound book and the doll dresses tucked into the bodice of my dress, I leaned into Mariah's mane and let her take me back to Elizabeth's at a pace much faster than I normally rode. I feared Lucais—or his helpers who, in my mind, had taken on the characteristics of the buzzards that had welcomed us to Mission—would step out of the woods and try to apprehend me. It was a dark fancy, and not a pleasant one.

Uncle Brett's car was parked in front of Elizabeth's house, and I was glad they were back from their assignment. Being with Reginald made me feel safer, even if I knew logically that was not true.

I rode into the front yard, dismounted, and quickly led Mariah to the barn where I unsaddled her and rubbed her down. She was as reliable as Elizabeth had promised. "Sweet, sweet girl." I gave her a handful of grain when I knew she was cool. When I was certain she was fine to turn out, I let her go and settled on an old bucket to examine the journal. I opened it and stopped, so disappointed that I couldn't even form a thought.

Whatever information was in the journal was beyond my grasp. It was in some kind of code I'd never seen before. I'd risked so much to get this journal and it was all for nothing. I picked up the bundle of doll dresses and turned to go into the house. I dreaded seeing the expectations of Elizabeth and my partner crushed. I'd barely gained my feet when I stopped short. Reginald stood in the doorway of the barn, but he didn't say anything.

"What is it?" I asked, dread creeping up my spine. He was upset. I could feel the dismay radiating from him.

"A child has been killed."

"Oh, no." It didn't matter that I wouldn't know the child—the death of a young person was always a tragedy. "I'm so sorry. Was it someone Elizabeth knew?"

"Yes. Hildy Morse."

"That can't be." I started toward Reginald, stunned. "There must be a mistake. I just saw Hildy not an hour ago. She was at the clearing behind Ruth's house, waiting for Ruth to come and play dolls with her." I held out the bundle of dresses. "See, she showed me where these were hidden and that's how I found the journal." I held it out in the other hand. "Reginald, the journal is in some kind of code."

"We can deal with the journal later. You have to hear me. I don't know who you met in the woods, but it wasn't Hildy." His face was in shadow and he spoke gently.

"It was her. She said her name, Hildy Morse. I had to tell her that Ruth wasn't coming back. See, she showed me where to find this!" I held the book out again as if it were proof of what I'd seen. Even as Reginald took it from my hand, I knew Hildy was dead. The little girl who'd visited me was a spirit. All of the signs had been there. She'd shown me the hiding place, but she'd made no effort to move the stone herself. Because she couldn't. She'd been there one minute and gone the next. No real child could have vanished that fast. "She was looking for Ruth to play dolls with her," I repeated.

But it was more than that. I understood now, though I hadn't at the time. Hildy was lingering, looking for her grown-up friend to help with the confusion. The child hadn't yet realized that she was dead. Her spirit didn't know where to go, and I'd been unaware that she needed my help. My heart constricted in my chest just thinking about the poor lost soul. I hadn't known Hildy Morse, but I felt her death acutely.

I offered Reginald the journal, but instead of taking it, he pulled me against his chest and held me. "Ah, Raissa, I'm sorry. Elizabeth is beside herself. First Ruth and now the little girl. It's a damn tragedy. This will be too much for her."

"You're right." When I was certain I wouldn't cry, we went back to Elizabeth's house. Her eyes were swollen and her face puffy from crying. She put a cup of coffee in front of me and poured one for Reginald before she sat down.

"What happened?" I hated asking for details, but I had to know. The child I'd seen had not shown any signs of injury. Often the dead wore their manner of death. A slashed throat. A head cleaved open. Not Hildy, though. She'd been as whole and perfect as a young girl could be.

"They said it was an accident, but that's not true. They said she was in her yard alone and fell into the well. I don't believe it." Elizabeth's dark eyes blazed.

The idea of a little girl tumbling into a well was painful, but I wanted to believe it was an accident. I was fully aware of the blackness of the human heart, but the monster who would kill a child would do anything. "Do you know someone who would hurt a child? Hildy in particular?"

"I don't know. It's a terrible thing. At least they can't pin this on Slater McEachern, since he's already behind bars." Bitterness etched her voice.

I decided against telling her that I'd seen Hildy, at least right now. "How was your visit with Mrs. Brooks?" I thought if I turned the conversation, Elizabeth could compose herself. She was on the verge of tears again.

"She's the one who told us about Hildy." Elizabeth jiggled the infant in her arms, an automatic maternal action. Even with Elizabeth's obvious distress, Callie cooed, kicking her feet and pummeling the air with her fists. She put a hand on her mother's chin and gurgled. The effect was almost instantaneous. Elizabeth drew in a long breath and when she exhaled, she was completely in control of herself.

Reginald and I exchanged a long look. He'd seen it too. The baby's touch had calmed Elizabeth. It would be more accurate to say it had numbed her pain. I stood up and reached for Callie. Elizabeth put her in my arms. The baby's hand pressed into my sternum. A sense of peace started in my chest and spread rapidly through my body. It was the most peculiar feeling, like putting ice on a burn.

I looked down into the baby's navy eyes and knew the exchange had been deliberate. A gift from an infant. "Hold her, Reginald." I offered the child to him.

He took her in his arms with a skill I hadn't anticipated. Reginald had grown up hard, an orphan on the streets and some time in a hellhole called an orphanage. He had no family at all, but somewhere he'd learned to hold an infant.

Callie reached up to capture his mustache in her little

webbed hand. She tugged on it and burbled, kicking her feet. I'd never seen such a happy child. Reginald sighed, and the tension in his face evaporated. Whatever Callie had, it was powerful.

I didn't believe in angels walking the earth or children conceived by angelic union, but what did I actually know about the realms beyond this one? Before this past summer, I'd convinced myself that the things I saw out of the corner of my eye, the shadows flitting through moonlight, were all my imagination.

A week at Caoin House had taught me better. The dead were not always dead. And they were not always honest or good. Sometimes they could be very bad, motivated only by malice and ill will. There were more variations on what a ghost might be than I'd ever anticipated, even after reading the fabulous ghost stories of Poe, James, Bierce, and Freeman. I'd come to Mission at Elizabeth's request because I'd assumed—falsely —that she was haunted. Why else would she call an agency that specialized in hunting ghosts? There was something supernatural at work in Mission, but ghosts, at least in my experience, could not conceive a child. So who did Callie belong to? And what was the infant capable of?

The child Reginald held had definite powers. Did it matter where they came from? Not to me or Reginald or Elizabeth. But it could matter greatly to Slater McEachern. If this child conveyed the power to dream the truth, as Elizabeth believed, she was essential to McEachern's future—to the jury verdict that would hang or free him.

"You asked about Gaylen Brooks?" Elizabeth dragged my thoughts back from the dark realm. "She had every reason to hate Ruth, but she didn't."

"I grew up in New Orleans around prostitutes and their

clients," Reginald said. "I've seen some unconventional arrangements, but nothing like what's going on in Mission."

"How do you mean?"

"Ruth worked for Lucais Wilkins," Elizabeth said. "He took a cut of everything she made, and he kept her working, even when she wanted a different life. Ruth was like an animal to Lucais and those men, to be used however they wanted, whenever they wanted. She couldn't escape them."

"Gaylen's husband was one of the men who frequented Ruth's house at night, wasn't he?" I asked.

Reginald nodded. "Apparently he was a very frequent guest at Ruth's. Enough so that the Brooks family was strapped for money all of the time. From what Gaylen said they were barely scraping by."

"What is her husband's role in Mission?" I knew he had an official capacity. He must have brought goods or a service to Lucais or Lucais would never allow him to continue so far in debt—if Gaylen Brooks could be believed.

Reginald nodded, intuiting what I was thinking. "Welton controls the loans at the local bank, at Lucais's behest. He says who gets a loan, or an extension, or some leniency on late payments. Only those who are unfailingly obedient to Lucais get any consideration. Lucais runs it but Welton is the face of what passes for the bank. And he's also in charge of the schools."

"So a man who frequents prostitutes and runs his family into the ground with debt is in charge of educating the children."

"Mostly the boys," Elizabeth said. "Girls don't often go to school, and those who do drop out when they're twelve or thirteen, of marriageable age."

"Twelve!" The calm Callie had bestowed on me evaporated in outrage.

"Train them young and they're less likely to rebel at a later date." Elizabeth's words were bitter. "It's abuse, but Lucais and the board approve the marriages. The parents of the young girls are often too afraid to speak out against the union."

"Isn't it illegal for a child to marry?"

"Not illegal if the parents consent. There's no one in Mission who would dare to withhold consent for a marriage Lucais arranged."

"And the mothers go along with this?"

"This is what they've been raised to know and expect. It's one reason a stranger like yourself is so dangerous. The women might begin to realize there's a different world outside Mission. They're given a rudimentary education of reading and numbers so that they're equipped to run households, budget, and sell eggs, cheese, or crafts." She leaned forward, elbows on the table. "Hildy wanted to learn. She loved history and reading."

Elizabeth suddenly pushed back from the table and stood. She paced to the kitchen window to look out. "Ruth told me about her friendship with the child. Hildy had a big imagination. She thought there were fairies in the woods and she loved stories about them. Ruth was helping her learn. I helped too. As far as I can tell, Hildy was the only good thing about Mission for Ruth."

"Do you think someone found out she was talking to Ruth?" Would they actually murder a child just for wanting to learn? The possibility notched my sense of unease up into something more akin to panic.

"I don't know," Elizabeth said. "Lucais has spies everywhere. You know he does. They watch the roads and drift by people's houses, making sure their 'laws' aren't being violated. They watch what you buy in the store and how you dress. Sometimes I'd swear they can tell what you're thinking. And they all report to Lucais."

I hadn't yet told Reginald about my brush with Lucais. I had to, eventually.

"There's no newspaper in town?" Reginald asked.

"None. And none allowed within the city limits. If you brought one here with you, it would disappear from your car. Such things are a danger. They put ideas into the heads of women and children. Ideas that can only bring punishment and suffering."

Something had been bothering me. "Why are you really here, Elizabeth?" Elizabeth didn't belong in Mission. She was educated, exposed to a bigger world. She was indeed a danger to the rule of law in Mission. It could only end with her being crushed. Why had she stayed so long? Waiting for her brother's return was an answer that was wearing thin.

"I don't have a choice. I have to help Slater McEachern."

"Even if it costs your life?"

"Even if." She retrieved Callie and held her close until the baby made a soft purring sound. "You should get ready for your dinner date, Raissa." She kept her gaze on her child.

I wasn't ready to concede defeat in my efforts to get Elizabeth and Callie to leave—with or without Slater McEachern. "I understand you want to save McEachern, but what about your child? If they kill you, what about Callie?"

Elizabeth leveled a gaze at me. "I've already told you. That's why you're here. You understand how special she is. You feel her. And if something should happen to me, I want you to raise her."

# CHAPTER 12

Hattie Logan had rigged an outdoor shower, and the water, warmed by the hot sun, felt fabulous. I washed my hair and changed my clothes, still opting for conservative dress though I longed for the shorter, cooler skirts of the modern world. In a small act of defiance, I wore a garnet necklace that had been my mother's and shoes with heels and several dainty straps. After broiling in the car for a week and sweating all night, I didn't care that Mission would be scandalized. I wanted—needed—to enjoy a few feminine pleasures. I had no idea where Michael Trussel intended to take me to dinner. I suspected it wasn't the small diner by the jail. That was far too public. It didn't matter where we went, I was vain enough to want to look nice, even though I had plenty of reservations about the evening.

I knew two things about Michael Trussel that made me believe our dinner was nothing more than an attempt to pump me for information. Michael was a former Pinkerton, and he'd been flirting or toying with the local law's kid sister, Melissa Gomes. If Michael truly intended to make a life in this area, he knew better than to play the Gomes girl false, which meant he had to have a business reason for spending time with me. Therefore, this was a set up to see what I might reveal.

Once I was clean and sitting on the porch for my hair to dry, Reginald sat beside me. He held the journal out to me and I took it with some reluctance. "It's some kind of foreign language," he said. "It's a language I don't understand."

My hopes faltered as I looked at the strange symbols that didn't translate into any language I'd ever seen written down. It wasn't a romance language. I knew a few words in those. "Do you have any ideas?" I asked. "Russian? Something like that?"

"I don't have any ideas, not yet. But that doesn't mean we can't decipher it."

"Time is running out. They'll try him tomorrow and likely get a verdict. You know it's a foregone conclusion that they're going to hang him unless we come up with something that refutes the murder charge. This," I shook the journal lightly, "is useless."

"Then why was Lucais out in the woods behind Ruth's house? Why would she keep it hidden if it wasn't important?"

I'd told Reginald about my encounter, and I could see it upset him. But it was over and done. Lucais hadn't threatened me. Not really. And now Reginald made a good point. "I don't know."

I handed the journal back to Reginald. "We can work on this when I get back from dinner. I won't be late, I assure you."

"Just be careful, Raissa. These are dangerous people. We don't know how this Trussel figures into the picture. Elizabeth said everyone in town knows he's dating the deputy's sister. I'm not thinking this is a smart move to go out with him."

"Tell me about Welton Brooks and the bank loans."

"It's a rigged system," Reginald said. "I felt sorry for Mrs.

Brooks. Lucais runs the law, the church, and the town. Welton loans money to people, so he controls who survives a bad year and who doesn't. Most who need a loan are already sliding down the slope of financial ruin. They become desperate if they can't pay their loan notes. It only takes a few months of missing a loan payment and they've lost everything. Mrs. Brooks is a nice woman, but she said her husband enjoys fore-closing on a family and putting them out in the road. She hates her husband, but she can't get away from him."

The power divide in Mission was bleak and clear. Those who curried favor with Lucais and Welton had an easier time of it than those who bucked them. Lucais's favorites got loan extensions, or help making the payments.

"Is there anyone who can put Lucais in his place?" I asked.

"No one in Mission." Reginald sounded bleak. "He controls this town. Everyone is terrified of him. His cruel streak is well known. From what I've gleaned, no one from out of town is interested in fighting Lucais. There's not enough gain for them."

"Is it possible Lucais killed Ruth himself?"

"That's what I was hoping to prove," Reginald said. "So far there's no evidence of that. Lucais is a brutal, cruel man, but Ruth was an asset. She made money for him. She kept men who otherwise might have looked for higher wages or better jobs from leaving the area. He would never let her go from Mission, but I don't think he would have killed her."

"And Welton Brooks? Could he have killed her?" He was Lucais's toady, and sometimes men like him took vicious plea-sure in stepping on those they felt were powerless.

"From what his wife said, he would never do anything to get on the wrong side of Lucais."

I let out a huff of frustration. "So neither is a viable suspect for Ruth's murder. Any other men or women who might want to kill her?"

"Gaylen as much as said that many of the wives tried to help Ruth out. They were by and large glad that she was in town to occupy their husbands."

I thought of Alex and the intimacy and joy we'd shared. Had he turned his attentions on another woman, it would have broken my heart. But Alex was a man who loved with his heart and his body. I didn't know if Lucais and Welton were capable of love of any kind.

I drew my attention out of the past. Reginald and I had to confront this moment, the present, and the things that were about to be set in motion early tomorrow morning. The trial would be swift and I had no doubt where it would end. Things were looking bleak. "The trial is tomorrow and we have nothing."

"We have to keep Elizabeth out of that courtroom." Reginald's pose was languid, leaning against the porch post as he swung a leg over the side railing. But the knuckles of his hands were white with tension.

"They won't let her in the courtroom door. Women aren't allowed to attend trials in Mission."

"That won't stop Elizabeth." Reginald had a good reading on our new friend. She was as willful as I'd ever dared to be, though she was far more reserved. There was a cold fire in Elizabeth, and when it came to justice for Slater McEachern, that fire burned hot. She claimed to have no romantic interest in him, and I took her at her word. Slater had been a friend to Ruth, and to Elizabeth at times. She was a person who stood tall for her friends.

The screen door creaked and Hattie came over to us. "If

you're hungry, I have some field peas and cornbread for supper. You're welcome to eat with me."

"We have something we must do, but thank you for the generous offer." Reginald was smooth. "Hattie, we never expected you to feed us. Please don't go to any trouble."

"No trouble. The garden made good this year. There's plenty of fresh vegetables, just not a lot of meat or sugar." She went back inside and the screen door shut behind her.

I made sure Hattie was gone before I spoke. "Where are you going, Reginald?"

"I have a plan." He grinned. "You'll find out about it later tonight if it works." He stepped back to the driver's side of the car. "I wish I knew where Trussel was taking you for dinner."

"Me too." I had a queasy feeling about being alone with Michael Trussel. "Has anyone mentioned any dining establishments near here?"

"There's the café in town, and then there's something called the Brass Kettle. That's what I'm betting on. I won't be far from you, Raissa. Just be careful and try not to give anything away."

I nodded. "That's my plan."

He got behind the wheel and drove away. I stepped up on the porch out of the sun.

"Are you two related?" Hattie asked from the shadows of the hallway. "Cousins like?"

"We're business associates. We're both working for my uncle. He sent us to look for some property for him."

"He's a handsome man and you're a pretty young woman." She wasn't making an accusation, just an observation. "There's been talk at the dry goods store. Mr. McKay doesn't like you much. He said you were uppity and that I shouldn't let you stay here."

The realization that we could make life difficult for Hattie hit me hard. "We can leave. We don't want any trouble for you."

"No, there's no trouble. I make ends meet renting out my rooms. I rent to all kinds of people and I can't let McKay and his vicious tongue take food from my mouth."

"Hattie, we don't want trouble," I repeated.

Hattie peered closely at my face. "What do you want? You're not here for the healing spring water or the church singing."

"It's like I said, my uncle sent me to look at some property, including Ruth's, to see if he might purchase it for a summer retreat." I decided to stick with my lie because it was the safest answer for Hattie, should she ever be questioned. Reginald and I would leave, but Hattie would remain in Mission. "Uncle Brett heard about the property but he couldn't come right now. I help him with things. He sent Reginald because he thought it was unsafe for a woman to travel alone. I can drive, but I understand I shouldn't do it here in Mission."

Hattie shook her head. "Don't let those men catch you driving or even thinking about it. They'd hurt you. Most of them have never driven a car. Can't afford one. Seeing a woman driving would be a punch in their gut and they'd definitely punch back."

"I hear you. Thank you for the advice."

"I'm brewing some fresh tea. We'll have a glass when it's done."

"That sounds terrific."

As I waited for my dinner date, Hattie and I chatted about fall gardens and the heat. Hattie went to check something on the stove and I sat on the porch for a moment longer. Beyond the clearing of the yard I saw something move.

Two watchers stood just within the shadow of the forest. They wore the overalls and straw hats of farmers, but they stood motionless, their hands hanging limply at their sides. "Who are they?" I asked Hattie when she returned.

"Bad men," she said. "Don't look at them. Don't acknowledge them. They watch and report back to Lucais. Their presence here is not good."

I hadn't expected her to speak out. A pang of guilt struck again—those watchers were here because of me and Reginald. Hattie didn't need this grief. Reginald and I had to leave. "Hattie, we'll pack up tomorrow. This is too much to put on you."

"Hush, now. If Olin was alive, they wouldn't dare lurk about my woods. They bully everyone in town, standing and staring when someone is out of line. They're only here because I'm a widow." Hattie's words were hot. "Now enough about those spies. You take yourself inside. It's not seemly for you to meet this man at the door like you're over-eager. And, Raissa, watch your step. He's been courting Melissa Gomes, the deputy's sister. If he's such a fool as to throw her over, the price is going to be high." She brushed past me and went into the kitchen.

I'd heard that before, and I took it for gospel. I wondered if Melissa Gomes was a buck-toothed horror that the whole town had to take her side, or if Deputy Gomes was so vindictive that no one wanted to get on his bad side. I went into the parlor and glanced out the window for one last look at the watchers. To my surprise, Hildy Morse was sitting on the edge of the front porch. She looked up at me and held up her dolly. "I can't find Miss Ruth," she said. In the blink of an eye she was standing at the window only inches from me. The speed of her movement made me gasp and step back. "I looked everywhere, but she's not here. Can you help me?" Her lips didn't move, but I heard her thoughts.

"Tomorrow," I promised her.

She remained at the window as if she wanted to come inside. She was only a young girl, lost and alone. She had no idea she was dead. I wanted to help her and I needed to question her. "Come back here early in the morning," I mentally told her.

"We're going to play dolls."

I didn't know if she understood me or not, but I put my hand against the windowpane and she smiled before she faded away. Gathering my composure, I hurried to the kitchen table and sat down.

I'd just finished my tea when I heard a car approach. I peeked out the kitchen window, moving the lace curtain back just enough to see Michael exiting the car. Hattie went to answer the door when Michael knocked, a formality that tickled me. Hattie had assumed the role of protector of my reputation.

Michael joined us in the kitchen for a glass of tea. He wore a suit cut to the latest fashion, and his hair was groomed and polished. He stared at me over the rim of his glass, and had I not known better, I would have thought he honestly fancied me. Snake charmer, and I wanted to be a willing snake. I missed the attention of a man, and Michael was smart and handsome and at ease with me. He included Hattie in the conversation and made her laugh, which warmed me.

When his tea was gone, he stood up. "We should get going. I don't want to keep you out too late."

"That's a good plan." I picked up my clutch. There was nothing in it but a lipstick that I'd failed to put on. Hildy's unexpected appearance had rattled me. Besides, Mission was a plain community. Face paint would not be favored. I preceded

Michael out of the house and waited for him to open the car door for me, allowing him the chance to be a gentleman.

"You look lovely," he said as he got behind the wheel. "That dress brings out the color of your eyes, yet somehow I think your regular wardrobe is a bit more...modern."

"It is, but I didn't want to offend anyone here or make them uncomfortable. When in Rome..."

"You're wise for your age," he said.

"How old are you?" Just because I couldn't wear my slacks and short skirts didn't mean I couldn't be a little bold.

"I'm thirty-two."

"Were you in the war?"

He hesitated. "No. I don't believe in wars."

I wanted to press, but I didn't. As foolish and impossible as it was, I wanted an evening without ghosts or guilt. Michael had stayed safely home while my husband had not. It's possible he was afraid to confront battle or to kill, or perhaps he was just a man who valued his hide more than his country. I didn't want to know or be forced to judge his motives. Alex had not wanted to go to war, but he'd felt it was his duty. When he'd gone to enlist, I hadn't fought him, though I wished now that I had. If only I'd tried to stop him... This was a mental game without a good ending and I pushed those thoughts away.

"Your face is expressive when your brain is busy. You're trying to decide if I'm a coward."

He read me too easily. "It's a question I ask often. Of many people."

"I was in medical school, training to become a doctor. I meant to go overseas when I could help the wounded, but I wouldn't have been a soldier."

Medical school was a twist I hadn't seen coming. "What happened?" The burden on my heart eased a little.

"I witnessed a robbery and gave chase. I apprehended the thief and turned him over to the law. After a few hours in detention, the man gave up his fellow thieves. A ring of outlaws that had been deviling the area was broken up and the leaders brought to justice. About a week later, I got a call from the Pinkerton Agency." His smile was wry. "My life's direction changed before I knew it. I thought I'd work for Pinkerton for one case, just to experience that life because it sounded...like an adventure. I completed the case, which was to track down a bank robber. I was hooked and stayed with the agency for nearly a decade. I traveled around the country. I saw the West. I never even thought of going back to the books, sick people, and diseases."

I thought about the Confederate ghost I'd first seen at Caoin House and how that one incident had rippled into a tidal wave of change in my life. "Was it fate or whimsy, do you think?"

"A philosophical question. Was I meant to be a detective instead of a doctor? I can't say. Are you a theologian or a scholar?"

"I was a high school teacher for several years, before I moved to Mobile to live with my uncle."

"I'll bet those high school boys thought they had died and gone to heaven when you walked into that classroom. All of my high school teachers crept out of the grave each morning to teach. When the sun set, they returned to their caskets."

"Educated by ghouls, were you?"

Michael threw his head back and laughed. As the wind swept his hair and the last glow of the sun touched his face, I felt his sexual attraction like a touch. Michael Trussel was a dangerous man. I was a practical, independent woman with a level head and a hard check on my desires. Still, there was no denying that Michael tempted me.

"Where are we going for dinner?" I focused on the basics of this date. I needed a quiet place if I intended to pump him for information.

Michael shot me a grin. "Across the county line to a little place I know. It's small and not so fancy but the food is good and we can get a gin fizz or maybe a Collins. I keep some good stuff there for special occasions."

I stilled my initial reaction. "So you *do* drink?"

"And so do you." He turned right down another dirt road. The lavender hues of dusk were setting in, and somewhere in the distance was a wood fire. The smell was pleasant and reminded me of long winter evenings reading books curled on the sofa in my parents' home. "You've earned your independence and the right to do as you choose. A drink does no harm."

I shot Michael a sideways glance. "That's contrary to the laws of Mission. Especially for women."

"Some women. Never doubt there's a hierarchy among the ladies as well as the men."

That was information I tucked away. "I suspect that Lucais Wilkins and his henchmen drink."

"I don't keep up with Lucais's bad habits and I urge you not to either." The dimple in his cheek came into play when he grinned. "The women in Mission are good for running a household. Other women are good for fun. I like a woman who's experienced life, has some opinions, reads books."

Unspoken were the words—and wouldn't expect marriage. "What a liberated view you have, Michael."

"The world is changing. Women can vote now, though I'll bet very few in Mission will register."

"As soon as I get back to Mobile I intend to register." The realization that Mobile was now home made me smile. Somewhere along the way, I'd stopped thinking of Charleston, the city I'd lived in until I came to visit my uncle, as my home. That issue had been settled in my subconscious.

I relaxed into the car seat. Michael was a good driver. He'd turned the headlights on and they swept the right side of the road as he made another tight curve. Two men were standing just behind the first row of trees. These were not the watchers I'd grown used to. These men wore hoods over their heads and faces.

"Stop!" I called out, and Michael slammed on the brakes.

"What the hell?"

"There are men in green hoods back there just in the trees. Like the men who watch me and Reginald all the time. Back up. I want to talk to them."

"That's a very bad idea, Raissa." Michael let the car idle in the road but made no effort to back up. "Those are dangerous men. You're an educated woman. I know you're aware of the white hoods, the secret society of the Ku Klux Klan and the fear they instill. They're meant to keep Negroes, and sometimes wayward women, in line."

"I know of them. Cowards." I'd seen their work.

"Perhaps they are cowards, because they hide their identity. This group, the Green Men, are much the same. They police the community and punish those who flaunt the laws of Mission."

As distressed as I was by the realization that an organized group was enforcing Mission's unique laws, it was a possible lead in the case we'd come to solve. "Was it one of them who punished Ruth Whelan to death with a meat cleaver?"

He sighed and put the car in motion. "You don't need to talk about this."

"Oh, but I do." He had no idea how much I needed to talk about this.

His jaw clenched and I couldn't tell if he was angry or worried. "Talk like that and Mr. Proctor won't be able to keep you safe, Raissa. Neither can I, if you poke that sleeping bear with a stick. Now let's just have a nice dinner. By the time we're finished, those men will have gone home."

# CHAPTER 13

The trees that hugged the road suddenly thinned, and Michael pulled into the rocky parking lot of a small wooden building that blazed with lights. Music filtered into the night, a jaunty dance tune that came from a live band. I drew back in surprise. "The woods around Mission are filled with surprises. Diners that serve a drink, a parking lot full of cars and only one mule-drawn wagon."

"There's an attempt to hold back the future in Mission, but it won't last. That never works. No matter how willful Lucais may be, he can't stop change."

I didn't comment, and Michael got out and opened my car door, offering a hand. Even when I stood safely on my own two feet, he continued to hold my hand as we walked to the front door. The delicious smell of grilled meat came from the back.

"This is the best bar-be-cue in four states, but they also have wood-grilled steaks and chicken."

"I like almost everything." It wasn't a lie.

The interior of the Hickory Pit was rustic and busy. There were only ten tables in the place and seven of them were in use. Michael pointed to a small table in a corner. Tucked away in a little nook, we had some privacy.

A middle-aged waitress placed drinks on the table. I took a sip, surprised at the combination of champagne and gin.

"It's a French 75," Michael said. "I grew fond of them working a Pinkerton case in New York. I taught Nellie how to make them for me." He held up his glass in a salute to the waitress. "Of course, we have to drink a number of them. Can't waste a bottle of good champagne."

He was teasing and I enjoyed it. "I've never been to New York, but I'd like to go. I have a...friend who lives there part of the time. I could visit her."

"That would be Zelda Fitzgerald?"

I was shocked, but I shouldn't have been. He'd been a Pinkerton. He had contacts and connections everywhere. "Yes. She has such a zest for life." Zelda had actually hired Pluto's Snitch to help her save a friend, a young woman who might have had brain surgery had it not been for our intervention. Reginald and I had saved Camilla from the probe of the surgeon once we'd figured out that she was possessed. It had been a very close shave.

"A very modern woman. And someone who makes no effort to avoid scandal."

I searched for censure in his tone but found none. "She would never deliberately hurt another person, but she demands the freedom to be herself."

"Her husband's books are excellent. A bit sad, don't you think?"

"I do." It surprised me that Michael had read F. Scott Fitzgerald's books. The novels were far too racy for a man who chose to stay in Mission, Alabama.

"I understand you're also a published author."

This time the shock made me carefully search his face in an effort to determine his motives. "Not yet. My first story will be published next month." My great love had always been literature, especially the stories of hauntings and ghosts from the masters such as Poe. Uncle Brett had encouraged me to try, and in a remarkable turn, I'd actually sold a short story to *The Saturday Evening Post.*

"In a very prestigious magazine. You're something of the master of ghost stories, from what I could find."

I didn't deny it. "You know a lot about me, so why don't you tell me about yourself?"

"I'd like an introduction to your uncle Brett Airlie. I'm considering another career change."

I showed no reaction even though I wanted to ask for the details. If he was playing me for an introduction to my uncle, I wasn't going to assist him. "I'd love to introduce you if you travel to Mobile. I'm sure Uncle Brett would find you delightful."

"I've always been interested in waterways. I know a lot about the submarines that were sunk in Mobile Bay and up and down the Mississippi River during the Civil War. Steam engines revolutionized river travel, and your uncle played a big role in that. The machine is going to change the way humans work and I want to be part of that change."

"Uncle Brett would be very interested in hearing your theories. He's an inventor also. Just let me know a time and I'll make it a point to be in Mobile to make the introductions."

"Perhaps over Thanksgiving. I like to be in a city for the holidays. This is a community that upholds family and if you don't have a family, well..." He shrugged.

"You're welcome to join us in Mobile. Our door is always open to business associates and friends." One thing for certain, if Michael was up to anything untoward, Uncle Brett would sort him out. And in the meantime, I might learn something beneficial about my case.

"Thank you." He reached across the table and squeezed my hand. "You travel a good amount to pursue your investigations, don't you?"

Again his knowledge caught me unprepared. "Yes, a bit. I haven't made it as far as New York City or San Francisco, but I'd like to." I played it casual, but Michael's thorough knowledge of me and Pluto's Snitch was deeply unsettling. Staring into Michael's placid blue eyes, I sensed something alert and dangerous hidden behind the façade of mild interest. Had Michael dived so deeply into my past because he truly wanted a meeting with my uncle or was there something else at work? Whatever his reasons, he'd worked extraordinarily quickly. Mission had no telephones or even telegrams. The flow of information was stifled by the isolation. Somehow, though, Michael Trussel had managed to find out plenty.

"I've heard you're here to look at property for your uncle. He trusts you to do such a job?"

"Uncle Brett is busy, and I can determine the value of a piece of land. Ruth Whelan's property is perfect for what he wants—a modest house, good water, and it's on a creek that's deep enough for a small boat. He loves his boats, as you can imagine."

"Do you think he'll bid on Ruth's property?"

"I think he will, but he may change his mind and want to go farther north, maybe into the Smokies." Now I wondered if he really had just come to pump me about my uncle's intentions. I wanted to think he was interested in more than a real estate deal, but I didn't know his true motives. "Do you know when the property is liable to go up for sale?"

He shook his head and signaled the waitress for another round of drinks. When she brought them, he ordered for both of us—a sample platter of the bar-be-cue with potato salad and baked beans. Normally it would have chafed me for a man to assume so much, but with Michael, I found it flattering.

"Where are your parents?" I jumped in with a question before he could.

"They're dead."

"I'm sorry. Any brothers or sisters?"

"I'm not close with my family. My brothers are successful businessmen. They frowned on my decision to be a private investigator in what they called a sordid profession of prying into the lives of others."

I couldn't help the grin that matched his. "I've heard that too."

"But you look into the secrets of the dead as well as the living."

There was no point denying it. "Sometimes the past is the root of a problem."

"Can you see dead people?"

Reginald had warned me not to reveal too much. For all I knew, if I admitted anything, they might hang me as a witch. "This isn't a conversation for now. When you come to Mobile, I'll tell you all about what I do."

"Agreed."

The food arrived and I realized I was starving. The delicious French 75s had relaxed my inhibitions. I reached for a rib and ate it while holding it with my fingers, enjoying the tangy sauce that had been cooked into the meat.

Michael followed suit. "There's nothing sadder than a person who tries to cut the meat off a barbecued rib."

"Sad," I agreed. We drifted into silence as we ate and

listened to the small band that played in a corner of the café. Banjo, fiddle, and guitar, the musicians laughed and teased some of the dancers.

"Do you like to dance?" Michael asked.

"I do. But I'm not all that good at it. I like to waltz."

"I figured you for a Charleston practitioner?"

"I've practiced in front of a mirror, but I look pretty awkward. I need a teacher."

"I can fill that position."

Was he really offering to teach me to dance the Charleston? "Surely not here?"

This time he really laughed. "No, not here. When I visit Mobile. I'm sure we can find a suitable place to work on your dance technique."

He sounded serious about visiting Mobile and that pleased me. "I'm stuffed." I pushed my plate back. I had to be careful with my emotions, but I also had to press him. "I heard about the little girl who fell in the well."

"Hildy Morse, yes, the whole thing is just terrible. Hildy was bright. And a handful. She didn't mind her mother. She was always running away from home. Mrs. Morse tried hard to keep Hildy safe, but the child had a wild streak. She loved the woods."

"How did she fall into a well?"

"I've been asking myself the same question. She was smart. And while she was wild, she wasn't careless or stupid. She had to be looking into the well. She must have been, to have fallen down it. But why would a child look into a well?"

"Could I see the well?"

"Why?" His eyes widened. "Do you know something about Hildy?"

"Of course not," I lied. "I'm just curious. You were a Pinkerton, aren't you curious?"

"Indeed I am. I'll pick you up tomorrow and take you to the well. I want to be sure Mrs. Morse isn't home—you can understand why having a stranger poking around would upset her. She'll be at the mortuary at nine preparing the body. We can go then."

It sounded ghoulish and almost cruel, but I wanted to see the well, to see if perhaps I could connect with Hildy to find out what had really happened to her. I didn't have to reveal to Michael anything I saw, and there was always the chance Hildy would show up at Hattie's house in the morning. But if she didn't, this might be a chance to learn something on my own. Reginald would be busy in the courthouse with the trial—which I couldn't attend because of my gender. But I could see if Hildy had anything else to tell me. Being at the location where she died might make it easier.

"What time does the McEachern trial start tomorrow?"

"It's been postponed." He reached for his wallet and laid out money for the bill.

"What?" I couldn't believe it. We had more time.

"I shouldn't tell you, but I don't see what it will hurt. There's some talk that Hildy Morse was murdered. If that's the case, it throws some doubt on McEachern as Ruth's killer. Folks aren't going to believe that there are two killers in Mission, a place where there's been only one murder in forty years, and that was over money. Lucais decided to postpone the McEachern trial until he determines what happened to Hildy. Shouldn't take long."

"Does Lucais Wilkins think Hildy was murdered? Was there evidence that she was murdered?"

"He hasn't said that, but he decided to postpone McEachern's trial until Hildy's death is settled. The town is too stirred up."

That was the first reasonable decision I'd heard in Mission. "Does he think McEachern may not be guilty?"

"Just the opposite. Lucais is certain McEachern is a cold-blooded killer, but he's afraid the town might believe otherwise because there's a dead child, one who may have been killed while McEachern was in prison. To hang a man, there has to be true community support. Lucais is just covering all his bases."

"What do you believe about McEachern? You're a Pinkerton, trained in investigative work. You live here and have heard all the evidence against McEachern, I'm sure."

"It doesn't matter what I think."

"It does to me." And I meant it.

"McEachern doesn't know when to mind his own business."

That wasn't an answer. It was more of a warning. "Do you believe he murdered a woman?"

"Someone did, and it's as easy to believe it's him as another."

"It's important to me that you answer me honestly."

He handed the money he'd laid out to pay the bill to the waitress. "In my opinion, there's not enough solid evidence to hang a man. The person who killed Ruth is right-handed, and McEachern is left-handed. I don't think he's guilty, but that won't stop Lucais from hanging him. There's something between those two and I'm not certain what."

"Is it Ruth's property?"

He shook his head. "There's something more than a piece of property."

"What's the physical evidence against McEachern?" I was pushing hard, but it was now or never.

"It took a strong person, someone who could really swing that cleaver, to kill Ruth the way she was killed. McEachern visited Ruth. He'd tried to buy her property but she didn't want to sell. He'd made statements in town that he meant to have it."

"There are plenty of stout men here in Mission and more than one with an interest in Ruth Whelan's property. The men are all strong from timbering and farming. Weak men don't make it here. Or weak women for that matter. If there were evidence of another motive, another murderer, would that make a difference?" I didn't mention the journal I'd found or my quickly growing suspicion that whoever had killed Ruth was after information, not property. Reginald had warned me to get information, not give it away.

"Probably not to Lucais. McEachern was a regular visitor of Ruth. Some folks said he was sweet on her, that he didn't like the way she made a living. The general opinion is that Slater McEachern killed her in a fit of jealousy when she refused to give up...prostitution."

"Had he offered to marry her or provide for her?"

"I don't know. Lucais thinks so. He believes McEachern pressed her but that Ruth didn't want to marry him."

"Is there something objectionable about him, something that would make a woman averse to a proposal?" I thought of his work-roughened hands, the slight brogue, the lilt of his voice—all things I found enjoyable.

"You'd have to ask a woman," Michael said. "Or maybe someone you know."

The jolt of fear that came with his words made me realize I'd grown too at ease with Michael. "I think we should go."

"Yes, it'll be late when we get back. I don't want to ruin your reputation."

"I don't live here so I don't have to worry about that."

"Live here or not, you still have to worry about what people think of you in Mission. *I* worry about it."

His words came to me as a rebuke and warning. I stood up and walked out of the little diner.

The night was pitch black, the moon and stars covered by scudding clouds. Michael's last remark in the diner had set my nerves ajangle. I couldn't be certain that Michael had threatened Reginald, but I also couldn't determine if his remark had been innocent. He knew a lot about me and my family. What had his research told him about Reginald? My partner could be in grave danger.

"When are you leaving Mission?" Michael asked as he handed me into the car.

"Soon. My business here is almost complete. I need to find the date when Ruth Whelan's property goes on sale in case my uncle would like to submit a bid. There are a couple of other sites I'd like to see in nearby locations, then we'll head back to Mobile."

"Then you and Mr. Proctor really weren't here on a case?"

I didn't want to outright lie, because it could prove dangerous to Reginald, Elizabeth, and me. "As you know, I have an interest in ghosts and such. I'm a writer. I find my best inspiration for a story comes from real life. When I heard about the brutal murder of Ruth Whelan, I wondered if it would make a good story. You know, how her spirit might linger. It's good fodder for a tall tale."

"Have you seen her?"

His question caught me off-guard. "What do you mean?"

"I know you have a gift, Raissa. I know what your investigation agency does. I know you can see and communicate with the dead sometimes. Have you had a chance to talk with Ruth?"

I settled back in the seat as he drove out of the parking lot. I had to figure out the smartest answer. "No, I haven't. But I'd like to. Perhaps she'd tell me who killed her." Was I drawing a target on my own back? I didn't know.

"How did you come by this gift? The more I know, the better I can try to protect you."

I wasn't certain I believed him, but lying about something he already knew seemed unwise. "I've always had it, though I convinced myself not to see for a time. My husband's death overseas...opened this door again."

"And do you see him?"

"Not often enough."

"You aren't over him, are you?"

I let the cooler night air lift my short hair off my face and neck. "No, I suppose I'm not. I wonder if I'll ever be."

"Probably not." Michael reached across the seat and took my hand. "I don't mean that to sound hard or cruel, but when you truly love someone and lose them, you're irrevocably changed. It doesn't mean you won't be happy again or find love, but this love for your husband will always be there too. Another layer."

He spoke as if from experience. "Have you lost a love?"

"I have, but it's a story for another time." He pressed harder on the accelerator and the car shot down the darkened road, the headlights creating a hole in the wall of trees that made the darkness so much blacker.

I was content to ride in silence, trying to organize my thoughts and emotions about the evening that had just passed. I had a gentle stirring of feelings for Michael. I couldn't deny it.

I found him attractive and intriguing. And also dangerous. I didn't know which side he played for—the truth or those in power. I couldn't risk Reginald or myself in an effort to find out.

We made a sharp curve a little too fast and something broke out of the woods in front of the car. The headlights illuminated a man who wore a strange green hood with eye and mouth holes cut out. He pointed a gun at us and pulled the trigger. The windshield of the car shattered, and Michael hit the brakes hard. The car slewed in the sand as he tried to hold it steady on the road. The trees and road and night sky swirled as the car went out of control. I gripped the dashboard, prepared for the inevitable wreck. The car's front wheels hit deep sand and locked. We were thrown into a slide that ended against two trees. The jolt of the wreck whipped my head into the dash with a solid crack. I fought the darkness that came down around me, but I was no match for it.

## CHAPTER 14

When I came to I couldn't move. My head throbbed and my body ached in places I never thought had feeling. It took me a moment to realize I wasn't paralyzed but that I'd been tied to a tree trunk in a sitting position. About five feet away, Michael had met the same fate. His head lolled on his chest, and blood covered his shirt. Had he been shot? I couldn't tell, but I had a terrible feeling that he was horribly injured, maybe dead. His body looked completely limp.

The headlights of Michael's car shone on us, and a figure stepped out of the woods. The man was a silhouette in front of the lights, but I could see he still wore something over his head and face: a green hood.

"What do you want?" I tried to fight my bonds but I was still weak and disoriented.

"You don't get but one warning here. Leave."

The voice might be familiar. Maybe the grocery owner, Vernon McKay, or even Deputy Gomes. I knew I was grasping at straws, but I had to fight. "Why should I leave? I've done nothing wrong."

"No questions. No answers. Get your fancy man and drive out of town tomorrow. You won't get another warning."

He walked out of the light and into the darkness. I waited for him to return, but he didn't. In the distance I heard other voices. I waited for as long as I could before I wiggled out of my bonds. I hadn't been tied tightly. There'd been no intention of holding me there. The rope was meant only to detain me until the men could get away. I hurried to Michael, who was beginning to moan. I untied him and eased him to a prone position on the ground. His eyes fluttered open and I read confusion.

"What happened?"

"We had a wreck."

"A wreck?" He tried to sit up, but I held him down with one hand. He was too weak to resist.

"Some man stepped out in front of us. He deliberately made us crash. He shot at us." I couldn't tell how badly Michael was injured or even if he'd been shot.

"Who?"

"I don't know. He was wearing a green cloth on his head. Like the men you told me about. The Green Men."

Michael stilled. "Are they gone?"

"Yes."

He inhaled and forced himself into a sitting position. "We have to get out of here."

"They left. We're okay for a minute."

"We aren't." He squinted against the pain as he sat up straight. "We have to get out of here. Can you drive?"

"If the car is operable, I can."

"Get me into the passenger seat if you can. If not, leave me and get out of town. Go to Victoria and get the sheriff. If someone else steps out in the road, run over them."

"Who are these people?" He was scaring me. I hadn't completely trusted Michael, but now I had no one I could turn to. If the men returned, intent on killing us, I wouldn't be strong enough to stop them.

"They're part of the church council. They run everything and they don't like strangers."

"Are you shot?"

"No, I don't think so. Just cut from the glass. Are you hurt?"

"Bruised, but nothing serious. Take my hand." I grasped both of his hands and set back on my heels, fighting my own pain. Finally I hauled Michael slowly to his feet. I saw his glasses on the ground and retrieved them. "Why did they attack you?" I tried distracting him with talk as we hobbled to the car. I could only pray it would still run. We'd slammed into the trees on the driver's side, which was badly damaged, but I hoped the engine hadn't been harmed.

"I wasn't abiding by their rules."

"Because you took me to dinner?"

"Yes."

"How did they know you weren't simply getting information out of me?"

He sank into the passenger seat. "Because they would have sent someone else for that mission. Someone they trust more than they trust me."

"And what about Melissa Gomes? Was this payback for betraying her with another woman?"

"Oh, believe me, that's going to be another level of pain."

He wiped his bleeding face on his shirt sleeve. "The deputy sets a great store by his sister, and the locals aren't going to appreciate the fact that I was taking you to dinner."

"Maybe you should talk to my uncle sooner rather than later."

"Maybe you're right."

He groaned and I wondered if he had internal injuries. This was no place to try to check him over. "Is there a doctor in town?"

"Not one we can go to. The doctor is part of this too. He can't be trusted."

I climbed through the backseat and over into the front until I'd wiggled behind the steering wheel. I had little hope the car would start, but it did. If the wheels hadn't been knocked askew, we might be able to go.

I put the car in gear and eased off the clutch and gave her some gas. The car lurched forward, making both of us cry out in pain at the harsh jolting, but we moved. I gave more gas and eased the clutch with more finesse. It took some patient maneuvering, but I got the car turned around and headed back toward Mission. The only place I knew to go was Elizabeth's. But if Michael was seriously injured, he'd need more medical care than I could give him. "Is there a doctor in Victoria we can go to?"

"I'm okay." Michael gripped the door to keep from being jostled as I lurched down the road.

I didn't believe it for a minute. We'd both taken some hard licks, but Michael had taken the worst of it. "Elizabeth can check us out and we'll decide from there." If we had to drive to Birmingham or even Mobile, that's what was going to happen. Somewhere we'd find suitable help.

I drove slowly down the road, the wind coming through the shattered windshield tossing my hair into my face. It was hard to see, and I diligently watched the sides of the road for any would-be surprises.

"I'm sorry this happened, Raissa." Michael was leaning back against the seat. He didn't complain, but I knew he was hurting.

"Me, too."

"They know you and your partner are here for some reason other than scouting property for your uncle."

"They know because you told them?"

"No. I keep my own counsel here."

We came to the turn off and I swung south on a wider road. "Who killed Hildy Morse and Ruth Whelan?" I asked.

"I don't know."

"Don't know or won't say?"

"A little of both."

I drove in silence for several minutes. "A man's life hangs in the balance. A man who may be innocent. How can you live with that?"

"No one is ever truly innocent."

He sounded defeated, and I worried that he was hurt worse than even he knew. "Tell me about Slater McEachern. No one else in town will."

"You need to stop asking about him or Hildy or Ruth or anything else. Mission views the things that happen here as no one else's concern."

"There's a bigger law, a larger system of justice than what Lucais Wilkins runs here."

"I wish that were true. The man controls everything in Mission. No one can stop him."

Michael's voice was growing weaker, and he sounded completely exhausted. "Tell me about McEachern." I repeated my request. I wanted to hear his opinion, but I also wanted him to keep talking. I was worried about a head injury.

"I haven't lived here all that long, but I'll tell you what I know."

I focused on the road, on driving with care and being prepared for anything as Michael's voice spun out the details of a man I only knew through prison bars.

"McEachern came down here from New England, where he'd managed a sawmill for a big company. There was some kind of family tragedy. Whatever it was prompted him to start a new life. He bought some land and set up a business of cutting and hauling timber. He was hardworking and minded his own business, up until the last few months. I don't know what happened, but Lucais got it in for him. The murder charge is the final straw. Lucais always wins, Raissa. That's what you have to understand. He always wins."

Not always. That's what I wanted to say, but Michael was agitated. Until I knew he was not in physical danger, I didn't want to upset him more. "And Hildy Morse? Who would hurt a child?"

"Depends on what that child saw. Hildy roamed the woods around Mission. She made the journey through thick woods from her home to Ruth's. It was possible she'd seen something she shouldn't have."

"Do you think Hildy knew who killed Ruth?"

"I don't know. I find it too coincidental that she accidentally fell down a well. The child was an aggravation to her mother, but she was smart. Too smart."

"So you knew her?"

"A little. Everyone in Mission knew Hildy. You'd be

standing at the grocery and turn around and she'd be there, hoping you might buy a sweet for her."

"She roamed about on her own. Where was her mother?"

"Mrs. Morse had her hands full with George Morse. Hard drinker. Never had money to pay the bills. Mrs. Morse took in wash and ironing. Sold jams and preserves from wild fruit she picked. She worked. Hildy was on her own a lot."

I was a little taken aback. "I thought it was against the law to drink in Mission."

"It's against the law when Lucais wants it to be against the law. George worked for him. Still does, I assume. That's the only way the Morse family has hung on to their farm. Martha does most of the planting and harvesting. She didn't have time to go chasing after Hildy all day long."

"And there's no school for the girls, I hear."

"Education is a bad word around these parts when it's associated with women, or most men, for that matter." He brushed at the blood that had dried on his forehead. "You're doubly cursed, Raissa. Not only independent, but wealthy and educated. Lucais wants you gone yesterday."

We passed through the town of Mission, a place of dark and empty buildings. It seemed almost a mirage, it was so unsubstantial and gone so quickly. When we came to the edge of town, I saw the two familiar men standing on the roadside. They wore the typical slacks, white shirt, and suspenders of the Mission men. Their hands hung at their sides and they watched.

"Who are they?" I asked.

"Doesn't matter. Just keep going." Michael had pushed himself up to a taller sitting position. "Whatever they do, don't stop. It's bad you're driving, so don't stop."

I gripped the steering wheel, afraid they'd step out in front of the car as the man in the green hood had done. Instead, they remained motionless and let us pass. At last I turned down the lane that led to Elizabeth's house, hoping that Reginald would be there. As cowardly as I felt, I wanted to leave. Not in an hour or ten minutes, but in that moment. I longed for my uncle and the way he could put my fears to rest.

"You okay?" Michael asked. He was staring at me.

"I am. But I'm worried about you, Elizabeth, Callie, and Reginald. I want to go home."

Michael cleared his throat. "It would seem Lucais's little ploy with the green hood has achieved its purpose."

The words scalded me, but not enough to overcome my worry and fear. "I don't care. Think me a coward. I came up here to help a man I don't know, and the only thing that's happened is that a child is now dead. What else will happen if Reginald and I remain?"

"I wish I could answer that."

We turned into the long driveway to Elizabeth's house. The narrow path was dark, pressed tight by trees and foliage. I'd only gone a short distance when a great fluttering rose up out of the woods, blocking out the narrow strip of visible sky. Something passed over our heads. "What was that?"

I stopped the car and got out. A dozen huge birds with vast wingspans burst out of the trees. The sound of their wings was like a storm, flapping wildly in an attempt to lift their heavy bodies up. They clipped the limbs and tops of the oaks in their struggle to become airborne.

A large black wing nearly touched my cheek as one of the massive birds swept past me, flying low along the roadway and finally lifting into the night sky.

"What the hell?" I brushed at my face. "What was that?"

"Buzzards," Michael said. "They're everywhere here in

Mission. I'd almost be willing to believe they're dark spirits, come to visit tragedy on the people of this community."

His words sent a chill down me. "Why would you say that?"

"I see them often. Always before something terrible happens. Now they're here, on the way to your friend's house. I'd take it as a bad omen."

# CHAPTER 15

Reginald had not returned, a fact that squeezed my lungs with worry. My immediate task, though, was Michael. He might be seriously hurt. I hadn't had a chance to really examine him, we'd been so intent on getting away. Luckily, judging from the way he got out of the car when I stopped in Elizabeth's yard, he was much improved.

Elizabeth gave one cry of alarm before she led him into the kitchen and began to clean away the blood so she could assess his injuries. Remarkably, his wounds were superficial. He'd slammed into the driver's door of the car hard, but his bruising was minimal. On the other hand, I had a goose egg on my forehead where I'd struck the dash, and my shoulder and ribs were already purpling from bruises.

"Looks like you took the worst of it," Elizabeth said.

"I guess." It didn't make sense. It was Michael's side of that car that took the hardest blow. Yet I was going to be the one who looked like I'd been in a battle of fisticuffs. Now that I was in a place of relative safety, I was exhausted. I wanted to lie down and sleep, if only for ten minutes. Elizabeth seemed to read my mind. She took me to her bedroom and covered me with a light quilt. "I think I should call the doctor."

I remembered what Michael had said—the doctor wasn't to be trusted. I wasn't hurt that badly. "No. Truly, I'm fine. I'm tired. If I can nap for ten minutes I'll be ready to go."

"Would you watch Callie while I tend to Michael?"

"Of course." I snuggled the baby against my body.

"If she bothers you, let me know."

The clean scent of a breeze riffling through pines came from Callie's dark curls, which were soft against my cheek. "She's fine right here." I was asleep before Elizabeth could even respond.

I woke up in the darkened bedroom hours later. The old house sighed softly around me, settled for the night. Everyone had obviously gone to bed, and I wondered if Michael had stayed or gone. And Reginald? Had he come here or returned to Hattie's? I thought to get up, but the baby was so warm and comforting that I lingered in the bed.

Callie had wriggled onto her back, and she entertained herself by reaching for her toes. She made the soft cooing sound that brought to mind the mindless clucking of roosting pigeons. When she turned her head to look at me, her soft gaze was like a touch.

Alex and I had planned on children. Three, a mix of boys and girls if we were lucky. We'd talked about the family we would have and the course our lives together would follow. We'd decorated, in our imaginations, the safe and warm house with a big, welcoming kitchen where I made our favorite dishes for the children as they grew up and went to school. Alex and I would grow old, sitting on the front porch, reading books and discussing anything and everything. We hadn't reached for an extraordinary life—only a happy one filled with love. He'd gone to war with a lingering kiss and a promise he'd be home as soon as the Kaiser's ass was thoroughly kicked. It was the only promise he'd failed to keep.

Emotion set a hard lump in my throat, but when I looked into Callie's eyes, the pain faded. The longing remained, and suddenly I saw Alex. He was lying on the ground, his uniform torn by the bullets that had pierced his chest and legs. The smell of blood was everywhere, and the dirt around Alex was pitted by shells. Cries came from the foxholes where other young men suffered and died. In the distance men shouted orders in German. I knelt beside Alex, capturing his hand and holding it as tightly as I could. Holding him to me even as he prepared to leave me. I was surrounded by screams and smoke and his fallen comrades.

"Please don't die," I begged him.

"It doesn't hurt," he said. "It doesn't hurt. Don't remember me this way, Raissa. Think of us on the porch, white-headed and content with a full life behind us." He coughed and blood bubbled at his lips.

"Alex! Don't go. Please. Just stay a while longer." I pressed his hand to my heart. "Please don't leave me."

"It doesn't hurt, I promise." He coughed again, pinkish foam gathering at the corners of his mouth. "I'll wait for you."

He meant he would wait for me on the other side, but that wasn't what I wanted or needed. He was my husband, the man who anchored me to life. He was the biggest part of my life, and I pressed against the wounds to hold the blood in, to keep him alive.

"I love you," he whispered. And he was gone.

Callie gurgled and kicked her feet, one of them thudding softly into my arm. Her little webbed hand brushed at the tears on my face. "It's okay," I told the baby quietly. And it was.

I'd seen my husband die, but I'd been able to be with him. He had not died alone.

Callie began a soft moan, a sound I'd never heard her make. She pumped her hands, but this time in what I assessed as agitation. "Callie." I whispered her name into the tiny coils of her ear. She began to make yet another new sound, this time with great urgency: "Uh-uh-uh-uh-uh." I leaned up on my elbow to see if anything was wrong with her. She turned away from me and looked toward a corner of the room, her little protest cry growing stronger. This, from the child who had never shown the first sign of any distress. When I tried to get her to look at me, she kept thrashing and turning to face the corner.

Outside the window I heard the rush of large wings.

I froze, and Callie fell immediately silent. A shadow fell across the window, and I realized that someone, or something, stood silently in the corner of the room.

"Who's there?"

I didn't expect an answer and I wasn't disappointed. The entity seemed to gain volume and solidity, tall and as big as a strong man. Dense. Impenetrable.

I pulled Callie into my arms and started to ease off the other side of the bed. Whatever this was in the room, I sensed it had great power.

"Stop."

The male voice that came to me was deep, commanding. My limbs stopped. I couldn't tell if I was held in thrall, or if I was so scared I couldn't move.

"Raissa James." It spoke my name and I realized I had to be in a dream, but this was not like any dream I'd ever had.

"Who are you?" I was startled by the sound of my own voice.

He stepped forward. The large set of wings attached to his back folded down, and he came to stand beside the bed. "I am Gabriel," he said.

He was nothing like the angels I'd been taught about in Sunday school. This man was a warrior. He wore a large knife sheathed at his waist, and the muscles of his naked chest rippled as his wings pumped lightly behind him. I had doubted Elizabeth when she'd claimed that an archangel was the father of her child. Now I no longer did. This creature was breathtaking, but filled not with light, but darkness.

Again, a large entity flapped by the window outside the house and little Callie made her uh-uh-uh sound. I thought of the buzzards. Were they really buzzards, or something else?

"What do you want?" I asked.

"I can show you the truth. Are you willing to see it?"

This wasn't a ride I wanted to take. I'd seen the truth of Alex's slow death on the battlefield. I'd held his hand as he took his last breath. I didn't want to see Ruth Whelan's brutal murder. But there was something I did want to see.

"Hildy Morse. What happened to her? Can you show me that?"

He came toward me and sat on the edge of the bed. My disobedient limbs refused to help me escape. "Take my hand." He held his out.

I didn't want to. I fought against it, but my own hand lifted and my fingers wrapped around his. Something akin to an electric shock rippled through my body and I had the most peculiar sense that I, too, had wings.

"You're attuned to the other truths," he said.

"I don't want to do this." Even as I held his hand a panorama of images swept through my head. Moments from the past, fragments of laughter, the scent of my mother's baking pound cake. The touch of Alex's hand on my thigh. My mind and body seemed filled with sensual fragments that were so intense I felt myself slipping into unconsciousness. At last the images stopped.

"You asked about Hildy Morse."

*I find myself outside a farm house. The yard is scraggly with weeds and bare patches and the back porch of the house sags. It's a place that needs a loving, caring hand. Wash hangs on a clothes line, and a thin woman in a faded dress comes out the back door and throws a pan of potato peels out to chickens that peck aggressively at the food and each other. The woman hurries back inside.*

*In a paddock with some of the fence almost down, an old mule stands in the shade, watching me. I'm pressed against the side of the barn, watching the house. I duck back when the woman looks my way. I'm hiding from her. When I look at my hands, they're strong, with hair on the backs of my fingers. Dark hair. My callused palms show embedded dirt, and my fingernails are rimmed in black. The tail of a white shirt hangs out of my pants, which are cinched tight at the waist.*

*From the other side of the barn, I hear a child singing a nonsense song. Her thin, young voice is clear and she carries the melody easily.*

*"Peepin' through the knothole of Grandpa's wooden leg, who'll wind the clock when I'm gone? Go get the ax, there's a flea in Lizzie's ear, for a boy's best friend is his mother." She finishes the verse with a burst of self-applause.*

*I peek around the corner of the barn to see Hildy drawing in the dirt with a stick. "This is the kitchen," she says as she marks off an area. "And here is my bedroom." She outlines another small section. "Where will my dolly sleep?" She continues drawing in the dirt.*

*Not twenty feet away is a well. The bricks that form the well are handmade, probably from slave labor. A bucket hangs at the top.*

*I step out of the shadows of the barn and she sees me. She looks up for a moment and then continues her play. She is not upset that I am there. I continue toward her. When I use the edge of my work boot to scruff away the wall of her playhouse, she stands up. Fear sparks in her eyes. She sees something in my face, in my stare, that scares her. She sees her fate coming.*

*"You better go away. My mama won't like you here."*

*I step into the pretend house she has drawn. Anger and stark fear show in her eyes.*

*"You'd better leave. My mama will shoot you."*

*I look toward the back porch of the house. There is no one there. No one to witness my actions. I grab the child by her shoulders, my fingers digging into her thin flesh. When she tries to fight me, I hit her. Hard. There is a snap and she slumps. She is not heavy as I carry her to the well. I drop her in, waiting for the splash before I leave.*

# CHAPTER 16

I woke up gasping for air, unsure where I was. The baby curled against my body, a little webbed hand pressed against my temple as we both slept. I forced myself to breathe, to calm a little before I rose. The dream was not a dream. While my body had slept, my spirit had lived a journey. I no longer doubted Elizabeth Maslow's version of the murder of Ruth Whelan. She spoke what was true and accurate. The horror of what she'd described was exactly as a woman had died. I knew this, because I, too, had witnessed a terrible murder.

Conversation drifted to me from the kitchen. Elizabeth's and Michael's voices rose and fell in a friendly manner. Michael was telling her about the accident that could have killed both of us, about the man in a green hood, about the danger that surrounded Reginald, Elizabeth, Callie, and myself. He didn't say it, but I knew that now Michael had been tainted by association with us. His focus was on others, though, and he urged Elizabeth to leave Mission for the baby's sake.

"There is nothing you can do for Slater McEachern," he

said. "The man sealed his fate when he went up against Lucais. He knew that and he did it anyway."

"He was trying to protect Ruth."

"And no one could do that. And now you can't protect McEachern. Cut your losses and get out of town. I won't be far behind you, but you have to get the private investigators away. They're in danger."

I eased out of bed, careful not to wake Callie. Not likely— she was sleeping soundly and at peace. When I stepped into the kitchen, Elizabeth and Michael stopped talking. Elizabeth studied me.

"You had a dream, didn't you?"

She knew. "Yes."

"Did you see Ruth's murder?"

I shook my head. "No. I saw how Hildy was murdered." The full horror of it was still with me and I know it was evident on my face.

She sighed heavily. "I'm sorry. That must have been awful."

I nodded but didn't speak.

"Did you see who did it?" Michael asked. It was odd that he didn't question the validity of my dream.

"In the dream it was me." My voice broke and I turned away for a few seconds before I found my control again. Elizabeth came to me and eased me into a chair at the table beside Michael. She stroked my hair, a gesture that gave comfort.

I looked at the kitchen clock and felt another shock. Only ten minutes had passed since I went into the bedroom to lie down. In a span of ten minutes I'd witnessed a murder and had a visitation by an angel. Time in the netherworld was elastic. I knew this from dealing with spirits, many who lived the day they died over and over for decades, if not centuries. They never aged or moved forward in time, stuck between the worlds of the living and the dead.

"Are you saying that you killed Hildy Morse?" Michael started to rise but Elizabeth signaled him to remain seated.

"No, that isn't what she's saying." She turned to me. "Tell us the dream."

Talking about the horror of what I'd seen made me relive it, but I told them, step by step. "I heard her body hit the water at the bottom of the well." I swallowed. "I hope she was dead before that."

"You hit her?" Michael picked up my right hand, examining the knuckles that could have been bruised and swollen in the car crash—or if I'd struck a young girl hard enough to break her neck.

"Raissa didn't hit anyone," Elizabeth told him. Michael was struggling to catch up with the truth that Elizabeth and I knew.

"Someone hit Hildy. A man. I merely relived it in the dream."

"Who? What man?"

I held out my hands, remembering the coarse, dark hairs on the knuckles of the person who grasped Hildy's thin shoulders and then punched her hard enough to knock her unconscious and possibly snap her neck. "He had dark hair. The killer had dark hair. His knuckles..."

"Almost everyone here does," Michael said. "Can you tell us more details?"

Elizabeth nodded. "Michael may not be on our side, but he isn't on theirs, either. He's marked by association."

She'd accepted Michael and was willing to share information with him. I began with what I had witnessed and what I had deduced. "Hildy knew him. She wasn't afraid of him at first, but when he deliberately scuffed away the outline of her pretend house...she was afraid then." She'd seen something in his eyes, some warning of what was to come, but she'd reacted too slowly. "It was almost as if she recognized him, but then realized he was someone else entirely."

Michael frowned. "Are you saying the killer possesses the bodies of people and forces them to kill?"

"I don't know what I'm saying. Only that Hildy knew him and wasn't concerned, until she saw something in his eyes. Something that frightened her."

"But she didn't run," Michael pointed out. "Or scream."

I remembered the paralysis of my dream, the inability to move my limbs. "Sometimes the body doesn't obey."

"Do you remember any more details about his appearance?" Elizabeth asked.

"He had a kind of big belt buckle. He wasn't wearing the suspenders so many men here wear."

"Shoes?" Michael asked.

"Work boots. But newer. Nicer than most."

"Shirt?"

I tried hard to pull up the memory of a shirt and finally got the sleeves and the tail hanging loose. "White. Starched. But he dresses slovenly."

"I know this man," Elizabeth said quietly. "It's the same man who killed Ruth."

"How do you know?" Michael asked.

Elizabeth and I shared a look before she answered. "I saw Ruth's murder in exactly the same way—as if I were the killer. And I know the killer is not Slater McEachern. That's why I can't leave town. Now Raissa has seen Hildy's murder. We have to find this man and see that the murderer is punished and an innocent man is set free."

"You're never going to get McEachern out of this." Michael was suddenly angry, and I recognized that his anger was coming from fear. Fear for all of us. "No one is going to believe this foolishness, that you dreamed the murder. You need to accept that and save the people you can."

"Do you know who killed them?" Elizabeth inhaled sharply and glared at Michael. "Do you?"

Something sparked between them. "I don't know, but I suspect. I think maybe you do too."

"But why would Lucais kill Ruth? She made a living breaking the law, providing those men what they wanted, but she was discreet. She gave Lucais his kickback, and she never challenged him. She never *talked*. She hardly went to town. More often than not I'd get her supplies. She stayed clear of town and gossip." Michael stood and paced the kitchen, his shoes echoing on the wide-plank floor.

"Don't wake Callie," I told him.

He stopped pacing and leaned against the sink, his gaze out the window.

He seemed lost in thought.

As worried as I was for Slater McEachern, I had other concerns. My partner hadn't returned, and Reginald was as vulnerable as the rest of us. "Elizabeth, where did Reginald go?"

"He didn't say." She tried to hide her worry, but I saw it. "He said he wouldn't be gone long, but he's been gone for a while."

"He said he wouldn't be far from me having dinner with Michael." I remembered that with a surge of fear. Had he been following me and Michael? Had the men in green hoods stopped him as well? Was he lying on the roadside injured? Dead? Was he in jail?

"I—"

Michael abruptly turned away from the window he'd been gazing out of and faced us. "Someone is out there." He jerked a thumb toward the window. "It's one, maybe two men. They're moving around the property."

The gut-punch of fear made me sit up straighter. "Who?"

He shook his head. "Too dark to see anyone's features, but I saw someone going inside the barn. It's likely the watchers. They know you're here, Raissa. They know I'm here."

"The horse!" I pushed back from the table. Cruel people often picked on helpless animals to inflict torment.

"Mariah won't let anyone catch her," Elizabeth assured me. "She's smart like that. She'll be out in the back field. They won't bother her. I see those creepy men around here a lot. They watch, but they've never taken any action."

"What if Reginald drives up?" If they were out there, waiting, they could shoot him when he arrived. I cast about for a reason for his absence. "He said he would be close to me, but maybe he changed his mind." I grasped at any reasonable excuse. "Even if he drove to Victoria for gasoline, he should be back by now."

"I can go and look for him." Michael needed a job, something useful. But taking off into the night in a car that might or might not run was foolish.

"Stay here, please." I had another thought. I'd seen Hildy murdered. Her neck snapped. What had the local coroner said about her cause of death? "Do you know if the ruling on Hildy's death has been given?"

"It will be accidental," Michael said. "They'll claim she fell into the well while she was playing."

"She was never a foolish child," Elizabeth said firmly. "She wouldn't play on the edge of a well."

"Maybe not, but that will be the official verdict. As soon as Lucais can get the word out that her death was accidental, he'll pick up McEachern's trial again. You two have to believe that no one in Mission is going to believe there is a killer loose, especially a child killer. They don't want to believe that. It makes them feel unsafe. The town is going to willingly believe that Slater killed Ruth and that Hildy fell into a well while she was playing in the yard."

That would make Hildy's mother's life a living hell of guilt and blame, but that was clearly not a concern. A plan was forming. A dangerous one, but perhaps a necessary one. "Is there a coroner in Victoria?"

Michael caught on quickly. "There is, but that doesn't do us any good. They'll bury Hildy day after tomorrow. No one will question the Mission coroner's ruling. Children die of accidents every day in Alabama."

"Does Lucais control him, the Victoria coroner?"

"I don't know," Michael said. "A body hasn't been autopsied since I came to live here. Ed Cleverdon rules on cause of death in this county. He's not a doctor, but for most people who die, it's pretty simple. Logging accident, mining collapse, heart goes out..."

"So there really is no way to prove if anyone else was murdered. If it vaguely resembled an accident, there's no further investigation." I tried to swallow my frustration, to think logically and not emotional.

"You're right, Michael." Elizabeth put the kettle on for more coffee. "Ed's a pleasant enough guy, but he has no medical training. He finds what Lucais wants him to find."

The minutes were ticking away and there was still no sign of Reginald. I was desperate for something to do, something I could control. "We need Hildy's body." Neither Michael nor

Elizabeth disagreed. "If her neck is broken, as I suspect, that will show she was murdered. At least it supports what I saw in the dream."

"She could have broken her neck in the fall," Elizabeth said. "That won't work."

I wasn't an expert on autopsies, but I'd read a lot of murder stories and studied the procedures of an autopsy for my first case. "We can put forth the theory she was murdered. It will at least be grounds to continue to delay McEachern's trial until we can provide a real coroner's report on Hildy's death. "It's the only thing we have right now. So we need a real, medical autopsy on Hildy."

Michael leaned forward. "But we don't *have* Hildy's body. Mrs. Morse isn't likely to just give us her child's body so some doctor in Victoria can cut her up to look inside."

His words made me cringe. The idea of Hildy cut up like an experiment was hard for me to take, but an innocent man's life was on the line and a child killer was walking free. "That's why we have to steal it."

"Oh, no!" Elizabeth grabbed my arm. "You are not going to try to steal a body!"

"Oh, but I am," I said. "*We* are. If we can get Hildy to Victoria, maybe an autopsy will prove a killer is still on the loose here. It could save Slater, or at least give us time to come up with something to save him."

Michael drummed the top of the table with his fingertips. "She's right, Elizabeth. We don't have anything else and if they bury Hildy, we'll never get permission to dig her up."

"This is too dangerous." Elizabeth put her hands on the back of a chair. "You can't attempt this. If you get caught...My God, Michael, you know what will happen. Stealing a body! They'll catch you before you get on the outskirts of town.

They won't wait for a trial. They'll string you and Raissa up right away. You won't help Slater McEachern one bit, and you'll be dead."

The cold truth of what Elizabeth said couldn't be ignored. Neither could the fate of Slater McEachern. "What else can we do? We can't prove Lucais killed Ruth Whelan, though we all suspect him. We don't have another suspect. Who else in town might want to harm her? We need a theory to investigate."

"Junior Albee was in town the day Ruth was killed, and the day Hildy was killed." Michael spoke with some hesitation. "The young man isn't right, but I never thought of him as a killer."

"Who's Junior Albee?" I asked.

"Deakle Albee's son. Deakle is a big wig in Victoria. He carries a lot of weight," Elizabeth answered. "Junior isn't right. Something happened to him a year or so ago. It was a big secret, but it was some kind of sickness—maybe a fever? Anyway, he came out of it...damaged. I've always viewed him as harmless. He wouldn't harm anyone, and especially not a child. Besides, he lives in Victoria, and no one would speak against him."

"Why would they protect Junior and not Slater?"

Elizabeth answered immediately. "Deakle is one of them. He has money. And power, and he leaves Lucais alone to run Mission as he pleases. Deakle is more a 'live and let live' kind of man. Victoria is different. No one man has a strangle hold on the town like Lucais has on Mission. In Victoria, there are more people, more money, more churches, and different ways of thinking."

"You have to understand the history of Mission," Michael added. "I spent some time figuring out how everything worked when I moved here. Lucais's family—the Wilkins family—was one of the first families to settle. Lucais's father owned the land the town is built on. He was a charismatic man who set up a church and those who bought—or were given—the property for their farms agreed to be a part of his church. Rankin Wilkins had a vision of a godly community where all who lived here had the same belief. He'd seen the conflicts that tore apart other churches or communities when doctrine was questioned. He made sure that those who settled in Mission were of the same mind as he was."

"I'm sure it sounded like a good deal for the men." I couldn't help my bitter tone. "Not so good for women and children, who are treated like property here. The men push their wives and daughters into virtual slavery. It works out well for the males."

"I'm not defending the situation, but that's been the lot of women for a long time, and not just here in Mission." Elizabeth spoke softly.

Michael and Elizabeth were both right. It wasn't even Lucais's fault, not fully. The Constitution had been accepted one hundred and thirty-three years ago almost to the day, and women had just gotten the right to vote. Not every state had ratified the 19th Amendment. Alabama had not. This was a systemic problem with the entire culture, not just the settlement of Mission.

"Tell us more about the Wilkins clan," Elizabeth said, smoothing over the raw emotion. "The more we know, the better we can plan. Since you've talked with some of the men, you probably know more than us women are ever told."

Michael thought for a minute before he spoke "Lucais keeps his finger in everyone's pie. If you own anything within the city limits of Mission, you're obligated to Lucais one way or the other. There's no such thing as a clear title, meaning a lot of people don't really own the land they live on. The power to control the land comes down from Lucais's father Rankin, who made sure the people here were financially obligated to him. Initially the plots of land were offered cheap. But there were strings attached. Lots of strings. And people didn't want to fight Rankin or Lucais. They learned quickly that it was not in their self-interest to buck the Wilkins family."

"What does Lucais want?" If I could figure that out—and Reginald had been taken by the Mission men—perhaps I could bargain for him.

"He wants control, and he intends to have it."

"That's why he hates Slater McEachern." I didn't understand the details, but I knew I'd hit on the truth. "Slater McEachern challenges Lucais's rule, doesn't he?"

Michael nodded. "McEachern is a disrupter."

"A what?"

"He wants to change the system Lucais has built. He wants—"

"He wants to run Lucais and his buddies out of town." Elizabeth finished the sentence.

"You knew this?" Anger was my first reaction. That she'd failed to be honest with me and Reginald and had essentially put us at risk. We would have come to help her anyway, but at least we would have known what we faced. With Reginald still missing and some strange watchers out in the barn, I wasn't happy with my client.

"Ruth and I suspected Slater was dabbling in things that he shouldn't have been." Elizabeth looked contrite. "I didn't know for certain, but I should have voiced my concerns to you."

"The night Ruth was killed, was Slater there?"

"He was. He was trying to talk Ruth into coming forward

with the names of all the men who'd used her. He thought she could convince Lucais to let her go. Use the list of names as leverage."

"And the journal. What is that writing?"

"I don't know." Elizabeth sank down into a chair. "I've thought and thought, but I can't figure it out. It has to be some kind of record of events."

"May I see it?" Michael asked.

We'd left the book with Elizabeth because we weren't certain of our privacy at Hattie's. She was an honorable woman, but there was no telling who might slip in and out of her house while she was doing laundry or in town. Reginald and I had agreed the journal was safer here.

"I'll get it." Elizabeth went into her bedroom. There was a soft exclamation, and she returned with the journal in her left hand and something else in her right—a large dark feather.

# CHAPTER 17

I stood up abruptly, staring at the feather. "Where did that come from?"

"It wasn't there earlier," Elizabeth said. "I would have seen it." Both Michael and Elizabeth turned to look at me. I was the only adult who'd been in that room.

I gaped at them both. "It doesn't make sense, but I think it's from, uh, from the dream." I wasn't certain how to explain what I'd experienced to Michael. I could hardly understand it myself. Reginald would understand, but Michael was another story.

"Gabriel was here. In my bedroom. You spoke with him. He left the feather." Elizabeth made statements that sounded almost like accusations. "He's never left physical evidence before."

"He was with me, but it was in a dream. And I did speak to him." My focus was on Michael, who was agitated, though he worked to hide it. I reached out to him. "We can explain all of this, but it's going to sound...crazy."

Michael stared at each of us in turn. "Gabriel? What are

you talking about? How did a buzzard feather get into your house and why does it warrant such a reaction?" he asked. "You two act as if you've seen a ghost."

"It's not a ghost and it isn't a buzzard." Now that he said it, the feather could easily have come from some of the giant black vultures I'd seen around Mission. They had a six-foot wingspan and they were powerful, though ugly, especially the ones with their semi-bald red heads. "Gabriel, this entity, was in my dream. *Prominently* in my dream."

"You dreamed of Hildy, and what else?" Elizabeth's tone gave me no clue if she was distressed for my safety or worried about what I might have seen.

"I saw Hildy, but also my husband. I saw Alex first. I was with him when he died on the battlefield in France." No matter what anyone said, I believed I had been there with Alex on that horrible day. I had been allowed to give him comfort. I had been with Hildy, too, though it hadn't really been me and she'd found no comfort from whatever presence I'd been inhabiting.

"Raissa..." Michael came toward me and I let him put a hand on my back. His warm touch was welcome, grounding me to this moment in time and place. "You're pale."

"What else did you see?" Elizabeth asked.

"No other dreams, but I saw him. Gabriel. He was in the bedroom with me and Callie. He's...magnificent." The sensual memory made me flush.

"And Gabriel is who?" Michael asked.

"An archangel." Elizabeth spoke softly but firmly.

"You believe an archangel was in that bedroom?" Michael had trouble grasping my truth. "You're dreaming murders and consorting with archangels? You expect people to believe that?"

"I do." I had come a great distance from where I'd looked askance on Elizabeth's version of events. "I doubted Elizabeth before. I thought it was merely an intense dream that she'd experienced. No one can truly dream the truth of a past event, or so I thought. Now I know the truth. The dreams come from Gabriel. And he's given Elizabeth and me a gift that can cut or heal."

Elizabeth nodded, and her shoulders sagged. "Thank goodness you believe me." She looked at Michael. "I know how impossible all of this sounds. I do. But you have to trust us, that we're telling the truth."

"You ask too much," Michael said. "You must all leave Mission now. As soon as Reginald returns, load up the car, take the baby and leave. The danger is only beginning. Ghosts and archangels are not going to protect you."

I had to make him understand. "I've seen ghosts intent on revenge, hungry creatures that feed on the sexual desires of men, evil spirits that reincarnated in a relative to claim vengeance. I've seen dead girls who couldn't talk because their throats were cut and their heads almost severed. I don't find it impossible to believe that an angel might visit, or that he might bestow the ability to divine the truth."

"And you're sure it was an angel?" Michael's fingers circled my arm. He didn't grip me tightly, but I felt his intensity.

"It had wings." I pointed to the feather. "Not white, like I expected, but darker. Light and dark gray, like storm clouds. I couldn't see him that well because it was dark in the room."

"I see." Michael let me go. He tried to hide his reaction, but he wasn't successful. He was upset. "As I said, we have to leave here. Now. All of us."

"We can't leave Reginald."

"We should. We must." He waved at Elizabeth. "Grab some

things for the baby. This place is not safe for you. We can leave Reginald a note. We can call your uncle to come and get you— all of you—as soon as we're at a place with telephones or telegrams. Hurry. There's no time to waste."

"We're not leaving Reginald. At least I'm not." I pointed out the window where Michael's car was parked in the darkness. "We don't even know that we *can* leave. Will the car run? Will we break down on a dark road, easy picking for those evil men or whatever it is you fear?"

From the bedroom, Callie's coos became more pronounced. There was excitement in her little chirrups and goo-goos. Elizabeth went to attend her.

"Raissa," Michael pulled me closer so he could whisper. "Lucais is not the real danger here. Not at all. We have to get away."

"Then who is the danger?"

He shook his head. "You have to trust me."

"No, I don't." Mule-headedness was a family trait, and I barely knew Michael.

"If you value your life and Elizabeth's and Callie's, you'll do as I ask."

Something in his eyes, his hand that grasped mine and held it, touched me deeply. I wanted to believe him. More than anything I wanted to run hard, away from Mission and the building tragedy. But I couldn't. "I'm not leaving Reginald."

"We can—" His response was cut short by the sound of shouting from outside. He stepped in front of me instinctively. "Stay here and start helping Elizabeth pack."

He didn't leave any room for disagreement as he strode out of the house. I went to the window that looked out on the front porch. To my intense relief, Uncle Brett's car slammed to a stop in the front yard and Reginald leapt out. Behind him came the sound of a gunshot and more yelling. Reginald ran to the porch. "Does Elizabeth have any guns?" He herded Michael back inside. "Hurry, if there are weapons, get them."

"Who's out there?" I asked, rushing to them both.

"A lynch mob." Reginald took a moment to grasp my hand for reassurance. "I drove through them. Men in green hoods. I believe if I'd stopped, they would have killed me."

"I know," I said. "They wrecked Michael and me. We're okay, but they gave us a warning to get out of town. They mean it."

Elizabeth, holding Callie, joined us. "I've gathered Callie's things."

"It won't do any good. They have the road blocked. If we try to get through, they'll wreck us or shoot us. Do you have any guns?" Reginald asked.

"In the bedroom. Two shotguns, a rifle, and three pistols."

I looked at Elizabeth. She had an arsenal for a woman who lived alone.

"When I came looking for Ramone, I knew it might be dangerous. I can handle a weapon if I have to."

"Good," Michael said, "because we all may have to. If they try to breach the house, we have no choice but to defend ourselves. They will hurt you. They will likely kill you and your baby. Do whatever you must to stay alive."

Michael was right, but he'd also said that a graver danger came from someone other than Lucais Wilkins and his minions. He would tell me, when all of this was over.

The windows were open, and we could hear the angry mob moving closer to the house. Reginald grabbed the guns and doled them out after he'd made sure they were loaded.

The pistol he gave me was heavy. "I'm better with a rifle," I said.

"The pistol is better for up close. Point it at the person and pull the trigger. You probably won't hit them but you'll let them know we mean business. This is our lives, Raissa. You can't hesitate."

When I lifted the gun to sight down the barrel, I knew I could use it if I had to. "Okay."

The first flicker of a torch could be seen at the edge of the yard. Reginald stepped onto the front porch. He fired a shot into the air and raised his voice. "You need to leave. We're heavily armed and we will defend ourselves."

There was no answer. The mob had suddenly grown quiet, which was somehow more frightening than their loud catcalls and yells. The lone torch remained where it was, and though it was impossible to see clearly, I guessed there were at least a dozen men.

"Leave now." Reginald gave them until the count of five. He fired the shotgun in the direction of the torch. There was a startled yell and the torch was dropped to the ground. "You want more of this, come and get it."

There was a surge of movement on the edge of the woods. I couldn't clearly see what was happening, but I knew we were being rushed by the men.

"Fire!" Reginald called out. Elizabeth's rifle blasted through the kitchen window. Reginald and Michael were crouched low on the porch, firing as fast their weapons would allow. I emptied the pistol in the direction of the men.

Bullets pinged into the wood near the parlor window and I dropped to the floor. Outside I heard shots hit the front porch and the side of the house where the kitchen was. The men were firing back, but we had better cover.

"Go again," Reginald called out. I'd re-loaded and emptied the six-shooter once again.

Two men cried out in the darkness.

"Luther's hit! Luther's hit," someone called out. "They shot him!"

"Charge again and see who else gets hit," Reginald called out.

"You'll pay for this!" The male voice came out of the fringe of trees.

"Bring it now," Reginald said. "You're cowards, jumping out of the woods, wrecking people, trying to harm women and children. Come on now and face grown men who are armed. Let's see how brave you are." He waited. "You'd better get going or I'll come after you."

"You're a dead man." A car's headlights cut the darkness and for a moment the hooded men were illuminated in the headlight before the car turned. There was cursing and grunting as our attackers loaded their wounded and the car retreated.

Reginald stood on the porch in the silence that followed. After ten minutes, he came back inside. "They'll ambush us on the road if we try to leave."

"Our best bet is daylight," Elizabeth agreed. "There's a farm road that goes around the property. We might be able to get on the other side of the blockade, but we can't do it in the dark. We can take Mariah, too, and drop her at Hattie's. She'll take care of her."

"I'd feel better if we could go now," Michael said. His gaze strayed to the bedroom and I wondered what he was thinking.

"At first light," Reginald said. "We only have one reliable car and we can't afford to bog it somewhere or hit a stump or hole."

Michael nodded. His gaze went not to the window but back to the bedroom. "We should stay awake."

We had a number of hours to wait for the sun. I didn't dare ask what he feared in our sleep, because I thought I knew. Gabriel.

"WHERE HAVE YOU BEEN?" I sat across from Reginald at Elizabeth's kitchen table. "I've been worried sick."

"Victoria. I went to ask a few questions, and for gas. It's a longer trip than I expected." He nodded to Michael. "I brought some in a can for you, but I don't know that your car will be going anywhere."

"I don't know how badly the car is damaged," Michael admitted. "Taking one car would be smarter anyway."

"How did you wreck?" Reginald asked.

"Raissa and I were run off the road coming home from dinner. By a miracle, neither of us were seriously hurt."

Reginald pointed at my head. The goose egg was still big, but it was going down. "They could have killed you."

What he said was true, but there was no point belaboring the dangers all around us. "Did you find out anything in Victoria?"

"Actually, a lot," Reginald said. "A young woman was attacked there. With an ax."

"Who?" Michael and Elizabeth spoke simultaneously.

"Is she alive?" Elizabeth continued.

"She's alive, but not easy to question. I did talk to some people who knew her. Her name is Mary Jane Brady. She's from out in the country, and she'd just taken a job as a clerk at the dime store in Victoria. I couldn't get a lot of information because there's something...hinky about what happened. I did find out the girl was struck on the shoulder with an ax, but she managed to get away. She's been hiding at her parents' home for months and she refused to talk to me. Several deputies arrived while I was outside the home. They said they were guarding her."

"Guarding her?" I asked. "So they fear she'll be attacked again?"

"Or maybe they fear she'll talk to the wrong people," Reginald said darkly.

"Did she see her attacker?" Michael asked.

"She won't say."

"So perhaps the person she saw is known to the police and someone they intend to protect." Elizabeth vocalized what we were all thinking. "They might want to prevent her from telling what she knows."

I shook my head in confusion. "But this is Victoria, not Mission." I could accept that a small village as isolated as Mission could be completely corrupt, from the lowest law officer to the judge. But Alabama had larger towns and cities where the justice system had taken root and worked. Supposedly. "Surely they're protecting her from a possible future attack."

"I came to Mission looking for Ramone," Elizabeth said. "His last letter to me was about a young woman—a girl, really —attacked by a man with an ax. It happened in Victoria. Not Mission. But Ramone said in his letter he was headed here."

"Did Ramone mention the girl's name?" Michael asked.

"He did. Daisy Evans. I tried to find her, but she was gone. I was told she'd moved away. It's hard for a woman to ask questions about such things, even in Victoria. No one would tell me what happened or where the girl had gone. And my brother was gone too. He'd vanished. I found two people who said they knew him and that he'd just failed to show up on a job building some cabinets. That wasn't like Ramone. He was a good worker and a skilled carpenter, when he wanted to be. They said he'd been talking about selling his wares up around Mission, so that's why I came up here."

"How does a murdered woman and child in Mission tie up with two women attacked with an ax in Victoria and your missing brother?" Reginald asked Elizabeth.

"I wish I knew."

It was time to spring my plan on Reginald and I knew he wasn't going to like it. "Reginald, I know we have to get out of town fast, but we can't leave without Hildy Morse's body. We need to get her to a medical doctor who can do a real autopsy."

Reginald stared at me in abject horror. "You think we're going to steal a body?"

"We have to."

"You want to add *body snatching* to the list of things we can be hanged for?"

"We need proof that she was murdered. I saw her murder, but no one is going to believe me." I rushed on. "She was slugged so hard I think her neck snapped and she was thrown in that well. I saw it, Reginald."

He drew in a breath slowly. "How did you see this?"

I looked to Elizabeth for confirmation. "I saw the angel and he gave me the ability to see things in dreams."

"Not an angel," Michael interjected.

Michael didn't know what I'd seen. I'm sure I sounded delusional to him. Who would claim that they'd seen an archangel, much less spoken to one? Not even the feather would convince him, because most people were completely unaware of the spirit realm. "I saw Gabriel, Reginald. He showed me what happened to Hildy in a dream. I lived it, just the way Elizabeth lived Ruth's murder."

"I don't know what's really going on here. The only thing I

know for certain is that we have to get out of this place," Reginald said, "before I start dreaming."

"We're hamstrung until daybreak." Elizabeth put on a pot of coffee. It was late and we were exhausted, but none of us would sleep with the possibility that the angry mob would return.

When the men were drinking coffee and discussing escape routes, I went into the bedroom with Elizabeth. "We can't leave town without paying Hattie. She'll be worried about us. Maybe we can get a message to her."

"She will worry," Elizabeth agreed. "But there's nothing we can do. You can mail her money. If you contact her now, you'll just put her in more danger."

Elizabeth was right, but it didn't ease my conscience. "I'm not even certain the post office will deliver a letter from me." It was foolish to be worried about a bill at a time like this, but it seemed like the only thing I could actually control.

Elizabeth fretted with the coffee pot. "We'll figure that all out when we're safe." She began piling baby things in the middle of the bed.

I realized then that for all of her calm behavior, Elizabeth was facing a drastic change and she was aware of it. "Will you ever come back here?"

She paused, holding a stack of diapers in her hand. "I love this place. This land. It's primal and wild. There are spirits in the woods. Ancient beings who guard the wilderness. They see a tragic future, you know. Not for us as individuals, but for the wild things." She looked down at the floor. "Ruth and I were close friends. I had someone I considered family here. She's gone, though. There's not a lot calling me back to Mission. To be honest, I don't know that I can come back. Those days may be gone."

"Tell me about your brother. He seems tied up in too much, Elizabeth. Tell me the truth this time. We've risked a lot to come here and help you."

"I did lie," she said. "I lied because of the ax attack. It happened right about the time Ramone disappeared. My brother would never do anything like that, but he's a Gypsy. We're blamed for many things. I'm sorry, but we've learned to lie to protect ourselves. It wasn't fair to you. I'm sorry."

"Is he a tinker? Was that the truth?"

"We are Romany. Ramone is a skilled builder, but he also sold goods. Pots, pans, weathervanes, things not easy to find. After the death of our parents, we inherited considerable money. He thought he could set out to take that and make his fortune." One side of her mouth lifted in a wry smile. "And have some adventure. That was, I believe, his primary focus. I had plenty of money, a safe place to live. He assumed I was protected in Chattanooga with the other members of our group. He said he would return for me, when he had made his mark. We would each marry and work our farms but we'd live side by side. We were very close. It's been two years since I heard from him. I've come to believe he's dead."

"He doesn't know about Callie, does he?"

"No. I would have written him, but I had no address."

Elizabeth had put the dark feather on top of her dressing table and I picked it up. For all that it had no vibrant hue—only the soft, silvery gray—it was undeniably beautiful. "I understand the power that Gabriel has." The memory of his presence hit me hard again. "He made no effort to touch me. I'm not even sure he's real. He could just be part of a dream. How do you know he's Callie's father?"

"I've been with no other man."

I didn't say it out loud, but I wondered if she could have

been drugged or coerced into forgetting. I kept thinking, why Elizabeth? I knew she had a gift. She could see creatures from the other realm, even if only in her dreams. But no one else knew that. No one could possibly discern that. And what would explain Callie's hands and feet? And Callie had the power to calm a person's fears. "You and Michael can come with us back to Mobile. We'll get a good doctor to look at Callie. I'm sure there are procedures that can be done to remove the webbing."

"Her life would be much easier if that were possible. I can't help but think about the hardships that await her if there isn't a medical solution. She'll be a freak; something for people to stare at."

"There are specialists in Mobile and even New Orleans, if we have to go there. We'll find someone."

Elizabeth put her arms around me and held on. "You've been a godsend to us, Raissa. I'm sorry I put you and Reginald in danger. I should have told the truth from the beginning but I was so afraid you wouldn't come, that you wouldn't believe me."

"How did you hear about us?" I asked. I'd meant to ask sooner.

"It was Deputy Gomes." She laughed softly without humor. "He'd gone to Montgomery for a meeting of his fellow law officers and someone had told him about Zelda Fitzgerald and Tallulah Bankhead and the way you'd helped another young woman who was their friend. Gomes was going on and on in the store about these detectives who could see ghosts. I went to Victoria and called Mrs. Fitzgerald. She was kind enough to give me your uncle's address. Of course Gomes isn't smart enough to put two and two together and figure out you're the ghost investigators."

At least one mystery was solved. "Do you really believe your brother is dead?"

"I do. Otherwise he would have found me by now, given me some sign. I should have left months ago, but travel by horse with an infant is not an easy thing."

"Unless he's involved in this deeper than you think." It was possible, and she had to be willing to confront that.

"I can't believe that Ramone would harm anyone, but wherever this investigation goes, we have to follow. And we have to be quick. The trial has been delayed, but only briefly. If we steal Hildy's body, the whole town is going to be up in arms and searching for us."

"They'll know it's us. It could be no one else."

"And if they find us before we get the autopsy results, they will hang us. All of us. My baby..." She bundled the clothing she'd piled on the bed in the bedspread, pulling the four corners together to make a sturdy knot. "We have to take Mariah over to Hattie's, like we did with Ruth's gelding."

"Good idea. Hattie sent a boy to take the chickens. They're gone."

"We'll leave at first light."

## CHAPTER 18

The car was jam-packed as we set off. I held Callie while Elizabeth held a lead rope. Mariah trotted contentedly behind the car as Reginald drove down a road that was little more than a track. It defined the borders of Elizabeth's land, and I watched the expressions roll across her face as she said goodbye to a farm she'd worked and enjoyed. She would not come back. Not willingly. This much I knew in my heart.

Reginald's clenched jaw reminded me how much danger we were in, though he'd been upbeat and cheerful to Elizabeth. I looked into the backseat at Michael, who rode beside Elizabeth. He nodded encouragement. "We're going to be okay."

The trees crowded close to the road, the trunks so thick the woods were as dark as night on each side of us. Anyone could be lying in wait. "Don't stop," I cautioned Reginald. "Whatever happens, don't stop."

He nodded and gripped the wheel tighter as the challenging road tried to wrest control from him. Up ahead, on the right, I saw something moving in the trees. I touched Reginald's hand. "Look there." I said it quietly, hoping not to alert Michael and Elizabeth until I was certain it was danger.

Reginald sped up. The car bumped and Elizabeth cast a worried glance at Mariah, who seemed able to keep up.

Whatever was in the woods increased its pace also. Michael leaned forward, pressing into the front seat. "We have to go back," he said.

"What?"

"We have to go back. Turn around. Quickly." He wasn't panicked, but he was firm.

"Why?" I leaned across the seat to ask him.

He pointed toward the woods, and I thought he'd also seen the dark shadow tracking us. Instead, he pointed to something closer—a green hood that had been fitted over the top of a small pine. The empty eye holes stared right at us. "They know we'll try this way out. They'll be waiting for us."

Movement deeper in the woods caught my eye. I caught what appeared to be the flutter of large, dark, wings, but I couldn't be certain. Though I was looking closely, I was completely unprepared for a wild rush of black wings and bodies that came out of the trees and flew over the car, missing us by only inches. The wake of turkey buzzards swarmed the car in a way I'd never seen that kind of bird react. It was almost as if they were attacking us. Their red heads, almost bald, looked dipped in blood.

"What the—" Reginald slowed in a small clearing and turned the car around. With the buzzards in pursuit, we headed back to Elizabeth's. We would not escape this morning. Maybe not ever.

"I've never seen a buzzard attack anything," Elizabeth said. "They're carrion eaters, not hunters." Little Callie had grown completely still. Her eyes were wide open, but she didn't fuss or cry.

"Could they have been poisoned?" Reginald asked. "They seem to be everywhere in Mission and they don't act like regular buzzards do."

"There have always been a lot of them. I call them the town greeters," Elizabeth said. "When I first came to town, there were dozens on that old lightning-blasted tree at the edge of town."

"We saw them there when we first arrived too," I said. "It was creepy, the way they sat on the tree and never flew away. They were watching. Just like the men who follow me and Reginald around town."

We'd left the birds behind, but their behavior had been strange, threatening. I turned to face Michael in the back seat. He didn't say anything, but he nodded, a sign to keep my courage up.

We arrived back at Elizabeth's defeated and worried. Michael was about to turn Mariah loose when I stopped him. I could ride her to Hattie's and get some help. On the horse, I could cut through the woods and fields. They couldn't follow me in a car because the woods were too thick. Reginald would have a fit, but no one else was nearly as good a rider as I was.

"You are not riding off on that horse." Reginald saw my hand on Mariah's lead rope and knew I was up to something.

"I can get help."

"Where? You can't ride that horse all the way to Victoria."

It would be a long and difficult trip, but I probably could. But I didn't have to. "If I can get to Hattie, she can help us create a distraction so we can make an escape. Maybe I can help her pile up some wood or old hay and start a fire, something that would draw the men over there. While they're busy we can escape."

"No." Reginald was firm.

"I can ride through the woods—"

"That's not safe." It was Michael who interrupted, not Reginald.

"I'm an excellent rider," I told him. "I'll be fine."

"It's not the horse." He stared at me. "It's the woods. Those buzzards. That wasn't natural, Raissa. Something dark is in those woods. The buzzards know it and I think they answer to it."

His statement took me aback. He might not believe in Gabriel, but he believed in something ugly and dangerous. Even so, I couldn't let him scare me off a plan that might save us all.

"Please put Mariah in the paddock. She needs grain and water," Elizabeth said. "Then come inside out of the sun. You're going to cook your brains. We can discuss this in the kitchen." Her tone was sharper than normal and I saw why. Standing at the edge of the yard, making no attempt to hide, were two men. They stood, hands hanging at their sides, watching. They didn't appear to be armed, but that was little comfort. As always, we were being closely observed.

I was tempted to go inside and get the rifle and shoot at them. Not to kill, but to let them know we weren't helpless. If they thought we were helpless, no telling what they would do.

Michael took my arm and walked me and the horse into the barn. We put a little grain out for Mariah and made sure she was free to head out to graze when she finished eating. Weaving my hand through his arm, he assisted me back to the house. We stopped in the front yard at the edge of the porch.

"Let's go inside." He was staring at the men too. One of them raised a hand and made what looked like a signal.

"What's he doing?"

"I don't know." Michael spoke to me but his gaze was riveted on the two watchers. The other man lifted his arm, curling his hand into a fist and bringing it down in a harsh manner.

"He's threatening us."

"Yes." Michael propelled me toward the front porch. "Go inside. If there's trouble, I need to be able to react quickly."

I stood for a moment longer, watching as a buzzard settled beside the men. Another bird lodged on a tree limb. The pose of the birds was almost a perfect duplication of the men's posture. Shoulders hunched, neck extended.

"Those aren't just birds, are they?" This was what frightened Michael in the woods. It wasn't the men in green hoods, it was something else. Something unnatural, as he'd said. The feather I'd found—he worried it was from something dark and dangerous.

"They're something other than birds." He didn't flinch when he said it.

"What?"

He stepped away from me, leaving me at the edge of the porch. "Go inside, Raissa. Now."

"Michael, I—"

A bullet sang over my head and struck the house with a fat plop. Reginald came to the door. "Get inside! Now!"

Michael and I both obeyed, rushing inside before another bullet was fired. I suspected the men of Mission were excellent shots. Hunting was how most of them ate—so it appeared they weren't aiming to kill us, only to keep us corralled in Elizabeth's house. They wanted us to know they could hurt us.

As soon as I could, I cornered Michael alone in the parlor. "What's going on with the buzzards? With you?" I caught his hand and held it between both of mine and felt the familiar frisson I always felt when we touched. I did have feelings for him. Small stirrings of attraction and desire, but my trust was not easily won.

"The birds—the buzzards—are messengers." He sighed. "I know you're able to see and feel things that others can't. Elizabeth is also a sensitive, but much weaker than you."

"What kind of messengers?" I looked up and Reginald was in the door. I waved him over to join us. "Please tell us."

"There's something dark here in Mission. It's part of the reason I'm here."

Any number of things could qualify as dark in Mission—killers who attacked the weak and helpless, men who ruled with iron fists, corruption of the justice system. "What? Just say it."

"What do you know about Callie's father?"

His question took me aback. "He's an archangel. Gabriel. He gives both Elizabeth and me the ability to dream what's truly happened."

Michael closed his eyes for a moment. "None of that is true."

Hot denial was my initial response, but I managed to hold it back. "Why would you say that?"

"The gift of dreaming the truth doesn't come from the thing you call Gabriel. It comes from Callie. *She* is Elizabeth's gift. She's touched with the Divine."

There was so much he wasn't saying. So much. "And Gabriel?"

He stared deep into my eyes, and I felt as if he were

touching something inside me. "Gabriel is no archangel. He's a great deceiver."

"How do you know this?" I asked.

"I just do. You have no reason to trust me, but you must."

"But—he has wings. The feather....I *saw* him."

"He is no angel, Raissa. He's treacherous and therefore dangerous."

I stared into Michael's eyes. He wasn't pretending. He was afraid for me. And for Elizabeth. But most especially for Callie.

"Do you believe Elizabeth saw the truth of Ruth's murder?" Reginald asked. He'd come to stand beside me. His arm brushed mine, a deliberate offer of comfort.

Michael nodded. "I do. The dreams come from Callie. She's an innocent. She reflects the truth without prejudice because she doesn't know what she's doing. She's merely opening a channel to a past event."

"But she is Gabriel's child," I said.

"I'm not so sure of that," Michael said.

"You doubt Elizabeth's word?"

He shook his head slowly. "I doubt her *knowledge* of what was done to her. That entity she calls Gabriel, we don't know what he's capable of."

"You agree he is...supernatural?" Reginald asked.

"I do."

"But he is not an angel?" Reginald continued, questions burning in his eyes.

"He is not an angel in the sense that you know angels— messengers of the divine, healers, those who bring comfort. He is none of those things. And he is a danger to Elizabeth and Raissa. They see him and experience him on many levels. If he gains a foothold in their heart or mind...he is dangerous."

I was about to reply when Elizabeth called out, "Coffee's made." She was standing at the sink and the men turned and headed to the kitchen. I looked through the open doorway and saw her at the hand pump—thank goodness she didn't have to carry water from a well or a creek. She was pressing the handle up and down and a flow of water gushed into the sink. Her head was slightly down as she worked.

Suddenly a shot rang out. Elizabeth stopped. It was as if she paused in her work to consider something. She stumbled backward a step or two and slowly turned to face us, confusion on her face. Her hand lifted to her chest as blood appeared at her shoulder like a rose—dark and intensely red. As it began to spread down her breast and torso, she slowly slumped to the floor.

# CHAPTER 19

T he men rushed into the kitchen and flew to
Elizabeth's side. Outside the house, I heard men
arguing.

"You stupid bastard, you shot her," one man said.

"Yeah, I got the bitch. She won't be troubling us anymore,"
another replied.

"That's murder, you dumb bastard. You'll hang for this."

I couldn't believe what had just happened—Elizabeth had
been shot standing in her own kitchen. I looked out the
window and saw the watchers running into the woods.
Stunned, I had to force myself to walk to the kitchen doorway.
Reginald held clean dishcloths to the wound and Michael
searched through drawers and cabinets for medical supplies. In
the bedroom little Callie began to wail—the first time I'd
heard the baby cry. This was an outburst of terror and loss, and
I hurried through the kitchen to pick Callie up.

She snuggled into my arms, still moaning softly as if she
understood what had happened to her mother. I paced the
bedroom, singing softly and rocking her. Gradually she calmed

and began the throaty noise that sounded like a purr. If I thought of Elizabeth, Callie grew agitated. I put up a wall between my feelings for Elizabeth and the baby. To keep Callie calm, I had to. When I could no longer ignore the desperation in the quick exchanges between Reginald and Michael, I took Callie into the back bedroom. I forced my mind to picture flowers and sunshine and the things of nature that gave comfort, and the baby was soothed.

She finally fell asleep and I tucked her on the bed, surrounded by pillows, and made myself go back to the kitchen.

"She's alive," Reginald said. His dark hair hung in his eyes and sweat covered his face and upper body. Michael, too, looked wrung out.

"We need a doctor," Michael said. "I did what I could."

"I can get one."

"No." Reginald was firm.

"Yes." I was calm. "I'm the best rider, the lightest. I can ride to Doctor Wainwright's office and send him out here."

"If they catch you, they won't hesitate to harm you."

I looked at Michael. "I don't think Gabriel will let them."

He was supporting Elizabeth's head in his lap as Reginald made compresses for her shoulder. "You can't trust Gabriel."

"I don't. But I believe I have more value alive than dead."

He didn't argue with that, and I knew I'd won. Whatever Michael knew about the entity that visited Elizabeth and me, he believed Gabriel would help us avoid harm if possible. *Why* was another matter, and something I could not think about right now.

"I can leave out the back of the barn. It won't take me long to get to Mission, and the doctor's house is just on the other side of town. I know he's in with Lucais and that crew, but even one of the watchers said himself that they shouldn't have shot Elizabeth. I don't think the doctor will refuse to help a wounded woman. I'll send help as quickly as I can."

"Be safe." Reginald had made a clean compress and he was pressing on Elizabeth's wound. The bleeding had slowed, but she was still unconscious.

"The baby is in the back bedroom. She's sleeping, but listen for her. If you hold her, try not to think about Elizabeth. It upsets her." My stomach clenched at the thought of leaving Callie. The mule kick of maternal love was unexpected. She wasn't my baby, but until Elizabeth was better, she was my responsibility. "Are you sure you can manage her?"

"There's a woman on the floor who's been shot and you ask if we can diaper a baby?" Reginald gave me a wry smile. "Get going. And hurry. We've almost stopped the bleeding, but I don't know what else to do. That bullet is going to have to come out."

"Raissa?" Michael spoke.

"Yes."

"Don't stop for anyone. Run them down if you have to. The horse will help you. Trust her."

I nodded and hurried back to the bedroom to find a pair of Elizabeth's dungarees that she wore to do farm work. I put them on with her boots and one of her shirts, and I pulled a brimmed gardening hat over my bobbed hair. This wasn't a ride for sidesaddle. It wouldn't matter how I was riding if I was caught, and I had much better control astride. I hurried out the back door, slipped over to the barn, and whistled up the horse. She came as if she had been waiting for me.

I saddled her quickly and mounted with ease. The minute Mariah felt my weight atop her, she snorted, ready for a run. I held her in as we walked out the back of the barn. I looked everywhere, but there was no sign of the watchers. Cowards that they were, they'd likely raced back to town, afraid there would be a murder warrant out for them. For shooting an unarmed woman in her own house. By god, I would see that they paid.

When we made the edge of the woods, I let Mariah have her head. She started down the trail at a brisk trot that shifted into an easy canter and finally an all-out gallop. I leaned low on her neck, twisting my fingers in her mane.

The mare was an athlete, and I felt completely secure in the regular saddle with both legs in use to steady my balance. We cut through the woods, relying on the angle of the sun for a northerly direction from Elizabeth's farm. When we came to a fallen tree, Mariah sailed over it, and I thought of a young girl in West Point, Mississippi, who'd ridden a silver white horse like a moon wraith. I didn't have her talent or style, but I had desperation. Elizabeth was counting on me to make this ride. So was Callie.

The footing in the forest was good, but I watched closely for holes. We followed a barely discernable trail that came out at a dirt road. I had no idea where I was, but I started down the path.

The road was empty for several miles, until I saw a farm truck up ahead. It was parked on the side of the road and a woman with two children sat in the shade of a tree, waiting for something. I approached with caution. She stood, and the fear was plain in her expression. When she realized I was a woman, she was shocked, but she also relaxed.

"How far to town?" I asked.

"Another two miles." She pointed in the direction I was going. "Hey, be careful."

I wanted to ask her what she knew of me, but I didn't. "Are you okay?"

She thought before she answered. "We are. Me and the kids are waiting. My husband went for some squirrels. You'd better ride on."

"Thanks." I took off at a trot, putting the distance between me and what could be more trouble.

I came to the main road and the lightning-blasted tree. The black limbs, stretching up into the blue September sky, made me think of a supplicant. The buzzards were gone. The road was quiet, unnaturally quiet, and I realized that there were no sounds of birds or small animals. It was as if a spell had been cast over the area by an evil enchantress. That was not a comforting thought.

As Mariah walked toward town, I looked through the woods, listening as hard as I could. I felt him, waiting and watching. Michael had soured my trust of Gabriel. What did he really want? Now I feared it was something sinister.

When I saw him, I wasn't surprised. Gabriel moved through the tree trunks, effortlessly keeping up with Mariah. This time there was no evidence of his wings—he wore pants, a white shirt, and suspenders like all the other men. He kept pace with me, never going slower or faster. If he wasn't an angel, what was he? What did he want? I'd ask him when I had a chance, but not now. He stayed too far away.

I circled around the town and tied Mariah at the back of Doctor Wainwright's house. I was lucky he wasn't busy and could see me right away. His maid led me to a small office where she showed me to a seat and gave me a much-needed glass of water. When the doctor came in, his consternation at my dress was clear. I was not behaving like a lady. My patience hit the danger zone.

"Elizabeth Maslow has been shot and we need your help. Now." I'd meant to ask for help, but his holier-than-thou attitude was unbearable. I would not ask, I would demand. These aberrant men had cowed the women under their control, but I would not have it.

The doctor stared at me. "Who would shoot Elizabeth?"

I had actually shocked him, and I backed down and softened my tone. "I don't know and I don't care, but if you don't help her, she's going to die. She's still bleeding and I've been traveling here for half an hour."

He grabbed a black bag from beside his chair and opened it to check for supplies. He pointed a pair of forceps at me. "You need to leave. Don't travel the main roads and get out of town as quickly as you can. Your life depends on it."

I had one chance to make a point with him. I wouldn't delay him, but I had to try to get through to him. "You're a doctor, sworn to do no harm. You know Slater McEachern is innocent of killing Ruth Whelan. They're going to execute an innocent man."

He snapped his bag shut and strode out of the room. I heard the front door slam and the sound of a car motor start. He'd left me to find my way back as best I could.

I jammed my hat tighter on my head and started out the back door, where Mariah waited patiently.

"Miss?"

I turned to find the maid wringing her hands. She was a young woman, my age or maybe a bit older. I'd paid scant attention to her—a silent woman in a plain dress of modest cut. Her hair was pinned on top of her head. "Yes?"

"Is Miss Elizabeth going to be okay?"

"I don't know, but I hope so."

"Who shot her?"

I could answer honestly. "I don't know. But I promise you, I'm going to find out."

"She's been kind to me and so many others. Please tell her Lindy says to call for any help she needs." She followed me out on the back porch and looked around before she spoke. "There's a place she can hide if she needs it. A safe place. I can look after her until you can get her out of town. Don't leave her at home. She isn't safe, but me and her friends can take care of her until she can leave."

"I'll tell her."

"They moved Mr. McEachern today."

This was news. "Moved him where?"

Tears formed in her eyes. "To a cabin in the woods. I heard them talking. They said he wasn't safe. Said some strangers had come to town to break him out of jail." She wiped her eyes. "That would be you, wouldn't it?"

"We did come to help him if we can."

"He didn't kill Ruthie. She thought a lot of him. A whole lot. She told me he was the only truly good thing that had ever come to her life." Her face contorted and she began to cry. "They killed her so they could blame him. This is all to get him out of the way."

"What's he in the way of?"

"Them doing whatever they want. He told them they were wrong. He said he was going to put a stop to them."

Slater McEachern had defied the rulers of the town. But would they really kill an innocent woman just to frame him? Why not just shoot him in the woods and pretend it was a hunting accident?

I faced Lindy. "Do you know where he's being held? Where this cabin is?"

She rubbed her tears with her fists. "I sure do. And I'll

draw you a map, but don't let the doctor know. He don't agree with what they're doing, but he won't stand up. They're too mean."

"I'll never tell, Lindy. But thank you."

I followed her back to the kitchen where she found a paper sack and tore it into a page. She worked on her map quickly. "Here's where we are. Here's where he is, for right now at least. They're afraid a lynch mob would get him and kill him before a trial. They need for everyone to believe he's guilty. If folks question his guilt... You better be real careful."

I studied the map until I had it situated in my mind. It wasn't much of a ride, and I could take another road through the woods to get back to Elizabeth's. "Thank you, Lindy."

"Make Miss Elizabeth get well. She's the only good thing left here in Mission."

I thought of one more thing. "Have you noticed anything... strange in the woods?"

Lindy looked at me strangely. "You see him too," she finally said. "He's always watching. He's there and then he's gone. I don't think he's a good man."

"You think he's a man?" The question slipped out.

"What else would he be?" she asked, giving me another curious look. "Just beware of him. He's up to something."

"Why would you say that?"

She shrugged. "You'd better get going. Fast."

"Are they burying Hildy Morse tomorrow?"

"They put off the funeral for some reason. Not smart in this heat. That little girl's gonna wilt and start to rot. Poor Mrs. Morse has taken to her sick bed. Hildy was a trial on her with her wild ways, but Florence Morse loved her baby girl hard."

"Thank you, Lindy." There was nothing else I could say. I

slipped out the back door clutching the map and mounted. Lindy came out to the steps.

"Ride safe."

"I will." I pressed my legs into Mariah's side and we were off. I cut across fields and plots of timberland to stay off the main road. Lindy's map was most helpful. I intended to check on Slater McEachern before I went back to Elizabeth's. If it was possible we could spring him from his confinement, we could all flee town at the first opportunity. It made a lot more sense to save a living man than steal a corpse.

Following the map, I turned into the woods and stopped. Gabriel stood in the middle of the narrow path. Mariah snorted and tried to spin and run but I held her steady in the road. The path had been empty only seconds earlier, but now he blocked it completely. There was no emotion on his face as he stepped toward me and touched the reins. Mariah instantly calmed.

I tried to calm the fear that fluttered hard in my chest. I'd once viewed Gabriel as God's messenger, someone who might help us. That had changed. When I looked into his eyes, I saw no warmth or humanity. "Who are you?"

"You know me. I'm Gabriel."

But I didn't know him. I'd assumed much, because of the way Elizabeth had presented him. She believed he was the father of her child. Now I wasn't so certain.

"Please, step away from my horse."

His dark wings spread, stretching out across my path. He reached for the bridle again and I clamped my legs around Mariah. She broke free of the enchantment he'd cast on her and spurted forward, causing him to step aside and let me pass. I grabbed her mane and leaned forward, freeing Mariah's back so that she could gather herself and run like the wind.

"You can't escape me, Raissa James," he called out.

I paid him no heed. I couldn't listen and allow my fear to grow. I buried my nose in the horse's thick black mane and inhaled the clean scent of a healthy animal. "Run," I whispered. "Run!"

We galloped through the woods, but I heard his laughter behind me. Overhead, the kettle of buzzards swooped low and silent, their huge wings casting enormous shadows on the sandy path.

# CHAPTER 20

Deep woods surrounded the cabin where Slater McEachern was lodged. I came upon the cabin so suddenly, it was almost as if the woods had spit me out at the front porch. We arrived there, both horse and rider, heaving and blowing in the broiling heat. Insects had feasted on my arms and face, and Mariah's neck was covered in blood where I'd swatted yellow flies, smashing dozens of them.

For a moment, I sat my horse in perfect stillness as I took in what was left of a yard. The woods had encroached. But the normal noises of the forest were silent. No wrens or finches flitting through the underbrush. No chatter of angry squirrels. No sign of anyone alive near the house.

My skin crawled when I saw the buzzards had beat me there and settled in the trees at the side yard. Even they were silent. Watchers. Messengers. Symbols of what? Who did they watch for? At first, I'd thought they were somehow connected to the town of Mission. Now, I was rethinking everything. They seemed part and parcel of the angel, Gabriel. They appeared to be his companions, if not a more nefarious bond as his spies.

The birds were one worry, but I was more concerned about armed men who might shoot first and ask questions later. When I walked across the patchy front lawn without a challenge, I could finally breathe. I was surprised that a guard hadn't been posted. I'd come upon the place so unexpectedly that I was easily within sight—had anyone been looking. It chilled me to think what the men were up to rather than guarding their valued prisoner.

"McEachern!" I called out.

"Go away, lassie!" His brogue was undeniable, and thicker than I remembered at the jail. He sounded exhausted and defeated.

I tied Mariah to a shrub and went up on the rickety porch. It took all of my courage to open the door and step inside. A big man reclined on a bed. In the relative darkness it took me a moment to see that he was chained to the wall with a band around his neck.

"You shouldn't be here." He sat up, but he didn't have a lot of room to maneuver. The chain was unnecessarily short.

I stood silent, taking in Slater McEachern. He was a giant of a man with dark red hair that curled in loops. He was greatly in need of a wash, and he was clearly embarrassed by his condition. He looked at the floor instead of me.

"I want to help you." I looked beyond him, giving him as much privacy as I could.

"You can't. No one can. Damn the lass, I told Elizabeth to stay out of this. The girl's too stubborn for her own good. She's going to get herself and that *bairn* hurt. And for nothing." He held up a hand to keep me back. "I'm *howfin*." He wrinkled his face as if he could smell himself.

I could understand his despair, and I didn't try to change it. I didn't know if I could help him or not. We all might be engaged in a fool's errand that would only end in disaster. But I had to try. "Who killed Ruth? If you know, tell me so I can prove it." That would be the most direct action to take to save him. I set about looking for a key to his chains as I waited for his answer.

He glanced up at me before looking away. "I don't know for certain. I've done nothing but think, and it defies any sane answer. I don't know who would do such a thing to a tender woman. She never harmed a living creature. Ruth was..." He fought for control. "She was a kind and decent woman. No matter what they say, she had more decency in her little finger than any of them."

The grief in his voice spoke more of a lost love than a lost friend. I went to the kitchen, where a jug of water had been left. McEachern couldn't reach it on the chain and I wondered how many hours had passed since he'd had anything to drink. I poured a glass and took it to him. He drank without pause, and I gave him another.

"Have you eaten?" I needed time to think of a way to help him. The chain was thick and sturdy. The metal collar around his neck, designed for slaves, would not easily be broken. No one had conveniently left a key laying about, which meant I wouldn't be able to take him with me.

"Not since yesterday morning. Feeding prisoners isn't a priority in Mission. If you run afoul of Lucais Wilkins, if they don't hang you, they'll starve you. They mean for me to die one way or t'other."

"I want to help you, but you're going to have to trust me." I took a chair from the small kitchen table and sat near the bed. The stench made my eyes water, but he couldn't help it and I wondered what kind of men would force another to live in such conditions when they could have easily allowed him to clean up in the yard. "Tell me about the night Ruth was killed."

"I saw her early that evening. I took her some wild grapes I'd picked in the woods. She made jams and jellies and some-times a bottle of sweet wine for us to share. Seldom an evening passed that I didn't spend some time with her. We talked. Lookin' forward not back." He hesitated. "Ruth wanted to change...what she was doing. She wanted to live quietly. Move into my gaff."

Reginald had the talent for reading people, but even I could see that Slater McEachern had been in love with Ruth Whelan. "You were going to marry her and pay off her debts, weren't you?"

"I was."

"Why would Lucais Wilkins care about that? He'd have his money."

"Ruth was his investment. She was worth more enslaved than free. Ruth could ne'er get ahead. Never pay the mortgage on her gaff. If she made a dollar, he took seventy-five cents. Said she owed him interest. She was trapped."

"But he couldn't have stopped you from paying her debt. Could he?"

"Seems no matter what I paid, the debt grew. Aye, Lucais was canny with contracts and debts. What he got Ruth to sign, when she was so desperate, he said it couldn't be undone. The man is an agent of Satan himself. Man kept a set of books, showin' the debt that never lessened."

A chill passed over me, and in my mind I saw Gabriel, reaching for the bridle of my horse. I remembered the journal. "Ruth kept records, too, didn't she? Records of those who paid her. You threatened Lucais with Ruth's journal, didn't you? You were going to expose him by giving out her accounts of the men who came to her and the dates. Evidence."

McEachern closed his eyes. "The town would have strung him up for sure. Lucais uses all his religious rubbish to bully people. He spouts the ten commandments as the basis for Mission, twaddlin' on about how adultery isn't tolerated. He dinnae believe a word of it, but a lot of the people here do. They truly believe that they're living life according to the way God ordained. Lucais makes a mockery of them. If they knew what he did, the fullness of his deceit, they would have made him pay."

"Look, we have to get you out of here before they come back." I couldn't bear to see him chained up in such despair.

"You plannin' on cutting off my head?"

He had a point. "No. We have to find the key or we need to be able to break or cut the chain." I stepped closer to him so I could examine the heavy links of his bondage. "Why couldn't they have just tied you up?" Frustration hit me so strong I wanted to cry.

"They have no love for me or my people or any from doon the road," he said. "Look outside for an ax. It's possible I can break the chain."

Glad to get outside into fresher air, I looked for the stump where wood was split. I found a splitter and a saw but there was no ax, nothing that would work as a tool to free McEachern. I took Mariah to the outside well and pumped water in a bucket for her. She drank and sighed.

By the angle of the sun, I estimated that it was near lunch time. Had the doctor saved Elizabeth? I had no intention of telling McEachern that she'd been shot. That her life was in danger. He couldn't help her, and the frustration might make him do something regrettable.

When I'd thoroughly scoured the yard looking for an ax to no avail, I went back inside and moved the chair back to the position I'd found it. "I'll be back. With an ax or a key. And a ride for you. We aren't going to just leave you here."

"Get Elizabeth and her babe to safety. That's what you can do for me. I'm nae afraid to die."

"But not unnecessarily." I wondered if he'd heard about Hildy Morse. "Slater, there's a killer on the loose. Someone killed a child. Hildy Morse."

He bolted upright and his forehead knotted in fury. "That wee sweet girl? How? Why?"

"We think she saw something she shouldn't have. She was hit very hard and thrown into the well in her yard. I believe she was dead before she went in the well." That was small comfort, but at least he wouldn't have the vision of her injured and drowning.

"Who did that? Who hurt a *wee quinie* in that way?" Chained to the wall, he was unable to do anything other than seethe. His clenched fists told the story of what he would like to do to Hildy's killer, and the idea of it made me happy.

"We don't know who killed Hildy. I only know it was a man." I stopped myself from going into the details of my dream. There wasn't time to convince Slater of the netherworld I sometimes saw and the things that lived there. "It was likely the same person who killed Ruth. There's also been attacks on women in Victoria." I waited to see what he would offer.

"I knew of one attack." He weighed his words and I wondered why. "A young man was accused. Junior Albee. The boy is...damaged in the mind. Daft."

Only a month earlier I'd spent a great deal of time in Alabama's state mental asylum. The plight of the mentally ill was a source of great sorrow, and one that left me without any solutions. For most, their days passed in restraint or oblivion. It was a sentence worse than death to be sent there. Yet a dangerous person couldn't be allowed to roam the streets and attack people.

"You know this man? This Junior Albee?"

"I do. When I can work him, I give him a job. He's reliable, just a little slow. He's found a talent in repairing motor cars."

"Is he capable of killing Ruth Whelan and Hildy?"

"He's strong enough, no doubt. In the past, he's been aggressive toward a woman, but he was provoked. Not Hildy or my Ruthie. Junior loved them because they were decent to him. Ruth gave him the kindness his own mother withheld. And Hildy played with him. She never noticed he was too big for her games." He tugged at the chain. "Now listen to me, Mrs. James, if it comes to them pointing the finger at Junior Albee or me, you let them hang me. I mean it."

"The boy means that much to you?"

"He's an innocent. If he did something wrong, it had no malice in't. Folks don't understand that. They're afraid of him, but the truth is, he's terrified of them. He never acts out unless he's being threatened, but the things that threaten him are... hard for others to see. They goad him. Junior gets agitated, but he's easy to calm. These bastards. Any excuse will do them to kill him, and him only a daft lad."

While Slater talked, I did a second, thorough search of the little cabin. If the key had been left, I couldn't find it.

"I'm going to get help." Time was ticking away from me. "I'll bring an ax and someone who can break that chain."

"And some food?" He gave a wry grin. "I'd rather die on a full stomach than an empty."

"Can you ride a horse?" I had an idea.

"Aye, I can stay on a cuddy. Learned as a boy."

I gave him another glass of water. I couldn't leave the container or glass with him or they'd know someone had been there. "I'll be back. I promise."

"Nae, dinnae put yourself in danger."

"It doesn't matter what I'm caught doing. If I'm caught, they're going to arrest me and possibly hang me." The words felt very real as I said them. "Now I have to ride. I *will* come back. If the men return, try to find where the key is."

He smiled, but it quickly faded. "Ruthie would have liked you, lass."

The pain of his loss was a knife in my already battered heart. I hurried out of the house and mounted Mariah. We had a lot of riding ahead of us.

# CHAPTER 21

When I arrived back at Elizabeth's, I found Reginald rocking the baby on the front porch. Michael was under his car, making sure the driveshaft and tie rods were solid enough to sustain a long trip. It was clear his focus was on imminent evacuation.

"How is Elizabeth?" I asked as I dismounted.

"Dr. Wainwright took her to his office to remove the bullet. He said the wound wasn't fatal. If she doesn't get an infection, she'll heal. Doc said she'll be back here before nightfall."

"How badly was she wounded? Will she be able to use her arm?"

"He thinks she'll have full use, but he gave us a stern talking to about the danger she's in. Not from the gunshot, but from her attempts to save McEachern." Michael had come out from under the car and was doing the talking. Reginald rocked and shushed the baby. "He told us to get her out of town immediately, before it was too late. The problem is, I don't trust the doctor. I'm worried that he might turn Elizabeth over to Lucais." He glanced at Reginald. "We had no choice but to let her go."

I unsaddled Mariah and turned her in the paddock with fresh water and hay. I would need her to be rested and ready before the night was over. I returned to the porch and had a long drink of water myself. When Reginald took Callie inside to change her, I motioned Michael out of earshot.

"Where's your horse?" I asked.

"I rent a room from a family. They're caring for him." His eyes narrowed. "What are you thinking?"

"We need to get that horse, and I need an ax."

"For what?"

"I found McEachern. He's in a house in the woods chained to the wall, but I think you can break the links with an ax." Michael would have to ride his horse and pony Mariah behind. That way both men could cut through the forest on horseback and we could pick them up on the road far away from any blockade. "We can save him. Then we can get the hell out of here."

Michael considered. "You do need to get out of here. Elizabeth too, but especially Callie. I've given it a lot of thought and she's the one in most danger. She is what this is all about."

"What are you saying?" Michael's clear-eyed intensity was scaring me.

"Callie is a special child. You know that."

"Her father is an angel. Of course, she's special."

He shook his head. "That doesn't matter right now. We can sort that later. The only important thing is to get her and Elizabeth to safety as soon as possible. And you're in danger too, Raissa. You're sensitive to things on the other side. There are forces at work—Look, we can't wait for McEachern. If I'm right, and we get Elizabeth and Callie out of here, the whole McEachern thing might blow over."

He was lying. He looked away from me as he talked, and there was a strain in his voice. Michael wasn't a very good liar.

Reginald came out on the porch, eyeing us both with wariness and curiosity. "You two look like you're ready to have a round of fisticuffs. What's going on?"

I'd hoped to win Michael to my plan before I had to confront Reginald. Time had run out, though. "I spoke with Slater McEachern. I want Michael to get his horse and lead Mariah to the place where he's being held. They moved him from the jail to an isolated cabin this morning. This is our best chance to save him."

"Why would they move him out of the jail?" Reginald hung on to the practical issues.

"They fear a lynch mob will break him out of the jail after Hildy's death. Emotions are high. But Lucais needs for Slater to be tried and found guilty. Lucais has to make certain that everyone in town believes he's guilty."

"Is there a guard?"

"No. He's wearing a slave collar and is chained to the wall. Michael can free him with an ax. Then both men can take a horse through the woods and we'll pick them up on the way to Victoria." I was spewing information because I knew any moment Reginald or Michael would object.

Reginald read the tension between us. "You don't like the idea, Michael?"

"I don't. I'd as soon steal that dead girl's body as try this. I say you take Raissa and Callie and get out of here now. I'll follow with Elizabeth."

"Why is Callie worth sacrificing McEachern and possibly Elizabeth?" Reginald asked in a calm tone.

"Gabriel is not her father," Michael said. "She's a gift from the divine and owes nothing to Gabriel."

His angry tone said it all. "What do you know about Gabriel? If he isn't an angel, what is he? If he isn't Callie's father, who is?"

"There's no time to explain."

"Gabriel is a dark entity." I spoke to Reginald, but it was Michael's surprised look that I followed. "I know that now. He's revealed that much to me. And he's up to something. What is it, Michael? You know, don't you?"

"I know that terrible things have happened since he appeared in Mission. I know that Elizabeth believes he's well intentioned, and that has put her in danger. If he's lied to her about Callie, what else has he told her? I don't know the answer to these things, but I know that his influence is seductive, insidious, and dangerous. Why have you changed your mind about him?"

It was a fair question. "He accosted me on the way to Slater McEachern. He grabbed Mariah's bridle, but he didn't try to detain me. While he didn't hurt me, there was something..." I remembered the way he'd reached for the bridle. His ability to control Mariah's reaction with just his touch. "He scared me. He..." It was hard to say, because in the strange world of Mission, this was the most damning thing I could point to. "He travels with the buzzards. I believe they do his bidding."

Almost as if I'd commanded them, we heard the loud flapping of wings. Dozens of turkey buzzards burst out of the woods and flew directly at the house. They came in low, their massive wings momentarily blotting out the sun. We all ducked reflexively as they swept by us. A black wing struck my face, and the smell of decay and carrion made me gag.

"Inside." Reginald herded us toward the front door.

"They'll report back to Gabriel," I told them.

"There's nothing to report," Michael said as he urged me toward the house. "Let's just be sure we don't give them anything."

When we were in the kitchen and I'd checked to be sure Callie was sleeping, I demanded answers.

"Michael, how is Gabriel connected with Lucais Wilkins?"

"I don't know that," Michael answered. "Lucais is a mortal man and Gabriel is an entity, whether from the realm of the dead or the dark void, it doesn't matter. He's dangerous to you." He paused. "And to Elizabeth. I regret that she embraced him and allowed him access."

"Access to her house?" Reginald asked.

"No, to her soul."

Michael's dark pronunciation affected Reginald as much as it did me. We shared a look of deep worry. "I agree with Michael. I need to take you and the baby out of here," he said. "We can't impact this until we understand it. Let's go to Victoria and call Madam Petalungro. She might have advice."

Madam was my mentor in the world of spiritualism. She was a deep trance psychic medium with real talent, and because of her fondness for Reginald, she'd always been willing to help me learn to manage my ability to communicate with the dead. At first, I'd been terrified of the ghosts I saw. Madam had helped me learn to take a breath, to see what they wanted or needed. Some were merely lost. Others were angry or evil or dangerous. And I was beginning to learn that there were far worse things than ghosts. For instance, this case had little to do with the dead or hauntings—that I could see. Madam's take on the situation would be very welcome.

Reginald pointed to the doorway to the bedrooms. "Make

sure you have everything Callie will need. We have to go. Now."

I shook my head. "I won't leave Elizabeth, and she won't leave Slater McEachern. He *is* a good man. He begged me to get her and leave. He's willing to be the sacrifice."

"And that's what you should do." Michael was emphatic.

"I can't without trying. Please. Take the horses, Michael. He can ride. I asked him." I got the map that Lindy had given me. "See here. If you cut through that trail behind the house he's in, it will come out on that road. We can be there with both cars, if yours is running."

"The car's okay," Michael conceded. "It'll get us to Victoria at least. That's not the worry. Getting out of Mission is what scares me."

But I wouldn't be deterred. "Good, the car is running. We can split up, take two different routes so that one of us is sure to get to Victoria and call the law. And my uncle. Uncle Brett will have federal agents here."

"The law might not respond in the way you hope," Michael said.

"I know. The local sheriff has abdicated when it comes to Mission. He allows Deputy Gomes to rule and I suspect he prefers not to hear anything about what happens here. That way he and the county commissioners can pretend ignorance if anything blows up. But if we press the sheriff and he realizes that innocent people are going to die, and that he'll publicly be held responsible, he'll take action. He'll have to." I had to convince them to try. To save Elizabeth and the baby, I would sacrifice McEachern. But only if there was no other way.

Reginald nodded and I knew he would stand with me. "Before you go off half-cocked, Raissa, I learned some things in Victoria that might impact your decision."

I hadn't even given Reginald a chance to tell me about his trip. I'd been too busy with my plans. "What did you find out?"

"Junior Albee could be the real killer. He's got a history of violence toward women. He was accused of attacking one girl, but he was never arrested. Instead, his family sought help from a priest. Whatever happened, he became very sick. The town was told he had contracted something and that the high fever had taken a toll. After that, he was never the same. More a child than a grown man."

Slater had painted a slightly different picture of the young man. "Have they ever arrested him?" If they had we could use that as grounds to legally force McEachern's release.

"No, and don't hold your breath. His daddy managed to keep him out of jail. The girl he attacked refused to name him. It was all swept under the rug."

"And there was an earlier attack of a woman in Victoria," Michael added. "No one pushed to find out what had really happened to her and it just was dropped. But that's a place to look, once we get out of here."

We were all clinging to any hope we could lock onto.

Reginald eyed me and seemed to come to some conclusion. "Raissa, can you watch Callie? I'll drive Michael to get his horse."

He was going to try my plan. It was more than I'd really hoped for. "Yes. She'll be fine. Can you get past the blockade?"

"That's the road into town. I doubt they'll be watching that as closely as the road to Victoria. We can try."

I nodded. "Be safe. I'll have everything ready for tonight when you get back."

# CHAPTER 22

The afternoon heat was stifling, and Callie was not her normal calm and cheerful self. The minute Reginald and Michael drove away from the house, she began to fret. I tried rocking her, walking with her, singing to her, taking her out back to watch the chickens. Normally the clucky birds, pecking and squawking, made her squirm with glee. I feared she was hungry, but she refused the sugar teat that I'd made, and I had no alternative. Elizabeth didn't keep cows or goats. Callie was breastfed, except now her mother was unable to feed and care for her.

As a result, Callie was irritable and unhappy. I had the sense of a little shock whenever she touched me with one of her hands. Not anything unpleasant, just a vibration. I'd held her in the past and never felt this, and I worried. Something was going on with her, and I didn't know how to help.

The watchers, both human and avian, were nowhere in sight when I looked out the windows. I'd taken Elizabeth's rifle, made sure it was loaded, and put it in the kitchen within easy reach. If I saw or heard anything that upset me, I meant to kill it. I'd never considered myself a violent person or someone who would deliberately inflict physical damage on another person or creature. But now I knew one thing for certain. If anyone threatened Callie, I would kill them. Maternal instinct or guardian, I didn't know or care. She came first, before the life of anyone else or my personal comfort.

Checking the edge of the woods for those silent—but armed—men one more time, I finally carried Callie out to the barn to see the horse. Mariah blew sweet breath on the infant's face and Callie laughed out loud. The spell of discontent was broken, and Callie's sunny nature returned. It was a relief to see her happy again. I could tell she missed Elizabeth, and dry nursemaid that I was, I made a very poor substitute. Hopefully, Callie's mother would be home soon.

While I didn't talk about it to the men—who carried their own share of worry—I was afraid Dr. Wainwright might try to hold Elizabeth as his prisoner, or even turn her over to Lucais and his thugs. Dr. Wainwright was involved with Lucais and the others, but I had no way to judge the depth of his commitment to their cause. Those men obviously meant to stop us from helping McEachern or even leaving town, with or without him. If Wainwright was in thick with them, he might give them Elizabeth.

In the shade of the barn, the exhausted baby finally fell asleep in my arms. When I started back to the house, she raised a hand, and the sunlight through the translucent webbing of her fingers was like a glowing map or work of art. Her hands and feet were strange, but they were also very beautiful, luminous. She touched my cheek and I had a sudden memory of playing in the roots of a huge oak tree when I was a child. I'd drawn farms and roads and used my dolls to set up my fantasy world. It was a moment of total satisfaction and safety. But it was long ago.

I took Callie inside and put her on the bed. She sucked a little on the sugar teat, and that seemed to soothe her. I was exhausted myself, and I crawled up beside her to try to catch a nap. The approaching night would prove long and dangerous.

"Your mother will be here soon," I murmured to the baby. "She's coming home. Just for you." A breeze slipped in the bedroom window and for the first time in what felt like months, I was cool. With Callie cuddled against me, I embraced sleep. I felt as if I were falling, falling into the depth of a deep well, into darkness that had no limit. I knew I was asleep, but the disorientation disturbed me. I realized I was dreaming, and I slipped beneath the spell of the dream.

*The rattling of the window shade draws me up, up from sleep into complete darkness. I'm no longer in bed, but upright and outside. The night is cool. I find myself in a dark garden filled with strange sculptures and hedges that take the form of predatory animals in the moonlight. There is a lion, mouth open, roaring anger at me. When I slowly turn, a large bear looms over me, paws ready to reach down to catch me. When I walk away, I find myself confronting a stone gargoyle upon a pedestal. In the distance is a woman holding a babe in her arms, weeping.*

*I am alone in the dreadful garden, but in the distance murmurs from a party spike the night. There is light laughter and the low rumble of conversation. When I look down, I wear a tuxedo, polished black shoes. I hold a heavy crystal glass filled with whiskey in one hand and a cigarette in the other. My hand is large, male, young, and uncalloused. I am not a working man, but an office man, or a man of leisure.*

*"Amory! Where are you?" A man calls out.*

*The name is familiar, and I assume it is mine. "Here, by the koi pond." I step near the edge of the pond where large fish swim relent-*

lessly back and forth. Though they are docile fish, they swim with the purpose and speed of sharks. One leaps from the waters and snaps at a bug, teeth clicking shut before it disappears back into the dark water.

A man steps out of the shadows. He also holds a cigarette and a drink. "Isabel is looking for you, old boy."

"Let her look." I don't want to see her.

The sound of girlish laugher comes to me and my body tenses. Isabel is right outside my range of vision. She steps into the moonlight and I realize we're on the grounds of Princeton. Nassau Hall is in the distance. I recognize it from photos Alex showed me. He'd attended seminars there, and we'd talked of maybe moving nearby so Alex could further his law education once he returned from the war. I am in a dream that mingles my past and someone else's. Whose, I can't say.

The woman, Isabel, is smiling as she walks forward. She is angular, slender, and I know the dress she wears. I've read it described somewhere. It hangs on her, draping perfectly as she moves. She is like the koi. She is one thing, but more than that.

"Isn't it grand to be perfect?" she asks. "That's the gift Scott gave us. We may not be nice people, but we have physical perfection."

"Perfect?" I don't understand.

"That's us, perfect physical specimens. Too bad he couldn't write us with a soul."

I realize that I don't like this woman at all. "Leave me alone."

"I can't." She walks around me with her long strides, her predatory essence. She wants to gobble me with one bite.

"You really should go." My temper rises, and I consider dousing her with my drink.

"I can't." She laughs again. "You know that if you really think. I can't go and neither can you. We're trapped here." She grins with pleasure at my distress. "Don't be a bore. Gabriel sent me. He's been looking for you. He says you're very naughty, hiding from him in dreams and stories. You can't escape him." Her voice has lowered considerably. It's *no longer light and flirtatious and feminine. Even as I watch her shoulders are hunching over. Her elegant posture is gone in a snap. Her head swings from side to side as she patrols me. She is changing into something dark and dangerous.*

*I look beyond her, across the campus green, and I see him. His dark wings flare and he seems to drink the moonlight that filters down on him, leaving darkness in his wake. Dread fills me. I start to leave, but my feet are anchored to the ground. It's as if they've grown roots. I tug and pull and twist, but I am unable to even lift a foot. Isabel sees my predicament and laughs. Her circles around me become closer, and I can smell something fetid about her.*

*"Don't fight him," she says. "You know you shouldn't resist. He can give you things you desire, things you didn't even know you desired." She traces fingers across my cheek. Her hand is cold, icy. "Isn't it lovely? We're the special ones, the golden girls and boys. We glitter, and your friend Zelda leads the pack. This is the world of her husband. You admired her, and him. You were seduced by his writing, her self-confidence and joie de vivre. Pretense, money, privilege, all so very different from the place your body resides, in that bed, in the bedroom, in the house in that backward little town of Mission, Alabama."*

*I'm not completely certain where I am. Or even if I'm asleep or awake. Is this merely a nightmare, a terrible dream of helplessness and fear? Or is this the real world that Gabriel offers? That idea is terrifying, and yet I can't move or run or stop what is about to happen. At any minute, Isabel will leap at me and take my life. She is becoming more craven, more animalistic as she narrows her circle, and I cannot move away.*

*When Isabel stops in front of me and faces me, her eyes are glazed by death. Clumps of hair begin to slip from her skull and dust the ground at her feet. When she grins, it is a death rictus. She reeks of death.*

*"Oh, dear, Amory, you're just a character created by your friend's*

*husband. Raissa is gone, replaced by a shallow man." She laughs and I gag at the smell of her breath.*

*"Gabriel can take you anywhere he chooses in your dreams. Even into a book. Even into a book where he's re-written the characters and the storyline. Here, in this place, Amory Blaine is merely fodder for Gabriel's dark fantasies."*

*I know where I am now. Somewhere in the pages of a fictional world of F. Scott Fitzgerald's* This Side of Paradise. *I'm a character I can't know or control in a world that bears no resemblance to the book or reality. Panic sets in and the woman laughs at me.*

*"What do you want?" My voice rises. "Tell me what you want, damn you!"*

*"Oh, I am already damned." She walks around me and leans to whisper in my ear. "I have everything I want, Raissa. I have you. And soon I'll have Elizabeth. But the greatest treasure of all will be little Callie."*

*"Have us? How? The minute I wake up, I'm free of you."*

*"Are you? Are you sure about that? What if you never awaken? What then?" She is whispering at my ear, and her breathe harbors the odor of rotted meat. She is a dead thing masquerading as a character in a story. Gabriel controls this. All of it.*

*"You have no power over me. None." I brazen it out, hoping that someone will come home and wake me up, or that Callie will cry. I have to escape, but as long as I'm asleep, I am Gabriel's victim.*

*"It doesn't matter. None of it matters." The creature that had once been Isabel, a polished character in a modern novel, drops to the ground. She crawls on all fours across the moonlit green. Her body moves in ways that give me anguish, her back arching in an imitation of a scorpion's tail. Any minute her spine will snap. Her head spins around backwards and watches me as she lopes away across the grass.*

*For a moment I am alone in the darkness, and I am glad. The gentle breeze flaps my dress hem against my calves. I am no longer a man, no longer Amory Blain, Fitzgerald's fictional character. I am Raissa James, wearing my proper dress. The man walking toward me is Gabriel, someone I had once supposed to be an angel. He has a terrible beauty in the magnificence of his physique and the handsomeness of his face. I realize now that Michael told the truth. This is no angel. I don't know what he is, but he is dark and dangerous and capable of blending the real world with the fantastic in dreams. He is fully capable of ensnaring me in his nocturnal machinations and I have no power to hold him at bay. I don't know who or what he is, but he is very dangerous.*

*"It's easier to give in," he says. "Trust me. You will eventually. They all do. Once I'm in your dreams there's no escape from me."*

*"I wouldn't be so sure." Madam will be able to help me. I know she will. I just have to get out of Mission—with my friends—and get to her for help.*

*Gabriel's wings flap lazily behind him. His eyes have taken on a strange yellow cast. "We'll see about that, Raissa. I have all the time in the world. And if you think leaving Mission will make a difference, you're wrong. Should you actually escape, you merely take me with you. Between you and Elizabeth, I have a free ride, until Callie is old enough to accept me. It won't be long, and I'll be waiting. Always, waiting and watching."*

The back door slammed and I sat up in bed, sweat pouring off me. Callie was wide awake, watching me. She put a hand on my chest, and the panic stilled. The terror was still there, but my heartbeat slowed to the point that I didn't feel like my chest would explode.

"Raissa?" Reginald called.

"In the bedroom," I composed myself as best I could.

He came into the room and sat on the edge of the bed. "Are you okay?"

"No. I'm not."

"It's Gabriel, isn't it?" he asked.

I nodded. I wanted to cry but it would do no good. "I don't know what he is or what he wants. He says he wants Callie, but what would he want with an infant? What is he?"

Reginald grasped my hand, worried at my obvious distress. "You're going to be okay. We'll figure this out. He told you he was an angel?"

I shook my head. "He has wings, but they're dark. Elizabeth told me he was an angel, but he's not."

"I've given this some thought, and while I was in Victoria, I stopped by one of the churches. I'm glad we have a few minutes alone so I can tell you."

"You don't trust Michael?"

Reginald shook his head. "I don't trust anyone here. Not even Elizabeth. Something evil resides here in Mission, and until we know where and who all is involved, we can trust no one but ourselves."

"Tell me what you learned in Victoria." I had recovered my balance, for the moment.

"I talked to a priest." He squeezed my hand. "The Catholics are better versed in demons and exorcisms. What I found there was...unexpected."

"Meaning what?" I swung my legs off the bed and stood. Callie had settled back to sleep, and the smile on her face told me that whatever Gabriel was up to, he hadn't yet infected her sleep.

"I grew up in an orphanage."

"I remember."

"Actually two different orphanages. One was Catholic, and there was an old priest there who told us stories about the different creatures God created. That's what gave me the idea to stop and talk to Father Kilroy."

"What are you talking about?" I had a terrible thought that I was caught in yet another dream, this one with Reginald.

"According to some Biblical scholars, God's first creation was the angels, immortal beings. Their beauty was equal to God's, and their every wish was met with fulfillment. It was God's pleasure to provide for his winged creations. He gave them many gifts, from the power to heal, to the gift of music, and on and on."

I'd done some time in Sunday school so I knew the Christian story of creation, but I didn't interrupt Reginald. He was headed in a specific direction and he would get there.

"According to the old priest in the Catholic orphanage, everything was fine until God created man, also in his image, but without the wings. But man was also mortal and needed more care, more attention, more nurturing, and when a man died, it grieved God. Some of the angels hated God's new creation of man. They were jealous, and they disobeyed God by tempting man with forbidden things. Each time man disobeyed God's rules, he was punished by the angels. They afflicted man with illness and greed and violence, hoping that man's behavior would disgust God and He would turn away from them."

This wasn't exactly the doctrine I'd been taught, but it was a parallel.

"Some angels were sent down to Earth to live among the mortals. God charged the angels with being examples to man, to show man the way of goodness and compassion. What God didn't realize was that his angels were as flawed by weakness as the men he'd created. The angels found the daughters of men to be fair and enchanting. These angels were tempted by the forbidden, and they slept with human women."

This hadn't been part of my religious upbringing, and I was

shocked. I had to be sure I understood what Reginald was saying. "The angels slept with mortal women?"

"Yes."

I'd never heard of angels bedding humans until Elizabeth made her claim, which I still had trouble grasping. With her, I'd assumed there was love, but the way Reginald made it sound... The idea was...terrible. It made a mockery of my understanding of the winged creatures of heaven, the golden, shining angels with their halos and beautiful choruses. "This can't be."

"I spoke with Father Kilroy in Victoria about this, and he believes it to be true. He confirmed that this doctrine exists. From the union of human women and these angels, these fallen angels, the Nephilim were born."

"Nephilim?" I'd heard the word but couldn't place it.

"The offspring of fallen angels mating with a human female. In ancient times, the Nephilim were thought to be giants, but whatever they are, they are an abomination." Reginald's words were soft, almost sad.

"Lucifer is the only fallen angel I've heard of." And Lucifer ruled Hell and the fiery pit.

"Lucifer was not the only angel who disgraced himself, but Lucifer was the Morning Star. God's favorite angel and his greatest betrayal. Lucifer's beauty was greater than any other angel."

"You learned all of this in a Catholic church?" I was a little shocked at the things I'd never been exposed to.

"Not the church. From the old priest. Who may have been crazy. But he convinced me there were things beyond what was taught, things that happened before the world of man dominated the earth. There was a time when good and evil were not such clear choices. That priest told me of things that no church wants to acknowledge. This is one reason I was drawn to Madam and her séances. I have always known there's a world counter to ours, an existence where shades and spirits linger, and many of them are lost there because they aren't interested in the light."

Reginald claimed that he had no "gifts" like second sight or the ability to see the dead. But he had other gifts I was just discovering. "That's why you're helping me, isn't it? To protect me."

"And to learn, Raissa. You have the true gift. But I can learn and become more sensitive. And I can help."

He had no idea how much he helped as it was. "And these Nephilim, do they have the nature of angels or humans?"

"Neither." Sorrow had crept into his expression. "They are wicked beyond redemption, and their goal is to corrupt the men of Earth."

"Wicked angels? Isn't that an oxymoron?" Reginald was so serious I tried to put a bit of lightness into the conversation.

"They're not angels, Raissa. Once they've fallen, they're demons."

# CHAPTER 23

Reginald's pronouncement was like a kick in my gut. I couldn't breathe or even think. How many times had Michael insisted that Gabriel was not an angel? Each time it was mentioned, Michael had contradicted the statement. Not an angel. That was all he'd said, but I understood now. Gabriel was not an angel but a demon. At last I found my voice. "You think Gabriel is a Nephilim?"

"No, I think he's a dark angel. A fallen angel."

"Do fallen angels still have the powers that were given the heavenly angels?" The hierarchy felt muddled and unclear. "Can he heal?"

"Angels heal and bring joy. Fallen angels tempt and bring illness and suffering. That's how Father Kilroy explained it to me."

"And there are fallen angels on earth, other than Gabriel?"

"Yes. In her work in New Orleans, Madam has dealt with at least one. They're treacherous and very dangerous. They can manipulate time and space."

"And dreams," I said, remembering the topiary and fictional Isabel galloping about on all fours.

"Madam can help us. I know she can, but we have to get to New Orleans. It's imperative we take that baby to Madam before it's too late."

"Too late?"

Reginald looked away to hide the despair in his eyes.

"You think Callie is Gabriel's child, born of a mortal woman, which would make her..." I couldn't say it. I looked down at her, her Kewpie doll mouth, the fringe of dark hair, and the smile that stole my heart.

"I don't know what she is, Raissa. According to the old priest, God and man waged a war to rid the planet of the fallen angels and their offspring. Supposedly none were left. Those that were found were cast into the pits of Hell." He hesitated. "I hadn't put this together with fallen angels. When I first met Madam, years ago, she battled with a fallen angel. It had attached itself to a woman in New Orleans. She became pregnant. She began to hallucinate. She came to Madam for help." He looked away from me.

I reached up to turn his face to me, but he refused to look at me. "What happened to her? To the child?"

"The woman was murdered before she could deliver the baby."

"Murdered by whom?"

He shook his head. "Madam believed the Catholic Church sent an assassin to destroy a great evil. I had just met Madam and I wasn't in her confidence. There were rumors, only rumors."

"And you believe this?" I knew there were spirits, a component of a living human that transcended the flesh. But a world of angels, fallen or otherwise, half-angel children, and murdering priests was not something I could easily grasp.

"I don't believe anything. I'm only telling you what the priest in Victoria made me remember. What Madam confronted and fought. What happened. The priest also said something else interesting."

"And that was?"

"That the town of Mission had no place in the county or the state, that it was a village that belonged nowhere."

"What did he mean?"

"I'm not a hundred percent certain, but the implication was that there was something unholy about Mission. Like a place that decent people avoided."

"There are decent people here," I protested. "Elizabeth, Hattie, the little girl Hildy."

Reginald didn't respond. After a moment he spoke. "I was taught that the Nephilim are superior in unusual abilities and wickedness. Their birth is a sin against the orders of God."

"Callie isn't wicked." I could see where this was going.

"Perhaps not yet."

It was the most chilling thing I'd ever heard Reginald say.

"You think the baby will grow to be wicked?"

"I think there's a murderer loose in Mission. I believe a good man may hang for a crime he didn't commit. For the life of me, I can't see any real benefit to McEachern's death. It's possible there is wickedness here merely for the sake of evil."

I drew back from him. "I won't listen to this."

"I won't continue. But I'm concerned what powers that baby may have. Or how they will manifest themselves."

Callie stretched and yawned. She pounded her little fists in the air and made the purring sound of contentment. When she turned her head to look at Reginald, he stood up. "We shouldn't be talking in front of her."

I nodded agreement. "Michael was able to get his horse?"

"He should be here soon," Reginald said. "Setting McEachern free is a crazy idea, Raissa. If it doesn't work, we could all be in grave trouble."

"I know." I did. "But we're already in a lot of trouble with few ways to escape." I was saved from further conversation when I heard a vehicle coming and ran to the window. "It's Elizabeth." I got up and hurried outside to see what the doctor had to say about her wounds.

Dr. Wainwright helped her out of the car. She was able to stand and walk, but it was obvious she was very weak.

"She lost a lot of blood," he said, directing his comment to Reginald. It was clear he wanted nothing else to do with Elizabeth or me.

"Can she travel?" I asked.

"It would be best if she didn't, under normal circumstances. Now, though, I think leaving would be your best bet. You're in danger here. All of you."

"Leave me," Elizabeth said. "I won't leave Slater McEachern to hang for a crime he didn't commit."

"She's been saying that, repeating it like a crazy woman," the doctor said with annoyance. "She can't know his innocence or guilt, and she'd better act to save her own hide and her baby. She's a fool if she doesn't think they'll hang a woman and do God knows what with that child. Everyone in town is terrified of it."

It, not her. She wasn't even a child to them. Yet they had

no clue how much reason they had to be afraid of Callie, if she was what Reginald thought she might be.

"Take Callie," Elizabeth said to me. "Take her and go. Hurry." She almost lost her balance but Reginald righted her.

"Take it easy," he said, supporting her up the steps. At the door he turned back. "Thanks, Doctor, but again, I ask how you propose that we make a getaway. We tried to leave and they blockaded the road. If they stop us, they'll kill us. The green hoods were out."

"Damn them," the doctor said with fierceness. "They've gone too far now. They think they can do whatever they please." He took a breath. "I'll help you."

"How?" I couldn't help myself.

"I'll create a distraction. Something on the other end of town. I'll draw them there and you can escape."

"If they catch you--"

"They'll kill me too. They'll kill anyone who gets in their way."

"Why would you do this?"

The doctor looked away and paused before he spoke. "I loved Ruthie. Slater McEachern wasn't the only man who cared about her. He was just the only man who had the backbone to try to save her from Lucais and the life he'd assigned Ruth to."

"Why didn't you do something?" I was in his face. I couldn't help it. Reginald couldn't stop me because he was supporting a very weak Elizabeth. "Lucais is going to kill an innocent man and you did nothing."

"I'm doing something right now," Wainwright said, his features going stiff with anger. "I'm going to get you on the road out of town if you're smart enough to go. That's what I'm doing, young woman. And you'd be smart not to cast hot grease on someone trying to help you."

His words cooled me down, but it did nothing to alleviate my anxiety. "How can you distract them?"

"Eight o'clock tonight, be ready to get out of town." Doc didn't look very happy about his decision.

"What's going to happen at eight?" I asked.

"There's going to be an explosion. While all the watchers and Lucais's henchmen are running toward that explosion, you get out of town. You hear me? You won't have long. You better take this opportunity."

"How are you going to cause an explosion?" Reginald asked.

"I have some dynamite and I know how to use it. Trust me. There'll be a boom big enough to bring everyone in the vicinity running."

I looked at Reginald and Elizabeth. "Can we get—"

"We'll be on the road at eight sharp," Reginald said. "Thank you, doctor."

"If you don't make a getaway, you've likely doomed all of us to the hangman's noose. They won't hold back on me if they know I tried to help you."

"Come in the house," Reginald said to me, already helping Elizabeth through the door. "Now, Raissa."

Reginald was never snappy unless he had a reason to be. I followed him in the door and Doc Wainwright got in his car and drove away.

"Can we get Michael and Slater McEachern in time?" I asked.

Reginald motioned me to help Elizabeth to bed. When she was under a light sheet, we left her beside Callie and closed the door. He drew me roughly into the kitchen. "Get on that horse and ride toward that cabin. Meet Michael on the way at old

Sawyer Road. Then start walking home." He was whispering. "I'll pick you up once I'm certain Elizabeth can be left alone. Tell Michael and McEachern if they intend to get away, they must ride hard for here. We'll leave as soon as they arrive. If they aren't here by five o'clock, we have to leave them."

"But the doctor said eight—"

"You see the evil spirits, Raissa. I see the evil in men. Doc Wainwright is setting us up. At eight o'clock, when we hear the explosion, every green hood and unhappy man in this area will be on the road waiting for us. They'll kill me, McEachern, and Michael and what they do to you, Elizabeth, and that baby I don't want to think about."

"Are you sure?" I didn't want to believe this. I needed to believe that someone was helping us, someone cared that justice was done.

"The doctor never looked me in the eye. He's not a murderer, but he's a coward and he's terrified of Lucais. He didn't leave any instructions for Elizabeth's care. He was only specific about the time we should make our escape. I'll bet the old bastard does have some dynamite. They'll probably blow up the road under the car."

"I'll be back as quickly as I can," I said, heading to the barn to saddle up Mariah for one last ride.

"I'd ride her myself, but you're the better equestrian." He tried for a smile but failed. Worry etched a furrow in his forehead. "We'll get out of here, Raissa, and when we get to Victoria and can contact your uncle, he'll be able to help protect us. I've learned one thing in the last few months and that's Brett Airlie has a mighty long reach where his niece is concerned."

The mention of Uncle Brett almost made me cry. He hadn't wanted me to make this trip. He'd been subtly opposed, without really voicing his opposition. I had known he was worried but I pretended not to notice. He knew that Sand Mountain was a dangerous, isolated place where the regular rule of law didn't prevail. Bad men took power and wielded it with brute force. Belief systems sprang up and took root. All of that my uncle knew. But he didn't know that a dark angel walked among the people of Mission, Alabama. And he didn't know—nor did I—what this entity wanted from Elizabeth Maslow and her daughter Callie or to what lengths he would go to get it.

# CHAPTER 24

Mariah was as fresh as if she hadn't already been ridden today, and she willingly galloped down the road. Perhaps she understood that our lives depended on her speed and good sense. When I came to the intersection of the roads where Michael would have to pass, I edged into the thick woods and waited, listening for pounding hooves. Michael's ride was far longer than mine, and I was relieved I'd beaten him to the crossroads. I had to stop Michael from going back to Elizabeth's to get Mariah. We no longer had the luxury of time. If we were to rescue Slater McEachern, we had to move with great speed. I felt the saddlebag again, making sure the mallet and tongs were still there. And the ax.

I sat on the cool ground, glad for a respite from the saddle and the sun. Mariah waited patiently. When I saw Uncle Brett again, I would ask him to buy her for me if Elizabeth agreed to give her up. In a city like Mobile, Elizabeth would have no need of a horse, and I shared a bond with the buckskin mare.

My nerves settled a bit as I searched my memories for

horseback rides and other pleasantness to pass the time. I was brought up short by the smell of something dead and decaying. The odor came from nowhere, but suddenly it was everywhere. A large shadow flitted over the dirt road in front of me. The watchers were with me. A buzzard settled on a tree limb across the road.

My heart clutched with fear, and Mariah, too, snorted and pulled back, away from me and the bird. The bird looked right at me and made a long, low hissing sound. The raspiness of its voice reminded me of Isabel in my dream, when she'd begun to change into something far removed from human. How close was Gabriel? Or whoever he was. He might be many things, but Michael was right. He was not an angel. At least not in the sense that I'd come to believe in the heavenly host.

"You can't win, Raissa."

I whipped around to find him standing not six inches from me. Mariah rolled her eyes and snorted. I gripped the end of the reins firmly so she couldn't get away. She wasn't leaving unless I was on her back.

"I know what you are."

"Do you?" he asked. "Are you sure?"

"You're nothing from heaven."

"Did I ever make that claim?" He was cold, but something very hot burned in his eyes.

"You led Elizabeth to believe you were something good, something holy."

"People always see what they wish to see, Raissa. You should know this, considering the work you do." He smiled, but it was chilling rather than warm. "You saw goodness in me too."

"And now I know better." I glanced down the road in the direction Michael would be coming.

"And yet you cling to the idea that someone will come to assist you."

He could read my thoughts, and that was more frightening than anything he'd said. I couldn't allow myself to think about Michael or our plan. "Why have you targeted Elizabeth?"

"She has a gift, and she was easy. All alone, knowing in her heart her brother was dead. Knowing there was no one else for her. You know how that feels, you've been there." He smiled, and a chill ran down my spine. "Since Alex."

I pushed past the instant anger. "Yes, being left behind is lonely...and painful. To lose the one you love is hard." Though I tried not to think about him, Alex was always in my heart. I missed him intensely. Suddenly he stood before me with his hand on Mariah's hip. He wore a white shirt with a rounded collar, an older style that was preferred by the law school where he was sometimes invited to lecture. His gray flannel pants were immaculate, his hair burnished in the sunlight that angled through the trees. I wanted to rush into his arms, to cry against his chest and beg him never to leave me again. But I didn't move. I knew this was a trick even as my heart seemed to beat with a newfound urgency.

"I miss you, Raissa." He smiled, and I ached with the pain of loss. How precious that smile was to me.

"I miss you too." I eased back from his hand. Alex was dead. He couldn't be here with me no matter how I longed for him. His time had come and gone. It was wrong for me to want to hold him in a half-life.

"Come for a walk in the woods with me."

I couldn't, and I knew it. Gabriel was manipulating me. Still, I couldn't stop the overwhelming desire to rush to Alex. He was as warm and solid as he had been in life. I pressed my face into his chest, surrounded by his distinctive smell of leather and books and coffee. "I love you." I wanted to beg him not to leave me, as I should have when he went off to war. But I didn't then and I didn't now. I knew he couldn't stay. Wasn't really there. This was the hellish magic of Gabriel. He took my dream and made it flesh—only to take it from me again.

In the blink of an eye, I was standing with my arms around empty air. I would not cry. I would not let Gabriel's tricks weaken me.

"What if I could return Alex to you?"

"From the grave?" I scoffed. "You might be able to manipulate my dreams, but you can't play necromancer."

"Can't I?"

"What are you?" I asked him.

"I am one of God's chosen." He grinned at my look of disbelief. "No, it's true."

"You're an angel." I waited to close the trap. "One that God has turned away."

"The things you might hear in a place called Mission. I thought you were smarter than to get embroiled in gossip." He was toying with me and enjoying it.

"Why are you here?"

"Hasn't anyone ever told you not to converse with demons?"

He scared me, but I couldn't let him see. "What if they have? It hardly seems I can stop you from talking, so you might as well answer my questions." I tried to think what Madam had told me would protect me from evil. She had warned me that there were things other than ghosts to be wary of. I'd encountered a female entity that I believed to be a succubus and also a strong, dark spirit that meant to have new life in the body of a descendant. Gabriel, though, was far stronger and more clever than anything I'd experienced.

"There's nothing you have that can protect you." Gabriel was once again reading my mind.

"Did Elizabeth bring you here?"

He considered. "I found Mission to be a place where I was welcomed, before she arrived. Once Elizabeth got here," his smile was truly terrifying, "Mission became irresistible."

"Is Callie your daughter?"

"What does it matter to you?"

I kept my thoughts away from Nephilim. "She's a remarkable child. She deserves two parents."

Gabriel was suddenly only inches from my face. "What do you know about her?"

"Elizabeth loves her. And the child has the ability to offer comfort by her mere touch." I wasn't going to lie—he'd know I was lying anyway. I focused on remembering the way Callie's little hand had touched my face and calmed me. If I was going to combat Gabriel, I had to be able to control my own thoughts and emotions. I had to learn to put up a wall that he couldn't penetrate. I'd never been required to think in this way, but knew intuitively that he fed off my thoughts and emotions. If he read my fears, I was in terrible danger. I would be completely vulnerable to him.

I put my hand on Mariah's neck. She no longer pulled away from him, but her eyes had taken on a distant look. She'd disengaged from this moment, had gone somewhere else. I understood this was the defense I needed too.

The place I chose was Uncle Brett's shipyard on the Bay of Mobile. I surrounded myself with the sound of men working, the salty smell of the air, the brownish waters of the bay that led to the aquamarine beauty of the Gulf. Several barrier islands—sugar sand beaches windswept by the stiff Gulf breeze —separated the bay from the gulf waters. Dauphin, Ship, Petit

Bois, Horn, the barrier islands had become one of my very favorite places on the planet. Uncle Brett had taken some friends and family out for several adventures. The wildness of the islands gave me such intense joy.

"Ah, you've figured a way to elude me. Or so you think?"

I didn't respond. I clung to one particular day on the beach. Hunting for shells. The tiny sand crabs. The call of the sea birds. I inhaled the beauty and held it inside me.

"Your plan to escape won't work. I'll never let Elizabeth take Callie. Wherever she goes, I'll follow."

I licked my lips and tasted the salt whipped off the tumbling waves that hissed along the beach. The sun on my face seemed to soak into the bone.

"Alex should be there with you," Gabriel said.

His attempt almost derailed me, but I pushed past that and saw Isabelle waving at me from the distance. She was wading barefoot in the foaming tide. I ran toward her. She and Uncle Brett were getting married. I wanted to help with the plans. She made my uncle happy, and I adored her.

The sound of a horse trotting came to me and I pushed past Gabriel so that I could see the road more easily. Michael rounded the curve on his fine horse.

"Michael!" I called out to him. "Hold!"

When I looked back toward Mariah, Gabriel was gone. One buzzard remained in the tree across the road. He'd report back to Gabriel, I was sure. Nothing went unnoticed. I led Mariah out of the woods and walked up to Michael's knee and handed him the reins. He'd have to pony Mariah to the cabin to free Slater.

I motioned Michael to lean down closer to me so I could whisper. "The ax, a bolt cutter, and some other provisions are in the saddlebag. Free McEachern and then you both ride through the woods toward Elizabeth's."

"How are you going to get back there?" he asked.

"I'll start walking back. Reginald will pick me up when he's sure Elizabeth is comfortable enough. We have to leave town as soon as possible. Elizabeth is there. She's stable, and Reginald says we must leave. He believes the doctor betrayed us."

"I don't like you walking alone on the road," he said.

I waved him away, "I'll be fine. If I hear anyone coming down the road, I'll duck into the woods. I promise." I could tell by his expression that he was seriously debating whether he could leave me alone. He had to. Otherwise the plan Reginald laid out would never work.

"Go! Get McEachern. Ride back to Elizabeth's down that woods trail on the map. We'll be packed and ready to go." I slapped his horse on the rump and Mariah too. They took off at a gentle lope. Michael looked back at me, but he kept going, the hooves of the horses digging deep into the road.

When they disappeared from view, I felt terribly alone and vulnerable. Mariah had been a lot of comfort. I'd learned something from her. I looked across the road to see the black turkey buzzard watching me. He clacked and hissed, as if cursing me. I loved animals and was never deliberately unkind, but I picked up a clump of clay in the road and hurled it at the bird with all my strength. It hit the tree limb but not the bird. He looked at me with great insolence, but then he spread his wings and lifted in to the air, at first clumsy and awkward, but finally gaining an updraft. He circled and then left.

# CHAPTER 25

L uckily, I'd worn the boots I'd found at Elizabeth's. I'd chosen them to protect my legs from the pinch of the saddle, but now they served an equally important purpose as I cut through the woods. I'd always enjoyed the outdoors, and I was well aware of the danger of snakes and ticks. I wasn't afraid of them, but avoidance and good boots were the best plan. My hope was that if I stayed deep in the woods—but still close enough to hear traffic on the road—the watchers wouldn't notice me. Perhaps they tracked me by scent or heat or movement. I couldn't say. They were not ordinary buzzards, that much I knew. They were preternatural creatures. I could only try to avoid their relentless spying by hiding in the dense woods.

The shelter of the trees held back the very worst of the sun, but I was in a hurry, which increased the oppression of the heat and humidity. My movement and sweat also drew yellow flies and other bloodsucking insects. A swarm of the flies surrounded my head, and I broke off a thick huckleberry limb to swat them away. Despite them, I kept moving as fast as I could.

I tried to imagine how far down the road Michael had gone. Another two miles to the turn off to the cabin where Slater McEachern was chained to the wall with a slave collar. Michael was a fit man, but would he have the strength to chop or cut the links of the chain that held McEachern? If not, would Michael have sense enough to abandon a lost cause and meet us for our escape? Would Elizabeth go without McEachern? Could I so readily abandon Michael? His fate was now sealed along with ours.

All of these thoughts swirled, but there was another more terrifying consideration that I tried to avoid. It was like a sore tooth, though, and I couldn't long resist worrying it.

What was Callie? Was she literally the child of a fallen angel and a human woman? Had Gabriel tricked Elizabeth into the ultimate betrayal? Was Callie's father a demon, as Reginald believed?

My religious instruction hadn't prepared me for any of these considerations. In my Sunday School classes, we'd learned that angels were good. I'd been taught that angels were our guardians. Archangels—those most powerful winged agents of heaven, were sent to us for protection. My memory on the order of angels was rusty, but I remember the seraphim, who worshipped God on the throne, and the cherubim, who guarded Eden after man had been banished. But there were nine orders in all. Of course, there was one fallen angel known as Lucifer, the morning star, the brightest of all the angels who defied and disobeyed God and was cast down into the fiery pit.

The Nephilim, by definition, would be the blending of mortal and immortal, a thing considered impossible in the Christian faith except in that one instance of the Christ child.

And if Callie was a Nephilim, was she also immortal? Was she evil by nature? I stopped my thoughts there, because it was impossible to consider how to kill a tiny baby that might be immortal. Elizabeth would never allow anything to happen to Callie. I would fight to protect that child, whatever she might have the potential to be. But what if she had been born evil?

A soft moan escaped my throat as I pushed through some brambles. I was almost ready to give it up and go to the road. Even if I only walked there for fifteen minutes it would give me a break from trudging through briars, scrub trees, and the fallen limbs that trapped my feet and made me stumble. I'd dropped my swat limb and now my hands were bloody from killing the beastly flies and gnats that found any piece of skin not covered.

When I paused to wipe the sweat from my face, I heard the sound of a car. It might be Reginald coming to retrieve me and my heart lifted. I eased closer to the road and crouched behind a clump of gall berries. I had a pretty good view of the road in the direction Reginald should arrive from.

The vehicle rounded the curve and I drew back. It wasn't Reginald. It was Lucais and several of his helpers. They all carried guns, and they were drinking and laughing as they drove toward town. One of them was trying to make a lasso out of a rope that had been tied into a hangman's noose. It was clear to me they were going to town for more help, and then they would return for Slater McEachern. It would seem Lucais had run out of patience. He meant to hang Slater and soon.

I considered running in front of the car, anything to slow them down and give Michael a chance to free McEachern and ride away. I wanted to do that, but I knew they'd kill me on the road. After they'd finished with whatever else they wanted to do to me. I might delay them, but I wouldn't stop them.

My body trembled and I accepted that I was afraid of Lucais and his men. Afraid of their power not to kill me, but to hurt me. They were men who would enjoy my fear and pain if they ever got the chance to capture me. Though Lucais could control them, he wouldn't. Because he didn't want to.

The car passed and my heart slowed enough that I could stumble out into the road and run. I had to get back to Reginald and Elizabeth before those men returned down this road. I couldn't help Michael or Slater. I didn't know if I could help Elizabeth and Callie, if anyone could. But Reginald and I had to leave this place. There was something far, far darker at work here than just a power-mad man who would stop at nothing to control everything around him. There was primordial darkness. Evil.

I hit a sandy place in the road and felt as if I were wallowing forward but barely moving. I was tired. Close to exhaustion. Slogging through the woods had drained me and fear had punched adrenaline through my muscles. Now that it was gone, I felt too tired to put one foot in front of the other, yet I continued as fast as I could. I had to get back to Reginald.

To avoid the sand, I stepped back in the woods. The shade revitalized me, giving me another spurt of energy to push harder. Surely Reginald would appear to pick me up at any moment.

A dark shadow sped across the yellow road. Wings flapped, but when I looked up at the slice of pale blue visible between the towering trees on either side of the road, I didn't see anything. Whatever this was, it was bigger than the other buzzards. This was the king buzzard.

When I looked back at the road, Gabriel was there, his

wings extended before he drew them in and wrapped them around himself.

"Tired?" he asked.

"Leave me alone." I kept walking away from him.

"I could help you."

"At what cost? And if you could, why haven't you offered before?" I was afraid of him, but I couldn't let it show. I couldn't let him into my thoughts, my emotions. He was exceptionally treacherous. I forced my thoughts away from angels and demons and babies. I focused on the hymns I'd grown up singing in Sunday school. I went through all the stanzas of "Blessed Redeemer" that I could remember.

The minute I stopped the song, Gabriel was right beside me again. "You can't shut me out, Raissa. Once I've penetrated your dreams, I can slip inside you any time I want."

He terrified me, but I fought it. Weakness was what he sought. "What do you want?" I wouldn't call him Gabriel. He was not an archangel.

"The same thing all humans want."

"And that is?"

"I want a family, children. Progeny." His wings fluttered behind him. "I want to inherit what was rightfully mine."

"Through lies and deception."

He laughed. "Humans use lies and deception every moment of every day. Why should I be different? You have taught me well."

I felt him prying at the cracks in my thoughts, seeking entrance again. Each time it seemed to get easier for him. I had to get away. "Leave me alone."

He didn't bother with a response. He just kept pace beside me.

"Don't think you and Reginald can escape with Elizabeth and Callie. I won't let you go. Reginald can leave. No one else."

I didn't want to ask but I did anyway. "Why Reginald?"

"He's a man with many talents, but none like you and Elizabeth have."

"What did you do with Elizabeth's brother?" I knew somehow that Ramone had run afoul of this entity. That had been the gambit that lured Elizabeth to this isolated, backward community where she was easy pickings. A lonely woman searching for her missing brother; a demon posing as a sympathetic lover. In hindsight it was clear how Gabriel had played my friend.

"Ramone." He said the word in the Romany language. "Ramone is my gift to Elizabeth. I could have killed him, yet I didn't. Ramone desires nothing as much as building a fortune. He's going to be mine eventually."

"Wanting to do well isn't necessarily greedy." I didn't know Ramone, but I'd never believe anything this demon had to say. He perverted the truth with every utterance. "Where is he?"

"What will you give me if I tell you?"

Never bargain with an entity. Those were urgent words repeated more than once by Madam Petalungro. Never bargain with an entity for any reason. *The dead lie, and their lies will seal the fate of your soul.* I heard the words as clearly as if Madam stood before me.

"I'm going to figure out a way to destroy you." I would suffer a terrible fate no matter what I said if Gabriel had his way.

"You are an ambitious young woman. First the vote, then destruction of an immortal. Are you brave or delusional?"

I didn't care that he mocked me. At least he'd stopped probing into my thoughts. And I could detect a hint of anger in his words. "How fitting that your vanguard is a wake of buzzards feasting on the rotted soul of this town. How delicious carrion must be to you. You walked away from a banquet and hunkered down to sup on a corpse."

"Had we inherited what was truly ours—" He broke off, realizing that I'd successfully goaded him into a response. Thus, he revealed a weakness. He was vain and aggrieved. He'd had the privileges of first creation, and yet he smarted at the creation of man. I would hold this close until the time was right when I could use it as a weapon.

"I believe when you were cast down you got what you deserved."

"You dare to judge me?"

His words were spoken in a soft tone, but there was fire and pain beneath them.

The ground before me dissolved and I found myself standing in the center aisle of a small chapel, flanked on either side by two coffins. I looked down at my feet in the flat black church shoes bought especially for a funeral. My parents, or what had been my parents, were inside the coffins.

A burnished red light illuminated the chapel, and between the coffins was an altar where red candles burned. When I looked around, I realized the windows were stained glass, but unlike any I'd ever seen. These windows depicted a horned creature with a forked tail. He vanquished men with halos. Blood flowed freely in each scene of victory for the horned one.

Around me I felt the presence of the dead. The unhappy dead. They crowded close, their hunger and desperation apparent. I wanted to run, but again, my feet felt rooted to the red carpet of this hellish sanctuary.

"Raissa."

"Raissa."

"Raissa." My name passed among them in gravelly whispers.

I remembered another bit of Madam's wisdom, now too late to apply. Never tell a entity your real name. In all of the stories dealing with demons I'd read, finding out the demon's name was an imperative, but he already knew mine. And Elizabeth's. And Callie's and Reginald's and Michael's. Whatever Gabriel was, that was not his real name.

"Raissa." The voice came from the front of the chapel, and it was no demon whisper fed with sulfur. It was a voice I longed to hear every day of my life. "Raissa, let me out! Please. Let me out."

My mother called to me. Suddenly freed, I stepped closer to the coffin on the left. The polished mahogany gleamed in the red light from the window and candles. A knock came from inside the coffin, and then a voice. Her voice.

"Raissa, I'm so alone. We miss you, your father and I. Open the lid. The key is by the vase of flowers on the altar."

I walked slowly to the altar. A vase of mums centered a beautifully embroidered cloth. Beside the vase was the coffin key, a z-shaped mechanism that locked the lids on tight. I picked it up.

"Hurry, Raissa," my mother begged. "Please let me out."

I moved slowly toward the coffin. My heartbeat thudded in my ears. I didn't want to open the coffin. I didn't want to know what was inside. What if it wasn't my mother? What if it was?

"Remember the crayons your father bought for you?"

The memory was one of my favorites. I was sitting at the kitchen table coloring while my mother cooked, waiting for my father to come home. The crayons had been my prized possession.

"Raissa, it's dark here. Let me out."

I rubbed the key in my left hand. I could open the lid. My mother would be with me. Then we could free my father. My family would be complete. But no matter the perfection of the scene I saw, I resisted. A whisper of defiance held me back. What was really in those coffins? My mother would never ask this of me. But I couldn't refuse her. She sounded so alone and afraid. She'd save me. Of course, she would.

"The dead lie!" Madam's voice came to me like a roar of wind.

"Raissa, remember the night you had such a high fever? Remember how I sat in a chair by your bed with cold compresses? We got ice from the ice house and filled a tub with water and put you in it. The doctor said we saved your life."

The fever's rage touched my skin again as heat coursed over me. More than anything I wanted my mother's touch, the comfort of her hand on my forehead, the sweet whisper of her breath as she leaned down to kiss me. "Mama." I moved to the foot of the casket and unscrewed the opening to insert the key.

I heard her shifting and banging on the casket now, eager to get out. Impatient that I didn't move faster.

"Raissa!" There was command in her voice now. "Let me out."

I inserted the key in the hole and turned it once.

"Yes, that's my good girl."

"Never trust the dead, Raissa. Not the dark entities." Madam fought against the pull of my mother's demand. "Don't let her out. It isn't who you think it is."

"Get out of my head!" I couldn't concentrate on turning the key as long as Madam yammered in my thoughts.

"Don't do it, Raissa."

I banged my head on the top of the casket. Madam was confusing me. She wasn't even here and yet she intruded. My mother was a prisoner and I could save her. I gave the key another twist.

The smell of Sulphur and decay came from the casket.

"I want out!"

The key slipped from my hand and fell to the floor with a clatter. I backed away.

"Let me out or you'll be sorry."

I turned from the altar and ran. I ran out of the sanctuary, out of the chapel, out into the air.

The sound of a car horn nearly split my eardrum. I recoiled and lost my balance, falling and rolling in the hot sand of the road.

"Jesus, Raissa!" Reginald hopped out of the car and ran to me. He pulled me into his arms and held me. I shivered in the brutal heat.

"I almost hit you!" he said. "You came out of the woods like Satan was on your tail."

I looked around me. Dust and sand from the yellow road clung to my sweating body. The stench of panic and fear was all over me. "My mother. She's in a casket and needs me to let her out." I didn't cry, but I wanted to. "Only I don't believe it was my mother. It was something else. Something dead and evil."

"Get in the car." He helped me up and almost carried me to the passenger side. When I was seated, he closed the door and got behind the wheel. It was a tight turnaround, but he managed it. He sped down the road at a dangerous pace, but I didn't care. The wind cooled my flushed and stinking body. The sun burned away the images of the horrific stained-glass windows, the twin coffins, just as they'd been set up for my real parents.

"It wasn't my mother." I looked at him. "Was it?"

"You know it wasn't. Your mother isn't locked in a casket. Nor your father. They may visit you, because they're watching over you. But they are free to come and go as they please, Raissa."

"It was Gabriel, or whoever he is. He put that in my brain."

"I believe you're right. He's very powerful and very dangerous. Did he say what he wanted?"

I bit my bottom lip. The pain kept the tears at bay. "He did."

"What? What does he want from you and Elizabeth?"

"He wants Callie. And he means to get her."

# CHAPTER 26

The drive back to Elizabeth's, with the wind blowing in my face and cooling my neck, helped me find my balance again. Somehow, I would have to figure out how to put up a barricade to prevent Gabriel from entering my mind, from manipulating my memories and visions. Whenever I thought of my mother inside the coffin, begging to get out, I felt as if I'd betrayed her. Betrayed and abandoned.

Gabriel had been able to use the people I loved most against me. I couldn't let it happen again, because each time my resolve to fight him grew weaker.

When we drew up to Elizabeth's yard, a quiver of something unpleasant pulsed through me, gone before I could truly feel it or attempt to understand it. I'd learned that sensation was something I needed to pay attention to, and I scanned the area for the watchers. Sometimes spirits presented to me in dreams or by sound or even by scent. But some came as a sensation, a knowing. Madam called it clairgnosis. She said it was information that entered the body through the crown and that it was a pure message, the highest gift. "Some sensitives who have clairgnosis believe it is the spirit world protecting them, offering warnings."

I didn't have the sensation often, but this time it had been strong. Danger was nearby, though not clearly evident. I needed to develop my skills, to hone this ability so that I could interpret the things I perceived from the other plane.

If Reginald and I could ever close this case, I planned on going to New Orleans for the month of October and studying with Madam. There was so much to learn, and right now I needed wisdom I didn't have.

"What's wrong?" Reginald asked as he stopped the car. "You look like someone walked on your grave."

"Don't say that!" My mother's plaintive scratching on the coffin hit me hard. The idea of her, buried, trying to get out, was like being flayed alive.

"Raissa, what is it?"

I drew in a deep breath and blew it out. "Something bad is going to happen."

"How do you know?" He was worried now. He didn't take my pronouncements lightly.

"I don't know *how* I know, I just know. How much longer do you think it will be before Michael and Slater get here?" We had to leave Elizabeth's house and fast.

"Not long. Let's get Elizabeth and Callie in the car. We want to be pointed south the minute they arrive."

"Yes. That's the plan." I got out of the car and strode across the yard. My legs were aching from riding the horse, a fore-warning of the pain that was to come. The front door opened and Elizabeth came out of the house. A handsome man with her same black hair and golden amber eyes assisted her, holding Callie in his arms. I stopped in my tracks. It had to be her brother Ramone.

"Raissa! Reginald! Look who's here." Elizabeth was ecstatic. "It's Ramone! He found me instead of me finding him."

Ramone leaned over to kiss Elizabeth's cheek. "I worried my sister needlessly, but it wasn't completely my fault. I'll explain everything once we're on the road away from here, but we have to hurry." He assisted Elizabeth into a cowhide rocker on the front porch.

"You have to hear what happened to Ramone," Elizabeth said. She couldn't stop looking at her brother, reaching out to pluck his shirtsleeve or touch his hand—just to be certain he was truly standing beside her. "He was held prisoner, but he escaped."

The joy in Elizabeth's face was like the sun rising over a frozen setting, warming everything into spring. Her love for Ramone was clear to see, as was his for her.

"Ramone, this is Raissa and Reginald, my new friends. They saved my life. Ramone is going to help us escape. He has an idea that could really work."

"That's a plan I want to hear," Reginald said.

"Come inside. I'll make some coffee. Or maybe the men would prefer a drink." She smiled, but I could see the sheer exhaustion in her face. She'd almost died, and here she was up and trying to play hostess.

"Sit down at the kitchen table and I'll make whatever you tell me. We just have to be ready to go when Michael and Slater get here." Gabriel had said Ramone was alive and that he would be a gift to Elizabeth. I knew that demons lied, but this time, I hoped he'd told the truth. Elizabeth had longed to reconnect with Ramone. If it turned out this was one of Gabriel's tricks, she would be devastated.

"Who is Michael?" Ramone asked.

I let Elizabeth explain about the former Pinkerton as I

made coffee for me and Elizabeth and poured a small amount of whiskey for the men. Ramone knocked his back quickly but declined a refill. "I need my wits about me."

Elizabeth held Callie on her lap while I loaded water and the full gas can into the car. Reginald's and my belongings were still at Hattie's, and that's where they would stay. There was nothing there—except some short stories I'd intended to work on—that I required. Hattie could mail those to me in Mobile.

Reginald checked over the engine and the gasoline supply. The tank was full and we should have no trouble getting to Victoria, or much farther if we didn't feel safe in the bigger town. I watched the men talk and work as I did what I could to prepare to escape.

I was rearranging the bags to tie to the rear of the car when I heard Ramone talking. "Do you really think McEachern is innocent?" he asked.

"I do," Reginald said. "More importantly, your sister is positive he's been framed. You should ask her about it."

"I didn't want to stress her. She told me she'd been injured but she wouldn't give details. Only that we would all escape together."

"I don't understand how she's up and about. She should be unconscious in bed. She came very close to dying."

"Do you know why she's so determined to save this man?" Ramone asked. "She's always been one to take in the homeless and the strays, the people society forgets, but she's never befriended a murderer before. Those people don't always repay her in kind, if you know what I mean."

"I do," Reginald said. "Offering a hand to some is seen as an opportunity to take the whole arm. Your sister has a keen ability to see things. I trust her judgement. And keep in mind that McEachern is an *accused* murderer. There have been other attacks on women in Victoria. By an ax-wielding man. It wasn't McEachern."

"Do you know who it was?" Ramone asked as he checked the tires on the car.

"We're going to find out." Reginald looked around. "How did you get here?"

I looked around too. There wasn't another car in evidence, or a horse. Ramone was lean and fit and likely walked in, but the convenience of his timing niggled at me. How had he suddenly appeared, just at the moment we meant to make our getaway?

"I hitchhiked up from Victoria. It's a long story." He glanced to be sure Elizabeth wasn't listening. "Not everyone welcomes a Gypsy salesman traveling through. I ran afoul of some men who thought it funny to keep me prisoner and make me work for them." He held out his wrists to show us scars. "When I wasn't working, they kept me tied up."

Reginald looked up at him in shock. "Like a slave?"

"Of a sort. But as I led them to believe I had no interest in my freedom, they grew lax and I was able to slip away. I caught a ride here. I'd heard that Elizabeth was looking for me. I don't trust anyone, so I got the farmer to let me out of his wagon at the edge of town going the opposite direction of this farm." He shook his head slowly. "He seemed like a normal farmer and I was tempted to beg a ride here instead of that long walk, but I just don't trust anymore."

"Smart thinking," Reginald said. He bent back to work.

"You mentioned that Elizabeth sees things...what kind of things did you mean?" Ramone asked. "Our family has always been gifted with special...talents. Some are not as—" He broke off when I slammed the car door. "Raissa, can I help you carry anything out?"

"That was the last of it. What are the gifts in the Maslow family?"

"I'm a gifted salesman. Something Elizabeth both appreciates and also disdains. In the past, I've used that skill to better myself rather than other people. I've learned a lot in the last year."

"Why didn't you ever write Elizabeth?"

"Most of the time, I couldn't. I was watched closely. But even when I could, I didn't want to bring trouble down on her. I see now that she managed to do that all by herself." His grin was wry. "Finding trouble is a true Maslow talent." His smile disappeared. "Elizabeth has a strong connection to the other side, the place of spirits." He watched me. "She tells me that you share that gift."

"Not the way she does. Elizabeth has..." How could I tell him that she'd conceived a child with a demon? I didn't finish my thought, but Ramone ignored the lapse and continued.

"Each gift is unique, special. Perhaps it's why you've been drawn here to help her."

"I don't know. I only know that if we get out of this place without further injury, we'll be very lucky. Who held you prisoner, Ramone? Elizabeth had given up on you. She thought you were dead."

"I almost was. It's been a hard journey, and not the one I expected. The important thing is that I'm free and here to help my sister and my beautiful niece. Callie is...incredible. When I hold her, it's like a deep peace touches me and all the pain and bitterness and loss of the past are more easily shouldered."

He perfectly described the effect Callie had on me. "We have to protect her at all costs."

"Protect her from who? From what?"

"There's a man who intends to take Callie."

Ramone sucked in a breath. "I had a sense that Elizabeth was in serious trouble. Thank goodness you and Reginald arrived to help her. What man is after her?"

"He's a very bad man. If he gets the child, I believe his goal is to corrupt her."

"An infant?"

"Turn her from the light to darkness." I couldn't be more specific. Ramone only needed to understand how real the threat was and how his niece had to be saved. "This is bigger than money or land or power. This is...eternal."

To my relief, he didn't laugh. "My niece won't be going anywhere with anyone other than me."

"Thank you." I didn't trust Ramone completely. He seemed sincere, and Elizabeth was aglow with the joy of seeing him. We certainly wouldn't leave him behind, and for Elizabeth's sake, I hoped he was what he said he was.

# CHAPTER 27

E ven though the day was fading, the oppressive heat had us all sweating. When we had the car ready and there was nothing left to do but wait, I went to the hand pump in the backyard and filled a bucket with water. I poured it over me, easing the sting of the yellow fly bites I'd gotten in the woods. Surely Michael and Slater would soon arrive.

Ramone went inside to check on Elizabeth and Callie. He came back to the door. "Coffee's ready," he said. "Come take a break. We can plan the escape route."

I'd been giving our escape some thoughts myself. I was worried about the horses and what would happen if we left them either free to roam or shut up in the pasture. Someone might not give them water, or if they were loose, they could run into the road on a dark night and be struck by a vehicle. I had come up with a counter-plan which would also ease the overcrowding in the car. When we'd considered our escape, we'd planned on Elizabeth, Callie, Reginald, Michael, and me. Now Ramone and Slater would be added to the mix, creating a very tight situation in the car. But I could ride Mariah and pony Michael's horse over to Hattie's. I believed Hattie would hide me, even lie to protect me. It would only be a day at the most. Once Reginald was in Victoria with access to a telephone or telegraph, he could contact Uncle Brett. I knew my uncle and his powerful friends. Aid would be on the way to me immediately, and anyone who dared to interfere would greatly regret it. The very idea of what Uncle Brett would do to Lucais and his lowbrow thugs gave me a jolt of visceral pleasure.

I went inside, calculating the best way to present my plan. Elizabeth sat at the table with a quiet and content Callie on her lap. She looked pale, with high spots of color in her cheeks. When I touched her face, she was hot. If infection set in from the gunshot, she might not live. I wondered why Doc Wainwright had even patched her up, since he meant to betray us and turn us over to Lucais. As soon as we finished this conversation, I intended to check her wound, no matter how much she protested.

Reginald pulled out a pencil and paper and began drawing the roads around Mission. Elizabeth added the log trails that timbermen had cut across the woods. The problem was that these roads were often in very poor shape and unreliable. If there was a creek to cross, the car would have to be powerful enough to drive through it. If the car became stuck, the passengers would be sitting ducks. The watchers, those ugly buzzards, would find us and before long Gabriel would be there, ready to...take what he wanted.

When a route had been selected, Reginald sat back. His brow was shiny with sweat. The kitchen was close and the day had been long and horribly humid. "I want to stay behind." I just said it.

"What?" Reginald was stunned. "That's absurd."

"No. I want to take the horses to Hattie's. I'll hide there until you can call Uncle Brett. He'll send real law officers here. I'll be fine until they get here."

"That isn't going to happen." Reginald's jaw set. He was not a man who thought that it was God's plan that women obey him. He never tried to impose his will over mine—except when he feared for my safety.

"It's a good plan, Reginald. No one will suspect I'm still here and I can look for evidence to prove Slater was framed."

"If you stay, they'll kill you if they find you." Ramone shook his head. "You're no match for these men, Raissa. You have a sense of fair play and justice and that will be your undoing."

Arguing was pointless. The others might go to Victoria, but Reginald would not abandon me, even if he knew it meant death. I couldn't put him in that danger. I let out a deep sigh. "Fine."

Reginald did a double-take, but he was wise enough to say nothing.

Ramone spoke. "How much longer before the men get back?"

"They're here," I said. I'd felt the pounding of the horses' hooves on the hard-packed dirt of the road to Elizabeth's house. I went outside to catch the reins of Michael's horse as he came to a stop and leaped to the ground. The man who remained astride of Mariah was broad shouldered and power-ful. He threw his right leg over her neck and slid to the ground.

"You were right. She's a bonny mare." He handed me the reins, but he turned back to uncinch the saddle and pull it from her back. He did the same for Michael's horse. Hefting both saddles, he went to the barn and put them away. A moment later I heard him splash into the rain barrel on the side of the barn. After days of being a prisoner, he could finally clean up.

I led the horses to the trough to drink, taking care not to let them have too much. I walked them back and forth across the hot yard as the men went inside to get Elizabeth and Callie.

When the horses had cooled enough to drink their fill, I put them in the paddock and filled the trough. There was grass and plenty of water. Reginald came to stand beside me. "They'll be fine. Your uncle will have someone here to get both of them tomorrow," he said. "I'm sure he'll bring them to Mobile if that's what you want."

He was correct. The horses would be fine. I sighed and turned away. "Are we going to make it?"

"I wish I knew the answer to that." He put his arm around my shoulders and pulled me close. "This is going to be a hard journey for Elizabeth and she doesn't look good. She may not make it. You need to be prepared."

I swallowed down my bitter denial and went into the house and called her to her bedroom. When she came in, she closed the door. "Where's Callie?" I asked.

"She fell asleep so I put her in the back bedroom where it was quieter." She steadied herself against the bed post. "Thank you for freeing Slater."

"It's Michael you should thank."

"I will, but you all played a role. He is innocent. I couldn't abandon him to those...evil men."

I wondered if perhaps we hadn't drawn him into far worse circumstances, but I didn't say anything. "The men are outside, ready to go. Let me take a look at that wound."

She put her hand over it. "I'm fine."

Her behavior gave me pause. "Come on. This is the last

chance for me to make sure it's bandaged securely for the trip. It's going to be hard, Elizabeth. The roads are little more than woodland trails. We may have to walk, even push the car in places."

Hesitating, she finally nodded and slowly came toward me, lifting her blouse so that I could see the bandage Wainwright had put on her after he stitched her up. When I removed the tape and eased the bandage down, I looked up at her in astonishment. "What the hell?"

"Ever since I had Callie, it's been like this."

I couldn't believe it, but my eyes weren't lying. The wound was almost completely healed. All I had to do was cut out the stitches, which I did quickly before they grew completely into her flesh. She didn't even flinch as I pulled them out one by one. "How?"

"It's Callie. She heals me."

This was another special gift the infant had. "Is she truly Gabriel's child?"

Elizabeth bit her lip. "I don't know. He said she was. He told me how we made love and she was conceived. He said she was my destiny. Mine and his. That she's...special. Unique."

"You don't remember the...intimacy?"

"None of it. I only know what Gabriel told me. He said she would be a special child."

"That she is. She definitely has abilities. Could she belong to anyone else?" If there was a way to separate Callie from Gabriel, we had to find it. I had to voice one suspicion. "Could she be Slater McEachern's child?"

"No. There's no one I remember. I just found out back in the fall that I was pregnant. I didn't know how far along or how it even happened. I had no memory." She radiated tension. "I had planned to move on from Mission. This is a very bad place. The trail of my brother went cold. No one knew where he'd gone or why. Ramone wasn't here, so I wanted to look elsewhere. But I was pregnant, and I hoped I could find out who the father was. I didn't want anything from him, but I wanted to be able to tell Callie when she was older."

"You had to sleep with someone to get pregnant. You don't remember?"

"Nothing. That's why it makes sense that she is Gabriel's. If he's an angel, there would be no necessity for the physical act to conceive."

"Who told you that?"

"Gabriel."

More than ever I needed Madam's wisdom and knowledge. "We have to talk about this, but not here and now. We have to go."

"I should stay. I could delay them. I could hold them off by showing how I heal. They would be afraid of me and give you time to take Callie and get away."

"Of all the people here, you are the last one who should stay. Callie needs you. I don't know what role Gabriel plays in all of this, Elizabeth, but he is not good."

"I've had my suspicions in recent days." She looked perfectly miserable. "Do you know what he really wants?"

I weighed telling her the full truth. She deserved to know at least the danger—we could sort the rest when we were safe. "He wants Callie, and that's the one thing we can never let him have. Let's go. Everything is packed."

A knock came at the door and I opened it to Reginald. "All good?" Anxiety etched his face. Every minute we delayed put us closer to danger.

"She's good to travel. Let's get out of here."

I grabbed the bag with diapers and clothes for Callie and headed out the front door and across the porch to the car.

"Where's Callie?"

The cry came from the back bedroom where Callie had been sleeping. Elizabeth sounded distraught. I dropped the bag and ran back into the house, where confusion reigned. The pillows arranged to block Callie safely on the bed were still there, but the baby was gone. McEachern and Michael came into the room and immediately began looking under the bed and any place she might have fallen.

"The bairn couldn't disappear into thin air." McEachern lifted the mattress off the bed. "She's too young to crawl, but she must have."

"Where is she?" Elizabeth looked at me and I realized we both feared the same thing. That Gabriel had somehow managed to slip into the house and steal the baby he claimed was his daughter, a Nephilim child with untold powers.

# CHAPTER 28

The pounding of horse hooves came from the paddock area. A wild whinny of terror galvanized me into action. Something was after the horses.

I grabbed the shotgun, which Reginald had left on the kitchen table, and hurried out the front door. If those damn buzzards were harassing the horses, I would shoot them without hesitation. I didn't care if they were fallen angels or lost souls trapped in carrion-feeder bodies. I couldn't take any more. The unrelenting tension of the past few days had me on edge and ready to explode.

As I left the house, the two horses careened around the paddock area in a terrible panic. I lifted the gun to my shoulders and sighted, still looking for the cause of the horses' fear. There was nothing to see. The sun was slinking down behind the trees in the west, but there was no sign of Gabriel or his feathered minions. Still, the horses spun and wheeled, showing the whites of their eyes as they scrabbled, too afraid to go out through the open paddock gate and into the fields and woodland pasture.

Moving stealthily, I headed to the barn. Something had to be in there. Maybe one of the buzzards had gone to roost so it could watch over us and report back to its master. Still holding the gun to my shoulder, I slowly advanced. I'd never shot at anything with the intention of hurting it. The idea of killing any animal was repugnant to me. These buzzards, though, were not mortal creatures. I'd come to accept this. They played around in the wickedness that festered in Mission. Just as Lucais Wilkins and his thugs did. I didn't know how or why they'd chosen to serve evil, I only knew they had. Even to me, my thoughts sounded delusional and twisted, but I knew the truth. I saw it. And I would do whatever was necessary to defeat it.

The light in the barn was dim as I eased through the cracked door. With the horses outside, there should not have been anything alive in the barn. Whatever was in there, I had to handle it by myself because everyone was busy searching for a lost child—an infant I needed to also be looking for. I stepped past the first stall and deeper into the barn. Outside the horses continued to spin, crying out in fear and desperation. They'd injure themselves if I didn't put a stop to this.

Sunlight filtered into the barn in shafts where the roof and walls had holes. Dust motes danced in the light, oblivious to the pounding of my heart or the presence of danger. The smell of hay was sweet and strong. Elizabeth had put a small stack of freshly cut grass in a corner for Mariah. I approached the hay with fear. Anything could be hidden behind it. A quick search revealed only empty corners.

There seemed nothing out of the ordinary in the barn. I glanced up in the hay loft, but the area I could see was empty. I could detect no movement up there.

Suddenly a strange sound came to me from beyond the

stalls and tack room. It sounded like a swarm of flies buzzing. The noise swelled until it was loud enough to drown out any other sound. The smell of decomposing meat hit me at the same time. The buzzards had dragged something dead into the barn. They were likely feasting on it in the far corner of the barn, hidden in darkness. They would be easier to shoot if they were all clustered together. One foot in front of the other, gun at the ready, I continued on.

A terrible, terrible thought came to me. Callie was missing. What if those vile buzzards had come in the window and taken her? They were big. Big enough to lift a fifteen-pound infant. Callie was so helpless, so dependent on others to keep her safe. Those birds were big enough to kill her with beaks and talons. Normal buzzards were not predators, but these were not normal birds.

My breath hitched repeatedly as I pushed on. I didn't want to look, but I had to. I had to. I couldn't turn and run away as every inch of me begged to do. There was no room in my life now for cowardice or fear. I tried to think about what I was doing as a scene in a book, as something safely within the pages of a story I would one day write. My mind wouldn't hold onto that fantasy. It skittered away like a rodent and I was left with hurtling images of what I was going to find when I made it to the flies.

Beneath the disgusting buzzing of the flies emerged another sound. This one was guttural, the sound of something still alive, gurgling to an end. Was it possible the buzzards had Callie and she was still alive?

"Callie!" I rushed forward, unable to stop myself. "Callie!"

I forced myself past the last stall to the back of the barn. The area was very dark with no sunlight. The drone of the flies had reached cyclone pitch and the smell gagged me. "Callie?" I wished for a lamp or lantern, something to cast light into the dark shadows of the barn.

I couldn't see, but I forced myself forward, shuffling my feet to be sure I didn't step on the infant. Something scuttled along the floor of the barn and the smell grew worse. The gurgling sound continued, but it was no longer desperate. It was almost musical now.

"Whatever you are in here, I'm going to shoot first and ask questions later." I pulled the hammer on the shotgun back. It was hard to miss with a shotgun. I aimed high and pulled the trigger. The kick almost knocked me down, but I managed to keep my balance. The blast knocked a chunk out of the side of the barn. Dying sunlight flooded in at a golden slant, revealing a scene that hit me like a kick in my gut.

Callie lay on the floor of the barn, surrounded by at least nine of the buzzards. They walked around her counter clockwise as if they were performing some kind of ritual. They made a gruesome hissing sound—the sound they made when they feasted on something dead. Leaned against the wall was someone—I couldn't clearly see. He was outside the golden circle of light, but it was a person. Or had once been.

Callie turned her head to face me and a cry escaped my lips. Her eyes were pure white stones. She turned toward me as if she were blind, unseeing. But she gurgled and waved her arms, calling to me. Welcoming me.

The buzzards stopped moving and turned, all at once, to face me. I lifted the shotgun. I wanted to kill them. To blast them back into the hellish afterlife they'd come from, but I didn't. The shot spread of the gun was wide and powerful, and I couldn't risk hitting Callie or the person against the wall—if he was even still alive. The body looked as if all life had been sucked from it and an empty sack left behind, forgotten.

I took a step toward Callie, and the birds closed rank, preventing me from reaching the infant. They watched me.

"You bastards, I'm going to kill you." I felt an insane urge to blast them, despite the danger to Callie, and I realized that something was trying to gain control of me. The same something that fed off and changed my dreams. Gabriel. He was somewhere nearby, manipulating this scene—and me. I couldn't let him.

The smell of something rotting hit me hard and I turned away to gag. I was barely able to control the impulse to vomit, and when I turned back to the scene, my heart almost stopped. The body against the wall had started to move. It twitched and jerked and moaned. Before I could even step back, it dropped on all fours.

I remembered the dream of the characters from a novel, how one of them had turned into a beast on all fours, gamboling about, snapping at the air and her own flesh. The man did the same, his back arching in a way that would have snapped a normal spine.

The thing came toward Callie, who cooed and kicked her arms and legs, completely oblivious to the danger that was coming for her. I tried to move forward, tried to get between Callie and the thing on all fours that scrabbled toward her like something half dead but unwilling to find a grave.

"Stay away from her." My voice was weak, pathetic, even to my ears. The beast shifted its focus to me, and in doing so, the light from the hole I'd blasted in the wall fell on its face.

"Ramone!" Elizabeth's brother looked at me with such malicious wickedness that I felt as if I gazed upon the lord of hell himself. He opened his mouth and his tongue poked out, a black and rotting organ.

"Callie," he said in a voice so raspy it hurt my ears. "My

little Callie."

"Stay away from her." My threats were empty and I knew it.

"She's mine, now isn't she?" Ramone's grin was cruel.

"She is not yours. She will never be yours." I talked a good game for a woman who couldn't move her body an inch. "Elizabeth and I will find you and destroy you if you touch that child."

"Elizabeth knows she's mine. Elizabeth wants me to take her."

"You lying piece of filth." I had to think of something to do, something that would break the spell that held my body rigid. If he picked up Callie, he could disappear with her and no one would know where to look.

"She's mine and she's a god. She'll rule heaven and earth before this is over."

"Where is Ramone?" The creature in front of me might be using Ramone's body, but it was not the brother Elizabeth had come looking for.

"Gone." He rose to his feet, manipulating his joints and stretching as if the spine-snapping postures I'd just witnessed were nothing. "He's gone for good."

"Why, Gabriel? Why are you doing this?"

"It's a war, and you know it. The only war worth fighting. You delude yourselves into thinking that the wars humans wage are about good and evil." He laughed like a deep rumble. "So foolish. It's always money for you humans. Always greed. The war that must be fought is in front of you now. You think Lucais Wilkins is the enemy, but he does my bidding."

I didn't completely understand what he was saying, but I comprehended enough to know that Callie and Elizabeth were in terrible danger. Gabriel was not going to let us go.

"I'm taking the child. She belongs with me." Ramone went toward the baby and the buzzards scuttled out of his presence.

As he leaned down to pick up Callie, I aimed the shotgun into the roof of the barn and pulled the trigger on the second barrel. Shot flew and struck the top of the barn. Pieces of roof rained down on Ramone. It slowed him, but it wouldn't stop him.

More light illuminated the interior of the barn, but that wasn't my goal. I heard running footsteps. Help was coming!

"Hurry!" I called out. "In the barn. He has Callie. Help!"

The big barn door creaked open and more light flooded in. I turned to see Michael in the barn aisle, running hard toward me. When I looked back at Callie, she was alone on the floor of the barn. She was no longer cooing and her eyes had returned to normal. Ramone slumped against the back wall, blood trickling from his head. I found I could move my feet and I ran toward Callie while Michael rushed to assist Ramone.

"Is he hurt?" I couldn't remember shooting him.

"He's out, and there's a gash, but he's breathing steadily. I'll get Reginald to help me put him in the car. We have to go. What were you doing with Callie out here?"

"I found her. And Ramone. It was Gabriel, possessing Ramone. He wants the baby, and he can manipulate the things I see. Or think I see." I glanced at Ramone, who was unconscious still.

Michael rose to his feet. "Of course. If we're going to make a run for it, we have to go now. Right now. Send McEachern and Reginald here to help me move Ramone. We can't leave him."

I started to tell him what I'd seen, to warn him, but Michael waved me on. "Go! They won't be far behind Gabriel."

# CHAPTER 29

By the time we'd loaded the still-unconscious Ramone into the backseat of the car and had everyone else squeezed in, the buzzards were back. They had found a roost in the branches of a wild cherry tree that was dying. There had to be a dozen of them, their ugly heads and necks naked-looking in the dying light of the day.

"He's not going to let us go, is he?" Elizabeth asked.

Her color was much better, her posture erect. I figured she'd probably healed from the wound, but I had no intention of mentioning it. Not here. Not after what I'd seen in the barn. Or thought I'd seen. Had I actually seen Gabriel possess Ramone, or had that been another of the fallen angel's tricks? To make me believe Ramone carried the taint of evil. My thoughts didn't matter because Elizabeth would never leave without her brother.

"We don't need Gabriel's permission," Reginald said.

"Lucais and his men answer to Gabriel." I needed everyone to be clear about the degree of danger we faced.

"Let me stay," McEachern said with his slight burr. "I can lead the men into the woods. I'm good at surviving."

"No." Elizabeth put a hand on the big Scot's shoulder. "No. We sacrificed too much to leave you behind now. We're all going, or none of us will leave."

"They don't even want you," Michael said to McEachern. I sat between Michael and Reginald in the front seat. Reginald was behind the wheel. "It's never been about you, Slater. You were merely the bait to keep Elizabeth here. The murders, the dreams, it's all been a trap for Elizabeth and Callie."

"How do you know this?" I asked him.

"It's the only thing that makes sense."

"Ruth Whelan was murdered to set a trap for Elizabeth and her baby?"

He nodded slowly. "Ruth and little Hildy. And Slater was set up to take the blame. Then Elizabeth dreamed the truth. It was all to keep her here until Gabriel could make his move."

"And Hildy?" Elizabeth asked.

"I can only believe that Hildy saw something she wasn't supposed to see. She was always larking around the woods. And she was smart."

"What are we going to do?" I couldn't think about Hildy. I had to focus on escape. We would have only one chance, and we had to get out of Mission and down to Victoria.

"Make a run for it." Reginald revved the car.

Even Callie was silent as Reginald punched the gas and the big car roared forward, rocks clanging from the wheels. Whatever got in our way, Reginald would not stop for it. He would run over anyone and anything that tried to slow us down.

I glanced into the paddock. The horses were gone. They'd finally found the open gate to the back fields and woodland pastures and taken off. They'd be fine until my uncle could send someone to retrieve them. We had Callie safely tucked in the back seat in Elizabeth's arms. The child was as even-tempered as ever, and she blinked her eyes and yawned. Ramone, too, was coming back to himself. He appeared to have no memory of what had occurred in the barn, but soon he'd have plenty of questions.

Michael's hand slipped over mine and squeezed. "If you've ever prayed, do so now."

We cleared the yard and were headed far too fast down the driveway. When we came to the road, Reginald turned right, toward Victoria, the car listing and sliding so that I was thrown into Reginald and Michael into me. The people in the backseat fared no better. A few bruises and bumps were nothing compared to what awaited us if we weren't successful in our run.

The hot and humid September day had not finished, and the slant of the sun threw long shadows of the trees across the road. I expected at any turn to see Gabriel and his harbingers of doom. Michael's hand gripped my elbow as he tried to steady me through Reginald's wild driving. I finally shut my eyes and let my body find its own balance in the laboring car.

"Next right," Michael said softly.

When the tires hit the smoother packed surface of one of the main roads, I finally let my breath out. From here on out, the road was not as winding or treacherous. We'd left the bogs of sand and mud behind. In the few days we'd been in Mission, there had been no rain, and the road heading out of town was better than what we'd faced going in.

We came to the lightning-blasted tree on the outskirts of Mission where the road to town forked north and where I'd first seen the buzzards roosting. The tree was empty, the woods around it unnaturally quiet. Gabriel and the birds were nowhere in evidence. Looking at the blackened trunk and limbs against a sky turning blood red with the sunset, I had a terrible premonition. Gabriel wasn't going to let us go. This race for freedom—it would never succeed. He and his minions weren't visible, but that meant nothing.

Swallowing my fears, I remained silent. Things were dicey enough without me making it worse with crazy premonitions.

Twenty minutes later, when we pulled onto the main road to Victoria, I didn't believe it. Mission was several miles behind us. Open road stretched in front of us. We passed a farm wagon headed home. It was the only sign of life.

"Ramone, where have you been all this time?" Elizabeth finally asked. "I searched and searched for you. It's been months since anyone remembered seeing you here in Mission. Who was holding you prisoner and where?" She spoke with weariness instead of accusation, but I was eager to hear his answer. The things I'd seen in the barn—it was another of Gabriel's tricks. He'd manipulated the images in my mind the same way he'd done with the characters from a book I'd read. I couldn't be certain Callie's eyes had looked like blank white stones, or that Ramone's body had snapped and twisted into shapes that would sever a normal spine and leave him para-lyzed, if not dead. I couldn't rely on what my eyes told me.

Ramone spoke clearly. If that horrible, raspy voice had ever come from his throat, it had not damaged his vocal chords. "The folks in Mission weren't all that welcoming to a traveling Gypsy. I'd swing through the outlying farms with my goods and wares every month, steering clear of town. But the man who owns the general store, Mr. McKay, made it clear I wasn't welcome to sell cheaper than his prices."

"Vernon confronted you?" Elizabeth asked.

"A little more than a verbal confrontation. When I was

parked on the edge of town, someone set fire to my wagon. I put it out before there was a lot of damage, but I got the message. The next day I left Mission."

"And went to Victoria?" I asked. Listening to Ramone's story helped pass the time in the car and even ease the anxiety of watching the side of the road, trying to pick out danger in the car's headlights as they swept the verge. Each mile we put between us and Mission allowed me to hope a little harder that we might escape.

"I was headed to Victoria for a carpentry job, just until I could resupply my wagon. That's when I was attacked and taken. For six months or better, I worked cutting timber. I couldn't get away. I managed to sneak out of the camp one night and made it to a river—I didn't even know where I was. I figured the river would eventually end up in a town so I let the current take me. I camped where I could and nearly starved to death by the time some trappers took me on their canoe. I've been trying to get back to Mission ever since. I've got some scores to settle."

"Do you know who was responsible for abducting you?" I asked.

"I have a pretty good idea. Then I heard Elizabeth was living on the outskirts of town and I found her farm. I've never been happier to see a person."

Reginald was so intent on driving that I couldn't tell if he was following the conversation. Michael, though, was half turned in the front seat to look at Ramone and Elizabeth. Slater McEachern sat behind Reginald and beside Elizabeth. He watched the roadsides with intensity. Like Reginald, he anticipated an ambush. He was like a spring wound too tight. The slave collar was still around his neck—Michael had managed to break a link in the chain that held him to the wall.

Wisely, they'd chosen to ride hard for Elizabeth's rather than worry about the metal collar around his neck. When we got to Victoria and could find a hardware store, we'd find some way to unlock the collar.

"What's your plan now?" Slater asked Ramone.

"To get enough money to set up a little shop where I mend things for ladies in the town. That was my goal, to have a little shop in a permanent location. The traveling was too difficult alone. Folks always need repairs. Pot handles, knives, those things that are still good but need a little fixing up. I have a knack for repair and that was my plan."

"Ramone was always handy," Elizabeth said. She put a hand on her brother's cheek. "I'm so glad you're here with us. I've been so worried."

"When you knew I wasn't in Mission, why didn't you leave?" Ramone asked.

Reginald took a sharp curve, and Elizabeth held her answer until we were on the straight-away again. Reginald hadn't slowed a whit, so I knew he felt unsafe. We were out of the woods, but not out of the reach of Gabriel and his watchers.

"I didn't intend to stay," Elizabeth said. "The weeks just drifted by, and I didn't know where else to go. I kept hoping Ramone would show up. Folks said they'd seen him up in the Knoxville area headed back south. Mission was where your trail went cold, and I hoped you'd come back there."

Elizabeth sent her brother such a look of love that I felt as if I were spying into her private life. I realized suddenly the loneliness and abandonment she'd felt for the months Ramone was missing. After the death of my parents and then Alex, I, too, had drifted through the days and weeks. I'd gotten a job teaching literature in the local high school, and that had saved me, given me a routine that demanded a certain level of discipline and self-care.

Elizabeth and Ramone continued their conversation, filling in the timeline for each other, learning the important events that had passed in their lives. Everyone in the car except Reginald was listening.

"Until I found you, it didn't matter where I was." Elizabeth smiled up at her brother. "Mission didn't welcome me, but I preferred a solitary life. Folks did leave me alone, for the most part. Things began to happen that I didn't understand. I still don't understand." She swallowed. "I met this man. Gabriel. Yet I couldn't remember when we met or even where he was from. We must have spent time together, but I...don't know. I lost time. I was confused by the events that were happening around me. Then I found I was pregnant. Moving was out of the question until the baby was born."

"And then the dreams started," Ramone said. "That's what fascinates me. How you began to dream things that actually happened."

"Raissa has done the same," Elizabeth said, throwing the focus on me.

"Not really." I didn't want the attention.

"But you did. You dreamt the murder of Hildy Morse. I'm certain it happened just the way you saw it in your dream."

I shook my head. "Tell your brother about what happened to you," I said.

Elizabeth nodded. "The dreams were comforting, at first. Then they became confusing. Then terrifying. The things I saw turned out to be real, yet I had no way of knowing any facts about the events I dreamt. I began to dread sleeping and dreaming, knowing that terrible things I saw turned out to be true."

I'd had my share of dreams lately, and I could only hope they were not true.

"Tell them about your dream of Ruth Whelan's murder." I wanted to watch Slater's reaction, and also Ramone's.

Elizabeth looked down at Callie as she recounted her dream, the horrific time she'd spent in the skin of a brutal murderer. When she finished, she turned to Slater. "That's why I knew you were innocent." She picked up his hand where the scar between his thumb and forefinger was welted and clearly visible. "This wasn't the hand that held the cleaver. You didn't kill my friend, and I couldn't let you hang for something you didn't do."

"I thank you for your belief in me," Slater said, "but you'd be better served to let them kill me than pursue you. You've put yourselves at great risk."

"And you're free now, and we're on the way to a town with several lawmen." Elizabeth clung to the hopeful outcome.

"These dreams, you'd never had them before?" Ramone asked.

"I've always had vivid dreams, but nothing like these."

"And this happened after you became pregnant?" Ramone was clearly trying to find a link between the events of Elizabeth's life that might explain her peculiar gift.

"Yes, the dreams became this thick web of connective tissue." She reached over and picked up one of Callie's hands. "Almost like the membrane between her fingers. The dreams connect everything. I just don't know how."

"I'm sorry I wasn't there for you," Ramone said. He put a hand on the back of her neck and squeezed in a gesture of comfort. "You're my sister, and I wasn't there when you needed me."

Elizabeth shrugged. "I made friends with Ruth, and it

wasn't so bad in Mission. Little Hildy—" Her voice broke but she quickly regained control. "Hildy was a godsend to me when she'd come over. She was like a sprite in the woods, popping up where no one expected her. And she loved learning. Science, geography, languages. She was a sponge."

"I'm so sorry." Ramone patted her shoulder. "How lonely you must have been."

"It was okay for a while. Callie was born and I had everything I'd ever wanted. Ruth, Hildy, and I, we had fun walking and talking, learning about nature. Then Ruth was murdered. I couldn't abandon an innocent man. I couldn't."

Ramone lifted Callie from Elizabeth's arms. The baby, whose eyes were perfectly normal now, cooed and gurgled at Ramone. Callie seemed to like her uncle, but then she liked everyone. "Take a nap, Elizabeth," Ramone said. "I'll watch the baby. You look done in." He grinned at her. "But don't dream, unless we have a happy, safe ending."

I craned my neck for as long as I could, watching the two of them interact. Elizabeth quickly faded into an uneasy sleep, and Ramone busied himself playing with Callie. What caught my attention, though, was Michael. He sat watching Ramone and the baby. He wasn't a gregarious man, but I had the distinct impression he pitied Ramone. I would question him about it when we got to Victoria and found a place of safety.

"Where exactly are we going?" I asked Reginald softly. The longer he drove, the quieter and sterner he seemed to get. "Do you have a plan?"

"A boarding house or inn. Just for tonight. Elizabeth is exhausted, and she needs care. So does Callie. Ramone and Michael can look out for them because we have work to do. You and I are going to find a working phone so we can get in touch with Mr. Airlie and Madam. We need help, Raissa. We may get to Victoria, but we are far from safe and I think you know that."

There was so much I needed to tell Reginald about what I'd seen in the barn. About what I feared. I glanced into the backseat to find Callie staring at me. Her eyes were deep and beautiful, as I remembered. I feared greatly for the safety of the child—but possibly I feared her powers even more. Nephilim.

# CHAPTER 30

By the time we reached the outskirts of Victoria, I was exhausted. We'd taken several backroads, at Michael's direction, in an effort to avoid a confrontation with Lucais and his men. They hadn't given up—we all knew this even though no one spoke it aloud—but we didn't know from which direction they'd come at us.

We all looked haggard, except Elizabeth, who'd awakened from her brief nap refreshed. Callie, too, was her normal, good-spirited self. The child was never cross. She was almost... preternaturally pleasant.

Ramone returned her to Elizabeth's arms as Reginald searched for an inn or boarding house in town that could accommodate so many of us. It was only about eight o'clock, but the town slumbered as if a witch had sprinkled a sleeping potion over the entire populace. As far as I could see, Victoria didn't have a hotel.

Main Street yielded nothing that vaguely resembled an inn, but we found a large, rambling two-story house on Second

Street, and Reginald pulled to the curb. A small sign on the corner said it was the Sand Mountain Inn. We had few belongings, except for the things we'd brought for Callie.

"Michael, could you come in with me to check on registration?" Reginald asked.

It was clear he meant me to stay in the car with the others. In truth, I didn't mind. I was happy not to answer impossible questions from someone who was not going to be happy to be disturbed in the shank of the evening.

Sleeping arrangements didn't matter. We could double or triple up, as long as we could move the car off the street. Lucais Wilkins would be looking for us, and it only made sense we'd head for the nearest town. Getting the car out of sight was the first priority. Then, if we could only sleep for several hours, we could think more clearly. Tomorrow we needed a plan to attack our enemies instead of hiding from them. But just now, hiding sounded like a smart and reasonable action.

I swung around on the seat so I could face Elizabeth, Slater, and Ramone. "You okay?"

They all nodded. Elizabeth had slumped toward Slater in her sleep, and she remained against his side. It was clear they had feelings for each other, though when they'd developed, I didn't know. It made me wonder if they'd been completely honest with me. I'd learned one thing about Mission, Alabama —nothing was as it seemed. The line between dreams and reality was broken and interspaced with segments that made no sense in the world I normally inhabited.

I felt Slater's gaze on me, and I turned away.

"Raissa, may I speak with you?" he asked. "I have family and they haven't heard from me in nearly a month. I'd like to post a letter to them."

"Sure, maybe the landlady of the inn will drop it in the mail for you tomorrow."

"I want to consult on what to tell my family. I don't want them coming here for any reason, so I want to reassure them that everything is okay. I know I've unduly worried them. They take the burden of my decisions on their shoulders."

I realized then that he wanted to talk to me about something he didn't want Elizabeth or Ramone to hear. "Sure. Let's go sit on the steps of the inn." There was a steep flight that would give me a view of the car while I talked to Slater.

When we took our seats, I saw Ramone and Elizabeth watching us. They looked pensive, so alone. I couldn't say for certain what was happening with Ramone, but I feared Elizabeth would soon be dealt a terrible blow. I couldn't believe that Ramone would harm his sister, though. I leaned against the steps. We sat for a full minute before Slater began to talk.

"There's something not right going on."

There was a lot not right going on. "What do you mean?"

"We need to keep going. We shouldn't stop here."

It hadn't occurred to me that the buzzards might follow us into Victoria. But, of course, they could. They could be watching from a dark corner of the lawn even now. "We have to rest," I told him. "Just for a few hours. Reginald and Elizabeth are exhausted. Michael, too. I'm tired, but I'm also afraid to sleep."

"I can drive," he said. "Let's keep moving." He looked up and down the empty street. "I don't like this."

His words filled me with foreboding. I knew too well the power that Gabriel had, when he decided to use it. Both Elizabeth and I could fall under the spell of his nightmarish dreams. "Have you ever dreamt anything...so real and yet so completely filled with nightmare images?" I was thinking of Callie, lying on the floor of the barn with her stone-white eyes.

"No. My gran told me stories, though. Visitations from strange people who passed through the highlands. They had... abilities, and sometimes they took a neighbor's child with them when they left."

His words hit me hard. "They stole a child?" Gabriel had said he wanted Callie. That she was his.

"In the tales my gran told, they did."

"Any particular child?"

He thought a minute. "I don't remember all the specifics, but she said they would pass through, as tinkers or farmhands or sometimes teachers or ministers looking to work. Maybe to preach for a few weeks to collect money, or bring in a crop. Then they'd leave. Some years they returned, but never after they took a child."

"Who were they?"

He shrugged. "Gran didn't know. She said they caught one of them down the road with a baby once. The highlands were a wild and unruly place then. The taking of a bairn was nae tolerated. Searchers went out by torchlight, tracking the woman they feared to be a fairy. It was believed that fairies would steal a human babe and leave a changeling in its place. But no baby had been left."

"Did they find the baby?"

"They did. Unharmed, or so it seemed."

"And the person who stole the baby?"

"They hanged her. But when they went back to the gallows the next morning, the noose was empty and the body was gone."

"You said the baby seemed unharmed. Was it okay?"

"She was...peculiar, from what Gran said. Never took to

people. She stayed in the woods and fields, alone, content. Folks believed she was a fairy child after all and that she slipped away from the humans to be with her own people as much as she could."

My heart was heavy. "Did she ever find happiness?"

"She and my gran were friendly. The girl, her name was Ilka, grew up to be a healer with great talent. I don't know if she was happy. She favored being alone and lived in a small house up on a rocky crag. She could see anyone approaching, and it was believed she'd slip away into the woods unless she chose to help them. Some she didn't want to help. Gran said she never refused, but she simply couldn't be found when some people came looking for help."

"What happened to her?"

"One day she was gone. All her goods still there. Her medicines she'd made up. Her clothes and things, all neatly in the cupboard. She never came back. Broke my Gran's heart."

His gaze drifted down to Elizabeth and I wondered if he was seeing her in the light of the story. She, too, was an isolated woman with special gifts. She'd drifted into Mission and her life had brushed against his in an unimaginable way.

"No trace of her was ever found?"

"Not her nor the bairn that disappeared at the same time." He finally met my gaze. "Do you know that baby is Elizabeth's? For sure?"

Suddenly I couldn't breathe. I started to bolt up, but he caught me and continued talking. "I'm not accusing. It's a fair question. She shows up out of nowhere and one day she has a baby."

"You never saw her pregnant?" I asked.

"Nae. Neither did Ruthie, but Ruthie loved her. Wou'na hear a foul word about her."

"What are these...people that passed through your area if they weren't fairies?" I thought of strange Hildy and her love of the woods and her fairy searches. She'd been fairy-like in her unusual behavior and love of nature.

"I canna say."

"Why your village and Mission?" Perhaps it was Slater that was the direct link.

"They seek the isolation, I think. Folks in Mission cling to themselves, they disdain and fear outsiders. The men control outside influence. The things that happen there stay there. No word gets out to the bigger world. That's where Ramone likely ran into trouble. Handsome man shows up under the guise of selling goods. You can't tell me the wives and daughters weren't slippin' out to dance with the devil. The menfolk in Mission hold their women by fear, not love or kindness. They'd be ripe pickin' for a man like Ramone."

Stupid, but likely true. People, no matter how isolated or repressed, would always take the opportunity for sexual pleasure if they believed they wouldn't be caught.

I nodded slowly. "Ramone may have left because he was in trouble. It would make more sense that someone set his wagon on fire for sleeping with his wife or daughter than because he sold a pot cheaper."

"Whatever his reason for disappearing, it's good they found each other again. I hope."

"Do you have reason to think it might be otherwise?"

"I believe there's a world beneath this one. Or above, or beyond. A place where things happen that can't be explained in this world. Some of that is good, like Elizabeth. Some is bad. I don't know how to tell the difference." He sighed, "Elizabeth looks happier than I've ever seen her. She made Ruthie's life less miserable. I put her on the side of good." He nodded at me. "You're a seer, aren't you?"

"Seer?" I didn't know the term.

"You see things on the other side of the veil. You see the dead."

"I do."

"And Elizabeth. What does she see?"

"The things that Gabriel wants her to see. She saw Ruth's murder. She risked a lot to save you." I couldn't stop myself from defending Elizabeth. She'd been a stalwart friend to Slater and Ruth.

"I wish she hadn't stayed in Mission. She came up to the jail only once and demanded to talk to me. Deputy Gomes was amused, at first. He let her speak to me at the window, much as I talked to you. I told her to leave me alone, but she wouldn't listen. She kept saying she knew I was innocent and she'd speak in my behalf." He shook his head. "Had she gotten on that stand and told the truth, they would have hanged her for a witch beside me."

What he said was true. "She's brave and determined. Does she love you?"

"She doesn't ken me," he said. "She's a bonnie lass, but my heart still grieves for Ruthie. We were to be wed."

The whole sorry story began with Ruth's murder—and the reasons for it.

"Why was Ruth killed?"

"The things she knew. The things she wrote down. She kept a journal of the times and the men. They feared she'd show others."

"Did you see the journal?" Slater might have the key to being able to read it.

"She wrote it in a secret language. She was afraid something would happen to her once she let Lucais know she had written things down."

"Why would she do that, Slater? Why put herself in harms' way like that? She should never have told Lucais and those men about her journal."

Slater's face twisted with grief. "She did it because Lucais said he'd never let her go to marry me. He said she was his property, and a mighty fine source of income for him. He didn't want her to stop with her...work."

It all came down to greed. Nothing so surprising in all of that. "He'll pay for what he did. I promise you that much. Lucais may have power in Mission, but the state of Alabama is much bigger and there are a lot more powerful people in Mobile and Montgomery. My uncle will bring the force of the law to bear against Lucais and his miscreants."

"You still have the journal?"

I only smiled. "It's in a very safe place, and soon my uncle will have it. He has the power to bring those men to justice."

"Have you called him?"

I didn't answer because Reginald and Michael came out of the inn. "They have three rooms. Raissa, you and Elizabeth and Callie take the first one. I'll bunk in with one of the men, and there's a room for the other two." He handed me a key.

I rose and started to the car to get Elizabeth and Callie. I knew they had to be exhausted. I was barely able to put one foot in front of the other.

"We shouldn't stay here overnight," Slater said to Reginald. "We should keep moving. I was telling Raissa. It's dangerous here. We haven't left them behind."

I kept walking and let Reginald handle it. When I got to the car, I gave Elizabeth the room key and helped her gather the baby's things. Ramone carried Callie as we went up to the inn. We passed Reginald, Michael, and Slater, still in discussion. I wanted to help get Elizabeth and the baby settled, then call my uncle. It would distress him, calling at this hour, but I had no choice. And then I wanted a chance to talk to Madam. I had so many questions.

When everyone was settled and Michael had been tasked with finding a way to remove the slave collar from Slater's neck, I met Reginald on the steps of the inn. The proprietress wouldn't allow us to make a long-distance call from her phone, but suggested we go to the police department. We had to go there anyway, so we moved the car and hid it behind a row of businesses in an alley. From there, we walked to the police station.

The first hint of fall swept down the street and made my skin prickle with the unexpected chill. The weather had been hot and humid for months. Now the seasons were changing. I could smell the coming winter. A few leaves drifted from trees and onto the sidewalk, a reminder of the shorter days ahead as the Earth tilted Alabama away from the sun.

"It won't be long, Raissa. This will be over." Reginald was worried but clearly trying to hide it.

"I have a bad feeling." I couldn't lie to tell him. As we walked, I told him about the barn, the buzzards, the baby with her white stone eyes, and Dream Ramone, dead against the wall. "Gabriel can make me see whatever he wants. I don't know reality from the dream, and at this point I have no idea who Callie's real father might be." I rubbed my face with both hands. I was tired. "I just don't understand why he wanted Elizabeth to see the truth about Slater. Why not just let them hang him and be done with it?"

"A question without an answer, at least right now."

"Slater says he knew about the journal I found at Ruth's.

The one Hildy helped me find." Dead Hildy. She'd led me to the answer I needed. "Ruth told Lucais that she'd made a record of the things she'd done, and with whom. That may be the reason she was killed. We'll have the evidence once we decipher the journal."

# CHAPTER 31

W e arrived at the bleak police station and I was struck by the sense of darkness even in the architecture. It was nighttime, and Victoria had few streetlights. Reginald opened the door for me. I stepped inside to confront a dour law officer sitting at a tall desk. "We're travelers and we need to use your phone to make a long-distance call. I can reverse the charges."

"Can you now, little lady?" He looked down at me as if I might be lying. "Who are you calling?"

"My uncle. Our car broke down and we need him to send some help."

"Where are you from?" He watched me too closely. My skin prickled. There was something not right here.

"Mobile. My uncle is Brett Airlie. He has a steamship company and runs supplies up the waterways for towns all over the state."

"I'm still not sure you can use the phone. We aren't a phone service for every Tom, Dick, or Harry. Maybe you should find the mechanic tomorrow morning and get that car fixed so you can leave." He spoke to Reginald. He'd assessed me as a mere woman and was done talking to me.

Reginald leaned in to him, excluding me. It was an action that bonded Reginald with the policeman and left me out. It worked, but it still chapped me.

"I'm in a bit of a pickle here, Sergeant." Reginald turned on the charm. "The car belongs to her uncle," he nodded his head toward me, "but I'm the one who hit a limb in the road. I need to explain to Mr. Airlie. I owe him that."

Reginald had wisely played on the scenario that he was doing the right thing in owning his actions. He was the responsible person—and it didn't hurt that he was male. A responsible female would not impress the lawman.

The officer gave him a conspiratorial grin. "The phone is over on the desk there. Leave me with a bill and I'll see that you're arrested."

"No sir," Reginald said. "I wouldn't do that."

I kept my mouth shut. I was tired and aggravated by the officer's unwillingness to let a woman use the telephone, but I was smart enough to remain silent. One thing about traveling with Reginald and working as a private investigator: I'd gotten a heaping helping of the inferior role that women were allowed by law enforcement, religion, banks, businesses, schools, and society in general. Our opinions were not welcome. We were, like children, to be seen and not heard.

Reginald made the call to Uncle Brett, reversing the charges as he'd promised. We had to let the phone ring a long time for Uncle Brett to rouse himself and answer it. In fact, it was Isabelle who finally answered and accepted the charges.

"Is something wrong?" she asked, her panic clear.

"You could say that," Reginald held the phone so I could also hear. "We're in Victoria. There are some bad people hunting for us." He lowered his voice. He didn't want to involve the police, and I was glad. The officer hadn't offered much hope in the way of being interested in our safety. We were strangers and not his business, or so it seemed.

"Bad people? Let me get Brett."

In only a minute Uncle Brett was on the phone. "Who's after you and what do I need to do?" He got right to the point.

"We need Madam." Reginald also dove in headfirst. "Can you get her up here as quickly as possible? We need you as well. Come by train. The roads will slow you down too much. We're in Victoria but we can't stay here. We aren't safe. We can meet you in Gadsden."

"I can try to get her, if her health permits. Don't bother meeting us, just find a safe place and stay put. I'll hire a car."

"We're using the phone in the Victoria police station." Reginald kept talking but his gaze was on the officer, who was too far away to hear our conversation but was looking peeved. "We don't have access to another phone. Can you send some state or federal lawmen from Montgomery or somewhere? Send them quickly. They need authority in Victoria and Mission, but the local law is...compromised. There's a lot of bad stuff happening, Mr. Airlie."

The officer had come out from behind his desk and was headed our way.

"I have to go. We're at the Victoria Inn on Second Street. Please hurry. It's not a good situation." He hung up the phone just as the officer stopped in front of him.

"All done?"

"Yes, thank you," Reginald said. "Is there an all-night diner nearby, perhaps? We need a place to wait for morning to get the car fixed. We'll be gone as soon as the repair is made." He winked at the lawman. "We're engaged but not yet married.

She comes from a good family. We can't risk anything that looks improper. She's a society girl."

I kept my eyes downcast as Reginald lied. He didn't want the officer to know where we were staying.

"You must be from the city." The officer took in his clothes. The heat had wilted the starch in Reginald's shirt, but the cut of his clothes told of a man who took grooming and appearance seriously. "What's your business here in Victoria?"

"We're looking for property for my uncle to buy," I said, before I thought to stop myself. The look he cast at me told me I should have kept my mouth shut.

"What kind of property?" he asked Reginald.

Reginald picked up the question without a pause. "A sanctuary or hideaway. Mr. Airlie has a very stressful life with his successful business. He needs a place in the woods to simply unwind. We found one property in Mission, but we're going to look on the outskirts of Victoria. I think Mr. Airlie might prefer to be closer to...civilization."

"I see." The officer looked from Reginald to me and back. "And that's all you're up to?"

"I don't catch your meaning," Reginald said.

"You sounded like you might be in trouble," the officer pressed.

"Only in the sense that I may have damaged the car." Reginald took in a long breath. "Mr. Airlie is a lovely man, but he expects people to treat his possessions with care. I fear I may have disappointed him. He said to take it to a mechanic. Can you recommend one?"

"Junior Albee has a little shop. The boy is slow, but he's a steady worker and he gets it fixed. Folks swear by him."

"Thank you." Reginald stoically didn't react to the name

we'd heard before in reference to attacks on women. "Might we have the address?"

"Sure." The sergeant found a piece of paper and pen and wrote down an address. "Get there early because he gets a lot of work. Folks can be the bumsucker, you know. Those who need a favor from Deakle Albee make use of Junior's shop." He chuckled. "Not a bad way to keep your boy in business, is it? But the word is that the boy is a solid mechanic."

"What is it that makes Deakle Albee worthy of being... toadied to?" Reginald asked. This had truly fallen in our lap and we'd pursue it in the morning.

"He controls a lot in Victoria. Staying on his good side is worth the effort. Like staying on mine can make life easier."

Reginald brought out his wallet and folded a bill. When he took the paper with the address of the shop, he passed the money. "Many thanks, officer. You've been very helpful."

We took our leave, and it was a relief to step back into the night. I glanced behind us to see the policeman standing at the window watching us depart.

"Your uncle and Madam will be here as quickly as they can." Reginald was eager to see Uncle Brett and Madam and I knew why. We were in grave danger. If Lucais or his brutish followers caught us, we would likely be killed. We weren't safe in Victoria, as I'd hoped we be.

"Can we hide in Victoria that long?" I was ready to drive down the mountain and meet Uncle Brett part way. We had Slater McEachern, a fugitive from the law, with us. Whether he was guilty or not, he was still an escaped prisoner. We could face serious charges against all of us. But Uncle Brett could protect Slater and us until we could uncover the truth. My uncle was a powerful man with powerful friends. That meant nothing in Mission, but it did in the statehouse, where ultimate power resided. "Slater says we should leave immediately. Just drive as far away as we can."

"He may be right. At first light tomorrow. Let's see how the others have settled in."

I was eager to get back to the inn. I was tired and hungry and worried. There was nothing to do but get through the long night ahead of us. In the daylight we could assess our danger more accurately.

We set out into the darkness, our footsteps echoing on the wooden sidewalk. Parts of Victoria had electricity, thanks to the dam on the Coosa River, but streetlights were few and far between. A breeze had kicked up, and it sent tree limbs whipping, blocking the light and casting shadows in the two lights down the street. I thought of the magnificent oak trees that lined the drive to Caoin House, my uncle's estate. With the Spanish moss dripping from their limbs, those trees had danced in the moonlight. But there had been other things on the lawn, too. Nocturnal things that had no place in the land of the living.

At the nearest streetlight a sudden gust of wind blew the maple limbs so that the light was blocked for a moment. It occurred to me that this might be an omen. I shook off the unpleasant chill that touched me and looked about the town.

Had we visited Victoria under different circumstances, I would have found it charming. It was a small town with brick buildings that were made to survive the frequent tornadoes that skipped across the top of Cumberland Plateau. Several churches with elegant spires gave the little town a sense of grace. It was at one of the churches that Reginald had talked with a priest.

"Let's walk by the church." I had a ridiculous idea that we'd gain protection against Gabriel on holy ground. Reading

*Dracula* by Bram Stoker had left me with foolish notions: that evil couldn't enter a church and a crucifix could ward off... vampires. But what about fallen angels and Nephilim? I didn't want to know if Callie was the latter. Because if she was, I didn't have a clue what we would do with her. If the things Michael had told me were true, and the Nephilim were born wicked, what would we do? Callie already had powers. That much I knew. But they seemed to be gentle and healing powers. What if, as she grew older, she also grew stronger and more corrupt?

I was nearly in tears by the time we walked past one of the churches. Reginald grabbed my arm and drew me to a stop.

"What?" I hadn't seen or heard anything out of the ordinary. The town was dead asleep. Not a car, not a wagon, not a person on foot was about. Then I heard it, the flutter of wings. There was a rustling in the trees and shrubs that cluttered the churchyard, but in the dark night I couldn't see what it was.

Reginald stepped in front of me, blocking me from whatever he'd heard in the churchyard. He sensed danger too.

"What is it?"

"I don't know. There's something there watching us."

As soon as he spoke, a large black bird flew out of the dense foliage at our heads. The foul smell of death rode on its wings. It swooped right at us and if we hadn't dropped to the ground, it would have struck us.

The danger had escalated. The watchers were no longer content to watch.

We regained our feet and inched backward into the middle of the street. I was praying for a car or pedestrians, even a dog, to walk by. In the distance I could hear several hounds baying, as if they understood evil was afoot. Animals had a heightened sense of the dead, and possibly of evil.

"Let's try to get back to the inn." Reginald had my arm in a tight grip. "I won't leave you."

His words chilled me, because he understood intuitively that whatever was watching us wanted something from me. Or wanted me.

We turned to go down the street and I stopped. Gabriel stood a block away in the middle of the road. He spread his wings, fluttering so that they were outlined in gold by the streetlight. There was an answering flutter in the dense shrubs and trees in the church yard. Reginald looked toward the church, zeroing in on what was happening there because he could not see Gabriel.

"Run to the inn," Reginald said. But there would be no running away for me. Gabriel would not let me run. I felt him in my mind, just behind my eyes, taking over what I felt and saw and heard and smelled. He integrated easily into my perceptions, probing into personal memories. I could feel him prying loose the anchors of reality.

"It's Gabriel," I said. "In the street. He's trying to get into my mind. He'll plant images that terrify me and render me useless to fight him."

Reginald's grip on my shoulder intensified and he snatched me behind him as he ran toward the church steps.

A flock of birds, large enough to be buzzards but also mixed with smaller birds like crows or ravens, came out of the churchyard shrubs. They flew directly at us. One large bird grabbed Reginald's hair and began to peck around his eyes. I took off my shoe and struck it as hard as I could. Blood spurted down Reginald's white shirt, and I hit the bird again, a solid thwack. It let go of him and we dashed up the steps and into the sanctuary. Reginald bolted the door behind us. Bloody and panting, we went to a back pew and sat down.

When I turned to Reginald, I wanted to cry. Blood was dripping down his face, plopping onto his shirt. His flesh was torn in a dozen places where the bird had savaged him. He used a handkerchief to try to staunch the flow.

"What are we going to do?" I asked.

"Wait here until daylight. They won't attack during the day." He put his hands on either side of my face. "Did he hurt you? Is Gabriel gone?"

He was gone, but not for long. I didn't think a church would hold him out if he chose to come in. There seemed no barrier, personal or religious, that Gabriel couldn't breach. But we had to find something. At stake was my sanity. I'd never been in graver danger. "He knows everything about my past, and he uses things against me. My parents' and Alex's deaths, the things I desire and fear. He can turn me inside out whenever he wants, and he knows it."

"We only have to last until morning," Reginald said. "We can do that, Raissa."

A pounding at the church door made me cling to Reginald as we both rose to our feet. I was afraid. Reginald might have been too, but he squared his shoulders and calmed me. "If it's Gabriel, he wouldn't have to knock."

I nodded and sank back into the pew. Relief had jellied my knees as soon as we'd entered the church and I wasn't certain I could stand. It might not be Gabriel, but who was it? Who would knock at a church door in the middle of the night? I turned in the pew and watched Reginald open the door with my heart pounding. Michael Trussel stepped inside the church, his face grave.

"Elizabeth, Ramone, and Callie have disappeared."

# CHAPTER 32

**B**efore we could ask a single question, the back entrance to the sanctuary opened and a man in pajamas, slippers, and a robe came toward us. A silent nun in a full habit followed him into the sanctuary. "Can I help you?"

"Father Kilroy." Reginald hurried toward him. "We're in trouble. We need sanctuary."

The drowsiness that had clung to the priest's eyes disappeared. "What kind of trouble? We keep a low profile here in Victoria," he said calmly.

"It could be...difficult for you." Reginald wasn't going to lie. "There are people after us. Lucais Wilkins from Mission and his thugs and someone else."

Father Kilroy nodded slowly. "I know of Lucais Wilkins and his deeds. When you told me earlier you were in Mission to help a woman, I knew you'd eventually run afoul of Wilkins. Last year a Catholic couple tried moving to Mission. Wilkins and his men set upon them and beat the schoolteacher nearly to death. His wife threw herself over her husband and that's what saved him."

"Because they were Catholic?" I couldn't stop myself from asking.

"Catholic and teachers," Kilroy said. "They wanted to set up a school for all the children. Wilkins keeps rigid control over what's taught in the Mission schools. He determines the curriculum. An outsider with a broader world view could not be tolerated."

I remembered what I'd been told about how Lucais controlled newspapers in the town.

"Can you help us?" Reginald asked.

"We're a small congregation, but we would never turn anyone away. Other than Wilkins, what do you fear?"

"A dark angel." Michael spoke with calm authority.

Father Kilroy only nodded. "When I spoke with Reginald earlier, I wondered about some of his questions. What does this...entity want?"

"He hopes to corrupt Mrs. James. She's a powerful sensitive." Michael took two steps closer to me.

"Meaning what?" the priest asked. "What are you sensitive to?" He addressed me.

"She sees and speaks with the dead," Reginald said. "She's also aware of other spiritual entities. Dark entities. She sees things we can't see or understand. She has the courage to fight them."

"If she were compelled to assist a fallen angel, she would be a formidable asset to him," Michael said.

The priest didn't doubt or question us. "What can I do?"

"Can we borrow a phone?" Reginald put a hand on my shoulder. "Call Madam. Get her help now. We can't wait until tomorrow. She must tell us how to fight a demon!" Reginald turned back to the priest. "Keep Raissa safe here. With you. She's in the most danger of all."

"You can't just leave me here." I wasn't about to let Reginald and Michael go hunting for the missing Maslows without me. They couldn't even see Gabriel if he appeared. They would be helpless without me. I understood I was the most vulnerable, and my presence might make them more vulnerable. But as Reginald had pointed out, I could see Gabriel when they couldn't.

"You're safer here. We have to get that baby," Michael said.

"Where's Slater?" I asked.

"He's at the inn," Michael said, "waiting for us. Father, can we send someone to bring him here?"

"I'll send one of the sisters," Father Kilroy turned to the nun. "Sister Rosamunde can bring him back."

She nodded and left as silently as she'd arrived.

"That's good." Reginald focused on me again. "You, call Madam. She'll have some advice. If there is anything she can tell us to use against Gabriel, we need to know it."

"You need me with you," I said. "You can't even see Gabriel, but I can."

"I can see him," Michael said quietly.

"How?" I asked him. All of this time he'd held this back. "Why didn't you tell me?" With the relief also came a sense of betrayal. "Who are you?"

He shook his head. "It doesn't matter. What matters is that I can. Father Kilroy, do you know how to combat a fallen angel?"

The priest nodded slowly. "I've read cases. I'll gather some things for you." He put a hand on my elbow. "Let me show you to the phone. Remember, someone at the switchboard is likely listening in."

It was good advice that I hadn't considered earlier. I followed him into a small office where there was a desk and a telephone.

"It's a call to New Orleans." I could only pray that Madam would pick up at midnight.

"No matter. Now let me gather some things for the men."

I placed the call to Madam and held my breath until her butler, Carlton, answered. He knew me, and when I told him the call was urgent, he understood. In her time, no doubt Madam had received a large number of urgent calls. "Are you hurt, Mrs. James?" Carlton asked.

"No. Not yet."

He cleared his throat. "She mentioned you this evening. She's been worried. She'll be relieved to hear your voice. I'll get her."

I waited, gripping the phone with white knuckles. Time ticked past me. At last Madam was on the line. "Raissa, your uncle called me earlier. We're very troubled. I'm packed to leave in the morning. Has something else happened?"

I explained what I understood of our situation, being as discreet as possible. "Madam, I may be compromised. Gabriel has been in my memories and thoughts already. I may have allowed him in."

"A dark angel, Raissa. You're in terrible danger. You're too sensitive, too susceptible to—"

Madam didn't finish, but I knew what she'd almost said. I was too susceptible to temptation, to being influenced by the forces of evil, especially if those evil forces tempted me with memories of my dead loved ones. The touch of Alex's hand. My mother humming in the kitchen. My father admiring my artwork. The things that had been taken from me.

"How do we defeat this?" I asked.

"Only light defeats dark."

"How?" I needed specifics. I'd faced some powerful evil, and I'd won. Sometimes by chance. This time, the risks were too high. If Gabriel managed to seduce me yet again with his dreams and visions, I might be lost forever.

"What does this entity want?" Madam asked.

"I believe it wants an infant, a girl child. One who may be Nephilim."

Madam's gasp said it all. "I never believed such things existed. They were always legends, stories."

"Maybe not. Michael believes it is me, because of my abilities to communicate with the dead and other spirits, that this Gabriel truly wants. I see what he wants me to see. Feel what he wants me to feel. He can immobilize me with just the visions he sends to me. How do I fight this?"

"You are the prize, Raissa. Not the other woman and not the child. Everything has led up to you being there, within his reach. He has told you, no doubt, that he wants a family. With you. He wants to father a child with you. You have always been the thing he wants because you have a special gift from the Divine."

She was scaring me. "That doesn't make sense. That would mean that Elizabeth lured me and Reginald here." That couldn't be right. Ruth and Hildy couldn't have been murdered in a scheme to get me to Mission. It was too much to take.

Madam's voice was urgent. "You cannot be alone with this entity. You *cannot*. Stay in the church. The father has the power of goodness to ward off evil. It may not hold forever, but it will be a barrier so you can prepare. Outside the church, you are vulnerable. Heed me, Raissa."

"Callie, the little baby, is missing, along with her mother

and uncle. I have to search for them. The child is innocent, Madam. I can't abandon her."

"Consider that this, too, is part of a ploy to put you in a place where you have no protection."

The idea that Elizabeth had used me, had endangered Reginald... It cut me to the quick, and I wanted to reject it. But I couldn't. Not completely. Madam could be wrong. She wasn't here in Victoria to judge and evaluate the things that were happening. But her intuitive skills were highly developed and I trusted her ability to read a situation.

"How well does this Gabriel know you?" Madam asked.

"He's been able to tap into my memories. To use them against me." I thought of Alex dying, of the church with my parents' coffins and the thing inside one of them trying to get out. "He knows too much. And he knows what weakens me."

"I'm taking the first train to Gadsden tomorrow. My health isn't perfect, but I'm much stronger, and Carlton is coming with me. We'll meet your uncle and Isabelle in Gadsden and drive straight to you. Stay in that church, Raissa."

I wished I could. I wished that Michael, Reginald, and I could wait for Uncle Brett, Isabelle, and Madam to come to our rescue. But Callie was out there. This gentle child was at the mercy of whoever had her. I didn't have a choice—I had to find her and protect her. I wasn't her mother, but that didn't matter at all. Whether Elizabeth had betrayed us or not, the baby was helpless. She might have powers, but they'd proven benign or healing so far. I had to keep it that way.

WHEN I RETURNED to the sanctuary, Slater had joined Reginald and Michael. His neck was raw where the slave collar had been, but somehow Michael had removed it. "Do we have weapons?" he asked.

"You can't kill him with a bullet," I said. "He's not alive like we are."

"On the off chance that a piece of lead may slow him down, I'll gladly carry a gun. As far as Lucais Wilkins is concerned, a bullet will stop him cold." He gave a wry smile. "We have few weapons to choose from, Raissa. What can defeat a dark angel?"

"Love." I said it as a joke, not a serious answer, but I instantly recognized the truth of it. "There is a possibility that Reginald and I were lured here. Madam thinks that Ruth's death was the first step in an elaborate plan to bring us to Mission where I might be vulnerable to Gabriel."

Slater looked confused, but Reginald knew exactly what I was saying. And Michael too.

"Why would someone kill a good woman to get you to come to Mission? Why not just send a letter asking you to come?" Slater asked.

"I don't know. I would have come to help Elizabeth with whatever problem she said she had. No one had to die," I said. "I don't know that Madam's scenario is true, but it's possible. Madam wanted me to tell you. So that you would be alert. She is arriving by train tomorrow as soon as she can."

"It's wise to be wary, but Elizabeth would nae do this thing," Slater said. "Not willingly. But we can't know who is controlling her now."

I loved that he defended her, as she had fought for him. His heart was pure. Could I say the same about Elizabeth? I remembered her walking with Callie, the way the baby adored her, her absolute devotion to Callie, and her long quest to find her missing brother. It did not seem possible Elizabeth could be so evil, but I had learned the hard way that the worst evil, the evil that could break a person, was evil that came from someone you assumed to be good.

"Did you see Elizabeth, Ramone, and Callie leave?" I asked. "Were they alone?"

Slater shook his head. "I fell asleep almost immediately. Ramone left the room without disturbing me. I don't know if someone woke him or if he heard something and got up."

That spoke for itself, until Michael added, "It's possible they didn't leave of their own volition. They may have been coerced."

Slater nodded up and down vehemently. "That's more likely the case. Elizabeth loves that bairn and she loves her brother. If they were in danger, she would do whatever she had to do to keep them from being hurt. Leaving may have been her way of protecting us, too."

"I agree. She would do anything to keep Callie safe. Even betray us," Reginald said.

Slater considered that. "She would. She would nae want to, but she would die to protect that infant. She would likely sacrifice all of us."

It was an assessment that stopped the conversation for a full minute as we all considered the danger to Callie, and to ourselves. "How can we find them?" I asked.

"We don't have to go anywhere." Michael spoke to me. "They'll come looking for you."

Michael's words terrified me. I heard the truth in his pronouncement and I didn't want to believe it. "If they're after me, then we should leave Victoria, maybe drive to Gadsden." I didn't want to stay where Gabriel could find me so easily. He could find me anywhere I went, but we didn't have to make it easy for him.

"It's pointless to leave," Slater said. "The die has been cast. We are here. No matter where we go, they'll be there. Mission was the most dangerous place we could have been, because Lucais and his followers have been corrupted. We've improved our position by coming here. We have the safety of the kirk around us." He hesitated before he went on. "If we leave Elizabeth, Ramone, and the baby, if they have outlived their usefulness as bait, he may kill them."

I shook my head. "He won't harm Callie, I hope." But I didn't know. None of us knew. Father Kilroy was listening, but he didn't offer any support for my statement.

Slater grimaced. "If his goal is Callie, then Elizabeth and her brother are expendable." His big hands clenched into fists of helplessness.

"We don't know that," Reginald said, trying to quell the rising emotions. "We proceed as if Callie and the Maslows are still alive. To understand their value, we have to know what Gabriel ultimately wants. I agree with Raissa. I believe it's the child. Callie has potential we can't even imagine. Her touch... she can heal. Think about the wound to Elizabeth. The gunshot was nearly fatal. When she held Callie, she healed." He nodded at me.

I hadn't had a chance to tell Reginald what Madame had told me. And I didn't want to in front of everyone else. "It's true." I'd given Reginald the details of her wound. "I took the stitches out before we left Mission. She was already healing over them."

"When Ramone held her, after whatever happened in the barn, he healed quickly." Reginald looked at me and I shook my head. I didn't want him to mention what I'd seen with the buzzards and Callie's white-stone eyes.

"The child is special," Michael agreed.

"The child is an innocent," Father Kilroy said. "She must be saved, for I assume she's never been baptized. The church Lucais installed in Mission doesn't believe in baptism."

He was right about that. But how did we do that? We couldn't trust anything Gabriel said—or anyone who might be under his influence.

Even me.

"Gabriel wants power," Michael said. "Power to turn the humans around him to darkness. He destroys their souls in his hatred of the divine creation. He craves their energy like a drunkard needs wine."

"But how does Raissa give him more power?" Reginald asked. The room was silent as we waited for Michael to explain.

"Gabriel—though that isn't his true name—wants to procreate. He wants progeny to rule the Earth. Raissa could give him children with vast powers." Michael had hit upon exactly the same thing Madam had said.

"No!" I hadn't meant to speak, but the thought was hideous.

"Not a chance of that happening," Reginald said stoutly.

"What if there was a way for Gabriel to draw innocents to him?" Michael seemed to feel his way into his explanation. "What if he needs those who are inclined to work for a better world? Those who speak out for the helpless? Elizabeth has a talent. She and Ruth both connected with Hildy, a little girl who saw things she could never understand. Hildy could hear the voice of nature, of the wild things. Ruth and Elizabeth were helping her figure out what that meant."

"And Raissa helps lost spirits find their way to move on," Reginald said. "She helps others."

Michael turned slowly to face each of us. "There are those who give and those who take."

"The givers are marked with God's blessing," Father Kilroy said.

"There was a time when people believed in miracles. Now, so many of the old abilities are lost," Slater said. "My gran knew a healer woman could bring a person back from near death. She came 'round with some travelers each summer. Folks were afraid of her, but not my gran. My gran said she was blessed with a gift from God."

"What happened to her?" I asked.

"I don't know." Slater sighed deeply. "One year she just didn't come back. My gran went into the woods and said a prayer for her. I was a tot, and the doings of the grownups didn't stick with me. That's all I remember."

The circle of stones at Ruth's place. It had been a sacred place for many years. I'd assumed the Indians had made it to worship their gods and beliefs, and that was likely. But it could also have served another purpose. Had Ruth and Elizabeth used it too? Women in touch with the power of healing and helping others?

As if he read my thoughts, Michael said, "It's fallen to us to stop this evil. I wish we could wait until tomorrow when your friends arrive, but I don't think we can."

"What are we going to do?" Father Kilroy asked.

Michael turned to me. "I'm sorry, Raissa. We can't talk in front of you."

"What?" I was outraged.

"You can't know our plans," he insisted. "If Gabriel is able to tap into your thoughts, your memories, you can't know what we're planning."

Reginald put a hand on my shoulder. "He's right. I hadn't

thought of it, but he is right. You can play an even more important role, Raissa, by thinking of false things. We'll create a plan for you to know, and hope that Gabriel will attempt to feed off your thoughts. While—" He stopped abruptly because even knowing there was a false plan was dangerous.

"I can focus my thoughts, I think." I saw real potential here. "I will let him know only what we wish him to know."

"He's outside," Michael said suddenly.

"How do you know?" I asked.

He shook his head. "I just know. It's my gift."

"Is there a place of safety for Raissa?" Reginald asked.

"In the cloister. The sisters will protect her with their lives." Father Kilroy was pale, but he was not a coward. "Prepare, men. The battle has come to us."

# CHAPTER 33

The four sisters who resided in St. Lucy's Catholic Church were older than I was. They moved about in the dim room I'd been sent to for protection like wraiths, lighting candles, murmuring prayers, and keeping a watchful eye on me.

The room was large and filled with a heavy wooden table and chairs, a hutch with dishes, and bookcases crammed full of leather-bound volumes. I took a seat in a chair beside a mullioned window where I had a good view of the churchyard and the street. The avian watchers were back. They made no effort to hide, roosting in plain sight in the branches of the oak trees that lined the front of the church. With a start, I realized that human watchers were there too, six of them, standing under the trees.

The men stood like vultures, hands dangling at their sides. Two held rifles. I wondered if it would do any good to call the police. I'm sure Father Kilroy had thought of it. I was pretty certain that no one was coming to rescue us. The only good news was that dawn was breaking. Light was spilling across the churchyard, and it was easier to see our foes. But also easier for them to see us.

I wasn't much of a smoker, but I wished for a cigarette, more for the comfort of Reginald's presence than for the tobacco. I was never as afraid when he was with me. Now it felt as if my heart constantly stuttered. Terror had me in its grip. I knew how powerful Gabriel was.

A big touring car pulled up to the church and I recognized that it belonged to Lucais Wilkins. He had at least five men with him, all heavily armed. They silently got out of the car, nodding to the men in the edge of the churchyard bushes. Slater, Reginald, and Michael had brought guns from Elizabeth's, but the supply of ammunition was very low. I suspected the Catholic church had little use for bullets.

"Those are bad men," one of the sisters said. She'd come up on my shoulder without my noticing.

"Yes, they are." I didn't say more because I didn't want to scare the sisters. They were in danger because we'd sought refuge in the church.

"My name is Sister Teresa. Will they kill us?" she asked.

"I hope not." I couldn't tell her the absolute truth but I wasn't going to lie. I had no doubt Lucais and his men would gut a nun as quickly as they would a deer or fish. These men were brutes, and in their eyes no life other than their own held value.

Another sister who said her name was Mary Margaret joined us at the window. We stared out into the street, where the rising sun was now giving definition to the rutted clay road and the buildings across the street. Gabriel suddenly appeared beside the car, but I knew the sisters couldn't see him. I feared he could see me in the window and I drew back.

"What is it?" Sister Teresa asked.

"It is possible you may have to restrain me."

"Why should we do that?" Sister Rosamunde, who'd retrieved Slater, finally spoke.

I had to trust that the sisters believed in good and evil. That they wouldn't think I'd lost touch with reality. "There's a dark entity trying to control me. I intend to fight as hard as I can, but I don't know that I can defeat him."

"Are you possessed?" Mary Margaret asked breathlessly.

"Not at this time, but it's possible I could be." This wasn't what I considered a possession, in the classic religious sense. But because I had no training in fallen angels, I didn't know if Gabriel was technically considered a demon. One fallen angel, Lucifer, had become the King of Hell. Stories of exorcisms were part of the fiction I enjoyed, where good could conquer evil in a ritual. I wasn't possessed in the sense that the demon was inside my flesh, making me scream and rant and curse against God. No, Gabriel was far more insidious. I felt the tentacles of his thoughts sliding into my mind.

"We have experience with possession," the third sister said. "I'm Ursaline. I've assisted in casting out demons." She was a serene woman, older than the other two. "If it becomes necessary, I'll restrain you. To keep you from hurting yourself or others."

"It may not be necessary, but if I jeopardize the safety of anyone here, don't hesitate."

They all nodded.

Sister Ursaline asked, "This dark entity, do you know its name?"

"It calls itself Gabriel, and claims that it's an angel."

"What does Gabriel hope to gain by harming you and the people you travel with?"

It was a question I'd struggled with. "Power, a connection

with a human, control of other humans to bend them to evil?"
I shook my head. "I don't know. A woman and a child have
been murdered."

"A child," the nuns whispered.

"A little girl. An innocent."

"And why are you a target of this Gabriel?"

I wondered if I should tell her the truth. She couldn't help
me unless I did. "I can communicate with the spirits of the
dead. I see them. I help them to deliver messages or understand what happened to them. I assist them in leaving
this plane."

"Your gift has drawn this darkness to you," Sister Teresa
said.

She was so calm, eerily calm. "You don't doubt me?"

She shook her head. "I've seen a powerful exorcist cast a
demon out. It's never without cost, but if the host is strong
enough, it can be done." She touched my chin and lifted my
face to the light from the window. "You're strong."

"He has another woman and her child. A child he claims as
his own."

The younger sisters gasped, but the older one didn't flinch.
"Nephilim. The greatest desire of the fallen angels is to create
their own children. To live among men and draw them to darkness. In the heavenly realm, angels know neither pain nor pleasure. Their jealousy of man, God's creation that can experience
pleasure, drove some to disobey God. It's why they were cast
out. If this Gabriel has lain with a human woman, the child is
an abomination."

"Callie isn't a Nephilim." I couldn't prove it, but I also
couldn't let them harm her because they feared her. "She's just
a little baby."

The nun walked away from the window, but turned back to

me. "He is coming. He is very close now. Remember, when the entity is attempting to gain entrance to your mind, there is also access to his emotions, thoughts, and desires. Use that access, if you can."

"How?"

"He'll reveal a weakness. Watch for it."

"You said you'd worked with possessed people. How do you cast out a demon?"

"I worked with a priest performing exorcisms." She was matter-of-fact about something that I'd only heard rumors about. Even Madam, for all of her experience dealing with spirits both good and evil, had never witnessed an exorcism.

"Did you cast out a demon?"

"I've witnessed successful exorcisms, but—" she broke off. "They're dangerous. It's difficult to get the church to sanction an exorcism, but some priests and nuns do them anyway, if the need is great. I'm here because a young girl died. We couldn't save her. We failed. My punishment was being sent here, to Victoria. But I know what to do if I must."

"How did you know the girl wasn't mentally ill?" I thought how close a young woman I'd been hired to help had come to an irreversible mental operation. Camilla had been possessed —by the spirit of an ancestor. And she'd almost had a probe tapped into her brain to make her docile and compliant. Luck-ily, we'd been able to prevent that from happening.

"Marcella had moments of lucidity when she begged for our help. She battled fiercely for her soul. I only hope she was freed from the shackles of the demon when she died."

I'd read an account of an exorcism in Italy. I'd considered that the details might have been exaggerated. Now I found myself believing they were true. The possessed man had broken the bones in his thighs and arms straining against the restraints that held him. The demon had been cast out, but the man had never fully recovered.

"When she died, where did the demon go?" This was a very personal question for me.

"A demon has no use for a dead body. They must flee or die also."

"If this dark angel comes for me, he will try to twist my thoughts and emotions."

She nodded. "We will restrain you. There are plants that can sedate you, too, but that would only delay the inevitable."

"Have you performed an exorcism in Alabama?"

She didn't answer for a long time. "Only one. On a young man who attacked a woman with an ax."

I knew who it was. "Junior Albee."

She nodded. "The young woman who was attacked accused Junior. There was an outcry against him. A mob was forming, claiming that Junior should hang. Junior's father arranged for the exorcism and paid the church. The young man was saved from the gallows once the sheriff was convinced his devil had been cast out. He was damaged, though. The ordeal affected his mind."

An idea had started to form in my mind. "Sister Ursaline, if I were to flee from here, what route would I take?"

"Father Kilroy said to keep you safe." All four sisters gathered around me. "We won't let you leave."

"It's just a question. I will stay here, but I have an idea. I need to know a secret way to leave, the details of what I would see on the journey. I may be able to trick Gabriel." I needed the information quickly. I could feel the pinchers of Gabriel's reach, like the legs of a roach, prying at my mind.

Sister Teresa nodded. "At the end of the hall is a door that leads into the back of the church property. Since the tornado two years ago, what was once a garden is now a wilderness. Deer and wild creatures come up to eat what we put out for them so there are trails that wind through the trees and thick bushes. You could take those trails."

"Tell me the plants I would see. The slope of the ground. What I might hear and smell?"

She supplied the details of the old wilderness garden that stretched behind the church into the deep woods. There were no neighborhoods nearby, only the thick forest.

"Is there a river or stream there?" I was visualizing a route, focusing completely on the sensation of being in the dense thicket. I imagined the limbs slapping at my legs and face, and the drone of bloodsucking insects. My body was still welted from my last adventure in the woods and it was easy to bring those sensations to the fore.

"Yes, a stream, shallow enough to wade through."

I could see my feet, in the short boots I wore, moving through the cool water of the running stream. I reached down and brought handfuls of water to my face to calm the bites from the insects.

Gabriel pried and poked around the edge of the narrative I mentally clung to. I would not let him dig deeper into my precious memories or the emotions that were mine and mine alone. He was an intruder, an unwanted thief coming to steal the essence of who I was and turn it against my friends. I littered the path with sounds and sensations, driving him out, forcing him to follow me on my imaginary journey.

"Are you okay?" Sister Luisa asked.

"Yes."

"Should I get Father Kilroy?"

"No. Don't disturb the men. They have to be able to concentrate and fight."

"Why do these men want to hurt you?" One of the sisters at the window stared down at Lucais and his men.

"Because they're evil." I had no doubt I spoke the truth. "They serve the darkness." I couldn't be distracted from leading Gabriel away. I could see he was looking at the church and then toward the thicket. He was tempted to follow my thoughts. If I could lead him away...he started toward the side of the church. "Where does this woodland path end?"

Sister Ursaline smiled. "A mechanic shop. The only one for miles around. Junior Albee runs it. He survived his ordeal, but he's a—"

"He's a little slow, but a good mechanic." I finished for her. "And so my journey through the woods ends up where I knew I'd have to go. Somehow, Junior Albee is also a part of this."

"You're only going to imagine going there, right?" Sister Rosamunde asked. "We can't let you leave."

"Only in my mind." I smiled to hide the lie. I would take Gabriel into the woods with my mind, but I couldn't trick him for long. He'd catch on that he was tracking only my thoughts. But that would give Reginald, Slater, and Michael time to hunt for Elizabeth and her family. "Could you leave me so I can focus on my journey?"

Sister Ursaline was not so easily tricked. "Perhaps we should restrain you."

"Sit outside the door. I can't leave. But I must concentrate hard if I'm to shift the danger away from the church. I simply want to keep everyone as safe as I can."

They all nodded and filed silently from the room. I heard the click of the lock.

Looking out the window, I saw Lucais ordering his men into a formation to storm the church. There was no sign of anyone else on the street. The day had broken, but no one was bustling about. Gabriel stood beside the car, and he seemed to be sniffing the air. Could I really deceive him? I had to try.

I closed my eyes and concentrated on opening the door and slipping down the cool corridor toward the exterior exit. I was on my journey to Junior Albee's shop. As I visualized myself stepping into the dim interior of the woods, I peeked out the window and was gratified to see that Gabriel was moving toward the woods.

# CHAPTER 34

I t chaffed me that I couldn't know what the men were going to do to rescue Elizabeth, Ramone, and Callie. Their plans were secret from me, but I knew they would try no matter how desperate their scheme. I didn't doubt that. Even if they suspected Elizabeth had lured us to Sand Mountain. Reginald would risk everything if he thought he could save her and Callie. Slater and Michael seemed equally dedicated to saving her and Callie.

I pushed my thoughts away from that, clinging to the sensation of going through the calf-high weeds and underbrush soaked with dew. I was being followed. Someone sly and silent was behind me, keeping pace with me, careless of the crackle of sticks or the angry cry of a mockingbird. Gabriel was with me, which made me question who had the Maslows. If not Gabriel or Lucais Wilkins, who? Where were they?

I felt Gabriel trying to edge into my mind, trying to bleed me of my secrets and thoughts. Using mental imaging, I leaned against a tree trunk to get my breath, and I felt intensely the warming of the day, the sweat moving down my back and between my breasts. I'd never considered sweating sensual, but I felt the response from Gabriel. He pushed harder into my mind. He was trying to physically locate me, but he was stymied. For the moment. I focused on the drone of yellow flies and their painful bites as three found exposed flesh on my bare arms and neck. The pain helped me shake free of Gabriel's menace. I plowed deeper into the woods in my mind. The longer I could keep Gabriel occupied, the better the chance the men had to enact a rescue.

I'd only gone a short distance when I realized Gabriel was back. This time with a lulling memory of a cool night on Folly Beach at Charleston with the ocean breeze lifting my long hair. It was before the war, before I cut my hair and my ties to my old life and stepped into the modern world as a high school teacher.

The sound of hammers turned me toward the boardwalk under construction. The workers' noise was muffled by the shushing sound of the surf. The day was so beautiful that it was almost painful to look out on the sand and cresting waves.

Plans for the pavilion were the big news in the city, but on this evening, the beach was deserted. A storm was moving in fast from the East, and I remembered the tales of pirate ships, shipwrecks, and danger that my parents had told me when I was little. I missed them, and the pang of loss almost made me stagger. Instantly I felt the push of Gabriel into my emotions. I forced myself away from the ocean and returned to the hot woods of Victoria, Alabama.

I tried hard to hold onto the feel of the tree bark against my back and hands, the drone of the flies. Birds cried in the distance, warning against my intrusion into their wild terrain. Pushing off the tree I started forward down a trail where brambles ripped at my bare legs above my little boots. Ferns hid roots that almost tripped me. I squeezed every bit of intensity—tactile, aural, and visual—from my imagination. Gabriel's grip loosened.

*Keep moving, keep moving, keep moving.* I settled on that mantra and pushed on, now going uphill, scrabbling in the leaves and tree roots. At the top of an incline, I paused to search for the trail. It had suddenly disappeared. Before it had been clearly marked. Almost too late, I realized this was Gabriel, exerting his will once more. He'd hidden the way from me—the way I'd created in my own mind. He was on to me, I feared, and this mental game I played with him. How much longer could I keep him focused on me?

For a brief moment, I mentally returned to the room where my physical body remained by the window, hidden from view from the street. The watchers, both vulture and human, remained at the front, but Lucais and his men, the touring car, and Gabriel were all gone. Were they chasing Reginald, Slater, and Michael? I didn't know. Couldn't know.

Gabriel, I hoped, was in the woods behind the church looking for me. Lucais, with his thugs and guns, was a serious threat, but not nearly the danger Gabriel could be if he decided to attack my friends.

The room in the church was very quiet, and I suspected the sisters had gone about their daily routine, trusting me to remain in the room. They'd locked the door, but I doubted they'd set a guard. It wouldn't matter anyway. I pried open the window. There was just enough room for me to slip out and drop into the shrubbery around the church. I'd reached my decision. There was no waiting for my uncle and Madam to arrive. Time was against us. Elizabeth and Callie would soon be lost to me, either through death or corruption.

I landed soft and crept through the thick vegetation,

taking care lest one of the human watchers saw me. The longer I could hide my location, the more help I would be to Reginald and the others. Slipping along the side of the church, I made it to the woods. The path wasn't hard to find. It was much as I imagined it. I started down it at a trot.

This time I meant to be found. No longer would I hide from Gabriel or his followers. Lucais Wilkins couldn't scare me anymore. Nor the buzzards. I'd come upon an idea, a way to win this battle. I had no clue if it would work and no one to ask. In an attempt to save the others, I put only myself at risk.

I'd had little sleep the day and night before, and I was exhausted, but I pushed deeper into the woods. *Come and find me. Come and find me, Gabriel.* I projected those thoughts as if I played an innocent game of Hide-and-Seek. Gabriel was behind me. I heard him. He could move as silently as a feather through the wind, so he was deliberately letting me know he was following me. Deeper and deeper into the woods. Farther and farther away from safety and my friends. I hoped he believed he was herding me toward his ultimate win. As long as he believed he was going to conquer me, he would follow.

The woods were every bit as difficult and treacherous as I'd imagined. It was September, but the heat was unrelenting, the insects ravenous. In the thick woods with underbrush there was no breeze. Sweat poured down my body, making me slick enough that some of the briars actually slid off my skin without snagging me.

I stayed on the trail and pushed hard, going as fast as I could. If I could make the mechanic shop, there was a chance the Albee boy might know how to help me. I doubted he'd been possessed by a demon, but he'd survived an exorcism. I believed he'd survived an attempt at possession by a dark angel. Perhaps he held some knowledge that might save me.

The truth I knew was that I was not really taking a risk by my actions. Gabriel would follow me to Mobile or New Orleans or Katmandu. No matter where I went, if he wanted me, he would find me. Here, with my friends near and my uncle and Madam on the way, I stood the greatest chance of survival. If I could only make it a little while longer. I knew one other truth, too. Gabriel was enjoying this hunt. He had the power to stop me at any time, just as he'd stopped me in my dreams. He could sink my feet into the ground like the deep roots of a white oak tree and I would be helpless to fight him. Until he did, I forced myself through the woods.

The path had narrowed as it came down an incline. At the base of the hill was a small creek, just as I'd imagined. I half-slid down to it and sank into the water. My body was raw from the bugs and brambles. The water was clear and cold, murmuring as it skimmed over boulders and rocks. I sank into the water and splashed it up on my face, wetting my hair. I could stay here forever, sinking beneath the cool water as it soothed my skin.

The pool was only waist deep, but I ducked beneath the surface, completely immersed, and finally came up for air.

Gabriel stood on the bank, watching me.

# CHAPTER 35

"Come out of the water," he said.

He didn't compel me, but I obeyed anyway because I needed time to think. The water pulled at my skirt and blouse, but there was no supernatural force slowing me. I clambered up the bank and sat down on a rock, removing my boots that had once been fashionable. I busied myself, trying to calm the pounding of my heart.

"You led me a merry chase." Gabriel came closer.

In all the times I'd seen him, I'd never really paid close attention to his features. He was handsome, incredibly so. His dark hair was a match for Elizabeth's inky curls and his brown eyes held a soft glow. Thin, masculine lips formed a sensual mouth. His features were symmetrical except for a small scar that ran from the corner of his eye to his jawbone and marred the left side of his face. It didn't detract from his beauty, but somehow enhanced it. How had I never noticed?

He touched the scar. "A battle wound."

"Angels have the power to heal, yet you choose to wear your scar. Why?"

"Perfection can be boring."

"How did it happen?" I wasn't feigning curiosity. Madam had told me that by accessing Gabriel's thoughts I might gain an advantage. When he talked about himself, he revealed things. He was vain. He'd shown me that. What else could I uncover? I had to find some way to defeat him, otherwise he would kill my friends and take Callie.

"A farmer thought I was flirting with his wife. He attacked me with a cleaver."

"And were you? Flirting with his wife?"

His smile was self-satisfied. "Eternity can be dull. We should never have been forbidden to mate. We were denied the ability to feel the pleasures of sex. Forbidden. Because that joy was to be special for the inferior creation of humans."

The meat cleaver was an added detail that brought me back to Ruth Whelan and her bloody, brutal death, but it was his anger at humans that I focused on. This was definitely a clue. Gabriel was involved in Ruth's demise. He'd laid it out there for me to discover, a puzzle he believed I was incapable of solving. Now I only had to figure out how it fit into the web of evil and blood in Mission. "Were you involved with Ruth?"

"No. Though she spoke my native language. Imagine her surprise when I answered her in Hebrew." He seemed to grow larger, to swell. "Just before she died."

It clicked. "The journal that Elizabeth had kept was written in Hebrew. Why?" I had to keep him occupied and his vanity would work to my benefit. He would want to show me how superior he was.

"Hebrew is the language of the angels. Ruth and Elizabeth are highly educated women, but only Ruth spoke my tongue."

"Yet you chose Elizabeth to be your mate. She said you're Callie's father."

"Why is that of interest to you?" He was toying with me, amusing himself because he knew I was afraid of him.

"It's forbidden for angels to...fornicate with humans. You put yourself at great risk of punishment in creating Callie."

He laughed, and it made him even more attractive. "Rules are meant to be broken. Not all angels follow the rules, as you surely know by now. Those of us who rebelled against the rules, well, we're here. At least those of us who survived God's retribution. We've remained here in isolated places, searching for those who desire what we can give them. Power. Wealth. Success. Believe me, most humans are only too willing to trade their souls for power and comfort."

I was no Biblical scholar, though I'd been exposed to religious doctrine. I tried to remember what Madam and the Sisters and Father Kilroy had said. Most of all, I had to keep him here, with me, even though I understood that when he stopped talking, he meant to hurt me. "Was it worth it? Being cast down?"

"There are benefits." He reached out and brushed his fingertips under my jaw. "The pleasures of the flesh are not to be denied. Soon, I'll show you. I'll push those memories of Alex right out of your head." He stepped back.

To lose my memories would be to lose my identity. Oh, he knew how to strike at my deepest fear. I lifted my chin. "You and the other fallen angels lost everything. What benefits could possibly outweigh your angelic heritage?"

"Here, no one checks my power. Humans are easily tempted with baubles, easily manipulated. They're weak and can't resist. You're a weak and inferior creation, and one day our Father will see it and put you aside. For now, corrupting you passes the time." He eased closer again. "So many questions to stall the inevitable. You will be mine, Raissa. No one is coming to save you. You took so many precautions to get me here, alone, so we could finish what we started." His thumb traced over my lips. I couldn't move away from him. My feet were anchored solidly in the rock. He was playing with me, teasing me, and I could feel my body respond even as my spirit rebelled against him.

"Are you attracted to all human women?" I found it harder to talk.

"Not all. Still, some are worth the risk."

"What risk? I can't move or defend myself if you desire to make me helpless. How is there a risk for you?"

"To enjoy the pleasure of a woman, I have to assume human form."

"You need a willing vessel?"

There was no answer, just the flutter of wings as the buzzards flew around me from all directions. It was as if they were driven mad by Gabriel, who had folded himself in his own dark wings. The fetid smell of death wafted from the buzzards' wings as they brushed my face, making me gag. I shut my eyes, praying for strength to combat whatever was coming at me.

A rustling in the woods told me someone was coming. I didn't dare look. I didn't want to give Reginald away, if it was him.

"Raissa?" Gabriel's voice had changed. It had more lilt.

I opened my eyes to face my fate. Ramone was standing where Gabriel had been. He wore the same clothes he'd had on when last I saw him. The scar from his eye to his jaw was much fainter than it had been on Gabriel. He licked his bottom lip. "Hello, Raissa."

"Not Ramone." I wanted to cry. This was Elizabeth's

brother, her family, the one she'd risked everything to find. "Don't take him."

"Oh, he's been mine for a while now." He held out his hands and turned them over. "Clumsy and earthbound, but with such intensity of feeling. Do you understand the joys of eating a peach, or kissing a woman, or feeling the cool water of a stream run across your flesh? It's exquisite—and this has all been denied me."

I recognized those hands, from my dream of Hildy and her death. It had been Ramone. He'd snapped Hildy's neck and thrown her in the well. He'd probably killed Ruth, too. Not really Ramone, of course, but Ramone guided by Gabriel. "Why would you even want us humans? We grow old. Our bodies fail."

"Eternity is not the benefit you may think." He paced around me, eyeing me like a heifer at an auction.

"You should leave. And leave Ramone too. He's of no use to you. Give him back to Elizabeth. She thought she truly loved you."

"As I said, humans are so easily tempted. But I need Ramone. He'll serve for this one last use. He won't last long now."

"Why not let him go?"

"I'm trapped in this flesh until I can set it aside. When I leave, his deterioration will be quick." He smiled as if he'd told a joke.

My heart sank in my chest. Ramone had never had a chance. Whatever tidbit of power or pleasure Gabriel had dangled before him, he'd grabbed it, hook and all. Now if Gabriel left him, he would simply die.

A realization hit me. If Gabriel had truly seduced Elizabeth, slept with her, and produced a child, it stood to reason that he had not appeared in the body of her brother. He'd used someone else. Someone in Mission. Someone he could take control of and then abandon.

"Who else have you corrupted?" I asked.

"You're very clever, Raissa. Clever and helpless." There was a hint of anger in his tone. "Come here," he said, and I couldn't resist him. My body moved forward, though I fought against it with everything in me.

My clothes clung to me, and his gaze moved over my body, lingering on my breasts that were too visible beneath the wet material of my blouse.

"Leave me alone. Reginald and my uncle will kill you."

"No doubt they'll try." Ramone was completely unmoved by my threat.

"Is it really worth it, the risk you're taking?" I wasn't certain what that risk might be, but I meant to emphasize it.

"To lay with a human woman is a pleasure I demand. It should have been ours."

"You have immortality. We die, and you don't," I said. Even though I was standing in the sun, I was cold. I'd underestimated the danger, and now it was too late to better prepare. Gabriel had immense powers. He had the power to make me desire him, and I could feel those primal needs, unwanted and terrifying, beginning to curl through my body. A sob escaped me, and he laughed.

"You're the one who brought me out here into the woods, where we could be alone." He stepped closer to me, blocking my view, even blocking out the sun so that a darkness fell around us. This was his power, and I feared he would soon immobilize me and pry into my mind with his visions and memories. And possibly worse.

"Let Elizabeth go," I said. "She only wants to raise her child in safety. I won't fight if you'll let her go."

He chuckled. "You won't fight for long, no matter about the woman and her infant."

"Where are Elizabeth and Callie?"

He didn't seem to understand my question.

"Where's your sister and niece? Are they safe?" I hoped to reach any part of Ramone that was left.

He came close enough that he could reach out and touch my wet hair. "I've been thinking about this ever since I saw you."

"Stay away from me."

"I can control your mind," he said. "Feel your feet sinking into the rocks."

I was planted in the stone as surely as if I'd grown there. I couldn't run or escape. He could do whatever he wanted. And he would.

"Come with me." Ramone held out his hand and I put mine in it completely against my will. Gabriel had taken control of Ramone, and Ramone now controlled me.

He led me deeper into the woods to a place where a bed of ferns had grown around the base of several sycamore trees. The leaves, anticipating fall, had just begun to shift to vivid reds and golds, the first sign that the relentless summer was drawing to a close.

"Lie down," he said, and I did. I had no will. My body obeyed him, but my mind was still fighting.

"Don't do this."

"If we should have a child, now that would be a masterful creation. Our child would be a Nephilim. Imagine the power our union would harness. The right that has so long been denied me would be mine."

I knew then that Callie wasn't his. I had no idea who'd gotten Elizabeth pregnant, but it wasn't an angel. No doubt she'd been tricked and seduced, but if Gabriel wasn't the father, then Callie was human. "Where are Callie and Elizabeth?"

"Waiting for you. They no longer interest me. You're the one I wanted. You never should have come to Mission, Raissa. Never. You aren't powerful or knowledgeable enough to fight me. You're going to lose your soul."

He said it with such relish. "Who killed Ruth Whelan? Please, tell me that."

"I did. In the body of Ramone. He has served me well, as I said. But he's deteriorating now. Perhaps your Reginald would make a suitable vessel. Or that Slater. He's physically strong. He'd last."

I shuddered and forced myself to keep him talking. "And Lucais Wilkins. What is he to you?"

"Lucais is a most loyal servant. He's been handsomely rewarded for his troubles. Now enough questions."

My body was pressed down into the ferns with enough force to knock the wind from my lungs. This was not going to be gentle or tender. This was going to be by force. If I survived this, I would be mentally damaged. Like Junior Albee. It wasn't the exorcism that damaged him, but the possession.

My fingers dug into the ferns as I grabbed them with everything I had, trying to hold my body rigid.

Ramone knelt beside me and began to slowly unbutton my blouse. "You with your modern hair, your desire for adventure and a career. This will be your lifetime experience," he said.

My fingers found a rock the size of an orange hidden in the ferns. I gripped it, but I didn't know if I could lift it. He controlled me completely, except for the tears that leaked down the sides of my face. I didn't want to cry, because I knew it would give him pleasure, but I couldn't help it.

"When I'm done with you, I'm going after your partner and the Scot. Then the nuns and priest. I'll wipe them all away."

I wanted to beg him to leave them alone, but he wouldn't listen. He had a foothold in this part of the world, and he knew how to use people to his own aims.

He opened my shirt and leaned down to kiss my neck and chest. "The human body is sweet," he said, taking his time. He kissed my lips and bit me with enough savagery to draw blood.

The pain shot through me, a white-hot bolt. My arm came up, rock in hand, and I smashed him as hard as I could in the temple. Blood spurted in my face, and Gabriel roared. "You're going to die, you stupid—"

"Samyaza!" Suddenly Reginald stood on the path not twenty yards away. "I know your name. Samyaza. You are a fallen watcher and you must abandon her. It is forbidden."

I had no idea what Reginald was talking about, or where he'd come from. I couldn't help him. Gabriel grabbed me by the throat and began to squeeze. From the branches of the trees around us, the buzzards took flight. They rose high into the air, swooping down toward Reginald. They screamed their fury at him and swooped low. He hit one with the butt of a rifle, and he held his ground.

"Let her go! Ramone, if you're in there, get off her now. I'll kill you." He raised the rifle to his shoulder.

Ramone ignored him, applying more pressure. "You'll die on this spot," he said softly to me. "He can't stop me."

"Samyaza," I repeated in a croak. When he released the

pressure slightly, I drank in air. "That's your name. You were never Gabriel. You lied even about that."

From down the trail a gun roared and a bullet hit the angel between the eyes. He grinned and tightened his grip, supreme in his victory. Not three second later, he fell dead on top of me.

"Raissa." Reginald was running toward me. I was no longer held in Samyaza's dark grip but I couldn't move because the dead weight of Ramone's body pinned me to the ground. I pushed at him, trying to scrabble out from under him, frantic to get the weight off me. Reginald grabbed his shoulder and threw him to the side. My partner reached down and pulled me to my feet, turning away to allow me time to adjust my clothes.

"Are you okay?" Reginald was shaken, but when the buzzards came at us, he discharged the gun again. One fell to the ground and the others soared high and disappeared among the treetops.

"Yes." I wasn't, but yes was easier.

"Raissa, he could have killed you."

I nodded. "But he didn't."

"We found Elizabeth and Callie. They're safe. She told me how Ramone convinced her to leave the inn and then she realized he was not her brother any longer. Ramone has been... gone for a long time."

"Gone?"

"Not dead, but not Ramone."

Tears pressed at my eyelids. I walked back to the creek and sank into the cold water, washing off the blood and brains, sinking beneath the clear, cold creek. When I came up for air, I realized my clothes were soiled. No matter how I rubbed at my blouse, the bloodstain remained. I gagged and Reginald waded into the water to hold me.

"I'm sorry about Ramone. He was hurting you."

"It wasn't Ramone. And it wasn't Gabriel. He was never an archangel, only a fallen angel. And now he's dead. It was the only way."

"I never trusted him, but Elizabeth was so happy to see him. He just showed up conveniently to attach himself to us, but I wanted to believe it was her brother, safely home at last."

"Poor Elizabeth." She had lost her best friends, Ruth and Hildy, and now her brother. How many other losses were in store for us?

Reginald helped me out of the stream and eased me onto a rock to sit in the sun. "What were you thinking, Raissa? He was going to kill you."

"I wanted to lead him away from you, so you could find Elizabeth and Callie."

"You did that. They're safe."

"What about Lucais and those awful men?"

"Your uncle will be here in a matter of hours. He has the influence to handle this. I'm still trying to sort out Lucais Wilkins's role in all of this. We'll know more when we find him."

"And Slater and Michael?"

"They're with Elizabeth. They're all in the church."

"I don't want to go there yet."

"Then let's just sit here in the sun for a little while. We both need to dry off, and it won't take long in this heat." He sat beside me but he didn't hover.

The complete lack of Gabriel in my mind was a shock. My mind and my body had been violated, but now there was an eerie calm. I felt the sun on my arms and back, and I heard the sweet music of a songbird. The woods were coming back to life, and so would I.

"Samyaza. How did you know his name?" I asked.

"Michael told me. Samyaza was the leader of the angels who were thrown down out of heaven for their lustful contact with human women. The men who are always at the edge of town or the woods—they're watchers, the Grigori, or what remains of the other fallen angels."

I looked back to Ramone's body lying on its side, eyes wide open and staring. "Is he really dead? Samyaza, I mean."

"Yes."

"But he was immortal." I was afraid to believe it was really over.

"At all times except when inhabiting a human body. He could mentally torment you with visions and dreams and false emotions in his angelic form. But he couldn't consummate the...well, unless he took a human form. When you hit him with the rock and he was momentarily stunned, I believed I could kill him with a bullet. So I took the shot."

"Thank goodness you came. How did you know where to find me?"

"The sisters told me about your questions, about your desire to know the wooded trails and where they would lead. It was the only way you could have gone."

I put on my boots and stood up. I couldn't think anymore. I didn't want to think. I needed to move, and the only place to go was the church. Reginald stood also and together we started down the path. My boots were ruined, but I had no option but to keep walking. We took our time, hiding from the afternoon sun in the shade.

"What's going to happen to Slater?" I finally asked.

"He's still a wanted criminal, but your uncle will intervene on his behalf. We still have Ruth's journal, remember? I suspect that once we can translate it and the names are revealed, there'll be great changes in Mission. Lucais Wilkins will face the consequences of his actions."

"I know who killed Ruth and Hildy. It was Ramone. Well, not Ramone but you know what I mean. But we can't prove it." We hadn't really accomplished the task we'd come here to do. We might save Slater, but that wasn't justice. Nothing would bring back Ruth or Hildy or reverse the abuse of the town's women and children.

"We aren't done here yet," Reginald said. "All of those men who worked with Lucais Wilkins will be charged with various crimes and punished."

Punishment wasn't necessarily justice. But there was one bit of good news I hadn't shared. "Callie isn't a Nephilim."

"Father Kilroy is talking to Elizabeth. Perhaps he can shed some light on who Callie's father really is."

Reginald's calm assurance boosted my spirits. I refused to think about Ramone's body, lying in the dirt beneath a sycamore tree. Or what Samyaza had tried to do to me. Or what might have happened had he been successful. It was too much.

"I want to spend some time with Madam in New Orleans," I said instead. "I have to be better prepared."

"I agree." He put a hand on my shoulder. "But you did a damn fine job without her help. You saved Elizabeth and Callie. Had you not lured Samyaza to the woods, we'd never have been able to save them."

"We couldn't save Ramone."

"He's been out of our reach for a long time. You have to accept that and move on, as does Elizabeth."

"I'm tired." I was suddenly weak-kneed.

"It's not much farther," Reginald said. He offered his arm for me to hold.

"Going somewhere?"

The male voice came from down the trail. Reginald and I stopped and stared into the gloom of dense shade. Lucais Wilkins stepped out into the sunlight. He had a gun pointed right at Reginald's heart.

# CHAPTER 36

"W here's the journal?" Lucais got right to the point.

"We don't have it," Reginald said. "Last I heard, Ruth Whelan had it."

"That's not what Ramone told us." Lucais cocked the gun and lowered the barrel. He addressed me. "I'm going to shoot him in the knee first. It'll cripple him for life, but maybe then you'll talk...Little Lady." The last two words were a sneer.

"We don't have it," I said. "I was at Ruth's house looking for it when you arrived, but I never found it. We lied to Ramone because we didn't trust him." The fabrications came easily. I couldn't let him shoot Reginald.

"I don't have time for this." He came toward us with an angry stride. "I want that journal." He whipped the butt of the gun into Reginald's face. My partner fell to the ground.

"Stop it." I moved in front of Reginald. "Stop it now. If we had it, we'd give it to you."

"Oh, you have it, and you'll give it up. And I'm going to

enjoy making you do it." He looked down the trail. "Where's Ramone?"

"He dead," Reginald said as he regained his feet. He was bleeding profusely from a cut on his cheekbone and a busted lip. "I shot him."

Lucais faltered. "He's dead?"

"He is. And so is Samyaza." I said the name and saw the instant reaction of fear. "He can't help you anymore. He was trapped in Ramone's body and we killed him." I threw the words in his face, unable to stop the angry flow from leaving my mouth. "You're going to swing for all the wickedness you've done now that your master is gone."

Reginald reached out to stop me, but I dodged his hand and got into Lucais's face. "You lost your protector. Where are the watchers? The buzzards? They're all gone, aren't they. Can't you feel it, how alone you are? How powerless." Out of the corner of my eye I saw movement on the trail. "You're done for and all of the people you've held captive in Mission are going to be free to make their own choices now. Your rule of terror is over."

Someone was coming down the trail. Lucais's henchmen? I didn't know, and I had only one chance to save Reginald. I ran at Lucais, hitting him as hard as I could with my body. I knocked him backward several steps as he fought to keep his balance.

"I'm going to kill your fancy man and then I'm going to wring your scrawny neck," Lucais said as he regained his footing and started toward me. As he pointed the gun at Reginald, I saw who was on the path. Slater McEachern lifted the shotgun he carried. I fell to the ground over Reginald, pressing him flat. The blast of a shotgun peppered the woods around me as Lucais cried out. The second blast cut short his cries. His body toppled into the detritus of the woods.

I got up and walked over to him as Slater came down the trail. "Tell me he's really dead," I said. Blood still seeped from his wounds, but his chest wasn't moving. His eyes were open. Still, I had to be certain. This man had caused such pain and hardship for so many. I'd begun to doubt he was mortal.

"He's quite dead. At last I've really killed someone and I'll take all the credit for it." He pivoted to offer a hand to Reginald. "Are you hurt?"

"Thanks to you and Raissa, I'm not," Reginald said as he gained his feet. "You saved her life, and mine."

Something fluttered in the trees nearby and for one dreaded moment, I thought it might be the buzzards returning to mourn the loss of one of their own. Instead, a red-tailed hawk perched on a limb. The bird gave a sharp cry. "Skree! Skree!" In a split second it had disappeared into the woods.

I looked back at Lucais's body. He hadn't moved—though I'd been a little afraid he might try to crawl off.

Slater put his hand on my shoulder. "Aye, lass, he's truly dead. He was a mean bastard. Loved to push his thumb into a wound and twist it."

"What about his men?" I asked.

Slater reloaded the shotgun. "The men from town will face the law, even if I have to track them down one by one. The others, the watchers? They're gone. They were outside the kirk, making sure we didn't leave. Then they all turned and walked away."

Judging from his face, Slater found it hard to believe. The enemy had simply withdrawn, except for Lucais, who'd come hunting on his own. He'd found us, but not with the outcome he'd anticipated.

"You really okay?" Slater asked Reginald. "You look a little pale."

"I killed Ramone," Reginald said. I knew this would weigh heavily on my partner, though he'd had no other recourse.

"Ramone was possessed by a fallen angel named Samyaza. That was Gabriel's real name. He was going to rape me," I said. "And he would have taken pleasure in hurting me. Besides, in killing Ramone, he also killed Gabriel."

"Ah," Slater said. "So that's the reason the watchers left. Their master is gone."

"Yes." I wanted to say more but I was too tired to talk. We still had a walk back to the church.

Reginald took my arm and Slater came to my other side. The two of them half carried me down the trail as the sun slanted toward afternoon.

When we arrived at the church, Elizabeth and Callie were waiting for us. Michael was nowhere to be found. Slater took Elizabeth aside and told her about Ramone, holding her as she cried. Callie slept on a blanket in the church sanctuary with the sisters watching over her.

I found a pew and slumped into it. I couldn't remember ever being so tired.

Father Kilroy moved us all into his quarters and poured wine. I thought I was too tired to drink, but I sipped a glass as we settled into his comfortable parlor. Sister Teresa brought in sandwiches for us, and I found I was ravenous. We all ate in silence, except for Callie, who kicked her legs and hands and cooed.

When the plates were cleared away, Elizabeth came to sit beside me on a sofa. "Reginald didn't shoot Ramone. You and I both know that. Ramone, my brother, had been dead for a long while. It was the fallen angel who killed Ruth, not my brother. Ramone didn't have a mean bone in his body."

"And Hildy." I had to tell her. "It was Samyaza using Ramone. I saw his hands."

"Yes. I know. We have to make Reginald understand. He can't carry guilt over this."

"Thank you. I know he's hurting." I was impressed with Elizabeth. Her brother had been shot dead, but she was able to look beyond the grief to see the truth.

"I'll talk with him." She sighed. "Ramone...I was so happy to see him when he showed up, but something kept bothering me. It was the timing, the way he looked at you and Callie. With you, I thought I was imagining a budding romance, which would have pleased me. I hoped he felt protective toward Callie. Like a good uncle. But that wasn't it at all."

"I don't know what happened to Ramone or when it happened. Anything bad he did wasn't your brother, Elizabeth. It was Samyaza."

"I'll be right back." She left the room and returned five minutes later with the journal. "Here. You take this. You have the resources to get it translated so we can prove that Slater is innocent of killing Ruth."

"It's Hebrew. My uncle can do this. There's a rabbi in Mobile who may help us."

"Will Slater face charges for killing Lucais?"

"He saved Reginald's life. And mine. He won't be punished." I knew Uncle Brett would stand by Slater.

Elizabeth looked around the room, checking to see that everyone was engaged in conversation and ignoring us. "Who is Callie's father? It wasn't Gabriel, or Samyaza, thank goodness. Did he tell you who Callie's father was?"

The notion that an angel was the baby's father had been

implanted in her mind. "Gabriel didn't say. But he did say Callie wasn't a Nephilim."

Elizabeth's face paled as a horrific thought struck her. "Did I sleep with my brother? Did Gab—Samyaza trick me into sleeping with my own brother?"

"No." I couldn't prove it, but it was cruel to let Elizabeth think such a thing when there was nothing we could do to change it. "The angel confessed that Callie wasn't a Nephilim, therefore it couldn't have been Ramone."

"Who's her father then?"

I suspected, but I had no proof. Lucais Wilkins and his henchmen were more than capable of drugging Elizabeth and doing whatever they wanted to her. She would have no memory of it. But that was a seed best left unplanted. "There are some things we'll never know. It doesn't matter who her father is. You're her mother. And I believe Slater would like to play a role in her life. She couldn't ask for a better father." I'd seen the way he looked over to be sure Elizabeth was not in distress. He cared for her. What man wouldn't? She was beautiful and had risked everything to save him.

"Callie and I were never the goal, were we?"

"I don't know that either. I think you were manipulated to get Reginald and me here, as Ramone was manipulated. But what the angel's intentions were, I can't say."

Elizabeth reached out and drew me to her. "Generous friend, I almost got you killed. And Reginald too. Can you forgive me?"

"There's nothing to forgive. And there's so much to be gained. Think what kind of place Mission can become without Lucais Wilkins's ruling it like the Kaiser."

Elizabeth shook her head. "While you were out in the woods, Slater and I talked. We want to come to Mobile with you and your uncle. We want to see about surgery for Callie's hands and feet. We want her to be normal."

"She has a gift." I knew that denying such a gift could be dangerous. "Please don't try to hide that from her."

"Never. But she can have her gift and also look like a normal child if the medical skill is available."

I kissed her cheek. "A perfect decision." Contentment settled into my chest. "Where did Michael go?"

She frowned. "He was here and then gone. I thought he might be in the woods with you." She reached into the pocket of her dress and brought out an envelope. "He gave me this for you."

I took the sealed envelope from her, but I didn't open it. The letter held sadness. Somehow I knew that, and I wanted privacy to read it. "I'm exhausted."

Elizabeth motioned Sister Ursaline over. "Is there a place my friend can rest?"

"This way."

I looked over the group, still talking and figuring out the loose ends. No one had called the law about Ramone's and Lucais's bodies. They were waiting for Uncle Brett. That would have to be done and dealt with, and then we could start the long drive home. I wanted time in Mobile to recover, and then I wanted to spend a month in New Orleans, writing more stories and studying under Madam Petalungro. Soon it would be Halloween, always a favorite holiday of mine. Then the colder celebrations of Thanksgiving and Christmas. Time and tide waited for no man. I was learning that bittersweet lesson.

As soon as I was in a small, bare room with a cot, I lit a candle and opened the letter from Michael. It was short, and direct.

"Dearest Raissa,

This is my good-bye. I was called to other duties. Never doubt you were brought here to defeat the fallen angel, and you did. Samyaza is destroyed. Now I must resume my work. No mortal woman has ever tempted me to rebel against divine rule, until you. Keep this secret. Remember that good and evil walk among you. Use your gift, and help Callie develop hers, if you can. Please care for Sir John Monash. He's a special creature too. He'll give you pleasure, and remind you of me when you need me."

There was no signature. I became aware that I was crying. The sense of loss was keen. I rethought Michael's appearance in my life, his skills, his willingness to help strangers in trouble. I should have known, but I hadn't.

The sound of a commotion drifted to me, and I knew Uncle Brett, Isabelle, and Madam had arrived. I washed my face in cold water, aware of my sunburned skin and the insect bites that made me look like a plague victim. Those would pass too. I went to join my family and friends.

# CHAPTER 37

U ncle Brett was up at dawn and at the police station. He'd told us to pack our belongings and be ready to leave. Slater had ridden back to Mission to pay Hattie the money we owed her and to retrieve Mariah and Sir John Monash. Uncle Brett had booked passage for the horses on the train for the trip to Mobile, where they'd stay in my uncle's stables. Elizabeth, Callie, and Slater would settle at Caoin House, also. For the time being, they would be guests of my uncle.

While the final arrangements were being made, I walked out of the church and into the woods. The bodies of Ramone and Lucais had been removed. The sordid story had been explained by Reginald. I'd given a written statement about Ramone's death. My uncle's persuasive personality and his power had made it almost certain Slater would be cleared of all charges. What was told to the residents of Mission didn't matter to me. The stranglehold Lucais held over the town, with the help of dark forces, had been broken. The residents could take charge of their fate and move toward a common good, or not—but of their own free will.

I walked down to the patch of delicate ferns where I could have died. Ramone was gone, but not the blood where he'd died. I was almost afraid to believe that we'd truly killed a fallen angel. I heard footsteps and turned to find Madam coming toward me like a very slow locomotive. She was not well, but she would not be denied.

"He's truly gone," she said. "How did you figure it out? That to kill him he had to be trapped in human form?"

"I'm not sure I had it all figured out. I hit him with a rock, and when it hurt him, I knew he was vulnerable. Reginald saw it too and took the opportunity."

"He saved your life."

"Yes." Madam took real pride in Reginald's accomplishments. "He did. You taught him well, to act with decision."

"What's your plan for the future?" she asked, making me think of Michael and his never-ending duties. He could be anywhere in the universe, but I'd once hoped for a visit in Mobile with my uncle. I'd hoped for a little more than that, if I were honest with myself.

"I want to spend some time at Caoin House. Then I'd like to come to New Orleans to study with you, if you'll allow it. Reginald and I both would like that."

"I was hoping you'd say that." She was tired. I heard it in her voice and saw it in her stance. I offered my arm as I assisted her back to the church. "I have something that requires your help," she said.

"Really?"

"Yes, it's a case that may interest you."

I was already interested. The chance to work with Madam on a case was more than I'd hoped for. "What is it?"

"There's a woman in the Quarter who's asking for our help. She's a well-respected brothel owner."

This was somewhat shocking, but I kept silent.

"Her name is Angelique. She's of Creole descent. Her mother and grandmother ran the same brothel for generations. Reginald will know the name. It's legendary in New Orleans circles."

"What's the problem there?"

"One of the girls who works there found a doll in an alley. She brought it into the house. Angelique says it's beautiful. Ceramic face painted like a courtesan, and a can-can costume, which made her believe it was of French origin."

"A little girl's doll?"

"Much more than that." Madam stopped and faced me. "They named the doll Brona, and at first the girls thought she was beautiful."

A doll didn't seem like a serious case, but I wasn't about to say that. "At first?"

"Three of the girls in the house have been brutally murdered since the doll's arrival. Angelique thinks it's cursed. Possibly by a voodoo spell. There are practitioners in the Quarter, you know. Perhaps a jealous wife or boyfriend has paid for a curse."

"Can't they just throw the doll away?"

Madam nodded, as if she'd been waiting for this question. "They have. Four times. Brona always comes back."

"What do you mean she comes back?"

"She's on the doorstep or somehow manages to get back inside the house." Madam was being serious.

"I would burn her."

"They tried. That's how one of the girls died. The fire jumped to her and burned her alive."

My first thought was that Uncle Brett would not be happy with this case. "Do you believe in voodoo?"

Madam thought a minute. "There is good and evil. There are humans who work to manipulate both. Voodoo is only one tool in using darkness for personal gain. There are many others and some in all religious beliefs. So yes, I believe."

"Could I have some time to spend with Uncle Brett first?"

"Of course. Carlton and I have already begun some preliminary work on this matter. I'm afraid I'm not up to a lot of leg work, so you and Reginald will bear the brunt of that."

"Count me in." Another rich opportunity to learn from Madam might never come along.

"Then I'll see you in October. I'm getting too old for all of this activity. It's time you and Reginald learned all you can to keep yourselves safe. Besides, the Halloween festivities in New Orleans are not to be missed." She took my arm again and we continued to the church and the long trip home.

# ACKNOWLEDGMENTS

It's impossible to thank all the people who helped with this book, but that won't stop me from trying. First and foremost, I want to thank the readers who have so generously given their time to read and comment on the manuscript. I am so fortunate to have a group of avid Beta Readers who willing read my stories.

A special thanks to editors Jennifer Williamson and Maia Larson. Thank you for the careful attention you've given my story. It is a far better book, thanks to you. And to Claire Matturro and Susan Tanner, such accomplished writers who also gave the book a careful read through and offered terrific advice.

Nothing in my book world would ever happen without Priya Bhakta, who is such a big part of my life. Priya is a genius at formatting and graphic design. And special thanks to Cissy Hartley of Writerspace, who designed the cover and so many other things that go into publishing and promoting a book.

The material I write about in the Pluto's Snitch books

requires talents and skills that I don't always possess. I'm fortunate I do have friends with those skills. Special thanks to Helene Buntman, DeWitt Lobrano, and John Edwards.

# ABOUT THE AUTHOR

Carolyn Haines is the *USA TODAY* bestselling author of over 70 books in a number of genres. She grew up in a rural Mississippi town with a family devoted to telling ghost stories and creating adventures. Her Scandinavian grandmother combined history and local legends for many bone-chilling evenings spent in front of a fireplace with a cup of hot chocolate. And it didn't hurt that she grew up in a haunted house where she first began to see spirits.

The Pluto's Snitch mysteries combine her love of spooky moments and puzzling mysteries. She is also the author of the popular Sarah Booth Delaney Mississippi Delta mysteries and the Trouble, black cat detective, multi-author mystery series. Haines lives on a farm where she cares for dogs, cats, and horses. She urges everyone to please neuter their companion pets to help cut down on the suffering of unwanted animals.

**www.goodfortunefarmrefuge.org**

Thank you for reading this book published by Good Fortune Farm Refuge. 100% of all proceeds from the sale of this book will be donated to the GFFR which helps pets receive loving homes and medical treatment.

**www.carolynhaines.com**
**carolyn@carolynhaines.com**

[f] facebook.com/AuthorCarolynHaines

[t] twitter.com/DeltaGalCarolyn

[o] instagram.com/carolynhaines

[a] amazon.com/author/carolynhaines

[g] goodreads.com/CarolynHaines

[BB] bookbub.com/profile/carolyn-haines

*The Trouble with Cupid*

*Year-Round Trouble*

## THE JEXVILLE CHRONICLES

*Summer of the Redeemers*

*Touched*

*Judas Burning*

## FEAR FAMILIAR MYSTERIES

*Familiar Tale*

*Bewitching Familiar*

*Thrice Familiar*

*Too Familiar*

*Fear Familiar*

## SARAH BOOTH DELANEY MYSTERIES

*A Garland of Bones*

*The Devil's Bones*

*Game of Bones*

*A Gift of Bones*

*Charmed Bones*

*Sticks and Bones*

*Rock-a-Bye Bones*

*Bone to be Wild*

*Booty Bones*

*Smarty Bones*

*Bonefire of the Vanities*

*Bones of a Feather*

*Bone Appétit*

*Greedy Bones*

*Wishbones*

*Ham Bones*

*Bones to Pick*

*Hallowed Bones*

*Crossed Bones*

*Splintered Bones*

*Buried Bones*

*Them Bones*

## SARAH BOOTH DELANEY SHORT MYSTERIES

*Shorty Bones*

*Bones on the Bayou*

*Guru Bones*

*Jingle Bones*

*Bones and Arrows*

*Clacking Bones*

*Enchanted Bones*